PETER RAVEN
UNDER
FIRE

From The Chicken House

I'm sorry, I can't be quiet about this book! I WAS
SWEPT AWAY by the excitement of being at sea
with Midshipman Raven in a real man-o'-war, with
spies, battles and pirates. And actually meeting
Napoleon! I can't wait to see what Peter Raven
does next. More please, Mr Molloy!

Barry Cunningham
Publisher

PETER RAVEN UNDER FIRE

MICHAEL MOLLOY

The Chicken House

2, Palmer Street, Frome, Somerset BA11 1DS

Text © Michael Molloy 2005
Cover illustration © Mel Grant 2005
Inside illustrations © Brian Saunders 2005

First published in Great Britain in 2005 by
The Chicken House
2 Palmer Street
Frome, Somerset BA11 1DS
United Kingdom
www.doublecluck.com

Cover design by Ian Butterworth
Designed and typeset by Dorchester Typesetting Group Ltd
Printed and bound in Great Britain

1 3 5 7 9 10 8 6 4 2

British Library Cataloguing in Publication data available.

HB ISBN 1 904442 44 7

Autumn 1800

Great Britain is in the seventh year of her bitter struggle with revolutionary France. Napoleon Bonaparte, hailed as the most brilliant European general since Julius Caesar, has established himself as First Consul of the French Republic and virtual dictator of France. He has the reputation of being invincible on land, but at sea it is a different story. . . .

Chapter One

THE DEAD OF NIGHT

The full moon had long set on the rolling Hampshire countryside when dense storm clouds blew in from the west, obscuring the stars. In the pitch darkness before dawn two riders walked their horses down a narrow, overgrown bridle path. The first of them carried a lantern. He was a burly countryman in a rough russet-coloured coat and wide-brimmed straw hat. The second wore a heavy cloak over the scarlet uniform of a colonel in the marines.

Both men were well-armed. They had carbines in the holsters attached to their saddles and both wore a brace of pistols in their belts. The colonel's heavy sword was curved like a cavalry sabre rather than the customary straight weapon. The countryman with the lantern had a double-barrelled shotgun slung from his shoulder.

They stopped and listened, but all they could hear was

the soft jingle from the metal bits as the horses tore grass from the ragged edge of the pathway. The colonel took a watch from his waistcoat and leaned forward to read the time by the soft glow of the lantern.

'Do you think he'll be there?' asked the countryman, a slight note of anxiety in his voice.

The colonel nodded. 'I'm sure of it. Is everything prepared?'

'Just as you instructed.'

'Pass me the lantern. And follow my orders if I give the signal.'

'I will, sir.'

Leaving his companion in the lane, the colonel urged his horse forward to a gap in the hedge which led into the wide courtyard of an abandoned farmhouse. A dimmed lantern hanging above its entrance cast a small circle of light on to the cobbles.

Despite the darkness, the colonel was familiar with the layout here. A row of stables was connected to the farmhouse, and a ramshackle barn completed the third side of the open square. The colonel doused his light, slid down from his horse and looped the reins over the shaft of a massive old farm cart with a broken wheel. Much of its load of hay had spilt on to the cobbles.

Then he stood very still in the darkness. He could feel the weather had changed; a sudden stronger breeze blew from the west, and he could smell the coming rain.

'Did you bring the money?' a low voice asked from

beyond the circle of light.

Remaining in the darkness, the colonel took a heavy leather pouch from the pocket of his cloak. Holding it at arm's length he shook it. The gold coins inside jingled, and instinctively he stepped away from the sound he'd made. The movement saved his life.

A musket blasted out of the darkness to the left of the lantern's pool of light; the shot thudded into the butt of the carbine on his saddle. The horse reared in terror, and tearing the reins free, it galloped blindly out of the cobbled yard. Two more shots rang out before a voice screamed, 'Stop firing, you fools! Give me more light.'

A figure carrying a musket darted forward, reaching out to turn up the wick of the lantern over the doorway. From where the colonel now lay, flat out on the cobbled yard, he discharged his pistol at the man and rolled quickly away to seek cover under the sagging edge of the wagon.

Two more musket shots rang out.

Five of them, the colonel calculated. Time to adjust the odds. Reaching up, he fired his other pistol into the straw spilling out of the wagon, and hurriedly scrambled away into the barn behind. The muzzle flash from his last shot caught the dry straw, and a lick of fire showed, then a sudden explosive brilliance — gunpowder mixed in with the straw had burst into a dazzling incandescence that illuminated the whole courtyard.

'Down on him,' shouted the hidden leader, 'before he has time to reload.'

Silhouetted against the flames, three men approached carrying muskets fitted with bayonets. The colonel thrust his hands into a full corn bin next to the doorway and withdrew two pistols that had been concealed in the grain. When his attackers were within seven paces of him he fired.

Grunting, two of the men sprawled at his feet, but the third came on, thrusting the wickedly glinting bayonet at his stomach. The colonel tossed his empty pistols aside and drew his sabre. With an upward sweep he parried the musket and swung the blade down to strike the attacker's neck.

As the man fell, the blast of a shotgun was followed by another single pistol shot. After a brief pause, his companion shouted, 'All clear, sir.'

The colonel wiped his sabre on the coat of one of the slain men and returned to the courtyard, where the flames of the burning straw were already dying down. The countryman turned up the lantern over the doorway and pointed with his shotgun towards the two other dead men. 'Both done for, sir.'

'Hardly my most elegant plan,' replied the colonel wryly, 'but effective for all that.'

'Good job we were prepared, sir,' replied his accomplice.

The colonel consulted his watch again. 'I've got to catch the mail coach to Portsmouth. I must hurry. You'd better clear up here later.'

'I caught your horse,' answered the countryman. 'We'll

make the rendezvous with time to spare.'

Colonel Beaumont looked up at the black sky. As he wearily hauled himself into the saddle, the first drops of rain began to fall.

Chapter Two

THE LATE ARRIVAL

In the pearl-grey light of the wet September morning, Midshipman Peter Raven took a chance in the driving rain. Clutching his hat firmly by the brim, he leaped from the steps of the stone jetty to land on the deck of the naval packet, HMS *Dolphin*, moored at the dockside in Portsmouth harbour.

The unworn soles of his new shoes slipped on the slick planking, but a humiliating fall was averted by the swift action of a stocky seaman with a leathery complexion and tarred pigtail. Standing at the waist of the boat, he seized Peter's arm through his boat cloak and steadied him with an iron grip.

'Thank you,' said Peter, quickly recovering his footing and taking a firm hold on the handle of the dirk he wore at his side.

The sailor put a knuckle to his forehead and grinned.

'Able Seaman Connors, at your service, sir.'

Although it was his first time on board a Royal Navy ship, Peter remembered to salute the quarterdeck. He was observing the custom practised by all ranks, whether they were boarding a first-rate man-o'-war or a humble little jack-of-all-trades cutter like HMS *Dolphin*.

'Get yourself aft with your sea-chest, Mister, then report to the captain,' barked a young man dressed in foul-weather tarpaulins who'd noted Peter's arrival as he supervised the loading of stores. Despite his authoritative tone, Peter judged the youth to be no more than a few years older than himself, and he'd not long reached his thirteenth birthday.

'Aye, aye, sir,' Peter replied, and his mind suddenly went blank. For months he'd been practising the correct terms used on board ships, boring his older sisters to distraction by insisting that they test him from one of his several books on seamanship. Now he'd fallen at the first hurdle. *Aft?* Luckily, help was at hand.

'This way, sir,' said Able Seaman Connors, easily lifting Peter's huge brass-bound sea-chest, which had been swung aboard before him. Connors hurried along the slippery deck towards the rear of the ship, the heavy chest casually balanced on his shoulder and his bare feet sure on the wet surface.

The *Dolphin* seemed excessively loaded with supplies. Amidships on the open deck, a variety of livestock was penned under canvas awnings to protect them from the worst of the rain. There were a dozen sheep and as many pigs, a few goats, hundreds of chickens and several bullocks.

'I'll stay here and wait for you, sir,' said Connors, putting Peter's sea-chest down near the livestock. 'That's the captain,' he added, gesturing for Peter to go ahead to the wheel, where an older man was talking to a junior officer.

When the young officer departed, Peter stepped forward and saluted. 'Midshipman Peter Raven, sir. My orders are to join HMS *Torren*.'

'Welcome aboard, Mr Raven,' replied the captain, who was in good humour despite the apparent chaos aboard his ship. 'I am Commander Payne, captain of this vessel. I understand you have dispatches for Captain Benchley.'

'Yes, sir,' answered Peter, pulling out from beneath his boat cloak an oblong of tarred canvas which contained the documents.

The captain nodded. 'Keep them with you at all times, Midshipman, and make sure your sea-chest is stowed somewhere handy. We don't want to have to go hunting for it when we come alongside the *Torren*, do we?'

'No, sir. I mean, aye, aye, sir,' replied Peter.

'In different circumstances, I could offer you more comfortable quarters,' continued Commander Payne. 'But, as you can see, we don't have an inch to spare. We have supplies and letters aboard for the whole squadron. HMS *Canard* was due to take half the load, but she had to sail yesterday with urgent dispatches. I'm afraid you'll have to make do and sleep on deck tonight. See you get some hot food. Carry on.'

'Thank you, sir,' answered Peter, saluting before he took his leave.

With no duties to perform aboard the *Dolphin* and with at least two days before they reached HMS *Torren*, part of the British squadron blockading the great French port of Brest, Peter decided to make the best of the situation. Leaving his sea-chest with Connors for safekeeping, he scouted about the *Dolphin* and found that the captain had not exaggerated.

Apart from the livestock, sacks of vegetables were stacked up with barrels and boxes of other supplies and crammed into every available space on the ship. The upper deck may have been jammed to capacity, but below was far worse. The claustrophobic stuffiness together with the overpowering smells of bilge and unwashed bodies made sleeping on the open deck far more inviting, despite the pounding rain.

After a thorough search Peter found just the sort of niche he was looking for. Set behind the mid-mast was a squared-off heap of hay bales – fodder for the livestock – covered with canvas and separating the bullocks from the sheep. With the help of Connors, who gladly pocketed the threepence Peter gave him, they raised the canvas covering to rig up a sort of low tent, its roof held up over the hay bales by two tea chests, and stowed Peter's gear at one end of it.

'You'll be nice and cosy in here, sir,' said Connors, Peter having jingled other coins in his pocket indicating he would be prepared to pay for any future assistance. 'Just you stay put, Midshipman, and I'll bring you some dinner later.'

Peter removed his wet boat cloak and hat, and tucked away in his snug new quarters he stretched out to read the book his mother had given him as a parting present. After a time the rain hammering on his canvas roof gave way to a gentler tapping, then ceased altogether. He could hear the shouted orders to get the *Dolphin* under way.

As the command, 'Cast off, aft!' told him the ship was actually leaving the dock, he stuck his head out from under the canvas flap and was just in time to see the figure of a naval officer, his cloak floating behind him like a great dark flag, make a heroic leap from the quayside to catch the port halyard and swing himself aboard.

Smiling as he thought how uncomfortable the new arrival's voyage would be compared to his own, Peter was disconcerted a few minutes later when the flap to his refuge was pulled aside and Able Seaman Connors gestured into the ample space.

'Would you like me to show the midshipman to other quarters, sir?' asked Connors with a treacherous smile so broad it exposed a missing tooth.

'Wouldn't dream of it,' said the new arrival as he threw off his cloak and hat to reveal the uniform of a commodore.

Peter began to rise and give an awkward salute, but the

man waved him down with an unexpected smile, saying, 'There's no need for the usual formalities under the circumstances, Midshipman.' And as he heaved himself on to the hay bales next to Peter, he added, 'My name is Commodore Beaumont, and who, pray, are you?'

'Midshipman Raven, sir,' Peter replied, slightly alarmed. Although he was not yet well-versed in all the ways of the Royal Navy, he was aware that Beaumont seemed exceedingly young to carry the rank of commodore, which was a peg up from captain. He knew it *was* possible, but very unusual. As a rule, officers served several years as lieutenants and then even longer as captains before reaching such an exalted rank.

Beaumont's rise from midshipman must have been amazingly fast. The commodore was tall with a wiry frame. His thick fair hair was drawn back in a club and tied with a bow at the nape of his neck. His well-formed open features were marred by a nose that had obviously been broken and set crookedly.

But there was something else about the commodore that caused Peter to question his status. Wanting time alone to think, he mumbled an excuse and left the makeshift tent to stand by the ship's rail facing into the bracing wind. He had seen Commodore Beaumont before, not many hours ago, and in strange circumstances.

Chapter Three

THE VOYAGE OF THE DOLPHIN

Peter remained at the ship's rail, pretending to take an interest as the *Dolphin* passed between the two forts flanking the narrow harbour entrance, but his thoughts were on other matters. They were soon in choppier waters and passing close to the gigantic looming hulls of sombre warships lying at anchor in Spithead. All about them an armada of small boats plied between the Royal Navy men-o'-war and the town, ferrying passengers and supplies out to the waiting ships.

Peter paid them scant attention. His mind was racing as he recalled where he'd last seen Commodore Beaumont, a little over forty-eight hours earlier.

Four days ago, following sudden orders that had arrived at his home, Peter had reported to the Admiralty in London, where a duty officer had handed him dispatches for the captain of HMS *Torren*.

The duty officer had instructed him to take the mail coach to Portsmouth. He'd warned him that the journey might take longer than the usual two days because the roads in parts of Hampshire were said to be mired with deep mud because of all the recent rain.

After an exhausting first leg that had taken from dawn to almost midnight, the second day of Peter's journey had begun with a curious incident. The coach had left the overnight inn well before dawn, and a few miles down the Portsmouth Road the coach stopped at a crossroads when a man with a lantern waved it down.

The only other passengers on board the coach were a middle-aged husband and wife, who continued to doze. But Peter, surprised that the coach had halted so readily at the man's signal, took a deeper interest. He knew highwaymen still plundered the coach routes, yet the driver had pulled up with no apparent concern.

Feigning sleep, Peter gripped his dispatches tight and watched through half-closed eyes. The light from the lantern revealed a man in the uniform of a marine colonel wearily climbing aboard after bidding farewell to a companion in a straw hat.

Peter was certain that the colonel who'd boarded the coach that morning was the same man who, less than an hour ago, had introduced himself as Commodore Beaumont of the Royal Navy.

For the rest of the coach journey, the latest passenger

seemed to have fallen into a deep sleep, the collar of his cloak pulled up to obscure his features. The woman opposite, having now woken, sniffed with disdain at every gentle snore he uttered.

On their arrival in Portsmouth, long after nightfall, the coach finally rattled into the cobbled yard of an inn. After exchanging a few muttered words with the driver, the man dressed as a marine officer hurried away. Peter, concerned with the arrangements to transport his sea-chest, had thought no more of the matter.

Now, here was the same man, but this time he was wearing the uniform of a senior naval officer. Where had he acquired it? He'd carried no luggage with him on the coach.

Another squall of heavy rain interrupted Peter's train of thought, forcing him to return to cover and take his place beside the mysterious commodore.

When he was settled in again, the man reached out and picked up Peter's book, which lay between them. Holding up the copy of *Voltaire's Letters*, Beaumont casually asked in flawless French, 'And how are you enjoying the provocative thoughts of this gentleman?'

'With great pleasure, sir,' Peter replied in French of equal fluency. 'Voltaire is a very funny man.'

Beaumont nodded with approval, and Peter was suddenly grateful for the tedious afternoons he'd spent conversing with the elderly members of an exiled French family who had fled the Revolution and now lived in his father's parish.

Beaumont grinned again. 'So, we have a midshipman who talks like a Frog and looks like a Don, eh? They'll have you reading them Napoleon's newspapers on *Torren*.'

Peter knew what he meant. Captured French newspapers were greatly prized in the ward rooms of the Royal Navy, providing they had a competent translator aboard.

As for him looking like a Don, Peter knew his coal-black hair and olive skin were features more typically Spanish than English, but his eyes were greenish blue, like his mother's. What puzzled him was how Beaumont knew he was due for the *Torren*. Perhaps Connors had told him.

'And where are you from, Mr Raven?' asked Beaumont genially.

'Richmond in Surrey, sir,' he answered politely but without further elaboration. Still worried by his mysterious companion, Peter was determined to give him the minimum of information. Although, he reasoned, even if the man were spying for the French, the personal details of Britain's most newly joined midshipman would be of absolutely no benefit to the French government.

When eight bells sounded midday, the *Dolphin* – her decks awash – was still battering through the mounting sea, heeling to port as she was driven on by the rain-filled wind. Peter was relieved that the heaving motion of the ship didn't make him feel at all seasick, a fate his teasing sisters had confidently predicted.

In fact, he was just starting to feel hungry when Able Seaman Connors, dexterously balancing a wooden tray,

brought them hunks of fresh bread and large bowls of thick
pea soup. By then, the young commodore had learnt that
Peter Raven was the only son of the Reverend John and Mrs
Emily Raven, that he had three older sisters – Jane, Kate
and Alexandra – and that since Mrs Raven had brought a
handsome dowry to the marriage the family was by no
means poor.

He'd also ascertained that Peter and his sisters had been
educated at home by the Reverend Raven, a scholarly man
who had given Peter a sound grounding in the classics,
mathematics and grammar. He had not yet attained his
mother's level of skill on the piano, but she had managed to
make him quite an adequate water colourist.

Of Commodore Beaumont, Peter Raven had learnt
nothing.

Prepared for the worst, Peter cautiously took his first
spoonful of soup and was surprised by how delicious the
thick smoky concoction was. He'd been warned endlessly
about how awful the food would be.

'So, you're Captain Benchley's nephew,' Beaumont stated casually, before starting his own meal. Peter almost
choked with astonishment. How could Beaumont possibly
know that?

The young man laughed at his evident surprise. 'Just a
guess, Mr Raven,' he explained. 'Appointing their own
midshipmen is one of the few acts of patronage allowed to a
captain. So, there was a good chance you'd be either a relative or the son of a friend.'

As Beaumont spoke, there came another drumming on their canvas roof as the rain fell even harder, and Peter gave his attention to his soup.

Fortune favoured the *Dolphin's* passage and a hard south-westerly wind blew her down the channel towards the island of Ushant. Despite her overflowing cargo, the handy little craft's broad spread of sail caused her to flash through the water, dipping and rising on the crest of the white-topped waves.

By afternoon the skies had cleared to a sharp bright blue with high snatches of ragged cloud. Peter and Beaumont had left the shelter of their makeshift tent and were taking deep breaths of the exhilarating sea air.

'Enjoy the flavour, Mr Raven,' said Commodore Beaumont. 'It's like imbibing the very best vintage champagne.'

Peter's only experience of champagne had been at a wedding performed by his father, and he'd found the chilled bubbly drink disappointing, rather like sucking a penny.

Beaumont moved along the deck to talk to Able Seaman Connors, who was seated out of the wind, methodically using a wet stone to sharpen a collection of cutlasses from the ship's store of small arms. When Beaumont finished talking to Connors he moved away to the rear of the ship.

For a time, Peter watched the crew going about their duties, then he moved along the slanting deck to where Connors sat stroking the stone on a steel blade with rhythmic precision.

'Ready for action, Connors?' Peter asked cheerfully.

'Always pays to be ready, sir,' he replied easily, carrying on with his monotonous task. 'It never does to underestimate the Frogs.'

Peter gestured towards the sails of the three British merchantman ships that were close-hauled and beating their way up the Channel almost within hailing distance of the *Dolphin*. 'They don't seem too worried by the enemy.'

'More fool them, then,' said Connors without rancour. 'The Frogs have got plenty of guts.'

'Surely they're not as brave as our lads?'

Connors gave a grim smile. 'It's only folks tucked up safe at home who says one of us is worth ten of them. You don't hear seamen talk 'em down so easy.'

'But we always best them in a fight,' challenged Peter. 'Even when the odds are heavily against us.'

'Not always. But what you say is mostly true, sir,' admitted Connors. 'And it's a curious contradiction.'

'Why so?'

'Because their ships are better than ours.'

'Better?' echoed Peter incredulously. 'French ships?'

Connors nodded. 'They're faster, with cleaner lines. I was on the *Temeraire* for a while and she handled like a beauty.'

'But we captured her from the French, all the same,' said Peter sharply.

'Now, there's the same contradiction,' said Connors, smiling. 'The problem the Frogs have is their seamanship –

not their ships.'

'Go on,' said Peter, intrigued. 'Tell me more.'

'Well, take their gunnery,' said Connors after some thought.

'Is it so different to ours?' asked Peter, anxious to learn all he could.

Connors did not answer immediately. Instead, he rasped the stone along the blade, then tested its edge with a thumb. Satisfied, he took up another cutlass and said, 'We fire at least two broadsides for every one the Frogs get off.'

'We're *twice* as fast?'

Connors nodded. 'Sometimes three times. Of course, we've got flintlocks and lanyards rigged to all our guns and the Frogs still use slow matches to fire their charges, but our drill is much faster, both on the guns and handling the ship.'

'Why is that?' asked Peter.

'British ships are always out on the high seas and our captains push the crews hard. The Frogs are mostly bottled up in their ports by our blockade.'

'Why don't they work harder? Surely their officers could manage it?'

Connors gave the question some consideration before he replied. 'The French lost nearly all their best officers in the Revolution. A lot of them were aristocrats.' Connors took the cutlass he was honing and pretended to draw it across his throat. 'The ones they have now . . .' Connors shrugged. 'Well, they just can't catch up with our lads.'

Still digesting this information, Peter moved further to

the rear of the ship and watched the flow of waves on either side of their creamy wake. As twilight approached, a leaden weariness began to seep through him. The last four days had been exhausting and his sleep had been constantly interrupted. Now, free of any duties, he thought longingly of the straw bales under the canvas.

Finding the makeshift tent unoccupied, Peter wrapped himself in his damp boat cloak, and remembering for a moment how much his mother would disapprove of him sleeping in wet clothes, he fell into a deep sleep.

He awoke ravenous in the pale chill light of early morning. The wind had dropped and the ship was on an even keel. Blinking, Peter consulted his pocket-watch. It didn't seem possible, but he'd slept for nearly twelve hours. Commodore Beaumont had already raised the canvas flap and was shaving. With a mug of hot water balanced on the straw bales, he scrutinized his face in a steel mirror while carefully drawing an ivory-handled razor across his sunburned jaw.

'That's probably the longest sleep you'll ever have in the Navy, Mr Raven,' he commented dryly as Connors arrived with two mugs of steaming coffee.

Dangling his legs over the edge of the straw bales, Peter accepted the hot drink gratefully and flexed his limbs. The weather had closed in again and he could feel there was more rain to come.

'We're making good time, gentlemen,' said Connors. 'The captain thinks we'll find the *Torren* by afternoon watch.'

Beaumont looked up at the milky-looking overcast sky. 'If the fog holds off,' he replied, wiping his face with a large silk handkerchief before taking a long swallow of his coffee.

'How would you gentlemen like a nice beefsteak and a bit of bacon for breakfast?' asked the seaman as if he were offering presents to children.

Beaumont laughed. 'Better rations on the *Dolphin* than a ship with the blockade squadrons, eh, Connors?'

'True enough, sir,' he replied, grinning. 'I've eaten more than my ration of rotten salt pork *and* washed it down with bad water.'

Peter pretended not to be taking much interest in their exchange, but he did notice an almost imperceptible signal pass between the two men. Beaumont barely raised his eyebrows before flicking his eyes in Peter's direction. Peter looked away, but at the corner of his vision, he was sure he saw Connors give the slightest of nods.

Suspicion flooded back into him. Was Connors in some kind of plot with the mysterious Beaumont? he wondered in alarm.

A sudden cry from the lookout made everyone on deck turn forward. Peter felt his heart beat faster, all thoughts of plots put aside by the awe-inspiring sight ahead.

A majestic first-rate British man-o'-war was bearing down on them through the misty sea.

Chapter Four

A VISITOR FOR THE
FIRST CONSUL

While Midshipman Peter Raven faced the prospect of a misty day on the rolling grey seas of France's western approaches, it was a clear morning in Paris. A bright sun warmed the cobbles as General Jean Ancre's carriage arrived in the courtyard of the Tuileries Palace to the clash of sentries presenting arms.

He strode across the marble hall with echoing footsteps to where an equerry, gorgeously clad in full dress uniform, gave an elegant bow.

'Good day, General Ancre,' the equerry murmured respectfully. 'The First Consul is taking his morning bath, but I have orders for you to join him immediately.'

General Ancre nodded but made no comment. Even though the First Consul, Napoleon Bonaparte, had appointed him to his present role in the secret service,

General Ancre had never met him before, as their contact had always been through letters. Throughout the years since the Revolution, fate had somehow conspired to keep them apart.

Ancre was familiar with Napoleon Bonaparte's achievements, of course. Who in Europe was not? He had studied Bonaparte's campaigns and his dazzling victories, and had no doubt that the Corsican he was about to meet was a military genius. But he was unsure of what other qualities the man possessed.

Those doubts didn't make Ancre's task easier. He did not suffer fools gladly, nor charlatans. Although he kept his opinions strictly to himself, General Ancre, a widower, no longer held many of the revolutionary ideals he had fought for so passionately in his youth.

Known to his army contemporaries as an outstanding soldier who had risen from the ranks, Ancre had surprised them more than a year before by writing a philosophical treatise on the importance of gathering military intelligence. To Ancre's astonishment, the article had been read by Napoleon himself, who wrote to him urging that he accept the job he now held. Consequently, General Ancre had spent the last year in the West Indies, keeping in constant touch with the First Consul through a series of letters. Napoleon's last communication had summoned him to Paris.

As the general marched briskly along the wide corridor behind the equerry, a voice that was not quite French roared out, 'Constant!'

'Coming, sire,' replied a harassed looking man who scuttled from another room carrying several newspapers. He was dressed in the striped waistcoat of a valet. Clouds of steam billowed out from the door as he entered.

Ushered on by the equerry, General Ancre followed the valet into the room and they, too, were engulfed in steam. Through the haze Ancre could make out the valet settling himself on a footstool and reading aloud to his master from one of the already limp newspapers. Napoleon was wallowing in a large deep bath of very hot water, gazing up at the clouded ceiling.

At the general's appearance, Napoleon held up a hand to silence his servant.

'Do you like hot baths, General?' asked the immersed figure in an abrupt and somewhat aggressive manner. The question was accompanied by a stare of startling intensity.

So it's true, thought Ancre. He does have hypnotic eyes. But he was determined not to be intimidated.

'Are you inviting me to join you, Citizen First Consul?' he replied easily. 'I think there is scarcely room in the tub for the both of us.'

As Napoleon considered the reply Ancre was somehow reminded of a cautious dog sniffing an unexpected bone. Then he gave a short laugh. 'The question didn't require an answer,' said Napoleon. 'I find a good hot bath is worth four hours' extra sleep to me.'

'I am from the tropics, Citizen,' replied Ancre. 'We

prefer our baths cold.'

'My wife Joséphine is also from the tropics,' said Napoleon, moodily slopping water on to the floor.

Constant hastily mopped the polished wood with one of the many large towels he had at hand.

'But you already know that,' continued Bonaparte. 'I understand you two are old friends. You were both born on Martinique.'

'We were not friends there, sir,' answered Ancre. 'My father was a gardener. I had no acquaintance with the rulers of the island. We did not meet until I came to Paris many years later.'

'Do you disapprove of rulers?'

Ancre answered the question carefully. 'No, sir,' he replied. 'But I think they should earn their privileges and the respect of each new generation.'

Bonaparte smiled for the first time. 'I see you are a diplomat as well as a soldier.'

Ancre responded with a slight bow.

As if coming to a sudden and vital decision, Bonaparte snapped out, 'Constant, I will dress immediately. General Ancre, if you will be so kind as to wait in the next room.'

Ancre made his way to a study where a large fire blazed, even though the day was pleasantly mild. He stood at the windows looking out on the geometric patterns of the great gardens below, until the First Consul of France joined him.

Napoleon was dressed in a splendid uniform with a long scarlet velvet coat, a court sword, and white gold-embroidered trousers tucked into short tasselled boots. His hair hung loose to his shoulders, framing his face.

Napoleon began to speak enthusiastically as he strode towards Ancre. 'General, how goes the peace with the Americans?' he asked.

'The people of our islands are delighted,' Ancre replied. 'They've suffered loss of trade for the past three years. Of course, the French privateers are less enthusiastic. They've been making enormous profits from the booty taken from American ships and now, of course, all that must stop.'

Napoleon shook his head. 'A sea war. It was a foolish, headstrong thing for France to do. We should have anticipated the Americans would never come in with us in our war against the British. Their agreement was signed with King Louis XVI. When we cut off his head in the Revolution we freed them from that commitment.'

'The war may officially be over but the privateers appear to have returned to their old habits of piracy,' replied Ancre. 'They continue to attack American shipping and everybody else, Citizen.'

'Excellent,' said Napoleon, rubbing his hands before the blazing fire, 'as I intend to go on squeezing the Americans for money, despite the treaty.'

He gestured for Ancre to be seated. 'So, have you found me the man I need?'

'I have,' the general replied.

'Describe him to me,' Napoleon urged. 'Leave nothing out. I trust he is brilliant, ambitious and quite ruthless?'

'He is all those things – and more,' Ancre assured him.

'Then tell me about him,' Napoleon demanded, impatient now.

'The title he has assumed is Count Vallon, after the Caribbean domain of Vallon, where he resides when not at sea with his fleet. Sometimes people refer to the place as Roc d'Or, or the Rock of Gold, but that is only the name of the ancient fortress that guards the harbour.'

'He pretends to be an aristocrat?' Napoleon asked with a hint of disappointment.

'He has no need to pretend, First Consul, he *is* an aristocrat. His family line is ancient.'

Napoleon cocked his head, smiling with renewed interest. 'What family is that?'

'His late father was the Duc d'Allorais. I suppose Vallon could still claim the title, although the Duc d'Allorais was executed during the Revolution with the rest of the family. Their estates were seized on behalf of the people of France, so there is now nothing for him to inherit. However, like all his ancestors before him, Count Vallon still claims to be the rightful heir to the Angevin Empire.'

Napoleon nodded, recalling the history of the Middle Ages. 'So, that would make Count Vallon heir to the thrones of France *and* England.'

'Exactly. And Vallon's father always took the claim seriously. The son was taught both English and French as a boy, and schooled in the history and customs of the English – I suppose as preparation for eventually becoming king.'

'Were they mad?' asked Napoleon mildly.

Ancre considered the question before answering. 'Well, Vallon's father was reputed to sleep in a bed with a mattress stuffed in equal parts with French and English soil.'

Napoleon shook his head pityingly. 'Aristocrats, Ancre,' he sighed. 'It was the right thing to do, taking off so many of their heads.'

Ancre smiled grimly. 'I always understood you were from a noble family, First Consul.'

'On the Isle of Corsica, we nobles were much closer to the ordinary people,' said Napoleon shortly. 'Go on, tell me more about this man Vallon.'

'He has a great love of music. He even has his own orchestra.'

'Does he?' said Napoleon, raising his eyebrows. 'That can't come cheap. And what else?'

'It is said he has exquisite taste. My intelligence agents report that he has built a palace in the Italian Renaissance style at Roc d'Or. It is filled with wonderful paintings and the finest furniture. Also, he manages to keep a notable chef and an outstanding wine cellar, even in the tropics.'

'What kind of a place is this Roc d'Or?'

'Originally, it was just a small town with a harbour. It was fortified by the Spanish over two hundred years ago as a refuge for their convoys from the South American gold mines. It stands at the head of what was once a jungle valley. But Count Vallon cleared and cultivated the land and made it into a vast and beautiful domain. The harbour defences are said to be impregnable; no one has ever broken through them.'

'Why is such a paradise not well known in France?'

Ancre shrugged. 'From what I have gathered, it seems Count Vallon does not seek fame. He is a brilliant organizer who has converted piracy into a highly profitable business.'

'In what way?'

Ancre noticed how keenly Napoleon had responded to the information that Vallon was a brilliant organizer. The First Consul also had the reputation of being gifted in that area.

'Pirates, or privateers as they're sometimes called, are usually feckless men,' Ancre explained. 'One might even say childish. In their need for excitement, they risk their lives to plunder ships, but then they sell their cargoes to clever, dishonest businessmen for a fraction of their true worth. Of course the businessmen make by far the greater degree of profit.'

Ancre could see he had the First Consul's full attention.

'Pray continue,' said Napoleon, leaning forward intently.

'Count Vallon has recruited many of these privateers and their boats. He now has a large fleet. He pays the captains and men a regular wage and bonuses from the profits, but while the plundering goes on, he hides behind a perfectly legal cargo business. He has set up a network of enterprises throughout Europe, North America and the Caribbean. He is even reputed to rob his own ships from time to time, just to keep up appearances.'

'A nice touch,' said Napoleon admiringly. 'And what cargoes does he carry?'

'Apart from stolen booty, the crops he produces in the domain.'

'Sugar?'

'Yes, and large quantities of laudanum and opium.'

'He grows poppies, eh?' said Napoleon, indicating that he knew the source of the pain-killing drugs.

'He does, sir. And he has a factory in the town which converts the raw materials before shipment.'

'Does he own many slaves?'

'Yes, both in the town and in the valley. Interestingly, he has many white slaves as well as blacks and mulattoes. And, as he lives in permanent danger from those who wish him dead, he pays a strong force of uniformed mercenaries as guards. He also has an artillery regiment to man the guns of the fortress.'

'What else can you tell me about this Count Vallon?' pressed Napoleon. 'Does he possess personal courage?'

'Beyond question, First Consul. At sea, he is known to be fearless, highly intelligent and unpredictable. An equal to, if not better than, any of the captains in the British Navy.'

'Why have we never seen this amazing man in France?' asked Napoleon, sounding almost jealous.

'He apparently travels extensively throughout Europe, but always incognito, pretending to be a plain man of business.'

'Always incognito?'

Ancre nodded. 'It seems he was involved in a damaging scandal when he was a young man and only escaped the consequences by accepting his father's banishment of him to Roc d'Or, which was originally part of the family estates in the Caribbean.'

'What kind of a scandal?' asked Napoleon with even keener interest. 'An unsuitable woman? Debts? Surely he wasn't a revolutionary?'

Ancre shook his head. 'The story is that as a youth he imprisoned several men who were late with their rents. When the wives and children came to protest, Vallon took them to the forest on his father's estate and had them tied to stakes and burned alive! When the news got out it took all of his father's influence to prevent him from being executed. As you can imagine, the people hated him – one of the reasons the Revolution was so successful in his region.'

General Ancre felt a sudden chill and rose to stand nearer the fire next to Napoleon.

'So, you see the problem, sir,' he added. 'Count Vallon is just the man you require, but unfortunately he is not altogether sane.'

Napoleon strode to the window and looked down on the garden for a time. Then he glanced up at Ancre, his face expressionless. 'Nonetheless, he sounds the right man for the job I have in mind,' he answered bleakly. 'Now let me tell you what I want you to do.'

Chapter Five

A SHIP OF THE LINE

'She's the *Torren*, sir,' a lookout with a spyglass shouted, and all hands on the deck of the *Dolphin* strained to gaze at the battleship looming towards them.

'What a lucky young fellow you are, Mr Raven,' said Commodore Beaumont, who'd appeared at the rail beside Peter and Able Seaman Connors. 'Of all the ships in the Brest blockade, we come upon the very one you require. A good omen for your chosen career, sir. Perhaps you have the Nelson touch.'

Peter glanced at Beaumont's smiling face, and again wondered how genuine were his credentials. It was almost a sacrilege to speak jokingly about Horatio Nelson. Surely no true patriot would talk disrespectfully about one of Britain's greatest heroes?

But keeping his thoughts to himself, Peter said, 'We haven't passed Ushant yet. Are we not still in the Channel?'

'You're right, sir,' said Connors. 'You'd think the *Torren* had come out to meet us.'

'Obviously they can't wait to have you aboard, Mr Raven,' added Beaumont with a teasing grin.

Despite the running sea, the two ships manoeuvred close to each other with well-practised ease. Peter's sea-chest was swung aboard the *Torren* before any of the supplies from the *Dolphin*. And to his surprise, he saw that Beaumont and Connors were also preparing to board the man-o'-war.

Waving away the offer of a bosun's chair Beaumont, with perfect timing, leapt across to the boarding ladder and nimbly clambered up the side of the warship. Connors followed him. Peter was next, and as he leapt he heard the wail of pipes and clash of marines presenting arms in the proper salute due to a commodore.

A lieutenant appeared to be expecting Beaumont, as Peter heard him say, 'The captain awaits you in his cabin, sir.'

Peter was ignored by the lieutenant, but a midshipman of about Peter's own age told him, 'One of the hands will bring your sea-chest. Follow me.'

Peter stood firm and addressed the lieutenant respectfully. 'Sir, I have dispatches from the Admiralty. I was expressly ordered to deliver them in person immediately I came aboard.'

This information seemed to put both the lieutenant and midshipman into a quandary, but Beaumont solved their dilemma by saying casually, 'Midshipman Raven may accompany me, Lieutenant.'

Relieved, the lieutenant left it to the young midshipman to escort them aft. Peter was puzzled by the discovery that Beaumont had obviously been expected, until he remembered the *Dolphin's* captain saying that HMS *Canard* had sailed the day before with urgent dispatches. Could she have carried word that the mysterious commodore was to join the *Torren*?

Outside the captain's cabin the marine guard presented arms, and Peter and Beaumont were shown into the spacious and comfortably furnished quarters.

Peter was surprised by how cosy the cabin was. It seemed more like the living-room of a country gentleman's house than the cabin of a warship. There were chintz curtains at the windows, upholstered easy chairs and a sofa. Like the furniture, the deck here was polished to a deep mahogany glow.

Peter hardly remembered his uncle, Captain Arthur Benchley, who now rose from behind the small writing desk and greeted Beaumont with a handshake. 'Commodore, I have been expecting you.'

Peter looked on, recalling that the last time he'd seen his uncle he had been seated on his knee after a Christmas dinner. He also had a vague memory of being given a half sovereign. Judging from the grim glance darted in his direction now, he did not expect any repetition of that generosity.

His uncle's dark hair was now shot with white, but his

face was still the colour of oak and his greenish-blue eyes, so like those of Peter's mother, looked as sharp as he remembered them.

'I took the liberty of bringing Mr Raven with me,' said Beaumont. 'I understand he carries dispatches from the Admiralty.'

'Mr Raven,' said Captain Benchley with no hint of warmth. 'Welcome aboard.' He held out his hand for the dispatches, saying, 'I will see you later, sir.'

It was a clear dismissal, but again Peter stood firm. 'Permission to speak, sir?' he requested nervously.

A deeper frown appeared on the captain's face, but he nodded curtly.

'I have something to report, sir.'

'Go on,' said the captain brusquely.

Peter almost wished the planks beneath him would part and he could plunge into the oblivion of the lower decks. But it was too late to back out now. Just as a lifetime's experiences are supposed to flash through the mind of those about to die, so Peter recalled the list of punishments a captain could impose for insubordination: flogging with a cat-o'-nine-tails, keelhauling, even hanging. Fortunately Peter's vivid imagination was tempered with common sense, so at least he didn't think it would come to that. Nonetheless, he was determined to do his duty, even though it could blight his career prospects from the very outset. 'I understand you were expecting Commodore Beaumont, sir,' he said. 'But I have reason to believe this man is an impostor.'

'Impostor?' replied Captain Benchley. 'Explain your-self, sir.'

Peter took a deep breath and continued. 'Two days ago, I was on the mail coach from London. Before dawn on the second day of the journey, this gentleman joined the coach at a lonely crossroads. But he was dressed in the uniform of a colonel of marines. He disappeared when we reached Portsmouth, and turned up again on HMS *Dolphin* just as we were about to sail. This time he was dressed in the uniform he wears now. I also suspect he has an accomplice: the man with whom he came aboard, an able seaman called Connors.'

'And why do you think Connors is his accomplice?' Captain Benchley asked almost mildly now.

Peter felt flattened. He realized how feeble his story sounded, but he pressed on. 'I saw them exchanging signals on the *Dolphin*, sir.'

'What sort of signals?'

'Just odd little facial exchanges, sir. Surreptitious expressions, really.'

There was a silence which seemed to Peter as if it was going to stretch into eternity. Finally, the captain said, 'This is a dashed awkward state of affairs, Beaumont.'

'Things could be worse, Captain Benchley,' Beaumont replied easily. 'You could have an idiot for a nephew. I think he might actually be bright enough to know how to hold his tongue.'

The captain shrugged. 'I suppose there's nothing for it.'

He turned his full attention to Peter and said, 'What I am about to tell you must go no further than this room. Do you understand?'

'Yes, sir,' answered Peter, relieved that no devastating punishment was about to befall him at the start of his naval career.

'Commodore Beaumont is on secret business for our country. For which he is allowed to wear any uniform he sees fit.' As he spoke, Captain Benchley broke the seals on the orders Peter had brought from the Admiralty.

'Ha!' he exclaimed upon glancing down at them. 'These are but confirmation of the instructions that the *Canard* brought two days ago. I am to expect you aboard, Commodore, and render you all possible assistance, unless vital blockade duties take precedence.'

Captain Benchley looked up with a smile. 'Well, Commodore. Unless she's required for battle, HMS *Torren* is at your disposal.'

'I'm obliged to you, sir,' replied Beaumont, taking the chair Benchley indicated while Peter remained standing at attention. 'But I feel I owe Midshipman Raven some sort of explanation.'

Looking at Peter, he said, 'I was dressed as a marine because immediately prior to joining the mail coach I'd met with some French secret agents whom I did not altogether trust, and had therefore assumed a different identity. That encounter has made my current business altogether more urgent. I knew my authorization from the Admiralty was on its way, but when I joined the coach I had no idea it was you who carried the necessary letter, Mr Raven. I'd thought the messenger would be even more delayed by the bad roads than you actually were. So I forged some more papers and sent them ahead with Connors. He's actually a Petty Officer, by the way. He dispatched them on *Canard* and waited aboard the *Dolphin* for me to catch up.'

'Good God,' exclaimed Captain Benchley, astonished. 'You actually *forged* those papers? They weren't from Admiralty?'

'That is correct, Captain,' Beaumont confirmed blithely. 'It's the sort of underhand thing we secret service chaps do, you know.'

Peter was deeply impressed. He knew Admiralty orders were sacrosanct. Beaumont must possess extraordinary coolness and nerve to risk such a course of action. Peter felt his previous attitude of distrust becoming one of admiration.

'What exactly can we do for you, Commodore?' asked Captain Benchley, now pouring a glass of brandy from a decanter and offering it to the commodore. 'I thought you chaps engaged in secret work preferred to use smaller, handier craft than one of the *Torren's* magnitude.'

Beaumont accepted the drink and sipped it thoughtfully before saying, 'A double-bluff. We know the French are just as clever as we are at the spying game. They wouldn't expect a first-rate ship of this size to be carrying British agents. I had intended Petty Officer Connors to consult with your signals officer to make certain arrangements before you put us ashore in your cutter.' He thought for a few seconds more, then came to a decision. 'Are you aware Midshipman Raven speaks excellent French, Captain Benchley?'

The captain smiled. 'I'm afraid my nephew and I are virtual strangers, Beaumont.'

The commodore addressed Peter. 'How is your knowledge of signals, Mr Raven?'

Peter realized this was not a moment for false modesty. 'I am competent, sir,' he replied confidently, glad of his hours of practice at the rectory.

Beaumont nodded, then continued. 'Can you handle a small boat?'

'I've only had occasion to do so on the river Thames, sir.'

The commodore looked to Captain Benchley. 'Perhaps Midshipman Raven could be given priority training in the handling of the ship's small boats, Captain.'

'As you wish, Commodore.'

Beaumont addressed Peter again. 'Midshipman, there may come a time when you will be called upon to perform a great service for your country that will be outside the usual line of duty. Will you be ready for such an eventuality?'

'Aye, aye, sir,' Peter replied, hoping he sounded confident.

'One more thing,' Beaumont added. 'You may one day see me in strange or altered circumstances. In no way must you acknowledge me until you have my permission to do so.'

'I understand, sir.'

Satisfied, Beaumont then reached inside his uniform jacket and produced a folded sheet of paper from his wallet. 'This is a code based on dots and dashes. It may be conveyed by flag signals or by lantern at night. You are to learn it by heart, Mr Raven, in the presence of no one save Captain Benchley. When not in use, he will keep it locked in his desk.'

'Aye, aye, sir,' replied Peter.

Beaumont nodded. 'Well then, I shall bid you goodbye, Mr Raven. Connors and I will be taking our leave of *Torren* in a little under an hour. But no doubt we shall see each other again one of these days.'

'Goodbye, sir,' Peter replied with a salute.

'Mr Claiborne!' shouted the captain, and the youth who had ushered them in earlier returned almost instantly.

'Show Mr Raven to the midshipmen's berth and explain his duties to him. In addition, he is to receive extra drill in signals and handling the ship's cutter. He is also to spend one hour with me each day at the beginning of the afternoon watch.'

'Aye, aye, sir,' replied Claiborne, before wheeling round smartly to lead Peter away.

Leaving the spacious well-lit airiness of the captain's quarters they descended by companionways through the lower gun decks and into a vast, shadowy, windowless labyrinth of strange smells and unaccustomed noises. The only light in the succession of claustrophobic spaces they passed through came from glowing lanterns in the crowded confines deep within the belly of the ship.

But Claiborne, totally at home in the confusing maze, easily negotiated the twists and turns. He clattered cheerily ahead, suddenly ducking down steeply laddered passage-ways and weaving past unexpected obstacles. Eventually, they arrived in the midshipmen's quarters.

It was an area filled at one end by a large mess table where two young men in shirt sleeves sat deeply absorbed, studying instruction manuals by the light of lanterns. Three others slept in bunks. Claiborne lit another lamp and ges-tured with it to a corner. 'Your chest is over there, Raven.'

Then he kicked the chair of one of the young men studying. 'Hey, Arrowsmith, aren't you even going to greet your relative?'

The fair-haired young man looked up with a pleasant grin. 'Hello, Raven, we've never met but it seems our mothers are cousins.'

Peter shook hands with the young stranger he judged to be a few years older than himself. 'Yes, sir,' he answered. 'I was told you were aboard. Our mothers correspond, you know.'

'No need to call me *sir*,' said Arrowsmith, then added hopefully, 'I don't suppose you know anything about trigonometry?'

'Well, a bit,' admitted Peter.

'I'm Fenton,' joined in the other student with sudden hope. 'Do you know what the refraction of light is?' He was a red-headed, broad-faced youth, younger than Arrow-smith.

Peter nodded. 'You know if you put a pencil in a glass of water it appears to bend at an angle?' he asked.

'Yes, everyone knows that.'

'Well, that's caused by the refraction of light.'

'It is?' said Fenton, impressed. 'No one's ever told me that before. But how do you calculate it?'

'He'll tell you later,' said Claiborne. 'I've got to show him over the ship first.'

'I thought there was supposed to be a schoolmaster aboard,' said Peter, knowing such an appointment was cus-tomary for the instruction of midshipmen.

'And a parson,' answered Claiborne. 'They were both drowned when a boat rowed by the captain's clerk over-turned. So was the clerk.'

'See you later, Raven. You can tell us about trigonome-try,' shouted Arrowsmith as they departed.

'You make friends fast, Raven,' said Claiborne when they'd left the midshipmen's mess and were making for the upper deck again.

'I hope so,' answered Peter as a shaft of light from above suddenly revealed the most terrifying face he had ever seen in his life.

Chapter Six

LIFE ABOARD THE *TORREN*

Standing stock-still in the companionway Peter stared at the face of a creature that could have been something out of a nightmare. The man's hairless head was sunburned dark-brown and his heavy features were shaped in a mask of livid pink scars. His hooked nose, blunt brow, hollowed cheeks and down-curved mouth could have been crudely shaped out of pink wax by some demented sculptor.

'Ah, Midshipman Raven, this is Mr Guttman,' said Claiborne. 'He's the best helmsman on board, and sure to be on the boat when you perform extra duties on the cutter.'

'Glad to make your acquaintance, sir,' said the man with a slight foreign accent.

Startled at first, Peter looked for a moment into the man's eyes and saw a kindness there that seemed at odds with his hideous appearance.

'How do you do?' he replied rather stiffly.

When they had hurried past and paused on the upper deck, Claiborne said, 'What do you think of our Mr Guttman?'

'He looks like something sent by the devil,' replied Peter, recovering from the shock.

'Yes,' said Claiborne with a mirthless laugh. 'Strange, ain't it? Seeing as the only truly devilish man we have on board is Lieutenant Blysse, and *he* looks like an angel.'

'What happened to Mr Guttman's face?' asked Peter.

But before Claiborne could answer, the lookout hailed from aloft, and Claiborne pointed towards a smudge on the horizon. 'Ushant,' he told Peter. 'Let's take a better look. We'll go up the shrouds, Raven.'

The challenge in Claiborne's words made Peter eager to prove himself.

Claiborne seized the nearest ladder-like arrangement of ropes and began to climb. Without hesitation, Peter followed. He already knew from his books of seamanship that the shrouds were the support ropes for the masts.

Peter had no fear of heights, and since he'd been a small boy and had first wanted to go to sea he'd always made a point of practising for this day: first, by constantly climbing the massive copper beech in the garden of the vicarage, then the tallest trees in Richmond Park and many others growing along the embankment of the Thames.

But the trees had never swayed in such an alarming and

exhilarating manner as this. All about him stretched great billowing canvas sails, and the taut ropes sang in the wind.

Peter didn't look down until Claiborne had led him to the topmost yard of the mainmast. Then he gazed below at the minute details of the distant deck. From up here the ship seemed quite small. Yet when he had been exploring the massive depths below deck, he'd wondered at her great size.

As they ploughed onwards through the broiling green-grey sea, HMS *Torren* pitched and swayed in a far more thrilling fashion than any fairground ride Peter had ever experienced.

The rocky island of Ushant, now in clear view, lay some way off the coast of Brittany, near the great French naval port of Brest. On the maps he had studied, Peter had always thought the shape of this part of France's coastline looked like a dog's head, open-mouthed and barking into the Atlantic Ocean, with Ushant just above its forehead like a biscuit someone had tossed.

'They say this is the crossroads of the world,' shouted Claiborne above the sound of the wind.

Peter nodded in reply. He'd heard the expression before. All the ships of northern Europe, be they westward or homeward bound, passed close to this point. It was where the English Channel met the deep waters of the Atlantic Ocean.

Spread out along the distant horizon, Peter could see the sails of the Royal Navy battleships, always ready for action. Peter knew similar scenes were repeated outside all the great ports of France, in the never-ending task of keeping the French fleet tamed.

These ships of the British blockade were maddening talons in Napoleon's flesh. As master of Europe, he might march his victorious armies wherever he desired, crushing all who opposed him. But on the high seas he was humbled, like a wolf kept in its place by an ever-watchful flock of eagles.

And so began one of the happiest times in Peter Raven's life. In the months that followed, he quickly settled down to life aboard the *Torren,* and grew to feel for it like nothing else he had ever known. There were times he missed his parents, and even his sisters, but the *Torren* became something quite different from a family home.

It was Peter Raven's first ship. All his youthful feelings of patriotism, good fellowship, and his heartfelt desire to serve something greater than himself were encapsulated in the way he felt about his new home and the shipmates with whom he shared her. Peter also learnt why HMS *Torren* was a happy ship.

'It's all down to Captain Arthur Benchley,' explained Claiborne one day when they were off duty in the midshipmen's berth. 'Mind you, he's not an easy-going man,' he added.

'More than forty years' service in the Royal Navy doesn't mellow those who command ships on the high seas,' added Fenton dryly, looking up from the letter he was writing.

'Keeping a battleship at a constant state of readiness calls for harsh discipline,' agreed Claiborne, who was lying back in his bunk idly plucking at the strings of a violin.

Arrowsmith sat up. 'I know he's our uncle,' he said, nodding towards Peter. 'But Captain Benchley has special qualities that make him a fine leader of men.'

'What do you mean?' asked Fenton.

Arrowsmith considered the question. 'He expects those of us who give orders to temper them with natural justice. And he's got a sense of humour.'

'He can be kind too,' admitted Fenton.

'I've not noticed him be particularly kind,' said Peter, who had earned a harsh reprimand that morning for sky-larking.

'Look how he treated Batt,' said Fenton.

Batt was a pressed-man who, although not very bright, had a willing and cheerful nature.

'What did he do for him?' asked Peter.

'Batt is hopeless at any task given to him,' said Fenton. 'It's not that he's sullen or resentful, just hopelessly uncoor-dinated.'

'Even when he's swilling down the deck his legs get entangled with the handle of the mop,' added Claiborne with a grin. 'But worst of all, the sound of guns terrifies him.'

Fenton nodded. 'When he first came on board the

sound frightened him so much he would just crouch down, hands clapped over his ears, utterly helpless.'

'A perfect victim for Lieutenant Blysse,' said Claiborne.

Peter knew Blysse, a burly, golden-haired young man with the pink and peach features of a cherub.

'Blysse picked on Batt the moment he came on board,' said Fenton.

'There's something wrong with Blysse,' said Arrowsmith. 'As far as Batt's concerned, he's like a cat torturing a mouse for amusement.'

'Was he always like that?' asked Peter.

'Before Batt came on board, Blysse tried to break Mr Guttman,' said Fenton. 'But it never got him anywhere.'

'Why?' asked Peter.

Fenton shrugged. 'Guttman seems to have some inner calm. Anyway, he was impervious to Blysse's bullying. He never showed any sign of discontent at the punishments Blysse handed out to him.'

'It was different for Batt,' said Arrowsmith. 'He went in terror, although Blysse was careful to make sure his cruelties didn't come to the attention of Captain Benchley.'

'How did he manage that?' asked Peter.

'Easy,' said Arrowsmith. 'Blysse never ordered Batt to be flogged or had him put in the gun deck leg-irons.'

'They're punishments that need the captain's approval,' said Fenton. 'But Mr Blysse had other ways to impose his bullying.'

'Such as?' asked Peter.

'Whenever Blysse was close to Batt, he'd give the order, "Start that man!" and Batt would get another blow,' said Arrowsmith.

Peter understood. Petty officers carried either rope ends dipped in tar or rattan canes to administer instant punishments. 'Didn't Captain Benchley notice?' he asked.

'He did eventually,' said Fenton. 'And it put the captain in a bit of a quandary. It's a bad business punishing an officer, and shocking bad for discipline all round. But Captain Benchley took steps to rescue Batt by putting him out of harm's way.'

Peter was intrigued. 'How?' he asked.

Arrowsmith grinned at his relative's impatience. 'Well, the captain doesn't usually tolerate cowardice, but he realized that poor old Batty was being picked on and was absolutely unable to cope with battle. So he made sure Batt was always under his nose by making him servant of the poop deck, a role the captain invented.'

'What duties did it entail?' asked Peter.

Arrowsmith shrugged. 'Oh, cleaning the brass-work, scrubbing the deck and tidying the rolled hammocks we store in nets to protect us against enemy musket fire.'

'So that was the end of the matter?' said Peter.

'Oh, no,' replied Fenton. 'Just the beginning. One day during gunnery practice the captain went sprawling over Batt, who was curled up in terror on the poop deck, a quivering ball of fear.'

'What did the captain do?' asked Peter, imagining how

furious his uncle would have been.

'Captain Benchley had an inspiration,' said Claiborne. 'And that's why the men love him.'

'Love him?' echoed Peter, puzzled by the extravagant claim.

'Like Nelson's crews love him,' answered Arrowsmith, nodding. 'The men we have on board *Torren* are a hard and rough lot, but most of them are human and fair. They all know battle's a different kind of torture for Batt. They think of him as a sort of ship's mascot, so they feel sorry for him and excuse his terror.'

'Seeing how scared Batt was,' said Fenton, 'the captain sent for the ship's carpenter and had him build a little refuge for him.'

'Really? Where?' asked Peter, astonished.

'In the rear structure of the poop deck,' explained Claiborne. 'And it was so cleverly done, nothing shows. Batt's hiding place looks like a natural swell of the woodwork. There's just enough space for him to sit in it sideways, and there's slits to let in air as well.'

'Now, whenever we clear for action or gunnery practice Batt goes and hides in there,' said Arrowsmith.

Claiborne laughed. 'Captain Benchley boasted that the arrangement kept Batt from under his feet, but everyone understood his real motive.'

'And that's why the crew loves him,' said Fenton. 'Captain Benchley could sail the *Torren* into Brest and fight every ship there and, to a man, we'd all follow him.'

*   *   *

As Peter became accustomed to the day-to-day routine on board the *Torren*, he gradually absorbed the mass of practical and theoretical knowledge he would need to pass his examinations and become a lieutenant. He was acutely aware that some poor fellows never did earn that promotion; there were five such men still in the midshipmen's berth who were in their thirties. They were hard-working individuals, but unable to master the mathematics and trigonometry required to advance to the rank of second lieutenant.

In his first weeks aboard *Torren* Peter learnt to appreciate the value of every division of the ship by spending time in the armourer's shop, the powder magazine, sail making, gunnery, carpentry, and especially with the yeoman of signals.

As Commodore Beaumont had requested, he was given extra tuition in using the ship's cutter and also received instruction in the handling of firearms and lessons in swordsmanship. He went aloft in foul weather with the topmast men to observe how the sails were controlled and secured by the miles of ropes and cables that were the sinews of the ship.

Each midday after eight bells sounded, Peter took his place with the other midshipmen on the quarterdeck and, weather permitting, read the ship's position with the aid of a sextant and his own calculations. These he carefully recorded in his midshipman's journal. When he was finally ready to seek promotion he would have to show this journal to an Admiralty Board.

After his first participation in the daily gunnery prac-tice, Peter caused laughter among his fellow midshipmen.

'Why doesn't the *Torren* carry enough powder monkeys to serve each gun crew?' he asked. 'Won't the guns run short of cartridges in battle?'

Still grinning, Claiborne explained. 'Powder monkeys running down to the magazine to fill their buckets with gunpowder is just another myth landsmen tell each other about the Navy. Like the story that we paint the lower decks red to disguise the blood of battle. They're painted red because that's the cheapest paint. They'd be painted sky-blue if the Navy Board could buy it for a farthing a gal-lon cheaper.'

'But there are plenty of boys on board,' said Raven.

'And they do a useful job mopping up the loose powder around the guns,' agreed Claiborne.

'So, who does bring the cartridges to the guns in battle?' Peter asked.

'You'll see the way of it when we strip the ship for action,' answered Claiborne.

Chapter Seven

LUCY COSGROVE'S ESCAPE
FROM NEW YORK

An ocean away from where Midshipman Peter Raven was learning his profession, Mary Van Duren, a pupil at The Trenton School for Young Gentlewomen, woke up with a start, her heart racing.

Sitting bolt upright in bed, she saw a slim figure silhouetted against the lace curtains of the dormitory window. Mary was about to scream when the figure leapt silently towards her and placed a finger on her lips.

'Shhhh,' hissed a familiar voice.

'Lucy Cosgrove!' whispered Mary. 'You gave me such a fright. What *are* you doing? And why are you dressed in those disgusting old clothes?'

'I'm running away,' answered the tall girl. 'I've finally taken more than I can endure from the Trenton family.'

'Anyone would think you were a child, not nearly

seventeen,' said Mary scornfully.

'The Trentons won't teach me Latin and I can't attend university without knowing it,' said Lucy, lacing her moccasins tighter. 'No wonder there are no women at Princeton.'

'Why do you want to attend university?' asked Mary. 'You could always be a professor's wife,' she added, deeply puzzled by Lucy's outlandish ambition.

'Maybe I'd rather marry the kind of man who'd prefer to have a well-educated woman for a wife,' said Lucy.

Such a thought was too unconventional for Mary to grapple with. 'They'll catch you,' she warned.

'Not once I get up the Hudson Valley,' Lucy answered grimly. 'I know the woods there.'

'Then you'll be eaten by bears or wolves,' Mary predicted with absolute certainty.

'Not if I get my rifle and knife.'

'What are you going to do with them?' said Mary more loudly. 'Shoot your way into Princeton?'

'Quiet,' said Lucy. 'You'll wake the others.'

Lucy was dressed in fringed buckskin. Her black hair was pulled back and tied with a leather thong.

'Where did you get those Indian clothes?' Mary whispered.

'Brought them with me in my trunk, of course.'

'They smell funny.'

'They smell of wood smoke. It's a nice smell.'

'Only if you're a backwoodsman. So, how are you going

to get to the Hudson Valley?' whispered Mary, both alarmed and intrigued by her friend's reckless intentions.

Despite her haste, Lucy asked, 'Do you even know where we are, Mary? I speak in geographical terms.' After all the years they had known one another, Lucy was still astonished by her friend's happy ignorance of the world about her.

'We're in New York, silly,' came the self-satisfied reply. 'Located on Stone Street in lower Manhattan, *and* the most fashionable part of the city, at that.'

Lucy gestured towards the window. 'Not so far over that way is the Hudson River. From there, I can get a boat all the way home to my grandfather's house.'

Mary was astonished. Having always lived in New York, she'd never been the slightest bit interested in how others got there.

'You mean to tell me that dirty old stretch of water leads all the way to your family estate?'

'Practically to the front door,' said Lucy. 'And, it might also interest you to know, the Hudson River is as clear as spring water when you get above the city and beyond the salt-water tide.'

'Really? I didn't realize that,' said Mary, genuinely astonished.

Perhaps this blissful state of unknowing was why Mary was so popular with Mrs Trenton, Lucy mused. The headmistress was a tyrant who made no secret of the fact that she held a deep distrust of well-educated women.

Mary had relished her lessons in dancing, manners, deportment, music and social etiquette. But any efforts to impart to her even the slightest amount of information on other subjects had been carefully rejected, like unwanted food pushed to the side of her plate. She had only roused herself to learn French because Mrs Trenton had told her no young lady could ever hope to win a worthwhile husband unless she'd acquired a proper grasp of the language.

Mr Trenton, the headmistress's husband, was supposed to have taught the girls French, but he'd been quite hopeless as he had barely any knowledge of the language himself. Luckily, the school employed a part-time French-speaking seamstress from New Orleans, whom Lucy and Mary had paid extra to teach them the language correctly.

'Well, goodbye, Mary,' said Lucy, quietly easing open the window. 'You're all I shall miss about this place.'

'They'll bring you back,' warned Mary.

'They may try,' replied Lucy. 'But I doubt they'll succeed. I'll see you when I visit my great-aunt in the winter, *and* I'll be learning Latin by then.' With that, Lucy threw a leg over the sill and climbed down the thick ivy clinging to the brick wall.

Unlike Mary, Lucy had an intimate knowledge of the darkened streets around Mrs Trenton's school, so was able to slip purposefully through the shadows.

At the corner of Pearl and Broad Streets, despite the lateness of the hour there were still lights burning in the Queen's Head Tavern, and Lucy could feel a brisk breeze that smelled of the ocean blowing from below the Battery.

At the otherwise deserted dockside she soon found the men she sought: young Ned Pullman and his older brother Sam. With the help of two deck-hands they were loading a cargo of large carboys filled with clear liquid on to their ancient sloop, the *Ginger*. Clearly they considered the content of the jars was best shifted at night.

'Hello, Ned, Sam,' said Lucy as she stepped out of the shadows.

Both brothers jumped like startled jackrabbits at the sudden soft sound of her voice.

'Damnation, Lucy!' grumbled Ned. 'You come creeping up on folks like that and you'll get a bullet through you.'

'Not the way you shoot, Ned,' Lucy replied with a grin. She had known the brothers since childhood and had often hunted with them in the Hudson River Valley.

'Did you bring the fare?' asked Ned, always the practical member of the family.

'One dollar,' replied Lucy, handing over the money.

'It's two dollars on the regular passenger boats,' grumbled Sam.

'Yes, but for that you get a decent bed to sleep in and meals provided. You said if I was to come I'd have to provide the dinners.'

'Welcome aboard,' said Ned, pushing her to sit out of the way of their labours.

*   *   *

Three days passed aboard the *Ginger* and Lucy enjoyed herself more than at any time during the previous term. She
fished for shad, and when they tired of eating fish Lucy borrowed Sam's old musket and shot rabbits, which she then
roasted on a fire close to the embankment.

The wind blew erratically and sometimes it was cold,
but the autumn scenery was spectacular with the trees turning to russet and gold. The lakes joined by the mighty river
teemed with fish, and as always Lucy was thrilled by the
rich wild countryside and magnificently forested mountains
rising up from the valley.

As they approached her grandfather's estate, the cold
weather gave way to a violent storm with a dazzling display
of lightning. An omen of things to come, Lucy told
herself.

'New Orleans!' exclaimed General George Cosgrove, slap-
ping the table at which he was seated with his friend
and neighbour Robert R. Livingston, the man who had
administered the oath to George Washington when he
was inaugurated as first president of the United States of
America.

The two men were sitting on the pillared terrace of the
general's magnificent house, overlooking the broad wood-
land of the Hudson Valley and the silvery river that flowed
through it.

Livingston nodded in agreement. Although he was rather
hard of hearing, there was no mistaking the general's words.

'New Orleans is the key to the future of the United States,' continued General Cosgrove.

Robert Livingston, a tall distinguished man with bold features and hooded eyes, pinched the tip of his nose between thin fingers. 'Yes, but there are those who say there should be more than one country in this great land, George, not just the United States of America,' he said wearily. 'The French want Louisiana back from the Spanish. The news is that since they've ended their war with us, Napoleon Bonaparte is about to acquire it in exchange for some tinpot kingdom he's going to invent in Europe.'

Louisiana was a vast tract of territory, with hardly any population apart from the tribes of nomadic Indians and the occasional fur trappers with whom they traded. Far greater in size than any European country, Louisiana stretched from Canada in the north to the Gulf of Mexico in the south. The wide Missouri and Mississippi rivers made it relatively easy to travel the length of this mighty wilderness.

'It would be better for us if this land could all belong to America, Robert, but if that is not to be, then we *must* stop the French taking New Orleans. At the very least we must continue to have access to it as the Spanish have always allowed us,' said Cosgrove, his mane of silver hair shaking around his handsomely fleshy face as he argued. 'The president agrees with me.'

Livingston sighed. 'The president still thinks the French can do no wrong, despite the sea war we've just finished fighting with them.'

General Cosgrove slapped the table again. 'Thomas Jefferson has a strange affection for the French, but he knows we must make a binding treaty with whoever controls Louisiana, so that we keep the right to ship goods from New Orleans port.'

'Have you ever been there?' asked Livingston.

'To New Orleans?' The general nodded. 'A strange place. It's unbelievably hot and humid, and below sea level. They can't even bury their dead. Any hole they dig just fills up with water. Bodies have to be placed in stone tombs above the ground.'

General Cosgrove slapped the table yet again. 'I have long thought, sir, that if the French do acquire Louisiana from Spain, we should make them an offer to *buy* New Orleans. France is broke. She's been fighting wars for so long there's nothing left in the national coffers. Selling us the rights to use the port wouldn't do them any harm, and it would greatly increase the money in Napoleon's treasury . . .'

Just then Barrington, General Cosgrove's butler, hurried out on to the terrace as if the British Army was once again coming up the Hudson Valley. He announced gravely, 'Mrs Hargreave is here, sir.'

'She's *here*?' queried General Cosgrove, somewhat surprised. The last communication he'd received from his widowed sister had been in the height of summer. She had made no mention then that she intended to visit. And she always preferred him and Lucy to visit her at the New York mansion she'd inherited from her late husband.

Before Barrington could answer, an upright, handsome, middle-aged woman swept on to the balcony. The two men rose to greet her.

'Good afternoon, Robert,' she said, addressing Livingston. Then, getting straight to the point, she told her brother, 'George, your granddaughter has run away from school.'

'I know she has,' Cosgrove replied shortly.

'*How* do you know?' demanded his sister, astonished. 'I came up river from New York on a private packet boat as soon as Mrs Trenton informed me. I doubt if anyone could have brought the news faster.'

General Cosgrove shook his head. 'Well, you're wrong, Lizzie. Lucy crept into the house yesterday before dawn and took her rifle and knife from the gun room. Jack Cobden recognized her footprints. He put two and two together and figured she'd come up river with those shiftless Pullman brothers. Jack's out tracking her now.'

'Cobden!' Mrs Hargreave exclaimed in disgust. 'That dreadful fellow. He'll just encourage her to stay in the woods. I blame you, George. Fancy appointing a gamekeeper to be nursemaid to your only grandchild.'

'Jack Cobden is *not* a gamekeeper, Lizzie,' said General Cosgrove. 'Must I always remind you he is my oldest friend, not a servant?'

Mrs Hargreave accepted the chair that Barrington offered her, and all three sat down.

'How can you say he's a friend?' insisted Mrs Hargreave. 'He lives in a mud hut in the wilds. He's nothing more than . . . than an animal.'

General Cosgrove held his temper and spoke slowly. 'Jack lives in a log cabin, not a mud hut. After the war, in which I must remind you he saved my life, he could have gone into business with me when I begged him to, but he wasn't interested in shipping.

'When Lucy's parents died of the fever there was no one to look after her. *You* were off gallivanting in France and my business took me away most of the time. It made a lot of sense to let a backwoodsman look after a child in those days.'

'But she's a *girl*,' protested Mrs Hargreave. 'He made her into a wild creature.'

Cosgrove gave a snorting laugh. 'I think that's more likely to be due to her great-grandmother's Crow blood.'

Mrs Hargreave sat up stiffly, avoiding Livingston's eye. 'Our mother did *not* have Crow blood, George,' she insisted. 'The black hair in her family comes from a Spanish ancestor.'

'If that fairy tale pleases you, Elizabeth, then you go on believing it,' said the general, sighing.

'I don't care what you say, George; you've failed Lucy, and failed her lamentably. But I plan to make a lady of her,' said Mrs Hargreave with iron determination.

'Go on,' said the general, interested to hear what she was proposing.

'Now that America's tiresome squabble with France has come to an end I shall take Lucy to Paris,' announced Mrs Hargreave with a triumphant smile.

Deep in the woods of the Hudson Valley, far from any farm, Lucy Cosgrove sat with her back against a great beech tree, watching her fire.

Suspended in its glowing embers, two plump wood pigeons were almost cooked to her liking, and propped against the tree was a Kentucky long rifle, which she had already cleaned. She was sharpening a twig of wood to test the edge of the knife she'd just honed.

Without looking up, she called, 'Come on out, Jack, the birds are about done.'

With feather-light footsteps a tall, powerful man, also clad in buckskin, stepped out of the shadows and crouched down beside the fire. The right cheek of his darkly-tanned face was marked with an old scar shaped like a starburst that had been made by an Indian arrow.

'I've brought coffee, sugar and salt,' he said by way of greeting, and unslung a leather knapsack from which he unloaded the supplies.

'I don't want to go back to that school, Jack. I want to go to Princeton University,' said Lucy when they'd eaten the birds and were sipping coffee.

'You're *not* going back to school,' said Jack, poking the fire with a long stick.

'I bet I am,' said Lucy with some feeling. 'Grandfather

will insist.'

'It isn't so,' said Jack. 'When I said I was going to track you I figured you'd like a few days to yourself. So I hung about the house keeping out of sight. Your Aunt Elizabeth turned up. She was angry as a kicked hive of bees. I couldn't help overhearing her conversation with your grandfather, as I was resting in a nearby tree.'

Lucy grinned at the image of Jack Cobden eavesdropping on her great-aunt from the bow of an oak tree. It would have confirmed her worst suspicions about him. 'What did you learn?' she asked

'You're going to Paris, girl.'

'Paris!' repeated Lucy, surprised. 'Hmmm, I wonder what Paris is like?'

'Well, I liked it fine, so did Ben Franklin,' said Jack after some consideration. 'And Tom Jefferson. Well, he just fell in love with the place.'

Lucy nodded into the fire. 'What about going to Princeton?'

'It's a lot easier for a girl to get into Paris,' admitted Cobden, raking the ashes of the fire with a long stick.

Chapter Eight

THE MIGHT OF HMS *TORREN*

Peter Raven soon had an opportunity to observe how the boys of the lower deck played their part in battle. Early in October, while the *Torren* was beating close to Brest, three French frigates made a bold show to create the impression they were coming out into the open sea. But it was only a feign to allow a fast sloop to slip away.

Nonetheless, HMS *Torren* responded wholeheartedly to the threat of the approaching frigates, and Peter saw the result of Captain Benchley's endless training put into practice.

The order '*action stations!*' reverberated around the ship, and in little more than ten minutes she would be transformed. As Peter had not yet been allotted a permanent battle station he was instructed to roam about the various decks to watch and learn. What he saw impressed and astonished him. Like some great beast roused from slumber, HMS *Torren* seemed to shake herself in preparation for battle.

A rolling drumbeat sent all hands scurrying to their stations as the entire crew burst into a frenzy of action. But there was no confusion as every man applied himself to his allotted task with impressive speed and efficiency.

The marines took up the positions from which they would direct their musket fire at the enemy. Under the bosun's directions, topmen scrambled aloft to man the sails and rigging and be ready to carry out repairs under fire. The armourer broke out and distributed the stores of cutlasses, pikes, short muskets, blunderbusses, pistols and axes, should it come to hand-to-hand fighting.

Wet sand was strewn across the decks to provide a firmer footing. Below, the carpenter and his team worked rapidly to make long continuous passageways of the gun decks by knocking down the bulkheads and rushing them to storage below the water line. Furniture from the ward rooms and captain's cabin was also hurried below.

When the carpenter's team had finished their dismantling they stood by below, equipped with sheets of lead and canvas, wooden beams and props, spikes and nails, ready to staunch any breeches made below the water line by enemy fire.

Peter saw what Claiborne had meant about the duties of powder monkeys. No boys were poised ready to run down to the magazine with buckets. Instead, relays of men had formed, ready to pass the correct weight of gunpowder cartridges to the variously sized guns. The boys stood by with mops, ready to sweep up loose powder and give a hand wherever else the gun captain saw fit.

Peter followed a chain of men that went below into the deep bowels of the ship, where the lead-lined flooring that led to the powder room was flooded with an inch or so of water. In the powder magazine the gunners' men, wearing felt slippers and with all metal removed from their clothing to avoid accidentally creating a spark, feverishly prepared fat cartridges of gunpowder. Their only source of light came from lanterns shining through the windows of another small sealed room overlooking the magazine.

Peter raced back to the upper deck and watched the gun crews stripping the protective coverings off the rows of cannon before they hauled them into position at the firing ports. He had never seen men engaged in such concentrated and desperate activity; the very air seemed charged with the electricity of battle.

Glancing at his watch, he noted that the whole preparation had taken ten and a half minutes and the *Torren* was now nothing like a slumbering beast. Peter was put in mind of a gigantic loaded pistol, primed, cocked and ready to blast a massive scythe of solid iron shot into an enemy.

Driven by the pace and excitement of the warlike activity, adrenalin surged through Peter's body, so that he too felt ready to throw himself upon the foe. Then, at the captain's orders, the drumming ceased and the marine band struck up a crashing rendition of *Hearts of Oak*.

At the rousing sound of the opening notes, the entire crew of the *Torren* sent a great roaring cheer of defiance rolling across the sea towards the French frigates. Peter Raven felt the hair on his neck rise and a swell of pride in his breast as he joined in.

The following day Captain Benchley sent for Peter. He stood uneasily to attention in the cabin while the captain finished reading a document. Then Benchley looked up and gave his nephew the briefest of smiles.

'As from this moment, I'm appointing you my midshipman, Mr Raven,' he explained. 'Your duties are to be at my beck and call at all times. Do you understand?'

'Aye, aye, sir,' Peter replied smartly.

Captain Benchley nodded. 'It means I may call upon you day or night. Sinclair, my servant, will fix you up with sleeping arrangements nearby. I think there's a vacant cubby-hole near my galley.'

When Peter returned to the midshipmen's berth Arrowsmith asked, 'What did Captain Benchley want?'

'I'm to be his midshipman,' Peter replied hesitantly, wondering if his friends might view this as a privilege. 'What do you think, Claiborne?' he asked. 'Will the crew think I'm being given special treatment because the captain is my uncle?'

Claiborne laughed. 'Wait till we go into battle for real, Raven,' he replied. 'The poop deck is one of the most dangerous spots on the ship. Not only have you got the

enemy cannons to put up with, but all the Frog sharpshooters will be doing their utmost to kill you and the captain.
There ain't no privilege in being the captain's midshipman.
Some might even say he was going out of his way *not* to
make it easy on you.'

Claiborne's answer mollified Peter's fears and he looked
forward to his new duties.

He found the captain's servant in the empty dining-
room and made himself known. Sinclair, a thin mournful-
looking Londoner, showed him around with a proprietorial
air. Peter was most struck by how lavish and spacious the
captain's quarters were in comparison to the cramped conditions most of the men occupied in the rest of the ship.

'That's because *Torren* is a first-rater,' Sinclair told him
with a knowing smile. 'She's one of the only ten ships in the
entire Royal Navy armed with more than a hundred guns.'

'And don't first-raters usually carry admirals?' asked
Peter.

'Yes, Mr Raven,' agreed Sinclair. 'Admirals direct the
operations of the fleet but the actual command of the ship is
always left to the captain, even though the admiral may
make a suggestion from time to time.'

'So, Captain Benchley occupies quarters fit for an admiral?' said Peter.

'That's right,' said Sinclair. 'A comfortable cabin, a dining-room, and even a separate bedroom. And his second in
command, First Lieutenant Crawford, has the quarters the
captain would occupy were there an admiral aboard.'

Peter mused on how varied life was in different parts of
the ship. Even the officers lived in fairly confined conditions, and the crew mess decks were truly Spartan with
their basic odds and ends of furniture crammed in between
the great cannons on the gun decks. But the captain lived in
another world of fresh air, elegant rooms filled with light,
and a welcome absence of unpleasant smells.

When Peter took his things up to his new quarters and
reported for duty, Captain Benchley instructed him to
introduce himself to his clerk who would explain the daily
tasks to be performed by the captain's personal staff. That
was how he first met Matthew Book.

Peter entered the captain's dining-room and found a
powerful figure seated at the table with his back to him.
He'd only caught glimpses of the clerk before. Mr Book was
dressed as an ordinary seaman in slop shirt and canvas
trousers, but unusually he wore buckled shoes. Most crewmen went barefoot, unless they were going aloft.

Before him was a heap of ledgers and documents. Seem-
ingly engrossed, the man finished making a rapid entry in a
leather-bound ledger. But he was aware of Peter's presence
and eventually laid aside the quill and rose to his feet. He
had to stoop to avoid banging his head on the low beams as
he turned to face Peter.

'Mr Raven,' he said in a deep melodious voice with an
accent Peter could not place. 'Welcome to the captain's
staff.'

It wasn't only the man's sheer physical size that

impressed Peter. Despite his awkward stance, Matthew
Book had the bearing of an aristocrat. Looking at his ebony-
black face Peter saw many things: intelligence, humour, for-
bearance, and a hint of melancholy.

Instinctively, Peter held out his hand. Smiling slightly,
Matthew hesitated briefly before taking it in his own. The
palm that engulfed Peter's was warm, dry and hard, and he
knew the clerk could have crushed his bones as easily as a
bundle of dry twigs.

'I wasn't expecting . . .' Peter said, his voice trailing
away.

'A black man to be the captain's clerk?' Matthew Book
finished for him with an even broader smile.

'Well, yes,' answered Peter, thinking it pointless to
avoid the truth.

'Perhaps you have gypsy blood, Mr Raven,' said the man
easily. 'I could see you were looking into my soul.'

Peter smiled back, knowing he had made a friend.
'Other people have said I look like a gypsy, Mr Book. Perhaps next time you take tea, you'll let me read your fortune
in the leaves.'

Matthew Book was the first black man Peter had ever
spoken to. Until he'd come aboard the *Torren*, where there
were at least ten among the crew, he'd only ever seen one
other.

Two years previously Isaac, the gardener and handyman
at his father's vicarage, had taken Peter to the fair on Ham
Common and they'd watched a prize fight between two

professional pugilists. One of the contestants had been as black as Matthew Book.

Matthew took Peter to the captain's galley where he introduced him to Perry, the captain's jovial, red-faced Welsh cook. They were joined by Sinclair and Batt, who was fussing over a mop-head that had come loose. Smiling meekly, Batt put a knuckle to his forehead when he was introduced but seemed too shy to speak.

'Would you care for a nice fresh cup of water, Mr Raven?' asked Perry. Peter was surprised to see the cook pump a lever on the wall and water gushing into the pewter mug he held. As he drank the water, Peter was sure it tasted a lot better than any other he'd had on board.

Perry chuckled with pride and banged the bulkhead. 'Wonderful, is it not, sir?' he asked. 'A new metal tank was installed for the captain at the last fitting out. Of course the rest of the crew still drinks from barrels, but they say all the newest ships will have metal water tanks fitted for everyone. Things are changing in the Navy, right enough. Look at the amount of fresh food the hands get. They eat like officers on the lower deck these days.'

Peter had to agree. He had come aboard HMS *Torren* fully prepared for the grim food his sisters had predicted, only to find that although the diet was monotonous it far exceeded his expectations.

But Sinclair sniffed. 'The food's good while we're on blockade duty, Perry. We're just down the channel from home where the supply boats can reach us easy enough. But you'll see things differently if we're sent on a long voyage. In a few months we'll be on salt beef and pork, with weevils in the biscuits. There'll be no chucking spoilt bread overboard then, you mark my words.'

'Mr Raven!' A shout summoned Peter to the captain's cabin.

He hurried off, and the others quickly returned to their duties.

Chapter Nine

DINNER WITH CAPTAIN BENCHLEY

Autumn turned to winter and the days shortened. Still the *Torren* remained on station with the Brest blockade. Peter was now well accustomed to his duties and knew those brief moments of opportunity in the day when he could snatch a few moments of warmth in the captain's galley.

One morning when he was there with Matthew Book, the captain summoned them both. Peter saw Matthew make a swift detour to his desk to snatch up a writing crayon and a notebook. He waited so they could enter the captain's cabin together.

Benchley seemed in a thoughtful mood. 'I heard two midshipmen talking yesterday,' he began. 'Claiborne told Arrowsmith that port wine was for bumpkins and gentlemen drank only brandy.'

Peter did his best to suppress a grin. Claiborne was well known in the midshipmen's mess for putting on airs and making preposterous claims about what constituted 'proper behaviour', but his ludicrous pretensions were more a source of amusement than anger among his mess-mates.

The captain continued. 'It is my duty to train midshipmen to be naval officers, and that includes the social graces. I fear I have been negligent. So, the following officers and midshipmen are invited to dine with me tonight at eight o'clock.'

Peter was glad to see Matthew ready to note down the names. 'Lieutenants Crawford, Wesley, Blysse and Westlake, Mr Matlock the surgeon, Captain Hepworth of the marines, and Midshipmen Claiborne, Arrowsmith, Raven and Fenton. Got that?'

'Aye, aye, sir,' replied Matthew.

'And tell the bandmaster I will want the string quartet to play.'

Peter could have sworn Matthew let out a quiet sigh.

'They are to perform a selection of Mozart, Handel and Vivaldi.'

'Aye, aye, sir.'

'As to food, what do *you* suggest, Mr Book?'

After a slight pause, Matthew answered. 'We still have a few ducks. I know an excellent preparation for duck livers, sir. Then you could have the birds roasted as the third course, followed by a baron of beef. The meat is well-hung. And we took some lobsters from the French fishing smack we stopped yesterday. With mayonnaise they would make a good second course.'

'What about pudding?'

'We still have apples and berries stored in sawdust. A pie with fresh cream, followed by nuts and a Stilton cheese?'

Captain Benchley looked at Peter. 'How does that sound, Mr Raven?'

'Magnificent, sir,' he replied, his mouth watering in anticipation.

Captain Benchley nodded. 'Mr Book, write out a list of those invited and give it to Mr Raven so he may inform them.'

As Matthew withdrew Captain Benchley opened his drawer and took out the code Commodore Beaumont had given to Peter. 'How are you with this now?' he asked.

'I know it by heart, sir,' Peter answered promptly.

'Quite sure?'

'Quite sure, sir,' he replied.

'Good, well done,' said the captain, putting the list back in his desk and turning the key. 'Remarkable fellow, Matthew Book,' he said.

'Indeed, sir,' agreed Peter a trifle awkwardly. His uncle was still something of a stranger to him and Peter was careful not to cross the line into familiarity.

'Mr Book was a gun captain when my last clerk drowned. He was an absolute master of the short-barrelled carronade,' mused the captain. 'I put the word out for any man who could read and write and he was the best of those who came forward, which was a great relief to me. My previous clerk always smelled like a dead dog, even before he drowned. I don't think he'd ever washed in his life. Matthew Book actually bathes. And that does make life more pleasant when you're living in such confined quarters.'

'I'm sure it does, sir,' said Peter as Matthew returned with the list of those invited to the dinner.

Peter went about the ship requesting the captain's pleasure and was made especially welcome in the midshipmen's berth, where Claiborne and Arrowsmith were engrossed in their studies.

'What's he serving us for supper, Raven?' Claiborne asked eagerly. 'Any decent wine?'

'What would a bed-bug like you know about wine, Claiborne?' Peter replied, adopting a mockingly superior air. 'Stewed toads, cheese rind and stale beer for you. The rest of us are having a feast.'

'Ignorant young landlubber!' shouted Claiborne as Peter hurried away to continue delivering the invitations.

'Be careful who you call ignorant, Claiborne,' Peter shouted back with a wide grin. 'It's *dinner* you're going to, not supper.'

'Champagne, Mr Raven?' asked Matthew Book, stooping to proffer a silver tray heavy with brimming silver mugs. He was dressed in the white jacket of a steward, as was Sinclair. So large was the captain's cabin, there was enough space and headroom for all the guests to stand. Only Matthew had to keep his head down.

Captain Benchley had been fortunate in gaining prize money in the past few years, so the dining table glittered with lavish silver settings and impressive plate, candlesticks and fine china. The string quartet played softly, and the sea was reasonably calm, allowing the guests to stand comfortably despite its gentle swell.

Claiborne nudged Peter and nodded at the silverware on the table. 'Let's hope some of the captain's luck rubs off on us, Raven,' he muttered. 'I wouldn't mind going home on leave with my pockets stuffed with money.'

Claiborne rather exaggerated a midshipman's share of any prize money, but there was the real possibility of some reward in the future. In time of war, captured ships brought into British ports were sold and the prize money distributed on a sliding scale of percentages among the crew. The admiral who commanded the squadron received the lion's share, whether or not he'd taken part in the action.

Knowing what to expect, Peter tried to appear nonchalant as he accepted the mug of champagne from Matthew.

'Bit soured, this vintage,' said Claiborne, his lips suddenly pursed.

'It always tastes like this,' replied Peter.

'Oh, does it?' said Claiborne, too surprised to continue the pretence that he'd drunk it before. 'I always thought it would be sweet.'

Peter's attention was then caught by the string quartet.

Although he'd never properly learnt the piano, his mother had encouraged his appreciation of music and he knew the violinist was making some awful sounds. But apart from Peter, only Matthew Book seemed to have noticed it above the buzz of conversation in the increasingly warm room.

Suddenly Matthew laid down his tray and hurried forward to catch the offending violinist as he toppled from his chair. The music trailed off, and Captain Benchley turned as Matthew swept the musician up in his arms.

'What ails the man, Mr Book?' he enquired. 'Even I could tell his playing was off.'

'The violinist is unwell, sir,' replied Matthew. 'Although his skill on the instrument is always somewhat limited.'

There was a murmur of alarm among the officers. With men living in such close conditions diseases often swept through ships, and rank was no insurance against infection.

'What does it look like?' asked Captain Benchley, concerned.

'He's drunk, sir,' Lieutenant Blysse stated contemptuously.

'Then he shall be flogged,' said the captain grimly. Although a largish ration of alcohol was twice daily distributed to the men on board British ships, drunkenness was considered a serious crime. Inebriated sailors unable to attend to their duties properly could put the lives of others at risk.

'I don't think he's drunk, sir,' said the ship's surgeon Mr Matlock, who was now leaning over the thickset young marine. 'He looks more as if he has apoplexy.'

Matthew laid the young man down and unclasped the over-tight collar of his uniform to reveal an angry red welt around his throat.

'This man was choking,' said Matlock, as the youth began to suck down deep lungfuls of the warm air.

'What is the reason for this?' asked the captain.

The cello player stood up, pale with fear at having to talk to the captain in these circumstances. 'He's wearing the wrong uniform, sir,' he stuttered. 'His own got spoilt early on and he borrowed one of his mate's, but it was too tight.'

'Well, that's put paid to the music,' said the captain rue-fully, as Sinclair assisted the youth from the cabin after receiving a nod from Matthew Book.

'May I speak, sir?' requested Matthew.

'Eh? Oh, yes. What is it, Book?' said the captain, dis-tracted by events.

'With your permission, sir,' he said, 'I could replace the bandsman.'

'You?' replied Captain Benchley. 'Play the violin? We don't want any jigs or hornpipes.'

'I think I can manage, sir.'

'Well, go ahead, give it a try. Good man.'

Matthew Book took up the discarded violin and after a muttered consultation with the cello player he began.

After the first passage of a piece by Handel, the captain nodded his surprised approval. 'What an astonishing man,' he muttered, and turned to his guests.

Peter was equally impressed. He knew from experience how difficult it was to play the violin and just how skilfully Matthew Book was performing on the instrument.

At the end of the meal Peter, as the youngest at the table, was called upon to propose the Royal Toast. He could feel his head ringing with the unaccustomed amount of strong drink he'd taken, even though Captain Benchley had instructed that the younger midshipmen were to be kept in short supply of the wine.

But Peter managed to speak up clearly, and the words, 'King George the Third, God bless him,' were echoed by the officers as Midshipman Collier came in from duty on the quarterdeck. His cloak and hat glistening with rain, Collier cast an envious glance at the table, which was still heaped with nuts, fruit, cheese and decanters of spirits, before he reported to the captain.

'Officer of the watch told me to inform you that there are odd signalling lights coming from starboard, sir,' he said, loudly enough for the entire table to hear.

Chapter Ten

THE WOUNDED MAN

'I shall come immediately, Mr Collier,' replied Captain Benchley, and he nodded for Peter to accompany him.

'There's no need to end the party quite so soon,' he assured the other men seated at the table. 'Mr Crawford, I'd be obliged if you would deputize as host and offer the gentlemen more of that excellent port or brandy.'

Pausing only to don their boat cloaks and hats, Captain Benchley and Peter hurried to the quarterdeck. The rain fell as a heavy soaking mist in the cold night air.

'Where was the signal coming from?' asked Benchley, peering towards the dark coastline.

The officer of the watch pointed, and gave the compass direction. 'There it is again, sir,' he added.

A single light flashed on and off for half a minute. The captain drew Peter aside, out of the earshot of the others on deck.

'Is that Beaumont signalling?' he asked. 'I must be sure. We had arranged to patrol this sector of the coast on this date.'

'It doesn't say if it's him in person, sir. But the code is certainly his,' replied Peter. 'The message says, "Stand by to pick up man from French vessel".'

'Bring a signal lamp,' called the captain. Then to Peter he said, 'Tell him we are prepared for a boat to come along-side.'

Peter did as instructed, and after a while a fishing smack came out of the drifting rain and positioned itself alongside the *Torren*. The misty outline of the vessel was just visible in the light from the storm-lanterns. An agitated French voice called out a few sentences and Peter translated.

'They want us to throw down a rope for a wounded man, sir.'

Captain Benchley gave the order, and a few moments later a shabby man, looking half dead, was hauled aboard. By the lantern's ghostly light, Peter recognized the ashen face of Petty Officer Connors, who had accompanied Commodore Beaumont on his secret mission all those weeks ago.

Muttered commands came from the fishing boat, and the only other sound they heard was the creak of her sails as she faded away into the night.

'Take him below,' ordered the captain.

But from where Connors lay on the deck, he had enough strength to reach up and clutch at Captain

Benchley's cloak. He felt inside his shirt and produced a cloth-wrapped bundle. 'The commodore ordered me to put this book into your own hands, Captain Benchley.'

The captain took the bundle and thrust it inside his own cloak.

'It must reach the Admiralty, sir. Even if the commodore and I don't,' said Connors in no more than a whisper. His head fell back as if he had fainted and Peter saw by the light of the lantern that there was blood seeping from a wound in Connors' side. Two men began to lift him but he came to again with a shuddering cough. 'Look inside the book's flap, sir. It shows the location for a rendezvous with the commodore.'

Captain Benchley nodded briskly and ordered Peter to accompany him to his cabin. The sounds of the dinner party drifted over to them as they stood over the desk and Captain Benchley opened the book.

As Connors had said, tucked inside the book's flap was a flimsy sheet of paper. On it were a series of dots, dashes and numbers.

'Can you make this out, Mr Raven?' asked the captain.

'I can, sir,' Peter replied. He studied the coded message and translated. 'The first part is a British Admiralty chart reference for the mouth of the river Seine with an exact location. The message says we are to rendezvous there at midnight in three days' time. It also says the *Nautilus Book* must reach the Admiralty.'

Captain Benchley scratched his chin as he flipped

through its pages. 'So, Commodore Beaumont is at the mouth of the river that leads all the way to Paris. And he delivers to us something called the *Nautilus Book*.' He paused, puzzled. 'Isn't *Nautilus* the Greek word for sailor?'

'And Latin, sir,' Peter replied, equally puzzled.

The captain continued to study the pages of the book. It was written in a code quite different to the one Peter had memorized. There were also measurements, some kind of technical sketch and a page of mathematical equations. Neither Captain Benchley nor Peter could fathom their meaning.

'Well, the book obviously contains important information,' said Captain Benchley. 'I shall send it under seal to the admiral in command of the squadron so that it can be passed on to the Admiralty, together with a covering letter explaining that I have left station to pick up Commodore Beaumont.'

A surge in the sounds of revelry coming from the dining-room caused Captain Benchley to frown. 'Time to bring the party to an end, Mr Raven.'

A fresh wind drove the *Torren* up the English Channel that night, and all the following day, until they were within sight of the French port of Le Havre. They lay off there, not far from the British squadron that was blockading it. Captain Benchley signalled them an excuse for the *Torren*'s presence, then settled down to wait for Beaumont.

They were a day early for the rendezvous with him. All seemed well, until early in the afternoon watch when the wind began to blow at gale force, and the *Torren* had to fight to stay on station.

Although the gale drove the rest of the British squadron further east along the Channel, it was essential that Captain Benchley keep the *Torren* close to the mouth of the river Seine. It took all his seamanship to maintain their position for the coming rendezvous with Commodore Beaumont, which was to be on the shore near a tiny village called Villerville.

By late evening the gale had dropped, but there was still a hard wind blowing. The heavily overcast sky promised a dark night and the captain was fretting. With such a strong wind it would be dangerous to risk taking the *Torren* into the ever-changing shallows of the estuary. The ship's cutter would have to do the job, but it would need a good deal of calculation and seamanship to bring the boat close enough to the shore to pick up Beaumont. And once that was done, they would have to find their way back to the *Torren*. Wind and current would have to be continually recalculated.

His nephew was skilled at the mental arithmetic required, and was the only one aboard familiar with Beaumont's secret code. Also, he had made splendid progress in handling the ship's cutter and was now as accomplished as any officer aboard in commanding a small craft. Captain Benchley decided to instruct Peter to man the boat with a crew of his own choice for the rendezvous with Beaumont.

'Would you like me to take a hand with the cutter, sir?' suggested Lieutenant Crawford respectfully.

'Thank you, Mr Crawford,' replied Captain Benchley. 'But the work will be done by Mr Raven.' Privately he was glad that Peter would be in charge of the cutter. Crawford was a fine officer and fully able to command a ship of the line, but Benchley knew the job in hand required other gifts. Crawford could never match Peter's exceptional ability to execute the fast calculations necessary in the dark and confusion aboard a small boat tossed about on a running sea.

As Peter was making final preparations for the landing party, Matthew Book brought him his boat cloak and a brace of pistols. All Peter had intended to take by way of arms was his midshipman's dirk. Suspecting the dagger may not be enough, he took the pistols gratefully and tucked them into his belt.

'May I make a request, Mr Raven?' asked Matthew, who was also carrying a large oiled-canvas sack.

'Certainly,' Peter answered.

'Take me along,' said Matthew.

It took Peter a moment to realize Matthew had spoken in French.

'*Vous parlez français?*' asked Peter.

'*Certainement*,' replied Matthew.

'Why do you want to come? It could be hazardous.'

'I'm guessing you'll take Mr Guttman to serve as helmsman,' said Matthew.

'Of course,' replied Peter.

Matthew nodded. 'Mr Guttman and I are long-time shipmates, Mr Raven. It wouldn't seem right, him going into danger without me along.'

'Then arm yourself, Mr Book. You are most welcome,' said Peter.

Smiling, Matthew Book held up the oiled-canvas bag and partly slipped out a formidable looking brass-bound blunderbuss.

'Armed and ready, sir.'

Captain Benchley called out as the cutter was swung over the side and into the foaming sea. 'I shall be looking for your signal some half an hour after the time of the rendezvous, Mr Raven.'

'Aye, aye, sir,' Peter replied, then put his mind to the demands of handling the small boat.

He had the best possible helmsman in Mr Guttman, and Matthew was steady as a rock. The others he'd chosen were all rated able seamen. They were experienced hands he'd grown to know in his months of hard training: Wilson, once a fisherman from Yorkshire; Casey, a cheerful young Dubliner, a good man in any crew; Jenkins, a dour and hard Londoner who had worked on coal ships; Prewitt, a Bristol seaman who was quick and clever and already marked out as a potential petty officer; and Van Gelder, a powerful Dutchman with forearms like gigantic legs of pork.

Peter sat in the prow as six of the men rowed them clear of the *Torren*. He then gave the order to ship oars and hoist the single sail. They were soon racing away from the *Torren,* which was already out of sight in the darkness.

Peter could hardly believe he'd been given such a huge responsibility. He now faced the greatest test of all he had been taught in the past months. But this was no comfortable exercise, where all he had to do was write down answers to abstract questions. He was in a small boat under sail, being blown across stormy waters towards an unfamiliar coastline. Men's lives were in his hands, and all his decisions would have to be based on the calculations his wits told him were correct. If he failed they could all die, and Commodore Beaumont would be left stranded on the shore at the mercy of the French.

Peter quickly forced such thoughts aside and gave his entire attention to the task at hand. Taking a diagonal course from the *Torren*, and making provision for current and tide, Peter estimated where Beaumont would be waiting.

'I'd say this tide was taking us ten compass points off our course, Mr Guttman. What do you think?' called out Peter.

'Nearer fifteen, I'm thinking, sir, with this wind,' replied Guttman.

'Make it fifteen,' said Peter.

Although it was hard to see any reaction, Peter thought

he could feel the men's approval at the exchange. Seamen wanted those in command to be decisive, but they also liked to think someone of their rank was trusted by those in command. No lights showed on the shore, but that was to be expected. According to the chart it was a desolate place where the estuary shelved gently into the countryside.

'Keep a sharp eye out to port,' Peter commanded the crew. 'We're looking for a red light flashing three short blinks and one longer.'

Although the weather had relented slightly, the sky was overcast with heavy rain-clouds so there was still no moon-light. It made it harder to find the coastline, but also lessened their chances of being seen. Not that anyone was likely to be taking a stroll in this bleak place on such a night, Peter told himself.

As the crew heard the first sounds of the waves breaking on the shore, Matthew, who had joined Peter in the prow of the cutter, called out: 'Red light flashing ten degrees off the port bow.'

Peter returned the flashes with his storm-lantern and instructed Mr Guttman to alter their course, all the time praying that their luck would hold. When he judged the cutter was close enough, Peter struck sail and ordered the crew to row for the shore. They could now see white breakers on a beach. By the light of his storm-lantern, Peter glanced at his pocket-watch. It was just after midnight.

On shore the red light signalled again. Almost instantly it was followed by flashes from musket barrels and the crackling sound of gunfire. Peter's heart pounded. Beaumont was under attack.

Chapter Eleven

MR GUTTMAN'S SACRIFICE

'How many men do you estimate are attacking Commodore Beaumont, Mr Book?' asked Peter in a far steadier voice than he'd expected to muster. His stomach churned with anxiety as he strained to see more musket flashes in the pitch blackness.

'I'd say about ten, sir,' replied Matthew steadily.

The red signal flashed again but this time there was, surprisingly, a volley of return fire from the red light's position. There appeared to be as many men at the source of the signal as there were attacking it.

As the cutter ground on to the shore the men leapt out and dragged it up the beach. Peter raged inwardly against the darkness as he flashed his lantern in the direction of the red light. His men carried muskets, but it had been so wet in the boat he doubted if any would be in a fit state to fire. Cursing his lack of foresight for not having them covered like Matthew's blunderbuss, he watched desperately for Beaumont's next signal.

A sudden hail of musket shot smacked on to the ground around them and thudded into the cutter. Peter felt his coat plucked twice as if by an unseen hand.

'Anyone hit?' he called out in an urgent undertone, aware of Matthew beside him, removing the canvas cover from his blunderbuss.

'Guttman's shot in the stomach, sir,' replied Prewitt.

'The rest of you call out your names,' ordered Peter, and the voices of his crew came to him in the darkness.

'Wilson here.'

'Casey, I'm fine.'

'Jenkins.'

'Van Gelder.'

'Matthew Book. I'm with Mr Guttman.'

Peter hurried towards the sound of Matthew's voice and could just make out Mr Guttman leaning against the cutter clutching his middle. It was clear the man was badly wounded and Peter was filled with sudden compassion for him, but he would not allow himself to forget the desperate business at hand.

'Get him into the boat, Mr Book,' ordered Peter, but Guttman shook his head.

'Too late, Mr Raven,' he gasped. 'I'm almost done for. Leave me here with a storm-lantern.'

Peter began to protest but Matthew seized the lantern from him and thrust it into Guttman's hands. 'Goodbye, shipmate,' he said, his hand resting for a moment on the man's shoulder.

'Goodbye to you, Matthew Book,' Guttman answered. 'And may God bless you. I hope you get home one day.'

Enemy shouts in the darkness wrenched Peter back to his duty. It seemed the French had been ordered to advance towards the beach. Peter felt no fear, but in the confusion a terrible sense of disorientation was threatening to overwhelm him. Then a familiar voice spoke out of the darkness.

'I suggest we leave, Mr Raven, before the enemy have time to reload their weapons!' Commodore Beaumont loomed up beside him.

'What about your men, sir?' Peter asked him urgently.

'I have no men with me, Mr Raven,' replied Beaumont. 'Just a pocketful of children's tricks.'

They heard the French crashing towards them as Beaumont struck a flint and held it to a fuse. When it began to fizz he hurled it towards the advancing French. A loud series of what sounded convincingly like musket fire followed.

Firecrackers, Peter realized. Beaumont was throwing fireworks at the approaching enemy.

'Back to the boat, men,' he yelled. Leaving Mr Guttman on the beach, they all scrambled aboard the cutter and began pulling strongly away from the shore with Matthew at the helm. Another ragged volley of musket fire came from the French. Then the boat crew saw an extraordinary sight: Mr Guttman had managed to stagger to his feet and remove the cover of his storm-lantern. The shouting Frenchmen who had surrounded him suddenly froze in horror as the fearsome apparition loomed at them out of the darkness.

Mr Guttman's action won the cutter only a few vital seconds, but it was what they desperately needed. A cursing officer cut Guttman down with his sword and shouted to his men to continue reloading their muskets. As they did so, Matthew released the tiller for a moment and let go with his blunderbuss.

The crashing report seemed more effective than all the enemy's previous musket fire. Mixed shouts of anger and groans of pain came from the men on the shore. Peter ordered the sail to be hoisted, and as the wind snatched them away he was grateful now for the clouds obscuring the moon.

There was no conversation in the boat on the journey back out to the *Torren*. Peter had to concentrate on the job of navigation, while Commodore Beaumont, beside him in the prow, lay stretched out in the fainting sleep of the totally exhausted.

With as much luck as good judgment, Peter located the *Torren*, but he felt no sense of pride in the seamanship he'd displayed that night. He was still sick with anger that he hadn't had the men keep their muskets dry. But for this oversight, he told himself, Mr Guttman might still be alive.

Peter roused Beaumont when they came alongside the

Torren, and as soon as they were back on board they hurried to the captain's cabin. If Peter had been less miserable himself, he might have noticed that despite his uncle's effort not to show any emotion, he was clearly relieved to see him safe.

'How is Petty Officer Connors, Captain?' was Beaumont's first concern as he stood before Benchley's desk.

'Quite well, sir. The ship's surgeon is pleased with his progress and there appears to be no mortification of the wound.'

'And the book he brought to you?'

'Passed to the admiral in command of the fleet and now well on its way to England, I trust.'

Beaumont, dressed in civilian clothes this time, sighed, and taking a mug of hot rum and coffee from Sinclair he sat down heavily on a chair. After handing another steaming mug to Peter, the captain's servant then withdrew from the cabin.

'You may take a seat, Mr Raven,' said Captain Benchley. 'Commodore Beaumont's presence speaks of the success of your mission.'

'Mr Guttman was killed, sir,' Peter reported numbly.

'The loss of good men is often the price we must pay for command, Midshipman,' Benchley answered with no apparent emotion.

'Mr Raven's conduct was splendid, Captain,' said Beaumont. 'The exploits of this night will never appear in the newspapers, but I shall mention him in my report to the

Admiralty.'

'What do you require me to do now, Commodore?' asked Benchley.

'I suggest you prepare the ship for battle, Captain,' replied Beaumont, scratching his unshaven chin. 'I have every reason to believe that two French frigates, each of a hundred guns, are to escort a schooner that will attempt to run the blockade at first light. And, as the rest of our squadron has been blown along the Channel, the *Torren* alone must stop them.'

'You're sure?' asked Captain Benchley.

Beaumont nodded. 'By luck, I received the information yesterday afternoon while I was about some other business altogether. The captains of the French frigates were fretting and anxious to be under way as they assumed, correctly, that our squadron would be blown off station. They didn't imagine *Torren* would stay here. But they were obliged to wait for a special order concerning the schooner. The order was expected from Paris just before dawn.'

'What cargo is the schooner carrying?' asked Captain Benchley. 'It must be valuable to deserve such a formidable escort.'

'I couldn't get that information,' answered Beaumont. 'But it must be of some great importance to Napoleon. The schooner has been disguised to look old and hardly seaworthy, but in fact she's as swift as a greyhound. The frigates have been ordered to sacrifice themselves if necessary to give her every advantage to escape. May I be so bold as to suggest a plan? You may accept or reject it as you see fit.'

'Please do so, Commodore,' Benchley replied.

'I have seen the schooner,' said Beaumont. 'She's called the *Estelle*. The French plan is for her to leave port *before* the frigates in the hope of conveying the impression that she is of no importance. She carries no guns. It will need careful timing but if we can get close enough to her before the French men-o'-war come out, we might board her swiftly and secure her as a prize before you engage the enemy frigates.'

'It might be possible,' said Benchley, nodding in agreement.

Peter listened, enthralled. Even thoughts of Mr Guttman's sacrifice were driven from his mind by the prospect of his first real sea battle. What struck him most forcibly about the conversation was the matter-of-fact way Captain Benchley unhesitatingly accepted that the *Torren* would engage an enemy of twice his own ship's strength. There was no empty bravado in his uncle's decision. Any other course was clearly unthinkable.

Captain Benchley remembered Peter. 'You may turn in, Mr Raven,' he said. 'You will be needed at first light. And well done.'

Peter saluted and left the cabin. In a few moments, still in his wet clothes, he was in his hammock. Before sleep engulfed him, he wondered what vital information might be contained in the mysterious *Nautilus Book* for which

Connors and Beaumont had risked their lives. But then he slept deeply, groaning occasionally as ghastly images of the injured Guttman replayed in his mind.

Chapter Twelve

THE TAKING OF THE
ESTELLE

Sinclair roused Peter with a cup of coffee, and finding him still in his damp uniform the captain's manservant fussed at his forgetfulness.

'You don't want to go sleeping in wet clothes if you can avoid it, Mr Raven,' he scolded as Peter stood in the captain's galley splashing cold water on to his face. 'By the time you're my age you'll have rheumatism something shocking. Here, I've brought you a dry shirt, at least.'

Sinclair had even warmed the garment before the cooking range, and Peter slipped it on gratefully.

'Always best to wear clean clothes in battle,' said Sinclair, clucking about like a mother hen. 'Better for you if you get hit. You wouldn't want dirty linen in a wound, would you, sir?'

'Certainly not,' agreed Peter, grinning as he gulped

down the last of the coffee. Then he hurried to the poop deck, where Captain Benchley and Beaumont were waiting in the first faint glow of pre-dawn light. The *Torren* was already prepared for action; Peter had been so deeply asleep that he'd missed all the activity. Captain Benchley had artfully positioned the ship so as not to frighten the French ships back into port, but hopefully close enough to cut off the *Estelle*.

The wind still blew hard, but with slightly less strength than the previous day. Somewhere down the Channel the British squadron would be clawing their way back along the coast to their station outside Le Havre. But for the *Torren*, their absence would have provided a perfect opportunity for the French ships to slip out, make a wide turning swing, and trust their luck that they'd miss any other Royal Navy ships as they made a run for the Atlantic.

'Tell the lookouts to keep a sharp watch, Mr Crawford,' instructed the captain, eyeing the clear sky that had been blown free of rain-clouds.

'Aye, aye, sir,' replied the first lieutenant, and he roared out the order to be passed on.

As the first rays of sunlight flashed across the sea, the lookout high on the mainmast hailed a sighting. All officers on the poop deck, including Midshipman Raven, raised their telescopes. They could make out the billowing sails of the *Estelle* illuminated by the pink and gold dawn light.

Captain Benchley called out his orders and the *Torren* dipped forward under full sail, straining every width of canvas to swoop down on the French schooner.

'Shall we have the band play something lively, Mr Crawford?' suggested the captain. And as the *Torren* flew forward, the wind singing through her rigging, the Royal Marines struck up *Over the Hills*.

This was very different from the action on the beach when Peter had picked up Commodore Beaumont. There was no confusion in his mind. Now he felt as if he were actually part of the ship. The blood pumped strongly through his veins, and each lungful of air made him feel even more light-headed than he had after drinking Captain Benchley's champagne.

'Dear Lord, grant that there be sufficient distance between her and the frigates,' Peter heard Captain Benchley mutter, and he knew he was praying that there would be time to cut out the *Estelle* before he had to engage with the two French battleships.

Captain Benchley's prayer was answered. There did seem to be just enough distance for Beaumont's plan to work.

'Are you ready, Mr Westlake?' shouted the captain.

'Aye, aye, sir,' confirmed the lieutenant who stood amidships with a party of seamen and marines armed to the teeth with cutlasses, axes, pistols and short muskets, ready to board the *Estelle*.

'I shall be approaching her from our starboard side,' warned Captain Benchley.

Peter tried to follow the captain's calculations as he

steered the *Torren* on a course to bring her alongside the *Estelle*. He also tried to imagine what the captain of the *Estelle* would do. With the wind blowing them in the direction of the *Torren*, there was no chance for the *Estelle* to put about and run back into the harbour at Le Havre. As the *Torren* bore down on her she seemed about to make a run for it, but then the French captain obviously changed his mind. He heaved to and prepared for the inevitable boarding party.

All on board the *Torren* could see that the two French frigates had left port with as much sail on as they could and were heading for them at full speed.

When the *Torren* was close enough to the *Estelle* for Lieutenant Westlake and his men to board her, Benchley ordered the gunners to stand by. As they drew close, a figure on the *Estelle* hailed them in English through a speaking trumpet.

'For God's sake, do not fire, Captain,' he shouted. 'We surrender.'

Captain Bentley shouted an order. 'Get your men aboard, Mr Westlake. Secure the ship and head for Portsmouth, smart as you can.'

There was barely time for Westlake's party to scramble aboard the *Estelle* before Captain Benchley ordered the *Torren* to come about and tack against the wind to face the frigates that were now bearing down on them. The lookouts shouted their names.

'The *Juno* and the *Hercule*,' repeated Captain Benchley.

Peter realized he'd been gripping the handle of his dirk so hard his fingers were aching. Releasing them, he took out the two pistols he had stuck in his belt. As he checked the flints and charges for the second time Peter caught a fleeting grin from Commodore Beaumont who stood, apparently at ease, beside Captain Benchley.

Peter could feel tension throughout the ship, as second by second all nerves grew as taut as a tightly wound rope. The only sound was the groaning of the sails and the band playing as if they were performing at a Sunday concert in the park.

'Mr Crawford,' said Captain Benchley conversationally to his second in command. 'I am going to pass between the enemy ships.'

'Between them, sir?' queried the officer, surprised by the decision.

'Yes, *between*,' said Benchley carefully. 'Have the crews divide to man both port and starboard guns. When we engage, the gunners are to fire at will, making every effort to destroy the masts and rigging of the enemy ships.'

'Aye, aye, sir,' replied the officer, recovering fast from his astonishment to pass on Captain Benchley's command.

Peter was just as confounded by the captain's orders. The orthodox action would be for the *Torren* to pass to the outside of one or other of the frigates so as to take the force of the enemy guns from only one ship at a time. By manoeuvring between them, the *Torren* would be vulnerable to simultaneous broadsides from both the *Hercule* and the

Juno if the French ships had manned their guns on both sides. Benchley was gambling that they hadn't.

Conventional tactics of naval warfare dictated that it was best to fight one-to-one, but Captain Benchley was about to defy that convention.

'Steer for the *Juno* head on,' he ordered. 'I want them to think I'm going to engage them alone at the first pass.'

The *Torren's* helmsmen made the approach as instructed.

Peter watched the bustle of the gun crews splitting on the upper deck and knew the same thing was being done on the decks below. Usually, when French and British ships went into action, only one side of their guns was manned. But he had often watched the crew of the *Torren* practise their present drill for fighting enemies from both sides during a fleet engagement.

'Keep her heading full on for the *Juno*, Mr Crawford. At my command, we slip between the two of them.' The captain's voice was steady as the beat was kept by the marine band, now playing *Blaze Away*.

Peter understood Captain Benchley's tactics. The French frigates would be expecting the *Torren* to pass to the outside of the *Juno*. So only the guns all along that side of the *Juno* would be manned, so as to concentrate all their efforts on causing maximum damage from their broadside directed at the *Torren*.

For Peter, the last few seconds before the *Torren* altered course to slip between the two French ships seemed to slow into a dreamlike haze. His glance swung from ship to ship as they ploughed on between the enormous frigates that were no more than the width of a narrow street away.

Captain Benchley's gamble had worked. Neither the *Juno* nor the *Hercule* had their inner guns ready for action. Their captains could only watch in horror, but their troops, armed with muskets, were swift to respond. The crackle of small arms rent the air as the marines on the *Torren* and the blue-coated soldiers on board the *Juno* all fired on one another. Flashes also came from sharpshooters in the rigging as both sides aimed for their enemy's officers.

Suddenly Lieutenant Metcalf, gun captain of the carronades on the port side of the poop deck, blundered into Peter. Musket shot had opened a deep wound across the lieutenant's forehead and blood was gushing down his face, blinding him and making a dreadful scarlet mask of his features.

'Who's that?' Metcalf cried.

'Midshipman Raven, sir,' Peter replied.

'Can't see, Raven!' gasped the lieutenant, trying in vain to wipe blood from his eyes. 'Have Arrowsmith take over my position.'

'He already has, sir,' said Peter, looking around for someone to take Metcalf below. But there was no one free.

'What's happening, Mr Raven?'

'We're about to open fire, sir,' shouted Peter.

The swell of a wave brought *Torren's* starboard side higher out of the water, and following Captain Benchley's order the gunners discharged a massive rolling volley of cannon fire into the *Juno's* masts and rigging. The next wave brought the port-side cannon up and another massive volley blasted into the *Hercule*. Both French ships just had to take the hammering blows while completely unable to retaliate.

'We hit both the Frog ships, sir!' cried Peter. 'And nothing back from them. Captain Benchley outfoxed them.'

The air filled with smoke and stinking sulphurous fumes from the guns, and all about Peter musket shot sang through it all like giant bees.

'Are we hitting them hard?' asked Metcalf.

'Very hard, sir!' Peter gasped as one of the *Torren's* cannon balls smashed its way through three men on the *Hercule* quarterdeck, spraying their life-blood across its sand-strewn planks.

'How are the French doing?' Metcalf asked as Peter quickly bound his wound with a handkerchief.

'We're coming about, and the French are sending men aloft to repair the tears in their sails and rigging. Their fire crews are throwing wreckage overboard, and the bodies of their dead.'

Metcalf tried to wipe his eyes clear but the blood kept flowing despite the improvised bandage. A sudden great cheer went up from the men on the *Torren's* upper deck.

'She's gone, sir!' Crawford shouted in exaltation. 'By God, we've done it!'

Sure enough, by extraordinary good fortune, the *Juno's* mainmast had been cut through by the *Torren's* cannon fire and had crashed down into her foremast's rigging. Moments before, her sails had been tautly filled with wind. Now, they flapped uselessly like the wings of a dying swan.

Until then, the French frigate had been an equal enemy, able to turn and direct her guns with devastating power. Now, she lay suddenly helpless in the water, at the mercy of wind and current as her crew desperately hacked at the ropes and broken spars in a frenzied attempt to rig enough of her remaining sails for her to return to the fight.

'Well done, Captain Benchley!' Beaumont yelled as the *Torren* once more came alongside the *Hercule*.

'Broadsides now, gunners,' shouted Captain Benchley. 'And aim low.'

This time, there was no firing into the French rigging.

'My God,' said Peter as the *Torren* gave vent to her full fury and smashed her fifty-five starboard guns into the main body of the *Hercule* in a single broadside. This time she received equal return fire; however, Captain Benchley's gamble had paid off. With the *Juno* floundering, her mainmast tangled into her foremast, she was unable to manoeuvre herself back into the battle and had to watch as the *Hercule* and the *Torren* slogged it out.

A seaman came to lead Lieutenant Metcalf below and Peter edged closer to the captain.

'Hard to starboard!' shouted Captain Benchley as the two ships clashed, and the British gunners raked the *Hercule's* stern to shattering effect. Coming completely about, the *Torren* managed to take the *Hercule's* wind and draw alongside.

The starboard gun crews on the *Torren* now abandoned their position and rejoined the port gunners as, side by side, the two ships pounded each other mercilessly.

'Our superior rate of fire is telling,' called Captain Benchley. But there was no denying the courage of the French. They fought on until the *Hercule* was a battered listing wreck impossible to steer, but still firing the few guns she could still bring to bear.

'Break off the action, Mr Crawford!' shouted Captain Benchley. Even he was caught up in the excitement now. 'Prepare to come about and engage with the *Juno*.'

A roaring cheer of approval went up from the men. Peter realized that most of those on board the *Torren* thought the captain had spared the *Juno* so he could take her as a prize along with the *Estelle*. They seemed quite unconcerned by the fact that, although the *Juno* was unable to manoeuvre, her cannons were unaffected and her crew would be filled with a raging need for revenge and more than ready to repel any boarders from the *Torren*.

Chapter Thirteen

THE BUBBLE REPUTATION

While the battle had raged between the *Hercule* and the *Torren*, the crew of the *Juno* had worked furiously to restore enough sail to allow them to steer their ship. Men wielding axes had hewn through the wreckage caused when the severed mainmast fell, and the topmen had restored what trim they could to their mizzenmast.

With a greatly reduced area of sail the *Juno* could still turn, even though her speed was no more than a few knots. And she could bring her guns to bear on the *Torren*.

'It's a damned pity they worked so fast, Beaumont,' remarked Captain Benchley as they approached their wounded foe. 'If the *Juno* had remained helpless she could have struck her colours with honour. Now she'll fight on and there'll be an even bigger butcher's bill.'

They studied the *Juno*, whose patchwork of sails looked to their professional eyes like a badly hung clothes-line.

However, it was clear she could manoeuvre, no matter how clumsily.

'I would consider it a privilege to lead a boarding party, Captain,' volunteered Beaumont. Despite his superior rank, he still had to allow Captain Benchley to make this decision.

Benchley nodded and grinned. 'Are you thinking what I'm thinking?' he asked. His face and uniform like all the others on deck was streaked with powder stains.

'What would that be, sir?' answered Beaumont, feigning ignorance.

Benchley raised his telescope before he replied. 'That we lay off and draw their fire by taking a broadside from all their guns. Then turn towards her stern, rake her decks and come alongside to board her before the Frogs have time to reload.'

Beaumont smiled his agreement. 'They'll be expecting us to keep battering her as they're already half-crippled. I doubt they'll be prepared for a boarding party just yet.'

Captain Benchley shouted his orders. 'Hold your fire until I give the command, Mr Wesley. Any crew that lets loose before I give the order will be sorry they were born.'

'Aye, aye, sir,' replied the lieutenant.

'Prepare boarders if you will, Commodore,' said Captain Benchley as the *Juno* loomed closer.

Peter stood at the captain's side as the crew of the *Torren* rapidly divided into those who would remain on board and the newly-armed men about to hurl themselves on to the decks of the French frigate. With his heart thundering in his chest Peter felt no fear, just a great sense of exaltation as if his entire being were a tightly balled fist eager to deliver a crushing blow to the enemy. In the midst of all this death, he had never felt so entirely alive.

Beaumont had chosen Fenton as his midshipman. In the coming struggle, Fenton would have to stay as close as he could to the commander of the boarding party.

Captain Benchley bore down on the *Juno*, waiting for the French captain to fire first so he could rake the *Juno's* stern with gunfire. As the *Torren* closed in, Peter grinned when he heard the men muttering the traditional chant uttered in the Royal Navy whenever a ship of the line was preparing to receive an enemy's broadside: *'For what we are about to receive may the Lord make us truly thankful,'* came the mocking prayer from the dozens of men nearby.

All at once the *Torren* was engulfed by the thunderous fury of French guns and the curious mixture of battle sounds: a loud humming as gigantic oak splinters smashed from the *Torren's* structure, musket fire crackling like burning wood, and the whirr of chain-shot tearing at the *Torren's* rigging. More shuddering thumps rocked her as great iron missiles crashed into the starboard side from the *Juno's* cannon.

As the enemy ship passed out of range the deafening roar ceased, but still the gun crews laboured in a frenzy to swab out the barrels, recharge the cannons with shot, and prime them before hauling them back to their firing positions. All was ominously quiet, as the *Torren* turned sharply on to the *Juno's* stern.

'Fire as she comes to bear,' shouted Benchley, and the *Torren's* gunners slammed a rolling salvo into the stern of the *Juno*.

'Stand by to board,' shouted Beaumont. He had leapt to the shrouds with the men, who roared in wild anticipation. The French gun crews frantically fought to reload their cannon with grapeshot as the *Torren's* intention to board the *Juno* became clear.

Taut with fear and exhilaration, every fibre of Peter's body was screaming for him to join Beaumont and leap on to the enemy deck. The grappling hooks thrown by Beaumont's men took hold in *Juno's* rigging and the two ships seemed to embrace slowly in a spider's web of ropes.

Just as Beaumont was about to give the order to board, Midshipman Fenton was thrown back on to the *Torren's* deck, struck down as one of the French ship's first charges of grapeshot blasted into Beaumont's boarding party. Beaumont was unharmed, but three other men beside Fenton were also hit.

'Mr Raven,' said Captain Benchley with his usual calm control. 'Take Mr Fenton's place beside Commodore Beaumont.'

'Aye, aye, sir!' shouted Peter. Within seconds his racing heart had propelled him from the poop deck to Beaumont's side in the shrouds.

As Peter's foot touched the gunnels, Beaumont ordered his men to board.

With a raging shout of exaltation, Peter swung on to the Juno's deck.

'Get to her lower guns,' Beaumont shouted to the marines and sailors in the boarding party, intending them to overwhelm the crews below, who were still pounding the *Torren*.

The fighting on *Juno* was at its most deadly. Peter was of average size for his age and was agile and swift. As space was constricted on the decks, the most effective method of dealing with the enemy was by gun shot. Men stood face to face and blasted each other at point-blank range with pistol, blunderbuss and musket. Accuracy was hardly necessary as the opponents were within touching distance. Handguns were simply thrust into the bodies of the enemy and fired.

After the initial deadly exchange, with no time to reload the discharged guns they carried, the French and British fought hand-to-hand, thrusting, stabbing and slashing with swords, pikes, cutlasses and hatchets. Only the marksmen in the rigging of both ships continued to pepper the bloody mêlée with sniper fire.

Peter shot off both his pistols, then held one to use as a club and drew his midshipman's dirk. A French sailor thrust at him with a pike, but he managed to sidestep and plunge his long dagger into the man's upper arm. A pistol was discharged close to his right ear and his head rang from the concussion. But all the while, Peter managed to stay close to Beaumont, who was using his sword to hack his way through to the French quarterdeck. It was vital for the commodore to reach it so he could take the French surrender, if it was offered, and bring their resistance to an end.

Matthew Book was on the other side of Beaumont, using the butt of his blunderbuss to club aside two French sailors armed with cutlasses. Bullets ripped through the air from the sharpshooters above them. Several determined looking French seamen blocked the route to the quarterdeck, but Matthew had saved the single mighty charge in his blunderbuss for just such an eventuality.

'Clear my path, Mr Book,' shouted Beaumont.

Matthew levelled the massive gun and fired.

The thick cloud of smoke blew away, and Peter gasped when he saw the deck now strewn with the torn bodies of the men who had obstructed the way.

Beaumont quickly rallied a group around him and pressed on. Never again would Peter listen to any ignorant talk of Frenchmen being cowards. Both sides fought with a ferocity he'd never begun to imagine.

As a young boy, Peter had always thought of battles as a series of knightly clashes with fluttering flags, glittering arms, skilful swordplay and chivalrous consideration. But this was carnage. He had no choice but to fight for his life. Dodging and thrusting with his dirk he fought tenaciously, but in a strange state of detachment, as if part of his mind had disengaged and was watching himself in a nightmare.

Even as he fought, Peter vividly recalled visiting a slaughterhouse. Isaac had made him wait outside in the jogging cart, but the sounds and smell of the frightened livestock had roused his curiosity and he had gone to the open doors.

Just as he had seen it that day, blood now ran everywhere. It washed across the deck and flowed into the scuppers. In the slaughterhouse, men had killed terrified beasts, but on the deck of the *Juno* men were slaughtering men. *Never*, as long as he lived, would Peter think there was anything romantic about battle. It was horrible and barbaric.

With Matthew using his blunderbuss to batter a path for them, Beaumont and Peter finally reached their objective — the French captain and three of his officers who were fighting on the quarterdeck, where there was space to use their swords.

This was more what Peter had expected of warfare. The Frenchmen were fighting crewmen from the *Torren*. The British sailors hacked at them with crude cutlasses but their blows were easily parried by the more elegant skills of the French officers. Then the odds changed. Two of the Frenchmen were hit by sharpshooters from the *Torren*'s rigging.

Beaumont pushed forward and engaged the captain. They were well matched swordsmen, but suddenly the Frenchman's shoulder was creased by musket shot and blood spurted from the wound. Even so, he gave no sign of wanting to break off the fight; however, Beaumont stepped back, saluted his opponent and thrust his sword down, releasing the hilt so that the blade quivered in the deck.

'I beg you to strike your colours, Captain,' he shouted

above the continuous roar of the fighting. 'No crew could have done more. Save those of your men who still live.'

The Frenchman's eyes flickered over the dwindling remains of his overwhelmed crew. With a brief nod, he lowered his own sword.

The order to surrender was carried throughout the *Juno*, and the fighting gradually came to an end as the French crew reluctantly gave up their weapons.

Peter wiped the grime from his face and tried to shrug away a nagging pain in his back as he watched the stinking smoke gradually blow away from the deck of the *Juno*. He longed to get away from all this carnage, but he knew he still had duties to perform.

Beside him, Commodore Beaumont looked across the deck of the shattered *Juno* and sheathed his reclaimed sword, reciting words Peter recognized.

'*Jealous in honour, sudden and quick in quarrel, seeking the bubble reputation . . .* What comes next, Mr Raven?'

'*Even in the cannon's mouth,* sir,' said Peter, wearily completing the line from Shakespeare. Then his knees buckled and he pitched forward to fall at Beaumont's feet. The spike of an oak splinter the length of a bread knife was sticking out of a bloody patch on his back.

Chapter Fourteen

FAREWELL TO CONCORDE

Lucy Cosgrove had never stood still for so long in her entire life. At her grandfather's insistence she was having her portrait painted before going to New York for an extended stay with her Great-aunt Elizabeth, prior to their visit to Paris. The artist Jacob Kellerman had promised the picture would be finished that day.

Every morning for the past nine days Lucy had posed for three hours beside the French windows in the drawing-room. They overlooked a magnificent view of the Hudson Valley in all its richest autumn colours. Her clothes had been chosen by her great-aunt and brought from New York by the artist.

Mrs Hargreave had provided Lucy with an expensive blue silk dress trimmed with lace to wear for the picture. It had a tightly corseted bodice that flattened her chest, and its full skirt was worn over a contraption of wire to make her hips look wider. Kellerman assured her it was the latest fashion. Lucy hated it, and absolutely refused to wear the straw hat her great-aunt had also provided. 'I would look ridiculous with that huge bow tied under my chin,' Lucy told him.

Wisely, the artist compromised and suggested she hold the hat at her side.

Finally, the long clock began to chime twelve, signalling the end of the session, and before it had finished Lucy pleaded, 'May I move now, please, Mr Kellerman?'

The painter shrugged his thin shoulders and lay down his brush. 'Why not, Miss Cosgrove? You have moved every thirty seconds for the past forty-five minutes,' he replied with a sigh. 'Pray, do not restrain yourself now.'

'May I see it?'

Before the painter could answer, the doors opened and General Cosgrove entered the room, deep in conversation with a stocky, raw-boned, black-haired man wearing a sea captain's uniform.

'I'm sorry, Mr Kellerman,' said the general, breaking off. 'I quite forgot you were working in here.'

'We are finished,' replied the painter. 'But for the final varnish, the picture is done.'

'My God,' said the general, studying the picture intently. 'You've captured her to the life, sir. I congratulate you.'

'Do I really look like that?' asked Lucy curiously, feeling nothing like the cool elegant figure Kellerman had depicted.

'What do you think, Cooper?' asked General Cosgrove, then realized he had made no introductions. 'I'm sorry, sir. Captain Ephraim Cooper, this is Jacob Kellerman, and my granddaughter, Lucy.'

'Delighted,' said the captain, touching a heavy gold ring set in his left earlobe before he shook hands. 'As for the picture, it does Miss Cosgrove's beauty absolute justice. You are a sorcerer, Mr Kellerman. There's magic in your brushes.'

Kellerman gave a slight bow. Suddenly, he didn't look quite as comical as he had appeared to Lucy throughout the past week. He was a young man, but his pale melancholy features, awkward bony figure, careless, paint-flecked clothes, and his old-fashioned powdered wig had made him seem middle-aged.

'Such detailed work. How long did it take you?' asked Captain Cooper with the practicality of a seafaring man.

'I came here some time ago in August to prepare sketches of the landscape from the window,' Kellerman explained. 'But I actually painted the view in my studio in New York and had the clothes Miss Cosgrove wears on a dummy there.'

'But the trees would have had their full summer foliage then,' said Captain Cooper, intrigued.

Kellerman smiled. 'I knew what colour they would be in the fall.'

'That hadn't occurred to me,' said General Cosgrove, impressed. 'You're a damned clever fellow, Kellerman.'

He bowed slightly at the compliment and continued.

'Next, I brought the canvas here where Miss Cosgrove could pose for me. The face and arms are always the most difficult part.'

'And how did you transport the canvas?'

'When dry, inside a long leather tube. When wet, in a large wooden crate. Oil paint takes a good deal of time to dry, so initially one must take care to protect the surface.'

'I wish you could paint me,' said Captain Cooper, 'but I fear there will not be time. We are to sail for Asia within the week.'

'Perhaps we could come to some arrangement, Captain Cooper,' said Kellerman, suddenly interested. 'I yearn to visit such exotic climes. I would happily exchange a portrait for passage aboard your ship.'

'Capital idea!' said General Cosgrove expansively. 'You can also paint me, Kellerman. Let's hope we don't have too stormy a passage.'

'You're going to Asia, Grandfather?' said Lucy, surprised by this news.

'I meant to tell you, Lucy,' said the general. 'I have pressing business in northern India.'

'When are you going?' Lucy asked.

'We shall all accompany you when you leave for New York in the morning, Lucy. We will then proceed aboard the *Hampton* on the following tide.'

'But Jack Cobden is still away,' replied Lucy, knowing that Cobden had personal business in Albany.

'Jack's not coming with me,' said the general. 'He'll

join you in New York in time to accompany you to Paris.'

'Does Aunt Lizzie know he's coming with us?'

'She will soon enough,' said General Cosgrove, smiling affectionately at his granddaughter.

Mrs Elizabeth Hargreave was ill-prepared to receive her brother and his boisterous companion three days later, when they came knocking on the door of her Manhattan mansion late in the evening.

As often happens when grown men are setting out on a new venture that involves a sea voyage, a spirit of boyish high spirits had infected Jacob Kellerman and General Cosgrove. It had increased at least twofold when the general had insisted that he and Kellerman should stop for rum punch at a waterfront tavern while the servants unloaded their luggage from the schooner in which they had journeyed down the Hudson River. Captain Cooper had declined their invitation to join them as he wished to prepare the *Hampton* for putting to sea the following day.

'I'm sorry to see you in such raucous company, Lucy,' said Mrs Hargreave when they were shown into her presence by her elderly manservant, Potter.

'I rather enjoyed it, Aunt,' replied Lucy cheerfully. 'The walk from the waterfront was bracing and I have always enjoyed hearing *Yankee Doodle* sung with such gusto.'

'They were *singing*?' asked Mrs Hargreave, looking aghast.

'Is this any welcome, Lizzie? Don't be so stiff-necked!'

roared the general. 'I promised Mr Kellerman a beefsteak for supper.'

'I have not seen such rowdy behaviour in this house since it was occupied by the British during the War of Independence,' she replied. She then instructed Potter, 'Please show General Cosgrove and Mr Kellerman to the dining-room, where they will be more comfortable. And have the cook serve them with what they desire.'

The general and the artist smiled happily at the prospect.

'What is in the large box I'm told you brought into my house, Mr Kellerman?' asked Mrs Hargreave.

The painter bowed low before answering. 'It is the finished portrait of your great-niece, ma'am. The finest work I have ever produced.'

'*I* shall be the judge of that when I inspect it later,' replied Mrs Hargreave. 'Now, gentlemen, if you will be so kind as to follow Potter . . .'

'What about Miss Lucy, ma'am?' asked Potter. 'Would she like to eat?'

'Miss Lucy will stay here with me. Bring some of the cold capon I had for supper and serve it in here.'

General Cosgrove laid a friendly arm on Potter's shoulder. 'And make us some rum punch, Silas, for we go to sea in the morning and we have many farewell toasts to make.'

Potter looked to Mrs Hargreave for approval. She nodded her assent to the request, saying, 'Take them away, Potter.'

'Let me look at you, Lucy,' Mrs Hargreave demanded

when the others had departed.

Lucy stood in front of the fireplace. She was wearing the blue dress and carrying the straw hat she'd refused to wear for the portrait.

'Your complexion is terrible,' the old lady sighed. 'Well-bred girls are supposed to be pale, child. I suppose you've been out in the woods hunting wild animals with that savage, Cobden?'

'Not so much,' answered Lucy. 'I've been having my picture painted and Grandfather wanted me to spend more time with him. Recently, I've been reading to him in the afternoons.'

'Reading what?'

'Children's books, mostly.'

'That doesn't surprise me.'

'Doesn't it?' replied Lucy. 'I thought it rather odd.'

'He doesn't want you to grow up. Well, he's a bit late. He missed most of your childhood when you were running wild in the care of that Jack Cobden.' She reached out, saying, 'Give me your hands.'

Lucy did so and Mrs Hargreave sighed again. 'As rough as sackcloth. But by the time we leave for Paris you'll be a lady.'

Chapter Fifteen

A LONG CONVALESCENCE

Peter lay on a stretcher next to the *Torren's* entry port. The weather was cold and the ship rode gently on an ebbing tide as they lay at anchor in Spithead.

Mr Matlock, the ship's surgeon, had removed the oak splinter from Peter's back, but he was unhappy about the wound's proximity to the boy's lung and had insisted he be taken to the Royal Naval Hospital in Portsmouth for further examination. Peter was waiting to be lowered on to the cutter that was to ferry him ashore along with several other badly wounded members of the crew.

'How are you feeling, Midshipman?' asked Commodore Beaumont, leaning over him. He had already been ashore, but had returned briefly to finish some business with Captain Benchley.

'I'm fine, sir. It just aches a bit when I breathe deeply.'

'It could have been worse.'

'Yes, sir. You know poor Batt was killed? Or at least he's missing. Apparently there was no sign of him in his refuge after the battle.'

'One of the perils of being in the service, Mr Raven. Unfortunately, we must all get used to losing comrades.'

'Yes, sir,' said Peter grimly, then asked, 'How is Petty Officer Connors? I thought I might be seeing him in the hospital.'

Beaumont shook his head, smiling. 'Connors is as tough as a rope's end, Mr Raven. He came ashore with me last night. I've given him leave to visit his married sister in Poole. Meanwhile, I shall have to make do with Mr Book here. He's been assigned to me.'

Matthew Book smiled at Peter. He was smartly turned out in white trousers, short jacket, waistcoat, and a hard straw hat. He had his gear already packed in a large canvas bag.

'The commodore's boat is alongside and ready for you to board, sir,' reported Midshipman Arrowsmith.

As Commodore Beaumont was on special duties he was permitted to come and go as he pleased, unlike the rest of those aboard the *Torren*. On active service, leave was rare for the crews of Royal Navy ships, including their captains, particularly when they were in home waters. Although the majority of the men on *Torren* were volunteers, at least a third had been press-ganged into service, and if they were given leave they could easily take the opportunity to run away.

On his return to the *Torren* after his shore visit, Beaumont had delivered orders from the Admiralty to Captain Benchley and had recruited Matthew before bidding farewell to his recent host. So now, the *Torren* lay at anchor, her crew able to smell the soil of their homeland but unable to put a foot on it, despite their recent victories.

Captain Benchley stood near Beaumont on the deck, which was bustling with men from the carpenter's shop. The sounds of hammering and sawing were everywhere as they repaired the damage done to the ship in the recent battle.

Beaumont appeared to recollect something and said in a loud voice, 'By the way, Captain Benchley, I forgot to tell you earlier: the *Estelle* was carrying a cargo of powder, flints and muskets. A vast quantity it seems. She, along with the *Juno*, should make a very handsome amount in prize money. You and your crew are to be congratulated on your good fortune.'

'And all the money safe in the bank for when we next get shore leave,' replied Benchley with a great show of satisfaction.

Peter realized the two officers had deliberately spoken within earshot of the men working on deck. It was hard enough for the captain, who at least had comfortable quarters, not to be able to go ashore. But for those enduring the hardships of the lower deck the frustration was far greater. However, the conversation between Beaumont and the captain would be passed around the crew of the *Torren* within minutes, and the thought of the money waiting when they finally did get home would be some sort of compensation.

'Crawford will get command of the *Juno* once she's repaired and we've taken her into the Royal Navy,' continued Beaumont.

'I'm delighted,' Captain Benchley replied with genuine pleasure, even though he'd be losing his second in command. 'There's no better man.'

The captain shook hands with Beaumont and saw him piped away with the regulation guard of marines giving their salute.

Captain Benchley glanced up at the rigging where swarms of men were checking and repairing the miles of rope that controlled the workings of the ship. He seemed satisfied by the progress being made.

'Lieutenant Westlake,' he called in a cheerful voice.

Westlake hurried towards the captain from the quarter-deck where he had been overseeing a gun crew. They were relaying a carronade, as the original gun carriage had been hit by a cannon ball from the *Juno's* broadside.

'Mr Westlake, it gives me great pleasure to appoint you first officer on *Torren*,' said the captain. 'I'm sure you will conduct yourself with your customary dedication to duty.'

'I h-h-hope I shall give you every satisfaction, sir,' replied Westlake, barely able to stammer out the words. Peter knew Westlake was a good officer and liked by the men, but he was still young and had been a lieutenant for only four years.

Peter saw that all the hands nearby smiled with approval, and he realized this was yet more theatricals intended to cheer up the crew. But one face was wreathed in thunderclouds. Mr Blysse, who had been a lieutenant for two years longer than Westlake, could not disguise his anger. He stood well back in the shadow of the mizzenmast, glowering jealously.

'Cutter alongside to take the wounded, sir,' reported Arrowsmith.

'Thank you, Midshipman,' replied Benchley. Bending slightly to take Peter's hand he said quickly, 'Give my love to your mother and sisters, Mr Raven, and my kindest regards to your father.' Then he straightened up and called out to his new first officer, 'As soon as the wounded are over the side, set a course for Ushant, Mr Westlake. We shall continue our repairs at sea.'

'Aye, aye, sir!' answered Westlake happily.

'Well, Raven, you lucky dog,' said Midshipman Claiborne, who had just rushed up with Arrowsmith to say goodbye. 'You're off to have Christmas at home.'

Arrowsmith grinned. 'And we're off to bob up and down outside Brest again.'

'I'll bring you back some plum pudding,' promised Peter, clutching the half sovereign his uncle had secretly pressed into his hand.

Peter Raven did not spend Christmas at home. Instead, he came close to death in the Royal Naval Hospital. The wound in his back had become infected and he succumbed to a fever which had so drained him of his strength that the doctors had feared he may not live.

But Peter was more of a fighter than they'd reckoned. In January, still desperately ill but stubbornly clinging to life, he was moved to a Hampshire village to recuperate in the home of a parson friend of his father. The air in those parts was famously considered beneficial, and while he was there his parents arrived with an unexpected companion.

'Matthew Book!' Peter said weakly, when he saw the unlikely trio standing at the foot of his bed.

'Mr Book visited us together with Commodore Beaumont, Peter,' explained his mother as she clutched his hand. 'The Commodore's duties have taken him elsewhere, but he gave Mr Book permission to come with us to visit you.'

'How are you, my boy?' enquired his father, and Peter could see both his parents were holding back their tears.

'Much better than I was, Father,' Peter replied, trying his best to sound cheerful and strong. But it was a forlorn effort.

Matthew studied Peter gravely before he spoke. 'May I look at the wound, Mr Raven?'

With some effort, Peter was turned on to his stomach and the dressing removed. With his face buried in the pillow, Peter could hear his parents murmuring a prayer at the sight of his back.

'I think I can help this to heal,' said Matthew, examining

the deep festering wound. 'But it will take time. Fortunately, I still have a few days of leave left before I must return to the *Torren*.'

'What could you hope to do, Mr Book?' asked Peter's mother doubtfully. 'The doctors have tried everything.'

'I know of a healing poultice used by the people where I was born. Will you permit me to apply it?'

'What does it consist of?' Peter's father asked anxiously.

'A kind of moss which fortunately also grows in England. I should be able to find some near here. The rest of the ingredients will be in the kitchen,' replied Matthew. 'Do I have your permission to try, sir?'

'Perhaps we should first consult the doctor who is caring for Peter here,' suggested his mother.

Matthew shrugged. 'I'd be very surprised if he would allow me to treat his patient, Mrs Raven.'

Peter, who was now lying on his side again, spoke weakly. 'Please let Mr Book try, Mother. I have already trusted him with my life.'

Mrs Raven clutched her husband's arm. 'You have our blessing to do anything you think fit, sir,' she said.

Matthew Book and Peter's parents spent the next forty-eight hours at the bedside, with Matthew and Peter's mother taking it in turns to change the poultice. Thankfully, the treatment proved remarkably successful. Even so, the village doctor was sceptical when he visited Peter a few days later and found the patient sitting up for the first time with noticeable colour in his cheeks.

But Peter's parents had no doubts about where their thanks lay. 'We shall never be able to repay you, Mr Book,' said Mrs Raven, clasping his hands in her own when he came in to bid them farewell.

'You never did tell me what you've been up to with Commodore Beaumont, Matthew,' said Peter, grinning.

Matthew laughed. 'You wouldn't believe it if I did, Midshipman,' he answered, grinning evasively. 'But if it works, you'll be very impressed.'

'Will you see the commodore again?'

'I'm sure we both will, Mr Raven,' said Matthew, shaking Peter's hand. 'Commodore Beaumont is like one of those tunes you just can't get out of your head.'

Peter still had some months of recovery ahead of him. As soon as he was pronounced well enough, he travelled in easy stages to the vicarage at Richmond to be with his family. Much to his embarrassment, his sisters now treated him like a wounded hero.

At long last he was pronounced completely fit and his convalescence came to an end. His mother made one final plea to try and persuade Peter to give up his career in the Navy, but he assured her it was all he had ever wanted to do, and reluctantly she had to accept it.

One fine morning late in the spring, she and his father waved goodbye with mixed feelings as Peter's horse-drawn post-chaise departed for London where he was to take the mail coach to Portsmouth and rejoin the *Torren*. The ship had been in the dockyard for some weeks to be refitted.

Peter was pleased to find himself heartily welcomed back by all on board, except the vile Lieutenant Blysse who barely managed a nod of recognition.

The crew of the *Torren* had been greatly reduced in Peter's absence. Because of the ship's long weeks in Chatham dockyard, many of her hands and officers had been allotted to other commands. But even with the crew at less than half strength, Captain Benchley was eager to return to sea duty. And there were still plenty of familiar faces aboard. Matthew was back in his role as ship's clerk. He laughed when Peter found him with Perry and Sinclair in the captain's galley and thanked him again for saving his life.

'You know what the Spanish say, Mr Raven,' he commented. 'Save a man's life and you're in his debt forever.'

'Surely it's the other way around, Matthew?' said the captain's manservant.

'Who can understand the sayings of foreigners?' said Perry.

The following day the *Torren* sailed. Perhaps as a lesson to the crew not to take anything for granted, Captain Benchley allowed them all to think they were returning to blockade duty, but when they came within sight of Ushant's rocky coast they continued to sail west, causing wild speculation among the crew about where they were headed.

When their course altered again and they headed south, Captain Benchley finally ended the arguments and wagers that had been struck about their possible destination. The *Torren* was to join the West Indies Squadron in Jamaica, where there had been a marked increase in the activity of French privateers harassing British merchant shipping. More welcome news was that the crew would be allowed shore leave in Jamaica.

Men were always less likely to desert in foreign ports. Suspicious of and ill at ease with other languages, British sailors rarely strayed far from their ships, preferring instead to gather in dockside taverns where the cosmopolitan owners usually spoke a smattering of all tongues.

Older hands aboard the *Torren* told the younger and less travelled members of the crew that the weather would be hot and the rum cheap. Hands who had been to the West Indies before were full of tales about the pleasures they would enjoy.

'Fruit like you've never seen before,' Peter heard Prewitt, now a bosun's mate, telling a circle of eager listeners. 'Nuts as big as your head and spiders as big as chickens. And they don't have any winter there.'

'No winter?' said a doubtful crewman who was a Londoner and fairly new to the sea. 'There's got to be a winter. You're telling us tall tales.'

'It's true, as God is my witness,' protested Prewitt. Seeing Peter listening, he said, 'You tell them it's the truth, Mr Raven.'

Although Peter was many years younger than these men, he knew they had complete faith in his knowledge of the world because of his education. Few of his audience had ever touched a book, and none of them could write.

'Prewitt is right,' he replied. 'We are heading for the tropics. They never see snow there.'

'It don't seem natural,' said the original doubter. 'Going to a place where there's no winter.'

'There's nothing natural about this ship neither,' joked another hand. 'What about the ghost?'

'Ghost?' echoed Peter. 'What ghost?'

'The ghost of Batt, Mr Raven,' said Prewitt. 'Morgan said he saw his spirit when he was on watch last night.'

'There's no such thing as ghosts,' said Peter quickly. 'My father told me. He's a clergyman, so he ought to know.'

'As you say, Mr Raven,' said Prewitt, but without conviction.

Peter smiled to himself. These men were prepared to take his word about the wonders of the natural world without question, but their belief in the supernatural could never be shaken.

Peter was thinking about the mystery of Mr Batt as he hurried to get his sextant for the noon sighting. He knew Mr Batt had disappeared during the action with the French frigate *Juno*. Matthew had told him that Batt's hideaway on the poop deck was empty and no one could recollect seeing him during or after the battle. Such happenings were not unusual; two other missing men were still unaccounted for. In the confusion and fog of battle, combatants often fell overboard. Most were rescued, but an unlucky few were crushed between ships or just swallowed by the sea, so Batt's disappearance had been long forgotten, until now.

Peter decided to report the sighting of a ghost to the captain at an appropriate moment, when he got on deck. Rumours spread fast on ships, and sailors were notoriously superstitious. Give a ship the reputation for bad luck and the crew could make it a reality by giving up in an emergency, just when they needed to be strong-willed and determined to press on.

On the poop deck, the weather was hotter than any Peter had ever known, with the blazing sun reflecting dazzlingly off its white surface. Waiting for the noon sighting to begin, Peter tested the caulking between the planks with the tip of his shoe. The mixture was made with tar and the teased-apart ends of rope called oakum. Softened by the overpowering heat, it yielded to his pressure.

As usual, the midshipmen gathered in the presence of the captain to calculate the ship's noon position. Peter could feel his skin prickling beneath his heavy woollen uniform, and he envied the ordinary seamen who went barefoot, wearing only loose shirts and baggy canvas trousers.

When the midshipmen had made their calculations and entered the results in their journals, Peter found the captain speaking to Lieutenant Westlake. He stood respectfully at attention nearby while the two men discussed the excellent time the ship was making. Eventually, the captain was free.

'Mr Raven,' said Captain Benchley. 'How may I help you?'

'I thought I should tell you, sir,' said Peter. 'The men

believe there is a ghost aboard the ship.'

Captain Benchley nodded. 'The ghost of Mr Batt,' he said, tugging on his earlobe thoughtfully. 'I've been expecting that,' he added, addressing Lieutenant Westlake as well as Peter.

'You did, sir?' they chorused with equal surprise.

'Oh, yes. In fact, I've seen the spectre myself.'

'You've seen the ghost of Mr Batt, sir?' exclaimed Lieutenant Westlake in a high-pitched voice that betrayed his youth rather more than he would have wished in his recently exalted position.

'I very much doubt it was a ghost, Mr Westlake,' said the captain dryly. 'Although he did seem very pale in the moonlight. We all know there are a thousand places a man could hide himself on board a ship the size of *Torren*. He must have stayed hidden since our battle with the French frigates, and even during the refit. Remarkable achievement, don't you think?'

'Shall I instigate a search for him, sir?' suggested Westlake.

Captain Benchley shook his head. 'We might hunt for a year and Mr Batt could still elude us. That would only make us look foolish in the eyes of the crew. Which of them spotted Mr Batt?'

'Morgan, sir,' answered Peter.

'What's he like, Mr Westlake?'

'A steady hand, sir. He acquitted himself well in the fight with the *Juno*, even though it was his first engagement.'

'How is he rated?'

'Ordinary seaman.'

Captain Benchley nodded again. 'Mr Raven,' he instructed, 'bring Morgan to me.'

Peter hurried away and found Morgan with a party shifting barrels of salt pork for the cooks. It was hot work and he was glad to break off, until Peter told him the captain wanted to see him.

'What does he want with *me*, sir?' the sailor asked anxiously in a strong west country accent.

'I don't know, Morgan,' Peter replied truthfully. 'But it's nothing to worry about.'

Nonetheless, Morgan looked awestruck as he stood before Captain Benchley on the poop deck and knuckled his brow in a respectful salute.

'Ah, Morgan,' said Captain Benchley in a friendly manner. 'Are you the fellow who saw the ghost of Mr Batt?'

Morgan nodded. 'Aye, aye, sir. It was me right enough. Plain as the nose on your face, he was. He just glided across the fo'c's'le, if you don't mind me saying so, sir.'

'Well, I'm delighted,' said the captain. 'When I was a midshipman on the *Achilles* we had a ghost, and that was the luckiest ship I've ever served on.' Benchley took a coin from his pocket and handed it to Morgan who gazed in disbelief at the half sovereign.

'That is to reward you for being so sharp-eyed. There's no one I like to have on board with me more than a lucky

Cornishman. From today, you shall be rated Able Seaman. Dismissed.'

Morgan hurried away grinning with pleasure.

'That should ensure we have a *lucky* ghost on board, Mr Raven,' said the captain quietly, with the hint of a grim smile in Peter's direction.

When Peter visited the captain's galley for a drink of water later in the watch, he found Matthew Book and Sinclair cutting up a gigantic and peculiar-looking fish that had a long spiked nose.

'What on earth is *that*?' exclaimed Peter.

Matthew grinned. 'It's a swordfish, Mr Raven.'

'Try a slice of it griddled for your supper. It'll build up your strength, Mr Raven,' added Sinclair, who still fussed over Peter's health even though he was completely recovered. 'You won't know it from a tender piece of steak.'

'You've had it before?' asked Peter.

'Many times when I was a boy, sir,' Matthew told him. 'We're getting near the Caribbean, my home waters.'

Chapter Sixteen

A LADY OF BREEDING

'But why do all the grandest people of France live only in Paris, Aunt Elizabeth?' asked Lucy, who was seated by the window in her great-aunt's sitting-room. 'It seems strange that they have all chosen to cluster in one place. The best families here are all settled along the eastern seaboard.'

'My dear child,' Mrs Hargreave answered distractedly as she sat at her writing desk composing a letter. 'An essential trait of the French is their conviction that all the best people in the world are either in Paris or on their way there.'

It was a long time since Mrs Hargreave had last been in Paris and she was well aware that much had changed. But in most essentials she was confident the French would always be the same.

'Do you think their Revolution was a success?'

Lucy asked.

Mrs Hargreave sniffed. 'I don't see how it could be. A "successful revolution" is a contradiction in terms.'

'What about our revolution?' Lucy asked mischievously, knowing her aunt had been in favour of that.

Mrs Hargreave laid down her pen. 'Ours was a war of independence for America. It was fought by gentlemen against that despot King George the Third. But our aim was to govern ourselves with the best men of our country, not hand it over to a bloodthirsty mob of murderous riff-raff.'

Lucy suppressed a chuckle. 'You liked King Louis the Sixteenth, didn't you?'

Aunt Elizabeth nodded. 'He was a great friend to America, and almost bankrupted France to supply us with arms and ships to fight the British.'

'How will it be for us, going to France now? After all, we've only recently made peace with the French.'

'They say the new man, Napoleon Bonaparte, is reviving the old ways in France. He wants to restore Paris as the centre of civilization, and instil a new sense of order.'

Mrs Hargreave had taken up her pen again as she spoke.

'Who are you writing to this time, Aunt?' Lucy asked.

'The American Ambassador in Paris,' she replied. 'I am asking him to instruct an agent to find us a suitable house to rent near the Tuileries Palace, to buy us a decent carriage and horses, and to engage trustworthy servants. Also, his wife can recommend the best dressmakers. You'll be needing them when you come out into society.'

'You've already bought me more new dresses than I want,' Lucy reminded her.

'You will need even more when we reach Paris,' Mrs Hargreave assured her confidently.

Potter knocked before entering the room to announce, 'Miss Lucy's Latin teacher has arrived, ma'am.'

Lucy had flatly refused to return to the Trenton School, and had said she wouldn't go to Paris either unless she could start learning Latin. Her great-aunt had finally relented and hired William, brother of the painter Jacob Kellerman, to tutor her during the months before their departure.

'Thank you, Potter,' said Mrs Hargreave with a disapproving edge to her voice.

When General Cosgrove had left for India with Jacob, he'd insisted on taking the portrait of Lucy with him, saying it would cheer him up to be reminded of his granddaughter during the long sea voyage. Having hoped to keep the painting for herself Mrs Hargreave was still aggrieved that she'd lost it to her brother. And quite illogically, she'd now added both Kellerman brothers to her list of undesirables, along with Jack Cobden. She'd been even more put out when General Cosgrove had insisted Cobden was to go with them to France.

'George, the man is a savage!' she'd argued. 'How can we possibly have him with us in *Paris*?'

But Lucy's grandfather had been adamant. 'There's plenty of savages left in Paris, Lizzie,' he'd retorted. 'If you doubt it, just ask to see the square where they cut off the heads during the Terror. So, if you're determined to take my granddaughter to the ends of the earth, I want a man along who I know can get her home if there's any trouble.'

'Well, Mr Cobden will have to wear proper clothes,' said Mrs Hargreave, realizing she'd never change her brother's mind. 'I don't want Lucy seen riding around Paris with him dressed in animal skins.'

'Jack has suits, Lizzie,' replied the general. 'Just not many occasions to wear them these days.'

Lucy stepped light-heartedly down the stairs to the ground floor and found her tutor taking snuff in the morning-room. In complete contrast to his brother, William Kellerman was fashionably dressed, plump, and brimming with good humour.

'Ah, Miss Cosgrove, your presence makes even this glorious spring morning seem more intoxicating,' he said, bowing with a flourish. 'How inappropriate that we should spend the few precious hours left to us on a dead language.'

'I'd far rather be outdoors myself, Mr Kellerman,' she replied, 'but if studying Latin is going to get me into Princeton. . . .' She broke off with a shrug.

'Does your great-aunt still disapprove?'

'I'm keeping quiet about it while she's so preoccupied, Mr Kellerman. Please don't say anything that will remind her.'

He drew back in mock horror, saying, '*Procul hinc, procul este, severae!*'

Lucy laughed. 'You're quoting from the Roman poet Ovid.'

Kellerman nodded. 'Excellent! And can you translate what I said?'

'*Far hence, keep far from me, you grim woman!*'

'You've made astonishing progress in these few months, Miss Cosgrove.'

The lesson ended two hours later when Jack Cobden called to take Lucy out to lunch. She told Potter to inform her aunt that she would return in the afternoon, and William Kellerman strolled with them as far as a tavern near the waterfront. Had Mrs Hargreave known her great-niece was lunching there she would have been deeply disapproving.

Lucy and Jack gave their order and took a seat at a table in a sunny bay window. Through the thick distorting glass Lucy could see the tall masts of ships, and thrilled to think how soon she would be aboard one of them.

'You've bought a new suit,' said Lucy, looking with approval at Cobden's well-cut broadcloth coat and the stock tied expertly about his throat.

'I've bought three,' said Jack. 'The moths had made a meal of my old ones.'

'Just a few more days,' said Lucy with a sudden shiver of anticipation. 'I can hardly believe it.'

'Paris will be good for you, Lucy,' said Jack, and sipped the buttered rum he'd ordered.

'Do you think so?' asked Lucy, stirring cream into her

coffee. 'Sometimes I think I never want to leave the Hudson Valley.'

Jack smiled. 'You can't just go hunting with me all your days,' he said gently.

'Why not?' Lucy asked almost fiercely.

'You'll find out soon enough,' he answered.

'What do you mean?' she asked. 'That's the sort of thing adults always say. *How* will I know soon enough?'

'Because girls grow up differently to boys,' he said easily. 'To tell you the truth, some boys never grow up. Look at your grandfather. But with girls, well, it can happen all of a sudden. One night they go to bed a girl and next morning they're more than halfway to being a woman.'

Lucy grinned at the notion. 'How would an old backwoodsman bachelor like you know about girls growing up?' she chided.

'Because I had sisters, Miss Know-it-all,' he replied.

'Sisters?' said Lucy, astonished. 'You've never told me you had sisters.'

'Two,' he said.

'What happened to them, Jack? Where are they now?'

'One was killed during the Indian wars, the other married a Scottish officer and went to live in Edinburgh.'

Before Lucy could ask any more questions, a serving girl arrived with the newspapers for Jack. 'Two English and two French, Mr Cobden,' she said.

Lucy and Jack sat reading avidly, not even stopping while they ate the thick broth served for their midday meal.

As they finished each of the newspapers they passed them to the other customers waiting to read them.

As they strolled back to her aunt's house Lucy tried again to raise the subject of Jack's sisters, but he had little else to say. 'Just remember not to take your elders for granted, young lady,' he mocked. 'And don't forget, most old people have more secrets than the young.'

They parted at the front door. Mrs Hargreave had reluctantly offered Jack accommodation in her house, but to her relief he'd already booked himself in at the tavern.

'How did you get on with Mr Cobden, Lucy?' asked her aunt.

'We read the latest newspapers from Europe,' said Lucy defiantly. She expected her great-aunt to be shocked, since she'd always told Lucy that newspapers were unsuitable reading matter for young ladies of breeding.

'Oh, good,' said Mrs Hargreave. 'Do tell me what was in them.'

'Why on earth would you want to know the news from Europe, Aunt Lizzie?' asked Lucy.

'The French keep changing Europe about,' explained her aunt. 'We don't want to arrive in France and appear unsophisticated by not knowing who's ruling whom.'

Chapter Seventeen

A NEW EMPIRE

With a heartfelt sigh, Charles-Maurice de Talleyrand-Perigord, Foreign Minister of France, read an invitation to dine with Napoleon Bonaparte.

'Bad news?' asked General Ancre, who was taking tea with him in a shaded pavilion in the garden of the minister's palatial home.

When General Ancre had returned to Paris at Napoleon's command the previous autumn, he'd expected to be ordered to take immediate action to contact Count Vallon. Instead, the First Consul had told him to do nothing until he received further orders. General Ancre had been quite happy with the arrangement and had even taken a long leave in North America, from which he had only recently returned.

The weather was delightful, a perfect late spring day, but the general did not much care for tea, which he

considered nothing more than musty hot water. Strong coffee, heavily sweetened with sugar, was his preferred drink
in the afternoons.

'I am invited to dine with Bonaparte this evening,' said
Talleyrand, an expression of distaste flickering across his
aristocratic features.

'So am I,' replied Ancre. 'But I thought you liked our
First Consul. After all, you helped to bring him to power.'

'Oh, I have nothing but admiration for Bonaparte,' Talleyrand hastened to say, automatically glancing about for
possible eavesdroppers even though the pavilion was in the
middle of a vast lawn.

Since the Terror of the Revolution, Paris had become a
city of listeners, and every man of power employed spies
and informers. Satisfied his words would only be heard by
General Ancre, Talleyrand sipped his own tea appreciatively
and continued.

'Napoleon Bonaparte is the greatest military genius
since Alexander the Great, a politician of skill and imagination – but when it comes to food, his taste is terrible!'

General Ancre bellowed with genuine laughter. It was a
pleasant release to express himself so unguardedly.

Like all dictators, Napoleon trusted no man completely.
He therefore only ever revealed part of his overall plans to
any one person. So, for the past hour, the general and the
French foreign minister had been piecing together what they
each knew of the First Consul's intentions.

The cautious behaviour of General Ancre and Talleyrand

was understandable. Since the beginning of the French Revolution, men had frequently changed sides. As the power of life and death passed from one faction to another, friend had betrayed friend and rival united with rival. And the killing went on, as if a deadly plague had infected the politics of the nation for over a decade.

Eventually, individuals as different as Talleyrand and General Ancre had united with Napoleon to restore peace to the nation, even though the price had been his dictatorship. There were still fanatical revolutionaries in France who would guillotine the heads off half the population, and Napoleon was the only person who could prevent them.

Napoleon had promised to unite the nation and heal the wounds of the past. He wanted a new France where a person's ability, whether aristocrat or peasant, would be the only thing on which they were judged.

The two men taking tea together in the pavilion were living proof that Napoleon was keeping his word. Talleyrand was an aristocrat who could trace his ancestry back to the year 990. General Jean-Baptiste Ancre was by birth a Creole peasant from the Caribbean island of Martinique.

'So, General,' said Talleyrand, suddenly coming to the point. 'What is the First Consul's ultimate intention towards the Americans?'

'He plans to make mischief in the Caribbean.'

Ancre's answer was blunt enough but not all that informative. Talleyrand nodded and after sipping more tea, he prompted, 'And . . .?'

'I do not know. But I have carried out his instructions to me *exactly* as he requested.'

'Which were?'

'To find him a skilful and ruthless pirate in the West Indies, and await further orders,' said Ancre casually.

Talleyrand's eyes hooded momentarily. 'So, how may I help you, my dear General?'

'Answer me one question, sir. What exactly is the state of France's finances?'

The foreign minister smiled. 'Have you ever been to England, Ancre?' he asked.

'Never.'

'You should try to some day. Napoleon intends to invade them as soon as he can. Perhaps you will have your opportunity then. They are a curious race. The aristocrats possess most of the power, and they rule the country through Parliament with a certain amount of help from the middle classes. Even so, they actually believe they are a free people. They are extraordinarily patriotic and loudly claim that all things English are superior. Yet their aristocracy is descended from the French nobility brought to their shores by William the Conqueror.'

'And how does that answer my question?' asked Ancre.

Having obtained the information he wanted, Talleyrand was taking his time telling what he knew. He wagged a finger for the general to be patient. 'The English teach their children rhymes with no apparent logic or meaning. Children go up hills and tumble down, dukes march troops nowhere, rings are formed then all fall down. But there is one verse of which I am strangely fond. If I remember correctly, it states:

Old Mother Hubbard,
Went to the cupboard,
To fetch her poor dog a bone.
When she got there,
The cupboard was bare,
And so the poor dog had none.'

Talleyrand smiled at his guest. 'Napoleon is Old Mother Hubbard and France is the dog. The cupboard of France is well and truly bare, my dear Ancre.'

'Not even a bone?'

'Not even a bone.'

The foreign minister rose awkwardly on his club foot. 'Now, I must delay you no longer, General. I'm sure you have much urgent business requiring your attention. For my part I must instruct my chef to prepare something edible for me on my return from our First Consul's dinner.'

General Ancre bowed. 'And I must see a certain boat builder.'

'In Paris?'

'Like me, he is also a visitor.'

General Ancre found his boat builder waiting for him in the apartment he had taken near the cathedral of Notre Dame on the Ile de la Cité. The young man had already spread out his plans on a long table close to the windows overlooking the river Seine.

'Monsieur Valerie,' said the general. 'Will you take coffee with me?'

'Delighted, General,' replied the young man.

General Ancre drank the welcome coffee while studying various aspects of the boat that Valerie had designed to his specifications.

'She will be swift?' asked Ancre.

'None faster.'

'You have altered the layout of the loading chutes. Excellent!' observed Ancre.

'I must confess, General. When I drew up the original plans, I thought you wanted the vessel built as a slave ship. When you assured me you had another kind of cargo in mind I made these changes.'

The general nodded. 'I think they will work very well.' He looked up at the genial young man. 'Have you guessed what she will carry?' he asked.

'I think you must intend to transport exotic fruits to distant markets, General. Hence the need for speed.'

Ancre chuckled. 'A rare kind of fruit, indeed,' agreed the general, smiling to himself.

Chapter Eighteen

THE MEN WHO CAME TO DINNER

Talleyrand raised an eyebrow at General Ancre as a footman added water to the First Consul's wine glass.

'Where was the worst cuisine you have ever eaten, Talleyrand? England?' asked Napoleon jovially as the footmen cleared the plates for the next course.

The foreign minister slowly shook his head. 'Contrary to popular belief, if one is very, very careful one can eat quite well in England. Beyond doubt, the worst food I have ever had to endure was in the United States of America.'

'America, Foreign Minister?' asked Joséphine, who was sitting beside Napoleon.

'Even now, the memory of a certain concoction of boiled meats makes me shudder, Madame,' Talleyrand replied. 'Who knows, I might have been a successful businessman in Massachusetts, had I not been driven back to our own dear France by the barbarities they practise in the kitchen.'

'I heard it was because the Americans wouldn't pay the bribes you demanded, Talleyrand,' said Napoleon, dryly.

Ignoring the insult, Talleyrand shook his head. 'Americans are incapable of a sophisticated point of view, First Consul,' he replied. 'I made a close study of them during my stay. I came to the conclusion that their naiveté makes them extremely dangerous. Rather like gigantic and enormously strong children, it would be best for us all to keep them in a vast playpen made with iron bars.'

'Surely not all Americans are the same?' said Joséphine.

Talleyrand laughed. 'They *do* vary, I grant you, Madame, but to appreciate the differences among them you must first understand where they come from.'

'Explain what you mean,' demanded Napoleon.

Talleyrand shrugged. 'Americans, at least those of any influence, are in the main simply two different sorts of Englishmen. Just as America is two different kinds of country.'

'I still don't understand,' said Joséphine.

Talleyrand continued. 'It's like this, Madame. Those in the hot southern states are quick-tempered, gambling, swaggering slave-owners who see themselves as cavaliers. Oddly, they usually refer to their blacks as servants, as if they had some choice about their employment. The men of the colder north are a quite different breed of Englishman. They're businessmen or farmers of the puritanical kind, who keep no slaves and tend to despise those who do. *Their passion in life is the making and keeping of money.'*

'That's why they were reluctant to give any of it to you, was it?' said Napoleon.

'Your Excellency jests,' said Talleyrand with a smile. 'Nonetheless, we must deal with them before they grow too strong. Or the day will come when it will be they who deal with us.'

Napoleon stood up, and holding out a hand to indicate that Joséphine should remain seated, he snapped out at the two men, 'Follow me.'

Talleyrand and General Ancre rose and hurried after him.

Accompanied by several footmen, Bonaparte led them up flights of stairs and along a corridor to a part of the palace Talleyrand had never been in. Taking a key from his pocket, Napoleon unlocked a large set of double doors off the long corridor. Inside the room was in total darkness, but a shaft of light from the corridor cut through its gloom. Talleyrand and Ancre were puzzled to see that the vast floor space was almost entirely filled by a low tank of water.

'Bring lamps,' Napoleon instructed the footmen, and minutes later the room was brightly lit.

The two guests looked about them, intrigued. Filling the wall at one end of the huge room was a gigantic map as tall as three men. It depicted the geography of North America, including the Caribbean, down as far as the northern edge of South America.

At the opposite end, side by side on a long table, were a dozen strange little contraptions that resembled boats, and some kind of lantern with a single long lens.

Napoleon nodded to a footman who had obviously performed the task before. The man lit the lantern and handed it to the First Consul. Then he began to apply a candle to the tapers held by the rest of the footmen.

Still puzzled, Ancre and Talleyrand watched the footmen apply their burning tapers to the boats before placing them on the water. After a brief pause, the little machines began to chug about the tank, driven by the paddle wheels set on either side of each one.

'What a wonderful entertainment, First Consul,' said Talleyrand as if the room had been made over as some sort of elaborate and expensive game devised for Napoleon's diversion.

Ancre saw a deeper purpose. 'Steamboats,' he said quietly.

Napoleon flashed a piercing gaze in the general's direction. 'As you say, Ancre. *Steamboats.*'

'They work on steam?' said Talleyrand, hardly able to disguise his indifference. 'Where are they from?'

'A young American engineer called Robert Fulton designed them for me,' replied Napoleon. 'I had a watchmaker make these models from his blueprints. Fulton's an interesting man, Talleyrand. He is not a businessman, nor a farmer or plantation owner. He invents things. Another type of American you may not yet have encountered.'

'Can the boats be made on a larger scale, Citizen?' asked Ancre.

'*Yes*, by God!' replied Napoleon with sudden enthusiasm. 'They can be made the size of frigates. You know what this means, Ancre?'

The general nodded, glancing up at the gigantic map. 'I think so. It means we will have the ability to navigate the great rivers of the American interior, First Consul.'

'Right, General Ancre. And the sea, gentlemen, *the sea*!' said Napoleon, striking his fist into the palm of his hand. 'With steamboats we shall defeat my two greatest enemies: Britain and the wind.'

Watching the boats churning across the massive tank, Napoleon continued with even greater fervour. 'On land, no one can oppose me. I am the master of all the armies in Europe. But on the seas, the British rule. They use wind as an ally. With steamboats I shall be able to direct navies as I do armies, and I'll easily be able to calculate when they will arrive at their destination. Steam-power is the weapon I need to forge a new empire in the heart of America.' He snapped his fingers, saying, 'Footman, turn off the lights.'

As the room plunged into darkness Napoleon directed a narrow beam of lantern light at the vast map.

'Here are the present states of America,' he said, playing the beam of light down the eastern seaboard. 'Beyond the Allegheny Mountains is the great western wilderness, where the Americans continue to push out their settlements. There are thousands more of them each year. And to bring their goods to market they send what they produce down the Mississippi River to New Orleans.'

He made a vast circling motion with the beam of the lantern over the huge territories either side of the Missouri and Mississippi rivers. 'Soon, all this will once more be ours. With the power of steamboats, we will make it a magnificent new country.'

He swung the lantern again, running the beam south-wards down the coastline to Florida, across to the island of Cuba, and stopped as the light shone on the island of Santo Domingo.

'And this shall be my stepping stone. I intend to send General Leclerc to begin operations. When my French army has dealt permanently with those untrustworthy blacks on Santo Domingo, I shall launch an attack on Louisiana from the island.'

Ancre leant forward to turn one of the steamboats that had come to the edge of the tank and was paddling furiously against it. 'My agents tell me that Toussaint, the rebel leader on Santo Domingo, is an exceptional man,' said Ancre.

Napoleon shrugged. 'Pah!' he exclaimed. 'These gilded Africans have not yet encountered French troops. We shall sweep them aside, Ancre.'

He swung the lantern around to play it on Talleyrand's face. 'What is your view on that, Foreign Minister?'

Talleyrand reached out. 'With your permission, Citizen?' he said, taking the lantern. He shone it down the length of the map, west of the Allegheny Mountains.

'I believe it is France's duty to create a new empire, and to keep the Americans in their proper place. But France is almost bankrupt. Who is to pay for it?'

Napoleon ignored his question for the moment and spoke to General Ancre.

'I want you to leave for the West Indies immediately, General. Tell this man Count Vallon that if he comes to me here in Paris with sufficient treasure, I shall make all his dreams come true.'

Now he looked at Talleyrand. 'You want to know how I shall pay for our new empire, Foreign Minister? The answer is simple. I shall buy it with pirate gold.'

Chapter Nineteen

THE RESCUE

Peter was still not accustomed to the dazzling blue skies and the incredibly pure colours of the sea. Used to the grey-green waters of the English Channel, he marvelled at the splendours of the tropical ocean. Deeper waters were a rich Prussian blue, but where coral grew just beneath the surface the sea was sapphire until it met the white sands of the beaches on the tiny flecks of islands they passed.

It was strange to think of the gentler seasons in England. Summer there was never like this, and then there was autumn when days shortened and the trees in Richmond Park shed their brown and golden leaves. But Peter felt no homesickness, even when he thought of Isaac roasting chestnuts on the bonfire in the vicarage garden.

After a long run south, HMS *Torren* had turned to head due west, passing through the Antilles and into the Caribbean. She was on the last leg of her voyage to

Jamaica and had made a reasonably speedy passage from England. Captain Benchley considered himself fortunate. The winds were capricious at the best of times, so the voyage could just as easily have taken the *Torren* three months instead of the six weeks that had passed since they'd left Portsmouth.

The voyage had passed in such a pleasant and easy manner, it would have been easy to forget that Britain was still at war with France, had the captain not kept the crew constantly running through their drills so they'd lose none of their edge. Even so, as each day passed it became harder to imagine that a French ship might suddenly appear and engage the *Torren* in desperate and bloody battle.

Then, one mid-morning, the lookout hailed the poop deck. 'Smoke on the horizon!'

The lookout gave the position, and all telescopes were trained on the dark smudge, like an inky handprint, where the intense blue of the sky touched the darker hue of the deep sea.

Captain Benchley cracked on all sail and headed for the black smoke that trailed upwards in a raggedly rising column. But he did not order action stations until he judged the *Torren* to be within half an hour's sailing of the burning ship. By then, the lookouts had reported three departing schooners on the horizon. There was no chance the *Torren* would be able to catch the faster ships. Instead, they made for the burning vessel which was clearly sinking.

As they drew closer, they could see that the ship, a

brigantine called the *Moon Star* armed with twelve cannon, must have put up a hard fight. But the price the crew had paid for their courage was dreadful. Bodies floated in the sea all about the burning vessel, and it was obvious that most of the men had not died in battle. Whole groups were still roped together, and the sea was stained red where the sharks were feeding on them.

'Mr Stanhope,' ordered Captain Benchley. 'Have your marines drive off the sharks with musket fire.'

The crackle of their guns continued as the *Torren* drew closer to the burning ship and the lookout shouted, 'There are people still alive on the deck, sir.'

'By God, he's right,' said Captain Benchley, snapping his telescope closed. 'Midshipmen Raven and Arrowsmith, organize crews to take survivors off immediately. Be quick now. She'll be going down quite soon.'

While the *Torren* lay off, two whalers were manned and made ready to be swung over the side. Lieutenant Blysse was supervising the launchings from on board the *Torren*.

Beside him, Matthew Book was studying the *Moon Star* through a powerful telescope and suddenly became agitated. As he moved off towards the captain on the poop deck, a violent blow struck him down.

'Oh! Sorry, Book!' yelled Blysse, who appeared to have been emphasizing an order with the marlinspike he was holding.

But it had not seemed like an accident to Peter, who had witnessed the incident from his seat in the stern of one of the whalers. It looked to him as if Blysse had actually intended to knock Matthew over the side, instead of which Matthew had fallen to the deck with blood flowing from his cracked skull.

Peter could do nothing for his friend. His boat was being lowered into the water, and he was soon wholly occupied as they pulled hard towards the foundering ship. The rescue parties scrambled aboard and hurried across the listing deck as dense smoke continued to pour from the forward hatch. Peter and Arrowsmith found more than a dozen people roped together and lying at the foot of the mainmast.

They shouted with relief at the appearance of the rescue parties, and gabbling in a mixture of Dutch, English and French, they urged the men from the *Torren* to cut their bonds. Judging from their seamen's clothes, most were crew members of the *Moon Star*, but there were also two extraordinary figures among them: a man and a woman roped side by side.

Both lay unconscious, and their features were so alike they had to be twins. The man's clothes were cut in the vanguard of fashion. He wore a dark jacket, buff waistcoat, snowy white linen shirt, a high starched stock at his throat, tight doeskin trousers and short gleaming boots. Even lying there among the wreckage of a battle he looked as if he could have fallen from the window display of a master tailor.

The woman wore a turquoise turban and a gorgeous matching dress. Although it appeared to be no more than a simple arrangement of silk, it could only have been created by the most skilled and expensive of dressmakers. Her feet were encased in delicately bejewelled oriental slippers.

But the physical appearance of the two was even more arresting than their clothes. Both had light brown hair. The man's was carefully arranged in a pomade of curls, brushed forward at his temples and forehead. The woman's fell in ringlets from beneath her turban. Their translucent paper-white skin was not used to being exposed to sunlight.

Brother and sister were tall and slender. Their hands were exceptional with long tapering fingers. Both had high-domed foreheads and long narrow faces with pronounced cheekbones, and small well-formed mouths. Despite their extraordinary similarity, the woman was quite beautiful and the man was handsome in a foppish kind of way.

As Peter bent over them the man's hooded eyes fluttered open to reveal irises the colour of bluebells. The only significant difference Peter could see between the faces of the brother and sister was that the man had slightly thicker eyebrows.

'I am Lord Percival Fitzroy,' he said in a high fluting voice. 'This is my sister, the Lady Anne. Who are you?'

'Midshipman Raven, Royal Navy, at your service, sir,' said Peter. 'Hang on there. We'll soon have you aboard the *Torren*.'

'An English ship. Thank God,' said the man and fainted again.

*   *   *

There was a gabble of interest among the *Torren's* crew as the survivors from the doomed merchant ship came aboard. Twins were deemed lucky by those who were most knowledgeable about sailors' superstitions.

They were carried below. Lieutenant Westlake moved out of his quarters to share with another officer temporarily while his cabin was made available to the guests. Lord Fitzroy was revived with a large glass of brandy and sat in a chair next to the open window telling his story to Captain Benchley. Standing at the captain's side Peter listened, enthralled and angered.

'I am the owner of the *Moon Star*,' he began, but paused to watch out of the window as the ship finally slipped beneath the waves, leaving nothing but a brief pall of smoke dissipating in the stiff breeze.

At last, Fitzroy continued. 'We were en route to Jamaica with a cargo of furniture and iron goods,' he said. 'Usually I leave matters of trade to my captains. We only came this time because my dear sister was recently widowed and her doctor advised me that the sea voyage would be good for her.'

'A doctor with radical ideas, sir,' said Captain Benchley.

Despite his recent trials, Lord Fitzroy managed to smile. 'He also advocates the new idea of sea bathing. I'm not sure if I would follow his advice that far, but I understand the Prince of Wales is persuaded.'

'What happened to the *Moon Star*?' asked Captain Benchley.

'We were set upon by three privateers,' said Fitzroy. 'You may have seen them departing. They flew British colours until they were upon us.'

'A common enough ruse,' said Benchley.

'Their leader was a clever monster,' said Lord Fitzroy bitterly. 'He flew a white flag to come within hailing distance. He begged us to surrender for the sake of my sister, who'd insisted on staying on deck. He gave his word as a gentleman that we would be treated with all the honours of war. When they boarded us it was another story. They plundered the *Moon Star*, and murdered for the enjoyment . . . forcing my sister to watch their depravities. But we were saved by your timely arrival, Captain. I'm certain the devil who led them was hoping we would die with you – our salvation – in sight.'

'Did you learn the name of their leader?' asked Captain Benchley.

'I most certainly did,' replied Lord Fitzroy bitterly. 'He introduced himself as Vallon – Count Vallon.'

Chapter Twenty

THE DINNER PARTY

Despite their recent close encounter with death, Lord Fitzroy's remaining crew were prime seamen and fit for duty. Captain Benchley, still short-handed on the *Torren*, was well within his rights when he pressed the men into service, and they seemed to take their fate philosophically. Like most crews they were a mixed bunch: an Englishman, two Irishmen, a trio of Dutchmen, a Norwegian, and five French-speaking Canadians.

After a day's rest, Lady Anne was well enough to dine with the captain. She bemoaned her luck at losing her entire wardrobe, as it had gone to the bottom of the sea with the *Moon Star*.

The *Torren's* officers were most amused by these twins, although they did their best not to show it. Even Lady Anne's voice was similar to her brother's.

The night of the dinner, Peter was visiting Matthew

who was being tended by Sinclair. Matthew was still unconscious, stretched out on a narrow bunk off the captain's galley, his head wreathed in a blood-soaked bandage. But he
had stirred a few times during the day, and the ship's surgeon had assured Sinclair that he would recover.

'Bad luck for Matthew, wasn't it, Mr Raven?' said Sinclair bitterly. 'And a strange coincidence, seeing as he'd just
had that trouble with Lieutenant Blysse.'

It was clear from Sinclair's voice that he, too, was sure
the blow hadn't been an accident. But he dared not accuse
Blysse of deliberate brutality, for fear of being flogged for
insubordination.

'What trouble?' asked Peter sharply. 'What are you
talking about, Sinclair?'

'Didn't you know, sir? Lieutenant Blysse nearly beat one
of the boys on the lower gun deck to death with that marlinspike he's taken to carrying around like a club. He had it
drilled out and loaded with lead.'

'No!' replied Peter. 'I didn't know.' And he recalled
being puzzled himself as to how a wooden marlinspike
could have delivered a blow hard enough to floor a powerful man like Matthew Book.

'Matthew saw Blysse beating the boy,' continued Sinclair. 'The surgeon got angry when he examined the boy.
When he found out that Matthew had seen what had happened he ordered him to give evidence to the captain. But
before he had a chance to speak out, we were involved with
the *Moon Star*.'

'Thank you, Sinclair,' said Peter, leaving Matthew's bed-side. He went to the deserted poop deck where he could be alone to think. The night was so clear the sky was filled with countless stars, glittering like particles of sparkling glass. Peter looked towards the stern at the ocean. The *Torren* was churning phosphorus in her wake, like a tail of glowing pale-green fire.

Peter asked himself what he should do. Could he put right the wrong? Sinclair's evidence was only hearsay. Everyone aboard knew Blysse was a vicious brute, but proving he'd tried to bash Matthew's brains out was another matter.

Peter had seen that incident, but it would only be his opinion that Blysse had acted deliberately. And now, para-doxically, if Matthew were to give evidence against him in the case of the beaten boy, Lieutenant Blysse could claim it was petty revenge for his own accidental blow.

As he struggled with the problem, Peter heard an odd sound from above. Looking up, he saw the dark shape of a man falling against the white of the foremast's billowing topsail. Oddly, there was no accompanying cry.

The body landed with a sickening thud on the foredeck. Peter hurried forward, but he already knew the man was dead. Something strange was happening on the ship. There was an absence of familiar noises and there were far fewer hands than usual on duty.

Peter hurried to the wheelhouse. The two seamen who had been on duty lay sprawled awkwardly on the floor. The officer of the watch also lay crumpled, half in the shadow of the quarterdeck. As Peter arrived, new hands were taking their place. He recognized them as seamen they'd rescued from the *Moon Star*. One of them, a swarthy, bearded French Canadian, was called Le Bonne.

'What's wrong with these men?' Peter demanded.

'Don't know, sir, they just fell down,' answered Le Bonne as he took the wheel.

Filled with foreboding, Peter hurried below. The *Torren* was like a ghost ship on the lower decks. Bodies lay everywhere, just as they had fallen. But there were movements nearby. He could hear scurrying footsteps, and he caught sight of moving shadows at the far end of the lower gun deck. But they vanished as he approached. Then came a long terrible scream from above, which ended abruptly.

Peter's place in time of trouble was beside the captain. He made for the dining-room, where the evening meal should still be in progress. Instead of hearing the marine string quartet and noisy conversation, the only sound was an eerie cackle of hysterical laughter.

The dining-room door was ajar, and Peter put his eye to the crack. The strange laughter was coming from Lord Fitzroy and his sister. They were standing either side of Captain Benchley who was sitting upright in his chair, the point of Fitzroy's sword pricking his throat. The other officers were sprawled face down across the table as if asleep. Members of the string quartet lay tumbled among their instruments.

Peter then realized what was amusing Lord Fitzroy and

his sister. Sinclair, dressed in his steward's uniform, lay on his back across the centre of the dining table, his mouth and unseeing eyes wide open. Blood drenched the front of his white jacket. The servant's throat had been cut and a carving knife plunged up to its horn hilt in his chest.

Peter recoiled in horror, and was seized from behind. An arm circled his chest in a powerful grip and a hand was clamped over his mouth. He was lifted from his feet like an infant and carried soundlessly to the deserted poop deck.

'Don't shout, Mr Raven,' a familiar voice whispered as he was released. Peter turned to see Matthew Book, his head still bound with the bloody bandage.

'What's happening?' asked Peter, bewildered. 'It's like some dreadful nightmare below.' Even when the *Juno* had fired all her guns at them he had not felt the sort of fear that gripped him now.

'The Devil has taken the *Torren*,' Matthew whispered. 'I recognized Fitzroy when I saw him on the *Moon Star*, but Blysse knocked me out before I could warn the captain.'

'What can we do?' Peter asked. Then he remembered it was he who should give the orders and said, 'We must rally the crew.'

'There is no crew to rally, Mr Raven,' said Matthew urgently. 'All we can do is save ourselves by hiding.'

'I can't hide,' said Peter desperately. Such an action was unthinkable. 'We must do our duty and try to save the captain.'

Matthew did not hesitate. His left fist flashed out, clipping Peter's jaw. It was a well-judged blow; had he used his entire strength it might well have proved fatal.

Peter crumpled into Matthew's arms, and he carried him across the poop deck to the refuge that had been constructed for Batt. Matthew pushed the unconscious Peter into the recess and clipped the door shut before slipping away at the sound of men approaching.

Chapter Twenty-one

THE POWER OF MUSIC

Peter regained consciousness with his head pounding and his throat dry as chalk dust. Reaching out in the darkness, his fingers encountered the thick felt padding that lined his confined quarters.

He felt a moment of panic, not realizing at first that Matthew had thrust him into Batt's bolt-hole. But thin strips of light shone through the slits cut at eye level in the small door, and fighting off a surge of terror Peter tried to peer on to the poop deck.

He could see very little until he managed to work free more of the felt from around the slit. By pressing his fore-head hard against the door he could then see out.

The quarterdeck was brightly lit with hanging lanterns, and men were bringing more from all parts of the ship to festoon the shrouds. So festive was the scene, Peter was reminded of Christmas decorations, but it seemed no goodwill was intended by the show of lights.

The schooners they had seen fleeing when they'd first approached the *Moon Star* were being guided back to the *Torren*. They were soon alongside and men were transferring aboard to replace the helpless crew.

In less than an hour the task was complete and most of the new men had hurried below. Two chairs were brought from the captain's quarters and placed to one side of the poop deck. After a few minutes, they were occupied by Lord Fitzroy and his sister.

Peter could see the *Torren's* crew being led on to the deck in shambling lines. They were roped together and being prodded forward by armed guards. The men appeared to have been sedated. But how? And why hadn't he and Matthew Book been affected? Nor, he remembered, had Captain Benchley.

Lord Fitzroy seemed to be in an excitable mood. 'Music, we need music,' he called out and gestured to Le Bonne. 'Have the marine band bring out their instruments.'

'The string quartet, sir?' asked Le Bonne.

'No,' replied Fitzroy, with a shake of his head. 'The brass instruments. Martial music is more appropriate for this event.' Then he added, 'But find me the young man who played the violin earlier and have him bring his instrument.'

While his orders were being carried out, Fitzroy conversed lazily with his sister, who fanned herself daintily in the warm night air. The couple could have been taking an evening's entertainment at Vauxhall Gardens in London.

Eventually, the marine band was assembled and the violinist was brought before Fitzroy. 'You played earlier,' he said, holding out his hand for the youth's instrument. The marine was still too drugged to make sense of what was happening and simply stood hanging his head.

'Can we wake them up?' Fitzroy asked his sister irritably.

'Pain may do the trick,' she replied.

'Beat him,' ordered Fitzroy.

Le Bonne had two men use a cat-o'-nine-tails. At the sixth lash it was evident that the youth was responding to the agony.

Holding up his hand for the flogging to cease, Fitzroy plucked the strings of the violin thoughtfully for a moment before laying it to one side. 'His ineptitude is an offence to the most noble instrument ever devised by man.' He looked to Le Bonne. 'Hang him from the yard-arm and leave his body as a reminder of what happens to all those who insult the gods.'

The marine blinked in disbelief, then he was dragged away, struggling and begging for mercy. Moments later the sentence was carried out. From his vantage point, Peter screwed his eyes shut and prayed for the murdered youth.

'You vile creature, that boy did nothing,' protested Captain Benchley who had been herded on to the deck with his officers. He alone among the captured men was distraught; the rest of the crew, still dazed by the opiates they'd been given, seemed unable to comprehend the fate of the violinist who now dangled above them.

'Well, I'm delighted someone is moved to passion by my gesture,' said Fitzroy to his sister, then he looked at Benchley. 'I'm afraid your men are still feeling the effects of the potion we administered, Captain. I shall wait a little longer for it to wear off. There is no pleasure in killing a man if he is unaware of what is happening to him.'

He turned again to Le Bonne. 'Have the other musicians flogged awake.'

The order was carried out until all the bandsmen, though still groggy, were ready to perform. But before the first note was played, Lady Anne looked up, saying, 'I do believe the rest of them are stirring at last, my dear.'

A few of the Torren's crew were starting to gaze about them in a bewildered fashion. One of them caught Fitzroy's eye. 'The man with such fine blond hair,' he said, pointing to Lieutenant Blysse. 'Bring him to me.'

Blysse was hauled before Fitzroy, who looked deep into his eyes, and called out, 'Captain Benchley, do you consider yourself a good judge of men?'

Benchley did not deign to answer.

'I gather from your silence that you do,' said Fitzroy. 'I pride myself I can read men like a book.' He glanced up to where the hanged bandsman swayed from the yard-arm. 'Take this lieutenant, for example. I took particular notice of him at dinner,' he continued. 'A British officer, from good English stock, and raised as a Christian gentleman.'

Fitzroy chuckled and looked at his sister. 'But I've known savages from the South Seas with more of the milk of human kindness in their veins. I can tell just by looking into his eyes.'

Fitzroy continued to study Blysse. 'Well, do you want a chance to live and serve me, lieutenant?' he asked, almost playfully.

'I would do anything for such an opportunity, sir,' replied Blysse, who had now recovered from the effects of the opiate and looked like a begging dog at his captor.

Fitzroy placed an arm around Blysse's shoulder in a brotherly fashion, saying in conversational tones, 'The problem is, Blysse, you have just proved you have absolutely no loyalty. Who is to say how quickly you would switch sides again, were the positions to be reversed?'

Less certain now, Blysse looked sideways at Fitzroy, who still had a friendly arm draped casually across his shoulder. He did not notice Lady Anne rise. As she approached, smiling, she took a small, razor-like clasp knife from her purse.

With a sudden sweeping motion she drew the blade across Blysse's throat. He staggered away, panic and surprise on his face as blood spurted from his neck. Then with a gurgling moan he pitched forward on to the deck.

Lord Fitzroy clapped his hands with pleasure. 'You are Justice herself, my dear,' he congratulated his sister. 'How rarely we see such treachery committed and retribution follow so swiftly. I am uplifted. Have the band play a lively tune.'

The couple strolled back to their chairs, and it was clear to Peter that the proceedings had not yet come to an end. Fitzroy ordered the ship to heave to and the *Torren* came about to face the light wind, a manoeuvre that brought her to a virtual stop. It was an easy piece of seamanship for her new crew to hold her position. Fitzroy then ordered that Lieutenant Blysse's body be thrown overboard.

'That will bring the sharks to us, I shouldn't wonder,' said Lord Fitzroy casually. 'Begin throwing the rest of the crew over the side.'

'Who do you want to go first, sir?' asked Le Bonne.

'Anyone!' Fitzroy screamed with sudden impatience. 'Just get on with it. I command you.'

The sea rail was removed from the quarterdeck and the bound seamen, still only half-recovered from their stupor, were prodded towards it at the point of pikes and swords, and thrust over the side. Only Captain Benchley struggled, but bound and unarmed he stood no chance. The threshing waters were already seething with sharks attracted by the scent of Blysse's blood, and they attacked Fitzroy's latest victims in a frenzy.

'More, more!' Fitzroy urged, until finally the whole of *Torren's* crew had been sacrificed.

'That's the last, sir,' shouted his second in command.

Fitzroy leapt to his feet screaming, 'I wanted a sea of blood! Is there a sea of blood?'

Before anyone could answer, two men armed with pistols pushed Matthew Book in front of him.

'We found him hiding by the wheelhouse, sir,' one of them reported.

Before his captors could toss him into the sea, Matthew fell to his knees and scrabbled for the violin and bow discarded at Lord Fitzroy's feet. Intrigued, Fitzroy allowed him to pick it up.

In one swift movement, Matthew swept the bow across the instrument's strings and a lingering note of incredible beauty filled the air. Fitzroy stood stock-still, his head cocked like a listening bird as Matthew played.

Although still numbed by the terrible events he'd just witnessed, Peter recognized the piece Matthew was playing. It was one of Bach's violin concertos. Through his spyhole he could just see Matthew standing beside Lady Anne Fitzroy. Entranced by his performance, she was waving her fan in time with the music. Lord Fitzroy, his rage finally spent, walked slowly back to his chair and slumped down as if exhausted. His face, like his sister's, was filled with rapture at the haunting music.

'There's no more to go to the sharks, sir,' Le Bonne reported.

Lord Fitzroy waved him to be silent. 'Get the ship under way. And tell the men to be as quiet as possible,' he ordered.

When Matthew had finished the piece, he bowed to Fitzroy and his sister's appreciative applause.

'You play very well,' said Lord Fitzroy. 'Do you know anything else, or did you just learn that one piece?'

'I know much more, sir,' replied Matthew. 'Is there any composer in particular who would please you?'

'Some Beethoven, I think,' said Fitzroy. 'I leave the selection to you.'

Matthew continued to play for more than an hour. Eventually, Lord Fitzroy fell asleep in his chair. Gesturing to the men who stood nearby, Lady Anne had him gently carried below.

'What shall we do with this one, my lady?' asked Le Bonne, nodding towards Matthew.

'Have him continue to play outside my brother's door,' she replied. 'If he wakes, the music will soothe him.'

'What then?'

She looked at Matthew. 'He has already made his choice. I think he would rather play the violin for my family than go to the sharks.'

Matthew bowed deeply. 'My lady, I beg of you, if my music is to continue to please, I must occasionally rest my hands.'

She considered his request and nodded. 'It would not do to play out of tune. Remember the fate of the other violinist.' She looked at Le Bonne. 'He may rest for fifteen minutes every hour.'

Before he followed them below, Matthew made a swift gesture with his hand towards Batt's bolt-hole, indicating that Peter should stay where he was. With no other plan, Peter obeyed.

*   *   *

Alone in the dark after the horrific events he'd witnessed, Peter sat trembling with grief and shock. But Matthew's playing marked the passage of time for him; he could hear the music coming from the captain's quarters, and by the second interval he knew two hours had passed.

A storm blew up. The calm of the tropical night changed as rapidly as Fitzroy's mood. Lightning crackled across the sky, and in the aftermath of the booming thunder a raging wind began to blow. Men were ordered aloft to take in some of the spread of sail. The ship rose and fell like a pitching colossus as she battled against the ever-mounting waves. Finally, rain lashed down in blinding sheets.

Watching through the slit in the wood, Peter suddenly saw Matthew. He was clasping a safety line to pull himself across the heaving poop deck, which was awash from the storm.

Holding on to the rear rail, Matthew sprang open the door to Peter's refuge and had to raise his voice to be heard above the storm. 'I've put one of the lifeboats over the port side. It's trailing by that line,' he shouted as he indicated a rope tied on to the rail. 'It's stocked with food and water and a compass. We'll head north-west for Jamaica.' He thrust a sailor's knife into Peter's hand. 'Cut the line with this when we're aboard. I'll take the tiller.'

Peter's mind was still in turmoil. He desperately wanted to understand what he'd witnessed earlier. 'What happened?' he shouted. 'Why were the crew unable to fight back?'

Matthew leaned closer to reply. 'The men who came

aboard from the *Moon Star* laced the water barrels with some kind of sleeping potion,' he explained. 'You, me, Sinclair and Captain Benchley only drank water from the captain's private tank. They hadn't got at that.'

'How did you know Lord Fitzroy would be so affected by music?'

'I've played for him before,' said Matthew. 'But he didn't recognize me.'

'Where?' asked Peter, astonished.

'I was born at Roc d'Or,' said Matthew. 'The man calling himself Lord Fitzroy is Count Vallon.'

'Vallon!' echoed Peter.

'Yes. Now, for God's sake, *go!*'

Matthew directed him to the rope where the lifeboat lay over the side. Peter seized hold of it, and gripping with his feet he began to swarm down. It was not easy. In the heaving sea the rope alternated between jerking taut and swinging loose as the ship rose and fell on the mountainous waves. When Peter finally managed to scramble into the lifeboat, he looked back up at the ship's stern looming above him, and through the shrieking wind he heard shouting on the *Torren's* deck.

Matthew had been seen as he was about to escape. He stood on the rail hugging two rolled hammocks he'd hauled from their storage nets as hands had reached out to claw him back. Hesitating only briefly, Matthew leapt into the broiling sea.

Peter twice saw him rise and fall on the great waves, but

the lifeboat was still tied on with the rope and as every second passed he was being dragged further and further away by the *Torren*.

Peter hacked at the line with the razor-sharp clasp knife, and was suddenly adrift. He watched for a moment as the *Torren* ploughed on through the tropical sea, leaving the lifeboat far behind in its wake. He searched about, trying to see through the blinding rain, but there was no sign of Matthew. There was nothing but the threatening waves that tossed the lifeboat about like a fallen leaf on a swollen stream.

It was the bleakest time of Peter's life. Apart from his family, everyone he cared for had been taken from him. All dead, his friends, his uncle and men for whom he would have laid down his life.

And the *Torren* herself was as dear to him as his father's house. Now she was in the hands of Count Vallon. It was some time before he could even contemplate the likely consequences. A first-rate British warship of more than a hundred guns under the command of a madman. The implications were horrendous.

When the *Torren* had disappeared over the horizon, Peter set about struggling to hoist the lifeboat's little sail, deciding it would be better to ride out the storm rather than wallow helplessly at the mercy of the mountainous waves. As the howling wind filled the small patch of canvas Peter fought to keep the small craft trimmed, grateful for all the time he'd spent learning how to handle the ship's cutter.

Blown onward by the relentless wind, Peter made a solemn vow. He would use all the skills the men aboard the *Torren* had taught him, and no matter what he had to endure, he would survive. However long it took him, he would one day avenge the agonies inflicted upon his shipmates.

As if he were putting his boyhood behind him, Peter Raven dedicated the rest of his life to this purpose. If it was the last act he committed on earth, Peter swore the day would come when he would take his revenge on Count Vallon.

Chapter Twenty-two

THE MAGIC OF PARIS

The day finally came for Lucy Cosgrove to sail for Paris. Her friend Mary Van Duren, escorted by William Kellerman, came to wave her off. Mary's father had allowed her to use his open carriage, and despite the blustery spring weather Mary had insisted the hood be left down so she could be appreciated in all her finery.

'My, what a big boat,' said Mary, looking up at the *Mermaid*, a three-masted merchant ship. 'How many more of them does your grandfather own, Lucy?'

'Six or seven, I think,' answered Lucy, distracted by the exciting bustle all around them. Mrs Hargreave was already aboard with her maid and Potter, her manservant, but Jack Cobden was on the dock supervising the loading of their party's mountain of luggage.

'Try to read for at least two hours a day, Miss Cosgrove,' William instructed. 'And remember, Latin is the universal language of scholars. If you should be confused by anything in the books I have given you, there is an entire section of Paris, known as the Latin Quarter, gathered about the Sorbonne.'

'What's the Sorbonne?' asked Mary.

'One of the great universities of the world, Miss Van Duren,' answered Jack Cobden, who had joined them when the last of the luggage was stowed to his satisfaction.

'Why, Mr Cobden,' said Mary, twirling her parasol and smiling demurely at the tall figure who carried a long polished case in his arms. 'My father told me you were a surprising sort of man.'

Jack swept off his hat with a grin and a bow. 'And you are as lovely and predictable as your mother, Miss Van Duren.'

'There's Aunt Lizzie at the rail,' said Lucy.

'Time for us to get aboard, Lucy,' said Jack.

After hurried embraces and handshakes, Lucy and Jack climbed the gangplank and stood at the rail beside Mrs Hargreave, waving as the *Mermaid* was cast off and got under way. Mary and William continued to wave, and William bellowed something which only Jack Cobden managed to hear.

'What did he say?' asked Lucy.

'*Medio tutissimus ibis*,' answered Jack, smiling.

'*You will go most safely by the middle way*,' translated Lucy. 'Another quotation from Ovid.'

'Ovid? Ovid?' echoed Mrs Hargreave, puzzled. 'Are the

Ovids another one of those Indian tribes?'

The passage of the *Mermaid* was swift and during the twenty-seven days it took to reach Le Havre, Lucy made her first conquest, Lieutenant John Mowbury, who was newly-commissioned in the Merchant Marines and one of the ship's junior officers. Lucy's lively and unconventional manner had captivated him from the first evening she dined at the captain's table.

The lieutenant's infatuation was obvious to everybody else on board, but Lucy was quite oblivious to his feelings. She simply enjoyed his company.

On the last night of the voyage, after the *Mermaid* had been cleared of carrying any warlike cargo by a frigate of the British blockade, Lieutenant Mowbury accompanied Lucy on a stroll around the deck. Fearing he may never see her again, he declared his true feelings.

Lucy almost laughed, but fortunately she saw the miserable expression on the lieutenant's face and realized he was serious. 'Oh, Lieutenant,' she replied gently. 'I am deeply flattered, but my feelings for you are those only of friendship.'

Fortunately, Mowbury was called back to duty just then, and the awkward incident came to an abrupt end. He marched away stiffly, and Jack Cobden stepped out of the shadows to join her.

Lucy turned to him in distress. 'Did you hear that, Jack?' she asked.

He nodded.

'Do you think I've hurt him?' she continued.

'He'll survive,' replied Cobden.

But Lucy recalled the lieutenant's downcast face. 'He'll soon forget about me, won't he?' she added anxiously.

'In about forty or fifty years,' Jack replied casually.

'And I thought falling in love was supposed to make people happy,' said Lucy ruefully.

'Sometimes it does,' said Jack philosophically. 'Other times it's about as much fun as a raging toothache.'

Lieutenant Mowbury was soon forgotten in the bustle of their arrival the following day. Jack Cobden had already surprised Mrs Hargreave with his gentlemanly manners at the captain's table. Now, he astonished her with his ability to speak perfect French.

'Have you been to France before, Mr Cobden?' Mrs Hargreave asked, affecting only the slightest of interest.

'Yes, Mrs Hargreave,' he answered briefly, as he retrieved the long package from his baggage at the dockside in Le Havre.

Mrs Hargreave would have liked to hear more, but she was too proud to question their taciturn companion any further.

It took them some days to reach Paris from the port, and when they arrived, Lucy was astonished by the grandeur of the house her great-aunt's agent had taken on their behalf. In contrast to the streets of the city – many of which were squalid with refuse – their new home was magnificent, and furnished with exquisite taste.

Lucy's only objection to her new way of life would have puzzled her friend Mary Van Duren.

'Must I really have so *many*?' Lucy asked her aunt during another long visit from the dressmaker. Her extensive dressing-room was already overflowing with stacks of boxes containing shoes, gowns, cloaks, gloves, hats, parasols, and lacy undergarments.

'A young girl in Paris can never have too many clothes,' Mrs Hargreave intoned in a pious-sounding voice, before addressing the young woman who was supervising their wardrobes. 'Mademoiselle Heloise, are you quite sure Miss Cosgrove's clothes should be so . . . so *insubstantial*?'

Without quite sneering, Mademoiselle Heloise assured her the style was absolutely correct. At the time of Mrs Hargreave's last visit to France, women in the best circles of society wore dresses fashioned from lavish amounts of heavy cloth, reinforced with whalebone corsets and topped with powdered wigs. Now, the latest vogue dictated that their natural hair be curled with hot tongs, and that they must wear dresses made of gossamer-light materials.

In the latter days of spring, Mrs Hargreave finally decided Lucy was ready to come out into Parisian society. Accordingly, she made the necessary arrangements with the American Embassy for herself, her niece and Jack Cobden to be presented to Napoleon Bonaparte.

It was to be at a morning levee where the great and the powerful would mingle in the Tuileries Hall of Ministers, and influential people new to Paris could be presented to the First Consul.

When Mrs Hargreave descended the stairs of their rented mansion on the morning of the reception, she was appalled to find Jack Cobden dressed in buckskins and cradling a long, brass-bound, mahogany box. Next to him, Lucy looked wonderfully elegant in a hooded blue velvet cloak.

Jack Cobden's costume may have horrified Mrs Hargreave but it was actually rather beautiful, and not the old buckskins he used for hunting. He wore a scarlet shirt beneath a honey-coloured fringed buckskin coat that reached almost to his knees and was gorgeously decorated with beads of many colours.

Tucked into his wide yellow silk sash he had a long, horn-handled hunting knife and an engraved tomahawk. His highly polished boots were worn over dark blue army breeches and his hat was made from a fox pelt; the tail of it hung down his back and the head stared angrily from above Cobden's broad brow. Although Mrs Hargreave insisted he was wearing the clothes of a savage, Jack Cobden looked every inch a nobleman.

'You can't go to the Tuileries dressed like that,' protested Mrs Hargreave faintly. 'Do you want Lucy to die of shame?'

'I think he looks wonderful,' said Lucy, trying hard not to laugh at her great-aunt's stricken expression.

'Before you ask me to change, Mrs Hargreave,' said Cobden grumpily, 'I want you to know this wasn't my idea.'

'Then, pray, whose was it?'

'Robert E. Livingston and Tom Jefferson thought of it.'

'The *President* asked you to dress up in this backwoodsman's garb?' Mrs Hargreave gasped incredulously.

Jack Cobden nodded as he tapped the long polished box he carried. 'I have a present for the First Consul, and a letter from Thomas Jefferson which he wanted me to present personally. They thought I would attract Napoleon's attention if I was dressed a little differently.'

'How well do you actually *know* Thomas Jefferson?' demanded Mrs Hargreave.

'Pretty well,' Cobden answered. 'We went to the College of William and Mary together when we were boys.'

For a moment, Mrs Hargreave seemed lost for words, but she rallied. '*You* went to college?' she managed to utter.

'I'm afraid so,' said Cobden, smiling for the first time.

Mrs Hargreave held up her hands and let them fall to her sides in surrender, but she was quiet in the carriage all the way to the palace.

Chapter Twenty-three

A BACKWOODSMAN'S SKILL

Despite Mrs Hargreave's misgivings, the strategy devised to catch Napoleon's attention proved to have been inspired. The combination of Lucy Cosgrove's startling beauty and Cobden's exotic buckskins caused a sensation: amid the fashionably dressed women and the men in glittering uniforms who thronged the great hall in the Tuileries, none attracted greater attention than the incongruous pair of Americans.

The First Consul's wife Joséphine Bonaparte was already in attendance at the levee. Talking animatedly with a group of people at the opposite end of the hall, she was unaware of the interest being taken in Mrs Hargreave's two companions. But when Napoleon entered the hall he immediately noticed Lucy and Cobden.

After exchanging some peremptory words with a few of the most important guests, he strode purposefully towards Mrs Hargreave's party. An aide from the American Embassy hastily made the introductions. After Mrs Hargreave was presented to him, Napoleon quickly passed on to kiss Lucy's hand, which he continued to hold as he gazed at her. 'Welcome to France, Mademoiselle,' he said. 'Aristocratic beauty such as yours is rare indeed, even in Paris.'

Undaunted by Napoleon's famously hypnotic gaze, Lucy did not blush as those around her would have expected; instead she grinned at him. 'A fine compliment, sir. But, I assure you, I owe my looks to my Red Indian blood.'

Mrs Hargreave raised her eyes to the ceiling in horror.

The First Consul, however, smiled his approval. 'I see you have the courage of youth, Mademoiselle,' he said, and chuckled.

But Lucy had more to say. 'That is indeed a compliment, sir, from someone who has achieved so much, and at such a young age.'

There were sudden intakes of breath from those nearby. It was well known that Napoleon liked to be considered the father of the Republic, not merely one of its younger sons.

For a moment he fixed Lucy with his intense gaze, then he threw back his head and laughed. 'Tell me, Miss Cosgrove,' he said, 'who is this *Coeur de Bois* you have brought me from the American wilderness? Will you translate for us?'

Lucy was familiar with the phrase *Coeur de Bois*, a term the French used for their own buckskin-clad explorers of North America.

'This is Colonel Jack Cobden, First Consul. And he needs no translator.'

Napoleon raised his eyebrows, and with a quick glance at Cobden's military breeches he asked, 'How is it you speak French, Colonel, and where did you serve?'

'I learnt the language as a child, sir. My nurse was from New Orleans. I served in the militia in the Indian wars and in the Federal Army during America's War of Independence.'

Napoleon nodded. 'An educated soldier *and* a wild man. Such contradictions are to be encouraged.'

'I have brought you a letter from President Jefferson, sir,' said Jack. 'He charged me to place it in your hands personally.'

Cobden passed Napoleon the document, and a gentleman who had limped across the hall to join them reached out as if to pluck it from his grasp. 'Shall I take that for you, First Consul?' asked Talleyrand, the Foreign Minister.

Napoleon shook his head and slid the letter inside his scarlet coat.

'And what is this box, Colonel Cobden?' asked Napoleon, tapping the brass-bound mahogany case. 'Is it a gigantic cigar, by any chance?'

This time, Jack Cobden laughed. 'No, sir, it is a present to you from President Jefferson.'

Still cradling the box in his arms, he opened the lid to reveal a fabulous rifle. Nestling in the blue velvet lining was also a powder horn decorated with chased silver and an oiled-silk bullet bag. The weapon was long and slender with an almost delicate walnut stock. Its steel barrel and metal-work were engraved with hunting scenes inlaid in gold and silver.

Napoleon nodded in appreciation. 'A beautiful toy,' he said. 'I shall enjoy playing with it some day.'

'It's more than a toy, sir,' said Cobden easily. 'Don't let the workmanship blind you to its real purpose. Guns like these have saved the life of many a backwoodsman where I come from.'

'You would trust your life to such a weapon?' asked Napoleon, sounding interested.

'I have, sir, many times.'

'But it is such a small calibre,' protested Napoleon, examining its bore. 'And it is a rifle. How can you take such a chance with a weapon that takes so long to reload?'

'If you had the time, I could demonstrate for you, sir.'

Napoleon looked about him. 'A splendid idea, but per-haps not in here. Let us go out on to the terrace.'

The crowd watched with hushed interest as Napoleon led Lucy, an astonished Mrs Hargreave, and Jack Cobden out into the Tuileries Gardens. Intrigued and chattering with curiosity now, the rest of those attending the reception followed them out into the early summer warmth.

Trees stood in blossoming splendour against a sharp blue sky, and a light breeze blew from the west. The First Consul, now thoroughly enjoying himself, took charge of the proceedings. Standing with his back to the mighty edifice of the palace, he indicated that Mrs Hargreave should join the other spectators behind them, but that Lucy and Jack Cobden should stand beside him. He gestured ahead towards the long path which forked around a circular fountain and divided the formally laid out gardens.

'This should provide us with a suitable range,' he said. 'Over what distance do you wish to shoot, Colonel Cobden?'

'It makes no difference, sir,' answered Jack. 'As long as I can see the target.'

Napoleon smiled mischievously. 'What about a *moving* target, Colonel?'

'Whatever you choose, sir,' replied Cobden.

Napoleon was looking about for inspiration when a smiling Joséphine joined them. She was accompanied by a footman bearing a large Dresden bowl filled with oranges.

'An excellent choice, my dear,' he said, pausing to introduce his wife. He then told the footman: 'Take the oranges beyond the fountain, and at my order throw them up in the air.'

'All of them at once, F-F-First Consul?' the youth stuttered nervously.

'No, just one at a time, my boy,' Napoleon answered with a patient smile. 'We don't want to waste them, do we? They've come all the way from Spain.'

Lucy noticed Napoleon's gentle tone, and saw the young footman respond by casting his master a look of hero-worship. As the youth hurried to carry out the order

Lucy glanced at Napoleon, who was dispassionately watching him walk towards the fountain.

Without taking his eyes from the blue-clad footman, he felt Lucy's gaze and answered her unasked question. 'Quite soon, Miss Cosgrove, he will be a soldier. If I wish the youth of France to obey me when I order them to face death, it is best that they love me.' Then, as Cobden began to load the rifle, he gave his whole attention over to the weapon.

Deliberately taking his time, Cobden poured in a measure of powder from the horn that he'd hung over his shoulder, then he opened a compartment in the stock of the rifle and took out a small square of supple leather.

'What's that?' asked Napoleon.

'Greased leather,' Cobden explained. 'It seals the bullet tight in the barrel and gives maximum charge to the powder as the gases expand. It also helps to keep the barrel clean when the gun is fired. The little squares of leather are kept in this compartment called the patch box to keep them free of grit.'

Cobden quickly rolled a small lead ball in the leather patch and, taking his time, he slid it home with the ramrod. Finally, he primed the pan with another small charge of black powder.

'Ready, Colonel?' asked Napoleon.

'As ready as I'll ever be,' replied Cobden.

'Throw,' Napoleon shouted to the footman.

The crowd gave a sigh of anticipation as the dot of an

orange showed against the blue sky. At the crack of the rifle, the target whipped away and the crowd sighed again, this time in admiration.

'A fine shot!' exclaimed Napoleon, impressed. 'Is it the length of the barrel that makes it so astonishingly accurate?'

'And the rifling,' answered Cobden.

'Of course,' agreed Napoleon. 'But, I would never arm troops with rifles. They take too long to reload.'

'These rifles are the exception, sir,' said Cobden, and as he spoke he draped the powder horn over Lucy's shoulder and placed a lead ball in her hand. 'Miss Cosgrove will demonstrate.'

Napoleon glanced at her in surprise. 'Another talent, Miss Cosgrove?' he asked, intrigued.

'Now, Lucy,' commanded Cobden, and she snapped into action with well-practised moves. She tipped powder into the long barrel and, one-handed, rolled the ball into its leather patch. One jab with the ramrod, and the ball was home. As she slapped the side of the rifle to drive a small amount of powder from the main charge into the firing pan, Cobden shouted, 'Throw!'

Lucy fired before the orange had even reached the zenith of its arc. Like its predecessor, it too was whipped away. This time the watching crowd cheered and Napoleon shouted, 'Magnificent!'

'Miss Cosgrove took about fifteen seconds, sir,' said Cobden. 'But I know a man who can do it in twelve, and at a run when he's in danger.'

'We believe you, Colonel Cobden,' said Joséphine. 'But, it is far too peaceful a day for more gunfire.' She turned to Lucy. 'Come back inside, my dear. All Paris is now clamouring to meet you.'

Elizabeth Hargreave followed the First Consul's party into the great hall. She walked beside Jack Cobden, smiling with such pride it might have been she herself who'd fired the last shot.

Chapter Twenty-four

COUNT VALLON'S MAN

General Ancre had spent a tiresome ten days waiting in the humid weather of New Orleans, and his temper was growing shorter by the day. Some weeks earlier, he'd sent the same message to different men scattered about the Caribbean, in Cuba, Santo Domingo and Martinique, and in New Orleans: all places where the elusive Count Vallon was known to have business contacts.

Going to these lengths was necessary because none of Ancre's intelligence agents actually knew the precise location of Vallon's domain. Only the count's sea captains were privy to that secret, so making direct contact with Count Vallon was impossible. But General Ancre had not revealed this fact to Napoleon when they'd discussed how well Vallon fitted the First Consul's requirements for a ruthless pirate and ambitious man to fund his plans for America. If Ancre was to maintain the First Consul's trust, he had to give the impression that he had everything firmly under his control.

The messages he'd sent were simple. They stated that General Ancre was authorized by the French nation to make Count Vallon a fabulous offer of wealth and immense power, and that he wished to discuss the matter with him face to face.

Weeks passed until the general finally received Vallon's reply, which he considered to be a masterpiece of snobbish rudeness. It commanded him to wait in New Orleans, where he would be contacted sometime in the second or third week of July by the captain of the schooner *Columbine*.

General Ancre had never been fond of New Orleans. He had a peasant's superstition that it might one day sink into the swamp upon which it was so precariously built. And he hated the heavy humid heat which seemed to invite the killing fevers brought by the hot clinging mists from the marshy tributary of the bayou.

In the second week of his wait, General Ancre was seated close to the wrought-iron railings on the first floor veranda of a guest house close to the banks of the wide and muddy Mississippi River, sipping a brandy after a meal of spicy prawns and rice. All along the narrow street other residents sat on similar balconies, relaxing in the warm night air. Drifting up to them from the thoroughfare below came the sound of music and a constant babble of voices in a rich stew of different languages.

General Ancre laid his hand on the wrought-iron railing.

Like all the fancy ironwork in New Orleans it had arrived as ballast in a ship from England. The ship would then have been filled with molasses, rum, hardwood, cotton, indigo, sugar, and rice – all the fabulous wealth of the American South and the West Indies – ready to return home. Ancre also thought about the most profitable cargo of all, slaves from Africa.

Born on the French island of Martinique, which had become rich from her sugar plantations, General Ancre had been taught that slavery had always existed and was part of God's will. But things were changing: more and more voices in Europe were questioning the right of one human being to own another, be they black, brown, white or yellow. Anti-slavery movements were growing everywhere, except in the places where vast profits were still to be made from slave labour, such as the sugar islands of the West Indies and the plantation states of the American South. On Santo Domingo, Ancre remembered, an extraordinary man – Toussaint L'Ouverture – had led an army of black slaves to freedom. But although slavery had now been banished in the French colonies, there was talk of it being reintroduced due to the demands of the influential planters.

The general sighed. He could only foresee a world of chaos for the future. Everything was so volatile. Because the war with America had ended and it was whispered that France and England might soon be at peace, some optimistic fools were speaking of a new golden age. But General Ancre was filled with foreboding.

The British trading classes and American businessmen were very similar. With a few exceptions, all they really wanted to do was to make themselves very rich. Because of this they were resistant to change: for instance, though many disapproved of slavery, few had any real desire to force their slave-owning friends and business partners to give up the source of their wealth. Mostly, they hoped slavery would just gradually fade away, but logic told Ancre that slavery was an explosive issue and its fuse was already lit.

Also, for those who, like Ancre, yearned for peace, there was another dangerous element to contend with: Napoleon Bonaparte. Clearly this ambitious man would not be content to remain merely a political leader. He was already taking on more and more of the trappings of royalty. Napoleon proclaimed that his ambition was to make France a peaceful and prosperous country, and that he himself cared nothing for personal wealth. But Ancre recognized that Napoleon craved only one thing: glory. And glory demanded conquest, and conquest could only be achieved through war.

Ancre felt a moment of utter weariness tinged with apprehension, but then he reminded himself that he had a plan of his own. A plan that might bring him some modest wealth and contentment in his old age. He thought of the ship he was having built, and which was nearing completion in Le Havre. His thoughts were interrupted by his agent's wife, a part-Spanish woman. 'There is a gentleman to see you, General,' she said quietly. 'He says he's the captain of the *Columbine*.'

'Show him up,' answered Ancre. Weary no more, he poured himself another brandy from the decanter.

Moments later, a gaunt white-haired man stood stiffly before him. His mahogany brown features were as seamed and cracked as a rocky cliff-face. He wore a broad hat with a white cockade in the band, long sea boots and a blue velvet coat with lace at his cuffs and collar. Slung from his shoulder, a wide leather belt held the heavy type of Scottish sword which Ancre recognized as a claymore.

'I am Alistair McGregor, captain of the *Columbine*,' said the visitor, speaking in a soft yet somehow menacing accent. He was clearly a Scottish highlander.

General Ancre invited Captain McGregor to sit down and join him in a glass of brandy, but the man declined. 'I have other business elsewhere tonight,' he answered tersely. 'I'll send a man at first light to bring you to the *Columbine*.'

'As you please, Captain,' Ancre replied with no discernible warmth. He had never much cared for highlanders. He respected their fighting qualities, but found some of them were prone to alarming swings of mood. Often embarrassingly affectionate, they could also be capable of sudden murderous hostility at some imagined slight to their honour.

This man was no exception, General Ancre told himself. He could see a dancing spark of madness in the man's eyes. He nodded politely but was glad of the small, multi-barrelled pistol he always kept loaded in his coat pocket.

Chapter Twenty-five

THE WILL TO LIVE

Peter fought to stay in his tiny boat with every last reserve of his strength as the howling wind drove him ahead of the storm. He battled hard to keep on some sort of course for Jamaica, but eventually he had no choice but to yield to the awesome power of Nature.

An overcast dawn brought no relief from the savage wind, which finally tore the sail free of the mast and sent it flapping away like a gigantic bird into the tumultuous sky. But Peter's resolve never slackened. Clinging grimly to the tiller and to his vow to hunt down and destroy Count Vallon, Peter's hatred fed his will to survive. But as he fought on through the day, time lost all meaning for him and the grey stormy light once more turned to darkness.

Although they had no way of knowing how close to one another they were, the storm was driving Peter Raven and Matthew Book in the same direction. Once in the raging sea, Matthew had given himself little chance of survival after failing to find Peter's boat. But, refusing to give way to despair, he clung to the rolled hammocks that were his life raft and paddled on, his arms laced through the ropes to hold him on if he fell asleep.

Matthew did eventually fall into a swoon. Although the storm lessened, the wind continued to whip up the waves about him. Eventually, he was jolted awake by a strange sound, somehow familiar yet totally alien at sea. As the sound grew louder Matthew was reminded of the great sea serpents and monsters he'd heard about in old sailors' tales. Staring apprehensively into the gloom, he could just make out a dark shape rising out of the turbulent water ahead of him.

With his sail gone and no oars in the little boat, Peter was at the mercy of wind and tide. Days passed, and his meagre rations were exhausted long before the storm gave way to calmer waters and a merciless sun. Doing what he could to keep his exposed face covered, he sang songs, recited poems, and passed in and out of consciousness, his thoughts drifting to summer days in the garden at home where the copper beech tree provided welcoming shade from a kinder sun.

Once, his mother seemed to be beckoning him. He wanted to run towards her, suddenly sure that the sea would be firm beneath his feet. But his mother's gentle invitation was wiped away as the hallucination changed into the cruel face of Count Vallon. Peter drifted into oblivion hearing again the screams of his shipmates, and his uncle, as they met their gruesome deaths in the thrashing water. Only his intense loathing for Count Vallon was feeding his tenuous grip on life.

Peter was too far gone to know it, but his little craft was floating within sight of a palm-fringed shore.

Chapter Twenty-six

A WELCOME FROM COUNT VALLON

G eneral Ancre's voyage on the *Columbine* took five days in exceptionally fine weather with favourable winds. For most of the journey Ancre chose to remain on deck, even sleeping in a hammock slung aft and only occasionally visiting his tiny cabin.

Meals were served by a surly oriental cook who appeared to speak neither French nor English. The rest of the crew, a recognizable mix of men from the tropics, were equally uncommunicative.

Captain McGregor remained as tight-lipped as he had been at their first meeting, and after making sure General Ancre knew little of the sea, or the navigation of ships, he did not speak to his passenger again.

Ancre, indifferent to the captain's hostility, made no effort to be civil either, so the two men journeyed in silence. But McGregor made a mistake that Ancre would never have done. He underestimated his passenger.

Unbeknown to McGregor, General Ancre kept a careful note of their route. He had a compass concealed in his coat, and an excellent watch. As Ancre could survive on quite short periods of sleep, he was able to keep an accurate record of the voyage, including all changes of direction taken by the *Columbine*. He was sure the information would enable a competent navigator to plot the exact course they had taken from New Orleans.

On the last day of their voyage General Ancre was on deck, watching as they approached a green, mountainous coastline. At midday, Captain McGregor took a sighting and altered course to sail south for a little over two hours. Then he gave orders for the ship to heave to, and fired a shot from one of the *Columbine's* twelve-pound cannons.

Lookouts scanned the coastline until a rocket soared into the sky. Making a careful note of the direction, Captain McGregor steered the *Columbine* directly towards the source of the rocket.

Even as they came closer to the coast, Ancre could make out nothing that looked like an inlet, or any place likely to be inhabited by humans. Then, as the ship was virtually upon the shore, he saw something so odd that at first glance he thought he must be mistaken.

A great section of the lush jungle growth that merged with the water's edge suddenly took on the shape of a vast, low, vine-covered fortification.

'Welcome to Roc d'Or,' said Captain McGregor, speaking the first words he had uttered to his passenger in the last four days.

The *Columbine* had been sailing parallel to the coastline, but now it began a sweeping turn to enter the narrow mouth of an unexpected inlet. Disguised by the surrounding rock formation and the lush tropical growth, the entrance was only fleetingly visible.

One side of the narrow inlet lay at the end of the fortified rocky spur, the other against a sheer mountainside covered in dense jungle. The long promontory, which rose and fell irregularly to form the outer harbour wall, was like a giant's arm growing out from one of the mountains, its elbow crooked out towards the sea.

As they approached, Ancre marvelled at how cleverly the vines and outcropping trees had been cultivated to hide the massive outer stone walls, in which cannon ports had been cut. This row of artillery was not the only line of defence. There was also a gigantic floating boom, which could be used to seal the mouth of the inlet. The blackened timbers of the boom were so wide a team of horses could pull a carriage across them, and great iron spikes studded the side that faced the sea.

General Ancre quickly appreciated how truly impenetrable were the defences of Roc d'Or. The mass of cannon could easily batter any flotilla of ships to pieces, no matter what their numbers. And if by some miracle invaders did manage to pass under the guns, not even a first-rate warship could ram its way through that tremendous boom.

Once the *Columbine* had slipped through the entrance, instead of the expected jungle landscape, a fine deep-water harbour and a bustling town were revealed. It seemed to Ancre that he had come upon a prosperous Caribbean trading port rather than the secret refuge of thieves.

Against the great camouflaged outcrop that disguised Roc d'Or from the sea, an ancient fort swelled out into the harbour. Ancre saw uniformed artillery men manning the battlements. They looked like well-trained troops, not a scruffy band of pirates.

Five ships lay moored against the harbour jetty: three sloops, a brigantine, and one mighty battleship which loomed over the others. Ancre had only expected an ancient crumbling fort, but this was obviously a thriving town, cradled at the feet of two steep forest-covered mountains.

Further inside the harbour was a dry dock, a shipbuilder's yard, and a huge emporium selling ship's supplies. Beyond the granite jetty and the large paved square, handsome white-faced houses lined the cobbled streets. Ancre guessed a pair of imposing brick buildings set on the front were warehouses. Another, equally tall and facing on to the square, was some sort of factory. Several taverns stood either side of an abandoned church. The marketplace, which occupied a third of the sun-drenched square, was thronged with people shopping for fruit, fish, clothes and wine.

Close to the foot of the mountain on the right, a narrow

sparkling river ran into the harbour. It flowed down from a valley, which Ancre could just see through massive open gates set in the fortified walls at the rear of the town.

The place appeared charmingly picturesque, except for a row of ten iron posts set at intervals of about twenty paces across the market square. The posts were crowned with large metal baskets containing the blackened skeletons of human beings. It was clear they had been burnt alive and the remains displayed as a warning to others.

The *Columbine's* crew moored the ship against the jetty. Seeing no reason to thank the surly Captain McGregor, General Ancre stepped ashore. He was greeted with a deep bow from a portly man with curly blond hair who was wearing a pale linen suit and clutching a wide-brimmed straw hat in a podgy hand.

'Welcome to Roc d'Or, General Ancre. I am Monsieur De Croix, Count Vallon's steward.'

The man stood beside an open carriage pulled by four beautiful chestnut horses and driven by a scarlet-liveried footman. Another footman saw to the general's baggage.

General Ancre took a seat in the carriage beside De Croix, and the driver flicked the horses with his whip. As they passed along the sun-drenched dockside, General Ancre looked with interest at the ships moored in the harbour. They were all dwarfed by the majestic battleship.

'HMS *Torren*,' said De Croix with a languid wave of his hand. 'Count Vallon's latest acquisition.'

Ancre was impressed. So the rumours were true. The

British had done their utmost to conceal the fact that they had lost a first-rate battleship, but eventually they had announced it had gone down in a storm with the tragic loss of all hands, and the news had been reported in the newspapers of Europe.

'Are these people happy to live in Roc d'Or, so far from the rest of the world?' asked General Ancre, noting how busy and populated the town was.

De Croix gave a hearty laugh at the question. 'My dear General, what could their *happiness* have to do with anything? They all belong to Count Vallon. Whatever you see, he owns.'

'And you?' asked Ancre.

'I am his *most* devoted servant,' replied the steward.

The drive out of town took them along a wide gravelled avenue which was shaded with lime trees and ran beside the river. Eventually, it turned to cross a fertile plain dotted with farms, vineyards, sugar plantations, and a vast expanse of poppy fields.

After a time the road began to climb gently as the land rose higher and higher. As they gained altitude the temperature grew noticeably cooler. It was pleasantly warm now, rather than hot, and the air seemed much fresher.

'This is a remarkable place, is it not, General Ancre?' commented De Croix, gesturing across the surrounding countryside.

'*Remarkable* is indeed the word,' replied Ancre. 'What exactly is its history?'

'The town was originally a haven for Spanish treasure ships. If the convoys were attacked and scattered, they would rendezvous here before they continued their journey. Of course, in those days the fortifications could easily be seen from a distance. That was long before Roc d'Or was acquired by the count's family. Also, in those days the jungle grew down to the town walls.'

'Were there no people living in the valley?' asked Ancre.

'Oh, yes,' replied De Croix. 'Native Indians. There are still tribes in the jungle on the other side of the mountains. But they never come into the valley.'

'Why not?' asked Ancre, already guessing the answer.

'Count Vallon and his sister Lady Anne discouraged them,' said De Croix with a mirthless smile.

'How?'

'They took great care to inflict unpleasant and painful deaths on those curious enough to climb the walls the count had built. It can't be seen from here, but there is a palisade at the foot of the mountains and a perimeter road, all patrolled by Count Vallon's militia guards. Any intruders were quickly captured and dealt with. The Indians decided that devils lived here. Perhaps they were right,' De Croix added lightly.

'Building a perimeter road and a wall all around this domain must have been a colossal undertaking,' said the general, impressed.

'Count Vallon can achieve an astonishing amount

when he puts his mind to a particular problem,' said De Croix silkily.

'How has he managed to keep the location of Roc d'Or a secret?' asked Ancre. 'Is it not strange that no one has ever betrayed him?'

De Croix shrugged, holding the palms of his fat little hands upwards. 'Quite simple. The count controls a vast network of business interests throughout the Caribbean, the Americas, Asia and Europe. In all these places, his secret agents constantly offer huge bribes to anyone who will reveal the whereabouts of Roc d'Or. Every so often, some fool succumbs to greed, and is immediately kidnapped, brought here and burnt in the market square. Rumours about Roc d'Or abound, but the secret of its location is always preserved. Believe me, General, it is a system that works.'

Ancre nodded, and having no more questions for De Croix he gazed thoughtfully at the passing fields of poppies and sugar cane tended by occasional groups of slaves. Finally, the cultivated fields ended and the rising ground levelled on to a wide, carefully landscaped plateau overlooked by distant blue mountains. In the middle distance, Ancre could just see the line of the palisade that kept the outside world at bay.

As they approached the high walls of a great estate, the gently winding road was flanked by rows of cypress trees. Entering between tall wrought-iron gates, they passed on through acres of formal gardens until they reached a magnificent Italianate villa. Built of buff-coloured stone and white marble, the vast mansion was raised up on a high point of land. The carriage halted at the foot of a wide flight of marble steps leading up to a long terrace fringed with orange trees.

At the head of the steps an imposing figure stood in the shade of a vast white umbrella held aloft by a footman. Ancre noted that the count's servants all appeared to be white, something he had never seen in the tropics before. The general looked for De Croix to make the introductions, but the man had slipped away, leaving Ancre to meet his host alone.

Count Vallon's black silk coat, and carefully arranged dark hair, seemed to emphasize his impassive, death-white face. As the general walked up the marble steps he made a shrewd judgement. Sweeping off his hat, he bowed low before Count Vallon and waited to be addressed first.

'We are happy to receive you, General,' said the count, speaking in a lighter voice than Ancre would have expected from such a tall man. Vallon looked over Ancre's shoulder towards the distant mountains while holding out his right hand.

Knowing he was in the presence of a man whose mind was unbalanced, Ancre deliberately pandered to the whims of his host. He took Vallon's hand with its extraordinarily long fingers, and lightly kissed the large ring offered to him.

Unsure of what title he should use, Ancre settled for a

term of address generally used for royalty. 'I am delighted Your Highness issued an invitation,' he replied.

'Odd, is it not,' said Count Vallon, with a strange darting motion of his head, 'that you, a Creole peasant, raised up by a revolution, should be received by someone of my ancient blood?'

Ancre shrugged. Guessing Vallon would not take him seriously if he were too obsequious, he remained respectful but spoke his mind. 'All powerful families must start from somewhere, Your Highness,' Ancre began. 'The English have an apposite saying on the subject.'

'Pray continue,' said Vallon with an indulgent smile. 'As you may appreciate, English matters are of some interest to me.'

Ancre repeated a couplet he had learnt as a boy.

'When Adam delved and Eve span,
Who was then the gentleman?'

Count Vallon nodded with the same darting motion. 'Ah, yes. Perhaps we were all equal then. If I remember correctly, that was the saying of the English Levellers and Diggers during their rebellions against King Charles I, was it not?'

'They were fond of *repeating* the saying, Your Highness,' said Ancre. 'But I understand it was of even earlier origin, and first used during the fourteenth century English uprising known as the Peasants' Revolt.'

Vallon gave a short cackling laugh. 'I bow to your knowledge of peasant revolts, General. And I must say, I like you more than I expected I would. You are not afraid to say what you think, even in the presence of royalty.'

Ancre gave a briefer bow this time.

'We shall dine at eight,' said Vallon, and gesturing to De Croix who had slipped quietly on to the balcony during the conversation, he added, 'Show General Ancre to his apartment. See he has everything he wants.'

The general followed the plump figure, who had changed into court dress, but in the style of a hundred years ago. 'Welcome to Villa Royale, General,' said De Croix as they ascended a handsome staircase lined with paintings and tapestries.

Ancre smiled at the steward but didn't answer. It was delightfully cool inside; open windows everywhere caught the light breeze and conducted it throughout the building. The general intended to take advantage of the pleasing temperature by taking a long cold bath and a siesta before dinner.

Having disposed of his baggage to a maid, Ancre lay in the bath contemplating Count Vallon's extraordinary self-control. Few men would delay a conversation that would inform them of a way to gain even more wealth and power. It made the general more determined than ever not to underestimate the man he had come so far to meet and bargain with.

When he had finished his long cooling soak in the great copper bath, two manservants appeared with huge white towels. They attempted to help Ancre dry himself, but there was still too much of the peasant in him to succumb to such an aristocratic custom. Waving the pair away he rubbed himself dry vigorously, then, overcome with a sudden delicious weariness, he lay back on a wide bed and surrendered to sleep.

Chapter Twenty-seven

THE PLEASURES OF VILLA ROYALE

G eneral Ancre awoke to the delightful sound of music. Although most of the tunes he'd heard in his life had been played by military bands, he did recognize a good orchestra when he heard one. Whoever was playing, they were equal in skill to any group of musicians in Paris.

He then noticed there were no mosquito nets around the bed. Along with having white servants, that, too, was unusual in this part of the world. Ancre knew that pleasantly cool climates existed elsewhere in the tropics, due to their height above sea level, but he'd never heard tell of one as delightful as this.

As he'd expected, all his clothes had been restored to a pristine wrinkle-free state while he'd slept, and hot shaving water was produced without him requesting it. The general was fastidious about his appearance, and had decided to wear uniform for the evening. Once he'd dressed in clean linen and his heavy dress uniform, he was glad the climate was so temperate.

He descended the staircase to be greeted by De Croix, who escorted him to a pillared reception room where the walls were decorated with magnificent classical frescoes. There, seated in front of tall open windows, an orchestra of white and black musicians performed a piece by Mozart.

Half a dozen gilded chairs were lined up in front of the players, but only the two grandest, with full armrests and scrolled backs, were occupied. Count Vallon was sitting beside a woman who looked so like him she could only be his sister.

General Ancre waited until the piece ended, then walked forward to bow. He was even more startled by the extraordinary similarity of the pair. Their long, white, bony faces could have been cast from the same mould.

'General Ancre,' announced De Croix, but Count Vallon waved him away.

'General, may I present my sister Lady Anne, the Princess Royal,' said Vallon.

Ancre bowed low and kissed her proffered hand. Like Vallon's it was exceptionally long and slender. 'I am honoured, Your Highness,' said Ancre.

'Do you like music, General?' she asked. Even her voice was like her brother's.

'Very much, ma'am, although I possess little knowledge of it.'

'My brother and I share a very special sensitivity to music.' She looked into the distance for a moment, her head jerking with the same bird-like motion Vallon had displayed earlier. 'There is a term to describe the condition. Do you know of it?'

'I believe it is called possessing perfect pitch, Your Highness.'

'Yes, perfect. . . .' Then she turned to Vallon. 'You're right, Henri. He doesn't sound like a peasant. I expected him to have dung on his shoes and talk like a coachman.'

'Such a description would have fitted my father, ma'am,' said the general, smiling.

'Your father? Is he here?' Lady Anne asked with another jerking turn of her head, her bluebell-coloured eyes flickering strangely.

Ancre was a fearless man under fire, but he found something deeply disturbing about this pair. 'No, ma'am,' he replied carefully. 'My father is dead.'

The Princess Royal indicated with her fan that he should lean forward so she could impart some confidence to him. General Ancre did so and she whispered loudly, 'I had a parrot and he died.'

'I'm sorry to hear that, ma'am,' replied Ancre gravely.

'It was poisoned by my enemies,' she said, her eyes narrowing. Then she smiled. 'But Henri caught them all and we burnt them on my birthday. Which was fitting, really. Do you want to know why we did it on that day?'

'I do, ma'am.'

'Because the parrot was a present that I *received* on my birthday.'

The woman was as insane as her brother. Despite the coolness of the evening, General Ancre now felt a sudden crawling sensation beneath the shirt on his back.

'So you approve of my orchestra, General?' interrupted Vallon, completely ignoring his sister's demented talk.

'I do not think I have ever heard better, Your Highness,' answered Ancre, glad to look away from the woman's eyes.

'It is a diverting pursuit,' said Vallon, 'which has given me many years of pleasure. Some men collect paintings, or books – even weapons. I collect musicians.'

'Collect them?' echoed Ancre.

'Oh, yes. For instance, I spent years looking for a good trumpeter,' replied Vallon and glancing towards the musicians, he said, 'Stand up, Henderson.'

A sad-looking man with wings of grey hair over his ears rose to his feet.

'An Englishman?' asked Ancre.

'An Englishman,' answered Vallon. 'I found Mr Henderson on a ship bound for India. He was the only thing on board of any value to me. But it was worth the trouble. He really has an astonishing talent.'

'Such a collection must afford you a great deal of pleasure,' said Ancre.

Count Vallon sighed. 'There are frustrations that only a connoisseur would appreciate. Only recently, I found something of immense value, only to lose it again.'

Ancre looked puzzled.

'It was a violinist,' explained the count. 'He had an astonishing ability. The kind one encounters only once in a lifetime.'

'But you lost him?'

Vallon nodded. 'He did not know I recognized him. But I knew instantly he was a boy born on the estates of Roc d'Or, of a wholly unremarkable family. None of the relatives had any talent, except as troublemakers. But one day when I heard the boy singing, I experienced a moment of divine inspiration. Do you know what I did?'

'I am eager to know, sir,' flattered Ancre.

'I brought him here and had him trained. Intuitively, I knew the violin was his instrument, and I was proved right. It wasn't easy. I had to burn his family to encourage him, but it was worth it. He could play like an angel. Then he ran away.'

'But you found him again?'

'On board the British ship you saw in the harbour.'

'So, he's back in the orchestra?' said Ancre, scanning their faces.

'No,' replied Vallon irritably. 'He escaped in a storm. But if he still lives, I shall find him. I have offered a large reward.' Then he was diverted by De Croix announcing that dinner was served.

'Ah, let us go in,' Count Vallon said eagerly. 'I am always famished after music.'

There were no other guests in the dining-room, although there were settings for a hundred people beneath the crystal chandeliers. Vallon indicated that General Ancre was to sit on his right side, facing Lady Anne.

Before the footman had served the first course, the count suddenly became brisk and businesslike. 'Now,' he said, 'what does the Corsican, Bonaparte, have to offer me? And what must I pay for the privilege?'

Ancre was ready with his answer. 'The First Consul knows you have been harvesting the richest ocean in the world for the past fifteen years,' he began. 'All he asks, in return for a fabulous prize, is that you give him the equivalent of two million pounds sterling in gold bullion every year for the next five years.'

'And where will I be expected to send this tribute demanded by the First Consul?'

'He wishes you personally to deliver the first payment to him in France, as an act of good faith,' replied Ancre. 'And if I may say so, Your Highness, it is hardly tribute, but rather a down payment.'

'Really? This is becoming more interesting.' Vallon nodded for the general to continue.

'Quite soon,' said Ancre, 'a French army will arrive in the West Indies to make a secure base from which to build France's new empire in America. But troops have to be paid and fed, so we must also make arrangements for a safe place to store the money which you will provide.'

Vallon gave a dismissive wave. 'There could be no safer

place for it to be stored than where it is now. In the Fortress of Roc d'Or. It can be dispatched from there when necessary.'

'You have *all* your wealth stored in Roc d'Or, sir?' asked Ancre, astonished.

'Certainly,' replied Vallon. 'Every king must have his counting house, General. I like to be able to see my fortune whenever I choose. That is why I insist it is all converted into gold coin. Now, how much does Bonaparte require as an initial deposit?'

Ancre suppressed a sigh of relief. There had been no way of predicting how a madman like Count Vallon would react. He could so easily have taken offence. 'Shall we say the equivalent of one million pounds sterling, sir?'

Count Vallon took a sip from the wine that had been poured for him. 'And what am I to receive in return for this princely sum?'

Ancre tasted his own wine before he answered. 'The kingdom of Louisiana, the return of your family estates in France, and one-tenth of the income of all those fabled lands of America when its new population begins to pay taxes.' Ancre smiled.

Vallon held his glass up to the light and swirled the wine for a moment. 'That is not all,' he said quietly. 'You are authorized to offer me something else?'

Ancre was impressed by Vallon's ability to judge him. He once more reminded himself he must not underestimate the man, then answered, 'The throne of England.'

Vallon showed no emotion. He merely looked Ancre in the eyes and asked dreamily, 'And what about the throne of France? That is also mine by right, you know?'

Ancre smiled and shook his head. 'Unfortunately, Count Vallon, Napoleon Bonaparte requires that for himself.'

Vallon drank his wine and said, 'I accept. I must have the title to the English throne – after all, it is my family's birthright. But I would not wish to live there. They are a contentious people and hardly worth the bother of burning.' He leaned forward, his eyes suddenly blazing. 'But Louisiana, an opportunity to build a new kingdom from the raw earth. That is a challenge worthy of my family's blood.'

He dwelt on that thought for a moment, then asked, 'And what are your plans, General, now that you have my answer?'

'First, I must go to Santo Domingo, and I have some other business to attend to in the West Indies. After that, I shall arrange passage back to France where I will inform the First Consul of your decision.'

'Then you shall be my guest aboard the *Columbine* for the voyage to Santo Domingo,' said Vallon. 'I, too, have things I wish to do there, and perhaps we can eventually make the voyage to France together.'

'I look forward to that possibility, Your Highness.'

Chapter Twenty-eight

DOCTOR ANTROBUS

Peter was nearly dead from exposure by the time the current finally carried his little boat into the shallow coastal waters of an island. A Doctor Antrobus noticed the drifting boat whilst he was out with some local fishermen. When he discovered Peter he had them carry the unconscious youth up to his house.

It was some time before Peter became fully aware of his surroundings, and he was never entirely sure how much time had passed since his escape from the *Torren*. Whenever he tried to recall any of the events in detail his mind seemed to cloud over strangely, but his new haven soon became familiar.

Doctor Antrobus's house was a white-painted clapboard building with a long veranda overlooking a small bay on the south-western shore of Santo Domingo. Goats grazed on the ground that sloped down to a beach of dazzling white sand fringed with palm trees, where fishermen dragged up their boats and dried their nets.

Palm trees also grew behind the shingle-roofed house, which had a yard, a lean-to stable for an elderly grey mare called Hippocrates, a vegetable garden, a chicken run, and a long low hut nearby that was occupied by the doctor's servants Jose and Maria and their three young children.

On the ground floor of the house, a wide hallway led to a living-room furnished with four comfortable chairs and a vast quantity of books in several languages. Floor-to-ceiling shelves overflowed with volumes and more were piled up on the floor and tables. There was also a kitchen, a dining-room, and the doctor's surgery, which was as cluttered with equipment as the living-room was with reading matter. Upstairs were four sparsely furnished bedrooms and even a bathroom with a large hot-water boiler.

Although he spoke perfect English, Dr Antrobus was German, and the island of Santo Domingo was inhabited by a mixture of races as rich and varied as any in the Caribbean.

In his first weeks on the island Peter's mind was mostly clouded, but he knew he had changed since his escape from the *Torren*. And the one feeling that never relented was his hatred of Count Vallon. It lay like a tightly coiled spring at the centre of his being.

At first, he'd hardly recognized his own reflection in the looking glass. He was much thinner, his cheekbones sharply prominent in his deeply tanned face. His coal-black hair was

no longer pulled back into a neatly combed club shape at
the nape of his neck, but hung lankly about his watchful
face.

The clothes his host had provided were clean, but very
worn: a frayed shirt once owned by a bigger man, and
ragged trousers that hung only to the knee. His brown legs
were bare and on his feet he wore the remains of his last
pair of uniform shoes. But he'd removed the silver buckles
his sisters had given him as a present.

Dark hair and brown skin of every shade were common
in the tropics, so Peter was able to go about unnoticed,
although he hadn't ventured far from Antrobus's house. As
long as he kept his blue-green eyes cast down, anyone who
bothered to give him a second glance took him for one of
the native boys who hung about the island scavenging to
survive.

The doctor never questioned his young guest, nor
forced him into unwelcome conversations, and for a long
time Peter was glad not to talk as he found such exchanges
difficult and exhausting. But gradually his energy and spirit
were reviving, despite the puzzling cloudiness that seemed
to fog his mind whenever he tried to think about escaping
from the island.

As Peter stayed on in his new home he developed a routine of going to his room after supper to read alone, but
one evening Dr Antrobus suggested he remain on the
veranda and read in his company. Peter took a chair but
found he couldn't concentrate on his own book. Looking

out to sea he asked, 'Doctor, who owns Santo Domingo?'

The doctor removed his wire-framed spectacles and placed his book on the table beside him. 'A complicated question,' he began. 'Since Christopher Columbus discovered Santo Domingo, thinking he'd arrived in China, the island has been colonized and then fought over by the Spanish, French and English. Currently, the French have got it back.'

'It's very beautiful,' said Peter.

The doctor nodded. 'Early European colonists thought it was the Garden of Eden.'

'So that's why everyone wanted it.'

Doctor Antrobus chuckled grimly. 'Not for religious reasons, I fear,' he said. 'People make fortunes here.'

'How?' asked Peter.

'From growing sugar, coffee and indigo. Planters grew fabulously rich from the labours of their African slaves. But no matter whose flags fly over its towns, the same difficulties remain.'

'Which are?' asked Peter, fascinated.

Doctor Antrobus absent-mindedly cleaned his spectacles on his shirt before he answered. 'At the height of the Revolution in France, slavery was abolished in all its colonies. Ever since then, the outraged French planters have been petitioning ceaselessly for slavery to be reintroduced.'

'Will they succeed?' asked Peter.

Antrobus shrugged again. 'To add to the woes of the

planters, the slaves here went into revolt and overthrew their masters. The insurrection was led by a remarkable black leader called Toussaint L'Ouverture. They gained control of the island, but then Toussaint did an extraordinary thing. He declared himself loyal to France. So, instead of Santo Domingo becoming an independent country, it remains a French colony. However, if France reintroduces slavery, who knows what will happen? There'll be more blood spilt, no doubt.'

Peter asked no more questions that evening. It was interesting to learn about the island, but he was still a midshipman in the Royal Navy and knew it was his duty to escape. However, whenever he tried to think of a plan, like stowing away on a neutral ship, his mind would wander. Some distant voice seemed to compel him to stay on with Doctor Antrobus. But buried deep inside him his hatred for Count Vallon stayed fresh and raw, and he knew he would have to leave Santo Domingo if he was ever to fulfil his vow to avenge his shipmates.

Living in this state of inner turmoil inevitably took the worries of Peter's waking moments into his sleep. In one vivid dream he seemed to hear Commodore Beaumont's voice ordering him to stay with the doctor. In another he told Doctor Antrobus that he'd been a cabin boy aboard a merchantman out of Boston. He'd begun to recall that as he'd told this lie, Antrobus had been toying with the fob dangling from the chain of his pocket-watch. But now Peter couldn't be sure whether that had been another of the vivid and disturbing dreams he'd endured, or whether it had actually happened. Had it not been for the kindness of Doctor Antrobus, Peter was convinced his conflicting thoughts might have driven him mad.

As the weeks passed, many visitors called at the house and Peter discovered that Antrobus was fluent in French, Spanish, Portuguese, and even a Nordic language Peter didn't recognize. He couldn't guess the doctor's age, but his lean wiry frame was still strong. Antrobus claimed the deep lines on his weather-beaten face were induced by a lifetime of challenging thoughts. For some reason, the doctor's usual expression was one of watchfulness, but sometimes in the evenings when he sat on the veranda with Peter and they read by the light of a large oil lamp his face relaxed and became more kindly.

For a scholarly man, Doctor Antrobus was also capable with his hands. He'd do repairs on the house while Jose stood by offering advice and assistance. Sometimes the doctor went off for a few days at a time riding Hippocrates who plodded along at a comfortable pace on the narrow paths.

As well as his many healthy visitors, poor people came to him for medical assistance. They displayed an almost mystical faith in his abilities and listened to his instructions with awe and respect. But there were some conditions Dr Antrobus couldn't cure. One day three men had been brought to the door suffering from yellow fever, a disease known to all as the scourge of the West Indies. Too sick

even to walk, they eventually began to vomit a black substance and their skin turned yellow.

In the last stage of their illness, wrenching convulsions
began and were quickly followed by death. Peter also
became mildly ill, but thankfully in his case there was no
vomiting, and after a few days he made a complete recovery. Days later, Peter thanked the doctor profusely for saving his life, but Antrobus only shook his head regretfully.
'The disease that devastates this island is a total mystery to
my profession; we doctors can do nothing. You cured yourself, my boy,' he admitted.

Then Doctor Antrobus broke his leg. It was a silly accident:
he'd tripped over one of the goats. Jose helped him to a
couch in the living-room, and under Antrobus's instructions Peter had set the break and bound on the splints.

The doctor was concerned by his lack of mobility until,
after some thought, he told Peter he would have to make
one of his deliveries for him. 'I just want you to take some
medicine to one of my regular patients,' the doctor
explained. 'Please wait if he wants to write me a note, but
don't linger in town. Things are unsettled in Port-au-Prince
and the unrest might spread, so I don't want you to delay
your return for any longer than is necessary.'

The following day, Jose saddled Hippocrates and Peter
set off on his journey with the special bottle of medicine.
Before he took his leave, Antrobus had handed him a
clumsy old flintlock pistol, a small, ornate powder horn

and a leather bullet pouch, saying, 'Don't rely on this too much. But it may be enough to scare away anyone who tries to steal from you.'

Peter smiled at the doctor's words. 'I hardly look wealthy enough for anyone to bother,' he replied ruefully.

The doctor shook his head in warning. 'Many people on this island are desperately poor. You will look wealthy enough to them.'

Peter examined the heavy old pistol. It had once been a gentleman's weapon, but it was in poor shape now, its parts worn and loose. He checked the flint and loaded the piece, then thrust it inside his shirt along with the powder horn and bullet bag. If the worst comes to the worst, he told himself, I can always use it as a club.

Chapter Twenty-nine

THE FACE ON THE QUARTERDECK

Peter was glad of the ragged-brimmed straw hat he had taken from the hallway in Doctor Antrobus's house. He was used to the island's brilliant sunshine, but in Port-au-Prince the dazzling light seemed even more intense as it reflected off the cobbled city streets and white buildings. They passed the cathedral, which Antrobus had told Peter was the oldest in the New World, and leaving the main thoroughfare they ambled slowly through the side streets close to the harbour.

Peter found the address written on the bottle. After tying the mare to a hitching ring set in the wall on the shadowed side of a narrow street, he climbed the staircase to a top-floor apartment. In answer to his knock, a thin old man with unkempt white hair peered around the ornately carved door. Clutching the collar of his long dressing-gown he glared at Peter suspiciously.

Holding out the bottle, Peter said a trifle nervously in French, 'I have brought medicine for you from Doctor Antrobus.'

The man's hostile manner immediately altered to one of friendliness. Smiling, he ushered Peter into a dark hallway which led to a lofty, sun-filled room full of dark wooden furniture. Rugs were scattered on the cool, tiled floor.

'Make yourself at home, young man,' the old man said in English, and taking the bottle he went to another room, leaving the door ajar. Although there was no sign of anyone else, Peter had the feeling there were other people in the apartment.

'Where are you from?' the old man asked through the open door.

Peter had rehearsed a story in anticipation of just such a question. 'Boston in Massachusetts, sir,' he lied.

'And I am from the dark side of the moon,' the old man retorted dryly. 'It has been many years since I was last in England, but I would hazard a guess that you're from the west of London.'

Oddly, Peter felt no fear at this accurate observation, sensing there was no hint of threat in the old man's voice. He was curious now. Glancing about him he noted that the furniture looked well-made and expensive. There were several musical instruments on the various tables and a harpsichord against one wall. Heaps of handwritten music lay scattered about the room. Light was flooding in through open French windows that led out on to a balcony. Standing in front of them was a large brass telescope mounted on a stand.

Peter crossed the room as he said, 'I spent some time in England, sir.'

As he passed the open door, he saw that the old man was sitting at a small writing desk next to a large unmade bed. He held a large magnifying glass and was examining the label on the bottle Peter had delivered.

'If you say so,' answered the old man. 'If Antrobus trusts you, that is good enough for me, even though you carry a large pistol inside your shirt.' Still examining the bottle, he added, 'If you don't mind waiting a minute longer, I want you to carry a message back to the doctor.'

Peter stood at the French windows where the balcony overlooked the harbour. The telescope was directed down towards the ships moored at the jetty. Leaning forward, he glanced casually into the eyepiece. Suddenly, he was trans-fixed.

It was as if his entire mind and body had received a violent blow. Standing upright he swayed briefly. Then a rush of black rage surged through him and he ran for the staircase, pulling the pistol from inside his shirt.

'Where the devil has the boy gone?' asked the old man, bewildered.

Two other men came out from behind the bedroom door, also looking puzzled. The slimmer of them, a scruffy looking individual with a ragged beard and half the upper part of his face covered with an unsightly tropical sore, answered. 'I was watching through the crack in the door. When he looked through the telescope it was as if he'd been bitten by a poisonous snake.'

'It's focused on a schooner called the *Columbine*,' said the old man. 'I spotted General Ancre crossing the jetty earlier and saw him go aboard. The ship's getting ready to put to sea.'

The two men hurried over to the telescope. The scruffy one looked through the eyepiece, but all he saw was an empty hatchway. Shrugging, he made way for the bigger man, who moved the telescope to examine the figures on the quarterdeck of the ship. He gave a sudden sharp intake of breath.

'Vallon!' exclaimed Matthew Book. 'Mr Raven saw Count Vallon.'

The scruffy man pushed him aside and looked through the eyepiece again. 'Which one is Vallon?' he asked urgently.

'The one in the blue coat. He's standing next to General Ancre.'

Swinging the telescope away the scruffy man raced for the staircase, shouting back over his shoulder, 'Wait here, Mr Book.'

When Peter had seen Count Vallon through the telescope, the hatred coiled inside him suddenly sprang to life, driving him forward with an irresistible force. He hurtled down the stairs three at a time, and once in the street he searched frantically for a way through to the harbour. Locating a narrow alleyway to the waterfront he raced towards the *Columbine*, weaving and bumping his way through the crowds thronging the busy concourse.

It proved a difficult passage. At the dockside elegantly dressed couples, some accompanied by their servants, jostled with soldiers, seamen, beggars and slaves, but all of them moved with the same measured ease in the exhausting tropical heat. The only people who ever ran in Port-au-Prince during the hottest hours were thieves and those who pursued them. Consequently, the sight of a ragged youth racing through the waterfront holding a pistol was cause for alarm. Peter cut a swathe through the sauntering crowd as they leapt aside, fearful that a volley of shots may follow.

Despite his haste, the *Columbine* had already cast off and was pulling away from the jetty. Peter, trembling with an all-consuming rage, fought to gain control lest his shaking hand spoil his shot.

He slid to a halt on the granite coping next to a dockside vegetable cart, just close enough to fire on Count Vallon, who was standing nonchalantly at the rail of the moving ship watching the small boats at work in the harbour.

With images of the terrible events he'd witnessed on the *Torren* racing through his mind, Peter did not hesitate. He cocked the pistol, rested the ancient barrel on a wheel of the cart and took careful aim. He squeezed the trigger. But no shot followed, just a sudden flash of gunpowder in the priming pan as the main charge failed to ignite.

Holding back his rage, Peter began to recharge the ancient weapon. But before he'd rammed the new charge home, Count Vallon was out of range and the *Columbine* was turning away into the harbour channel. Another shot was impossible. Helplessly, Peter lowered the pistol.

'Don't worry, Midshipman Raven,' said a familiar voice behind him. 'There'll always be another day.'

Peter swung round. The only person close by was a scruffy man with a ragged beard, his face deformed by a hideous sore. The man grinned, showing yellowing teeth. In an instant, Peter recognized Commander Beaumont.

Neither of them noticed General Ancre slipping away through the alarmed crowd.

'Give me the gun,' ordered Beaumont. 'And don't speak until I tell you to,' he added in an undertone. Taking the pistol, he seized Peter by his ragged shirt and dragged him back through the curious crowd.

'I have the wretch, citizens,' Beaumont called out to the puzzled onlookers. 'He is an escaped servant. His master sent me to bring him back.'

The observers on the dockside quickly lost interest in the pair, but nonetheless Beaumont kept his hold on Peter until they reached the shadowed alleyway.

Back in the apartment, Peter was astonished to find a smiling Matthew Book dressed in smart clothes and looking every inch a man of substance.

Beaumont introduced the elderly owner of the rooms to Peter.

'This is Richard Brindles, once of the Royal College of Music, London, but known to the people of Santo Domingo as Professor Manichi. Mr Brindles, may I present Midshipman Peter Raven. Like Matthew Book, he's a survivor of HMS *Torren*.'

'What is this place?' asked Peter, bewildered.

'My dear Raven,' said Beaumont. 'Your wits *must* be fuddled. I would have thought it was obvious. You are in a nest of spies.'

Peter looked from Matthew Book to Beaumont. A light breeze stirred through the brightly lit room. Once more the butchery aboard the *Torren* flooded into his consciousness. Suddenly the terrible images in his mind changed, and he remembered the storm and the scorching sun when he was adrift in the little boat. But, superimposed above all this, as if painted by a giant's hand, was the image of Doctor Antrobus's watch fob, swinging like the pendulum of a clock. Then the floor seemed to come up to meet him and he was engulfed in darkness.

Chapter Thirty

PETER RAVEN'S PAST

Peter could hear an insistent voice calling his name, but it was mixed with other voices from the past: his mother on a summer's day in the walled garden of the vicarage, Isaac shouting a warning to keep away from the water's edge on the Thames embankment, and Captain Benchley calling him to his duties.

'I command you to open your eyes, Midshipman Raven,' said Doctor Antrobus.

Peter blinked awake.

He felt incredibly alert and immediately realized he was lying on a wicker couch on the veranda of the doctor's house. It was night. Insects circled in the light of the lamp. Matthew Book and Commander Beaumont were standing beside him, and the doctor was sitting on a chair next to the couch.

'I was in the musician's apartment,' said Peter, and

feeling his hatred rise again, he added, 'I saw Count Vallon escaping. Is there no way we can pursue him?'

'All in good time, Mr Raven. Count Vallon is part of a bigger game I must play out.' The commodore was still wearing the scruffy clothes, but he no longer had the hideous sore on his face, and the yellow stain on his teeth was gone.

'How did you know the way here?' asked Peter, accepting a glass of sugared lemon juice from Doctor Antrobus.

'I've been here before, Mr Raven,' said Beaumont.

'But why are you so far from home, sir?' asked Peter, bewildered again.

'Don't forget we're in the Navy, Midshipman,' answered the commodore, smiling. 'The whole world is home to us.'

'Why here?'

'I came to the Caribbean because these waters are infested with French privateers. It seems Count Vallon is their leader,' Beaumont began. 'My orders were to find their base and inform our West Indies Squadron of its whereabouts. The *Torren* was on its way to reinforce the squadron so they could set about destroying the privateers and stop them plundering our merchant ships.'

'But the *Torren*—' Peter began, then he remembered something. 'I dreamed you ordered me to stay with Doctor Antrobus.'

'That's right, Midshipman,' answered Commodore Beaumont.

'I must confess, I haven't tried to escape, sir,' said Peter. 'Even though I knew it was my duty.'

'I'm aware of that, Mr Raven,' said Beaumont gently. 'However, you were acting under my orders *not* to escape. Don't reproach yourself.'

'How could that be?' asked Peter, even more puzzled.

Beaumont looked up at Doctor Antrobus. 'You explain it to him,' he said.

'How much do you wish him to know?' asked the doctor.

'Everything,' replied Beaumont.

Peter looked at Antrobus expectantly.

'A long time ago, in Austria,' the doctor began, 'I and a young man called the Marquis de Puysegur studied medicine under a brilliant doctor called Franz Anton Mesmer. The marquis found that by getting patients to focus on a bright object he could put them into a trance-like state. He could then hold a conversation with the patient and suggest things for them to do when they woke from the trance. And they did do the things he'd suggested, but had no memory of being instructed to do them. The marquis could command a patient to take certain actions or to forget things. I used the technique to "mesmerize" you, Peter.'

Peter looked alarmed. 'How does it work?' he asked.

'We don't really know,' said Antrobus. 'All we know is that some people are more susceptible than others.'

'Stupid people?' asked Peter.

Antrobus shook his head. 'No. On the contrary. People with vivid imaginations appear to be most responsive to the technique.'

'And you did that to me?' asked Peter, wanting it confirmed again.

'Yes, Peter,' Doctor Antrobus answered with a reassuring smile.

'Why was it necessary to put me in a trance? Didn't you trust me?'

'In our line of work we trust nobody, Midshipman,' said Beaumont. 'But to begin with, the doctor had no idea that you and I were friends.'

Doctor Antrobus continued. 'When I found you, Peter, you were half dead. Even so, you gave nothing away and would tell me nothing. I put you into a trance and you told me you were off the *Torren*. When I questioned you further it also transpired, much to my astonishment, that you knew Commander Beaumont. Eventually, when I made contact with Beaumont, he confirmed your story. He ordered me to keep you mesmerized so you would be content to stay here with me.'

'All that time?' asked Peter, incredulous.

Antrobus smiled. 'It has not been as long as you think.'

'Why didn't you send me to Jamaica?' Peter asked Beaumont. 'Surely that could have been arranged. I could have joined another ship.'

Beaumont shook his head. 'Two reasons, Midshipman,'

he replied briskly. 'I wanted you restored to the best of health. You nearly died after escaping from *Torren,* and then to cap it all you caught yellow fever. I thought it better for you to recover fully before you took up any new duties. So I suggested the doctor keep you in a sort of trance.'

'You said *two* reasons, sir,' said Peter.

Beaumont nodded. 'Yes. Well, I'm afraid you would have proved an awkward embarrassment to our country, Midshipman,' said Beaumont.

'Embarrassment!' said Peter. 'Why?'

'Because the whole world believes you perished on HMS *Torren* in a storm. Your name was on the casualty list published in the newspapers. If you'd turned up out of the blue in Jamaica, it would have started all sorts of stories about the true fate of the *Torren.* You know how quickly rumours flash around among sailors. The French would have had a field day saying the British always lie. I decided it would be better for the time being if you remained "lost at sea".'

'So my parents think I'm dead?' said Peter quietly.

'I'm afraid so,' replied Beaumont. 'Still, you can always look on the bright side.'

'What bright side, sir?' asked Peter.

'Surely it's better to be alive and have everyone think you're dead, rather than the other way around?'

Peter had to smile, if a trifle bitterly, at Beaumont's lack of sentiment. 'I suppose so, sir,' he answered.

'Besides,' said Beaumont, 'now the war is nearly over, you'll be of much greater use to us if everyone thinks you're dead.'

'*Is* the war nearly over?' asked Peter, amazed.

The commodore nodded. 'Preliminary talks have already been arranged. We're going to swap a few island territories between us and the French, then we'll all be friends again.'

'What use will I be to you when the war is over, sir?' asked Peter.

Beaumont scratched his bearded chin before answering. 'Our war is never over, Midshipman,' he replied gravely. 'We fight a secret war that goes on forever.'

'A secret war?' echoed Peter.

Beaumont nodded. 'But no medals are awarded, there are no victory parades, no memorials, and no pretty maidens looking upon us as heroes. Just the knowledge that we serve our country. Do you want to join us?'

'I suppose so,' replied Peter bleakly. 'What else can I do? Now that I'm dead, that is.' Then a thought occurred to him. 'If Count Vallon is a privateer, killing him won't be an act of war, will it?'

'No, Midshipman.'

'Then I'm with you, sir.'

'Good,' said Beaumont briskly. 'I'm glad that's settled. Now, see if you can stay out of trouble for a bit. In your short career in the Royal Navy you've twice been at death's door. I shall leave you with Mr Book while I take a bath.

You will want to hear his equally extraordinary tale of what happened to him after you two parted company on the *Torren*.'

Chapter Thirty-one

THE LIFE AND TIMES OF
MATTHEW BOOK

When Beaumont and the doctor left them alone, Peter looked up at Matthew. 'I haven't had a chance to thank you for saving my life, Mr Book,' he said. 'How did you survive the storm? I thought you must surely have drowned. How did you get here?'

Matthew rocked back in his chair. 'It was a close-run thing, Mr Raven. The storm nearly did put an end to me, but the rolled-up hammocks I clung to saved my life. They were just buoyant enough to keep me afloat. But then I had a truly strange piece of good fortune: I came upon an abandoned cattle boat carrying six cows. The crew must have been swept overboard when she lost her mast, but she was still afloat. I thought I must be going mad when I first heard cows bellowing above the sound of the wind.'

'A cattle boat!' echoed Peter.

'I know it sounds incredible,' agreed Matthew. 'Even so, there was no means to steer her by. But like you, the current brought us to Santo Domingo. There was even money aboard,' said Matthew indicating his smart clothes with a sweep of his hand. 'When I reached the island I was in rather better condition than you, Mr Raven.'

'Full of cow's milk,' said Peter, managing a grin. 'Commodore Beaumont told me you've led an extraordinary life, Mr Book. Will you tell me more of it?'

'Going back how far?' asked Matthew, smiling.

'All of it, from when you were a boy,' said Peter. 'That is, if you are of a mind to tell me. But I have no wish to pry into anything you want to keep private.'

Matthew shook his head. 'I was born a slave, Mr Raven. Slaves do not have private lives.'

Peter struggled to sit up to make a point. 'My father is a friend of William Wilberforce, Mr Book. I was brought up to believe that slavery is an abomination against humanity.'

'You are fortunate in having such a father, Mr Raven. William Wilberforce is a great man. A time will come when he will be honoured all over the world.'

'My father says Mr Wilberforce will eventually win Parliament over and slavery will be abolished throughout the West Indies, just as it is in Britain,' said Peter. Then another thought occurred to him. 'If you were born in these waters, is your family still enslaved on the islands, Mr Book?'

'My family are all dead,' said Matthew softly. 'Killed by Count Vallon.'

'Vallon!' exclaimed Peter with deep loathing. 'But, of course, you knew him before he took the *Torren*. I remember you saying the devil had control of the ship.'

Matthew smiled bitterly. 'I knew him. And I played for him on many earlier occasions.'

'Please, I beg of you,' urged Peter. 'Tell me your story from the beginning.'

Matthew shrugged. 'It will not take long. I was born on the estates of Count Vallon. My parents worked the land as slaves. As a boy, I was singing one day when Count Vallon passed by. He noticed my voice.' Matthew paused for a moment. 'Do you know what perfect pitch is, Mr Raven?'

'Yes, I believe so,' replied Peter. 'Isn't it the ability to hear when people are singing or playing musical instruments perfectly in tune? I understand it's common to have a good ear for music, but few people are lucky enough to have perfect pitch.'

Matthew shrugged. 'It is arguable whether perfect pitch is a blessing or a curse.'

'How could it be a curse,' asked Peter, 'to hear music exactly as God intended it to be played?'

Matthew shook his head again. 'Yes, it is wonderful to hear music played in proper pitch. But, sadly, most notes we hear in this world are out of tune.'

'What do you mean?'

'Did you hear that?' asked Matthew, gesturing towards the back of the house.

The only sound Peter had heard was the creaking of the

gate on the goat enclosure as Jose went to do the evening milking. 'Do you mean the gate?' he asked, puzzled.

'Yes,' said Matthew. 'The notes made by the hinges are flat.'

'But it's a gate, not a musical instrument,' said Peter, still confused.

Matthew shook his head. 'All sounds are part of the musical scale. Most people just don't apply the idea of music to them. But for those of us like me, and Count Vallon and his sister, Lady Anne, who are cursed with perfect pitch, it is almost physically painful to hear the noise of the world around us. You see, it is filled with everyday sounds that are hideously flat or sharp.'

'So when Count Vallon heard you sing, he knew you too had perfect pitch?' said Peter.

'Yes,' replied Matthew. 'He had me brought to his house and tested me further. When he was sure, it was decided I would be educated and learn the violin.'

'Did you go away?'

'I received my education in Vallon's mansion, the Villa Royale at Roc d'Or. You knew my teacher.'

'I knew him?' said Peter, intrigued.

Matthew nodded. 'Do you remember Mr Guttman?'

'Of course. The seaman who was killed the night we picked up Commodore Beaumont at the Loire estuary.'

'Mr Guttman was the original violinist in Count Vallon's orchestra. Vallon had him brought from Austria, where he'd been a famous musician in his youth. Otto

Guttman taught me for more than five years – English and German as well as the violin. He was a brilliant teacher.'

'What about your family?'

'At first, I used to cry for them. It seems my mother and father kept asking for news of me, so Vallon had them burnt to death. But I did not learn of that until later. Meanwhile, Vallon instructed that I be told they didn't care about me. But Otto Guttman was a kind man and he became my family.'

'What happened to his face?' asked Peter.

'When he'd taught me all he could about the violin, Vallon gave him to his sister as a plaything. But she didn't like the way he looked, so she altered him with a knife.'

'Dear God!' exclaimed Peter. '*She* did that? Why didn't it kill him?'

'Who knows?' said Matthew. 'But he lived. And when his face healed he quite amused her. She used to have him led about on a chain to frighten the servants in the villa. She called him her special ape.'

'That monstrous creature,' said Peter forcefully. 'She's as vile as her brother,' he added, remembering what he'd seen her do to Lieutenant Blysse on the *Torren*.

'Oh, yes,' said Matthew. 'And she's always been so. It was well known in Vallon's domain that Lady Anne had been sent to the island several years before her brother. The story was that as a child she'd murdered a maid and had been sent to the Caribbean to avoid her being locked away in an insane asylum. A few years later her brother followed her.'

'How long was Mr Guttman her "plaything"?' asked Peter.

'A long time. But when I was old enough, he and I escaped by crossing the mountains into the jungle. Then we headed south. The journey was hard and took a long time, but eventually we found a settlement, and finally a ship that would take Otto Guttman. So, we became seamen.'

'Why didn't you play the violin to live?'

'Count Vallon has spies everywhere. He would have heard about it. Besides, we couldn't survive on land, Mr Raven. No one would suffer Mr Guttman's presence or give him lodgings. He was made an outcast. People shied away in horror at the sight of him in the streets. But we discovered sailors were more tolerant. They're more used to their own kind being maimed.'

Peter nodded, recalling that there had been other disfigured men aboard the *Torren*. Naval battles caused many terrible wounds.

Matthew continued. 'We found that Mr Guttman was accepted on ships, and eventually he was recruited in England without him even having to volunteer.'

'You were taken by a press gang?' hazarded Peter.

'One day, when we were parted for a few hours, Mr Guttman was pressed into service on a British warship. So I joined the same crew as a volunteer,' said Matthew. 'Something of an irony, don't you think? Otto Guttman being forced into a new home after he'd been rejected by so many.'

Peter nodded. 'When you got here to Santo Domingo after the storm, how on earth did you find Commodore Beaumont?'

'I was looking for him, Mr Raven. Remember when you were in hospital recovering from your back wound and I'd been seconded to his service?'

'Yes, you wouldn't tell me what you'd been doing.'

'It wasn't much,' said Matthew. 'Petty Officer Connors was still on sick leave and Commodore Beaumont needed another strong hand in case of trouble. I travelled north with him for a time. He was on some secret business. By the time his work was done, we thought you'd be at home recuperating with your parents, so we called on them in Richmond and they told us how ill you were.

'Then the commodore received orders to leave for the West Indies immediately, but he gave me permission to go with your parents to visit you. Before he left, he told me that if I ever needed to I could contact him in Port-au-Prince at the home of Professor Manichi. So, when I was washed ashore, I already knew where to go for help, and fortunately the commodore was on the island. He recruited me back into his service. I'm a Petty Officer now.'

'That's a truly amazing tale,' said Peter. 'Fate has dealt us both a strange hand, Mr Book.'

When Beaumont and Doctor Antrobus returned to the veranda, Peter could see from their attitude that important decisions had been made.

'Do you feel fit enough for sea duty, Mr Raven?' asked

Beaumont.

'Aye, aye, sir,' Peter answered.

The commodore gestured for them to remain seated and pulled up his own chair. 'Did you notice anyone else with Vallon on board the *Columbine*, Mr Raven?' asked Beaumont.

'Yes, but only briefly,' replied Peter. 'A soldierly-looking man, but he'd gone by the time I tried to shoot Vallon.'

'That was General Ancre. Head of the French Naval Secret Service in this part of the world,' said Beaumont. 'According to Professor Manichi, he has some business with Count Vallon.'

'What business would that be, sir?' asked Matthew.

Beaumont shrugged and held out his hands, palm upwards. 'That's our problem, Mr Book. We simply don't know. But, it must be something of great importance.

'We know that Vallon controls the most successful French privateers. He commands a fleet of ships and roams at will to raid shipping. If General Ancre has business with him, then that means Napoleon has business with him.'

'Why would Napoleon want to have dealings with a disreputable privateer, sir?' asked Peter.

'That's the big question. And for the moment, I don't know the answer.'

'Perhaps the French want to persuade Count Vallon to lead his fleet of privateers against the British,' Doctor Antrobus suggested.

Beaumont nodded his head. 'That's a possibility, but we

already know that Britain and France are working towards a peace agreement.'

'And, if there is peace,' said Peter, 'the privateers will no longer have free licence from the French government to raid our ships.'

Beaumont lightly tapped the rail of the veranda. 'It's a conundrum, right enough. And we're not going to find the answer here on Santo Domingo.' He swung around and looked at Peter and Matthew. 'Tomorrow, we sail for Port Royal, Jamaica.'

'To what purpose, sir?' asked Matthew.

'I've been told of a ship there and a crew of cut-throats of whom we may soon have need.'

'And will we be going after Count Vallon, sir?' asked Peter.

'All in good time, Mr Raven.'

Chapter Thirty-two

A RIDE IN THE COUNTRY

It was late morning and Lucy was in her dressing-room trying on her new riding habit.

'What do you think of it, Brigit?' she asked her maid, who was tidying the dressing-table.

Brigit gave a very Gallic shrug. 'Ladies do not look right riding horses, Mademoiselle,' she replied. 'Surely it is better to go in the carriage.'

'Riding is wonderful,' Lucy replied. 'I never really tried it until I came to Paris. Have you never ridden then, Brigit?'

The maid laughed. 'I grew up on a farm, Mademoiselle. I often rode the plough horses.'

'Didn't you enjoy it?' asked Lucy.

'No,' Brigit answered firmly. 'I always wished I was in a carriage, like the gentlefolk.'

Lucy smiled, and just then there was a knock on the

door. 'Enter,' Lucy called, and Potter came into the room bearing a silver tray. He offered it to Lucy, who took the cards on it.

'Three gentleman callers, Miss Lucy,' he announced.

Lucy read their cards. 'Tell them I'm not at home please, Potter.'

'Very well, Miss Lucy,' he replied, and departed as Mrs Hargreave came into the room.

'Lucy,' she began, 'there are three young men in the morning-room. One of them is playing the piano and another is reciting poetry.'

'What is the third doing, Aunt Lizzie?' asked Lucy.

'He appears to be ignoring the other two,' she said. 'Who are they?'

Before she answered, Lucy took one more look at herself in the long mirror. As her great-aunt had predicted, she no longer despised clothes. 'The one playing the piano is Henri Dupré. The poet is Charles-Louis Malfonte, and the snob is the Marquis Salciarre. They all want me to go to the same ball with them.'

'What are you going to do?' asked her aunt.

'I'm going riding with Jack Cobden.'

'Oh, must you?' said her aunt sitting down heavily.

'Yes, I really must, Aunt Lizzie,' she replied.

'Why?'

Lucy took her great-aunt's hands. 'I truly love my new life here in Paris, Aunt, but sometimes it does feel awfully restricting.'

'Restricting!' said Mrs Hargreave, knowing that Lucy was on the go most days from morning until the early hours. 'I can't fathom you, child.'

Lucy wondered if she could ever properly explain her feelings to her great-aunt. Jack Cobden understood. Growing up in the Hudson Valley had bred in Lucy a love of gigantic vistas, but Paris was a city of narrow streets. Occasionally, she couldn't help yearning for the open spaces, epic landscapes and immense solitude she had known since her childhood.

She'd told Jack Cobden how she felt and he'd suggested they go riding in the surrounding countryside. It was something she'd never done at home, but she turned out to be a natural horsewoman. She'd even learnt to ride side-saddle, although it irritated her to adopt such an unnatural pose. Nonetheless, she was soon giving Jack Cobden a run for his money when they tore across open fields and leaped fences with an abandon that would have caused her great-aunt to swoon, had she been there to witness such recklessness.

One hot day they had ridden further to the south-west than they'd ventured before, and eventually stopped by a meandering river. After tying their horses to a tree overhanging the riverbank, Cobden reached into his saddlebag and produced a rough picnic of bread, cheese and slices of ham.

After they had eaten, Lucy took off her riding boots. Hitching up the long skirts of her riding clothes, she paddled in the cooling shallows of the stream, thinking about a party she had attended the previous night. One of this morning's callers, Henri Dupré, had told her he was hopelessly in love with her. They'd only spoken for a few minutes, and the youth's ardour still baffled her. As Lucy wandered back and forth in the cool water, recalling the incident and her own embarrassment, Jack Cobden stretched out on the warm grass and seemed to go to sleep.

'Have you ever been in love, Jack?' Lucy eventually asked. She remembered the incident when Jack had mentioned his two sisters and realized that although she'd known her protector all of her life, she actually knew very little about him.

'Sure,' he replied, looking up at the clear blue sky.

'You have?' said Lucy, surprised, and a little resentful. 'Why have you never mentioned it?'

'Because it's none of your business, young lady.'

'But you're supposed to be my friend,' Lucy pleaded. 'Friends don't have secrets from each other.'

Cobden chuckled. He let his eyes close again as he lay with his hands clasped on his chest. 'Don't they?' he answered. 'Wait a few more years, and you'll soon be keeping plenty of secrets from me.'

'How often have you been in love?' she continued. 'Just the once, or plenty of times?'

'More times than I can count,' he answered lightly.

'But wasn't there anyone special? Someone you cared about more than anyone else?'

'Why do you want to know?'

'Because I want to know what it will feel like when it happens to me.'

'I can't say what it'll be like for you,' said Cobden. 'It's different for men.'

'How is it?' she persisted.

'Most men act kind of stupid. Like Lieutenant Mowbury did on the voyage to Le Havre.'

'Do they all act stupid?'

'Yes, but in different ways. Some act as though they've been gut shot, others recite poetry, some can't stop grinning.'

'But how does it *feel*?'

'There's plenty of time to find out – you're still only sixteen.'

Lucy laughed. 'Jack, I'm nearly *eighteen*!'

He sat up at that and did his own rapid calculation. 'So you are,' he replied. Then he unhitched the horses as Lucy pulled on her tight boots.

On the ride back to the city he was even less talkative than usual.

Chapter Thirty-three

NANCY'S HOUSE

When Matthew and Beaumont took their leave of Doctor Antrobus to go to Jamaica, they hired one of the fishing boats from the beach to take them by sea to Port-au-Prince. Once there, they visited Beaumont's lodgings to collect his sea-chest, then he led them to a schooner in the harbour.

Matthew and Peter watched from the dockside as the commodore appeared to haggle with the captain, a wide-shouldered swarthy man with a large stomach and a long oiled moustache. The transaction didn't take long, and Beaumont waved for them to join him on board.

They were shown to a pleasantly airy cabin while the schooner got under way. Most of the crew were Indian or black and the captain commanded them in Spanish, which he shouted with great gusto.

A smiling steward served them at the cabin table with

a lunch of boiled chicken and a delicious concoction of spicy rice. The captain joined them with a silent nod, and after several mouthfuls he took a sip of the lime juice and rum in his glass and gave a great sigh.

'My dear fellows, think how perfect this meal would be if we had ice to put in our drinks,' he observed in a gentlemanly English accent.

Matthew and Peter looked at him in astonishment. Beaumont smiled and said, 'Midshipman Raven, Petty Officer Book, allow me to introduce the Honourable Richard Harington, Lieutenant of His Britannic Majesty's Royal Navy.'

As good manners dictated, Peter and Matthew began rising to their feet, but Harington waved them down. 'No need to stand on ceremony here, my dear fellows. Delighted to meet you both.'

Despite Harington's reassuring words, Matthew still looked slightly ill at ease, and Beaumont realized that it must be difficult for a man used to a world of such vast divisions between ranks to be seated comfortably at the same table with them.

'Mr Book,' he said swiftly, 'when we are alone with fellow members of the service, such as Lieutenant Harington here, you can forget the deference expected of you in the past. You and Mr Raven are now part of a secret brotherhood. You're one of us. We have more in common with each other than with anyone else, perhaps more even than with our own families.'

'Quite so, old chap,' agreed Harington gravely. 'I'm sure my dear old papa would set the dogs on me if I turned up at home with this moustache.'

With no duties to perform aboard the schooner, Beaumont, Peter and Matthew enjoyed their cruise, as the weather was perfect and a fair wind sent them coursing towards Jamaica.

On the third day of their voyage, Beaumont shaved off his villainous-looking beard, after which he produced from his sea-chest some appropriate civilian clothes for Peter and himself which he'd bought in Port-au-Prince. Peter's jacket was slightly large, but on the whole it fitted rather well.

The ship approached the harbour of Port Royal late at night, and while they were still a fair way off, Harington lowered a rowing boat. Beaumont didn't want suspicious eyes seeing three newcomers arrive aboard a Spanish schooner.

They rowed ashore, where they tied up the schooner's boat amid the confusion of moored ships. As the commodore led them through a quiet narrow street Matthew carried Beaumont's sea-chest on his shoulder. Bright with moonlight, the port was occasionally made noisy by the sound of revels coming from the taverns.

'It doesn't look like much of a place, Matthew,' said Peter, unimpressed.

'Port Royal was once one of the pearls of the Caribbean, Mr Raven,' said Beaumont. 'But they suffered a bad earthquake here which knocked the heart out of the old town.'

They eventually arrived at a boarding house where, despite the lateness of the hour, a young black woman answered their knock. She was clearly in charge of the establishment and knew Beaumont.

'Take the chest to the second room on the left at the top of the second flight of stairs,' she instructed Matthew. 'There are rooms either side of Mr Beaumont's chamber for you other gentlemen. Do you want some food?' she added.

'No, thank you, Nancy. We had supper with Harington,' answered Beaumont.

'El Mustachios,' she said with obvious affection. 'Is he as fat as ever?'

'Even fatter,' replied Beaumont with a grin.

'How long will you require the rooms?'

'A few days, maybe longer.'

'The only other guests at the moment are two American brothers called Jacob and Elijah Culpepper.'

'What are they like?' asked Beaumont.

'They're from the north. Rich and close-mouthed. One's fat and one's thin, both are bald. They're waiting for someone. I'm pretty sure they're expecting to do some kind of business deal.'

'Good, they won't be wanting to engage in idle conversation, then.'

'Who are you going to be while you're here?' asked Nancy.

'English businessmen, I think,' replied Beaumont. 'I am a wealthy trader. My young companion Peter is a relative, and Matthew a servant. But I might have to become a British officer at a moment's notice.'

'So, I shan't be joining you for the meals you take here,' said Matthew, smiling.

'You can eat in the kitchen with me, handsome,' said Nancy. Then to Beaumont she said, 'The American brothers think I'm from New Orleans. What language should I speak in front of them, French or English?'

'Oh, English, I think. We'll turn in now. I shall be out early: I have to call on the admiral of the West Indies Squadron, and I'm not sure I'll be entirely welcome.'

The following morning, Matthew was taking his breakfast in the kitchen with Nancy, and Beaumont had already departed to pay his call on the admiral. Peter was alone in the dining-room when the American brothers took their place at a table furthest from the windows overlooking the street. They barely nodded at Peter and did not speak to one another, even when they both looked suspiciously at the dish of pork and fried eggs a servant girl called Pearl had brought them. Peter tucked into his own portion hoping he'd be able to eavesdrop on the two men if they did speak.

They wore dark woollen clothes and already seemed uncomfortable in the morning warmth. Finally, the thin one said, 'I might buy one of those white suits folks wear about here.'

The fat one shook his head. 'Why waste money? We'll be gone soon. Just loosen a few buttons.'

The thin brother pulled out a fob watch and flipped it open. 'He's late,' he said grimly. 'I can't abide doing business with a man who can't keep an appointment.'

But as he tucked the watch away, another man entered the dining-room. Peter almost choked on a mouthful of pork: it was General Ancre. Although Peter had seen him only fleetingly on the deck of the *Columbine*, the general's strong features were unmistakable. He was dressed in light linen clothes and greeted the two brothers warmly as he glanced about the modest room, displaying no apparent interest in Peter.

'Gentlemen,' he began. 'When I suggested you stay here I had no idea it would be so modest. I am sure there must be an establishment in Jamaica more suitable for such eminent visitors. I have a carriage outside. Permit me to take you somewhere on the island more comfortable.'

'We don't hold with fancy hotels, General,' replied the fat brother. 'This does us fine. Let's get down to business.'

Peter was suddenly aware that the Culpeppers were watching him with hostile eyes. His breakfast finished, he had no excuse to dwell longer. He rose and with a polite nod in their direction he departed.

Chapter Thirty-four

BEAUMONT'S NEWS

Matthew beckoned to Peter from a doorway further along the corridor. He hurried to him, and entered the room to find Nancy with her ear pressed to the wooden wall. Peter did the same and found he could hear the conversation in the dining-room quite clearly.

'How much can you guarantee to supply, gentlemen?' asked General Ancre.

'If the price is right, we can fill as many ships as you can send,' replied the thin Culpepper.

'And you're sure you do not want to come into this venture as partners?' asked General Ancre. 'You realize we are going to revolutionize the way of life in these islands?'

'Just pay us cash on the barrel per shipment. We're more than happy with that arrangement, sir.'

'As you wish,' replied Ancre. 'I don't want you to feel you've been cheated of a golden future.'

'General Ancre,' said the fat Culpepper. 'Our father Augustus J. Culpepper taught us to be happy with our pockets full of silver. There's plenty of fools looking for gold.'

'Then you can expect my ships on the date I mentioned in my letter. Shake hands upon it.'

'We'd like you to sign this contract as well,' said the thin Culpepper, hastily.

The sound of doors opening and closing told the eavesdroppers that General Ancre had departed and the brothers were returning to their room. Nancy instructed Pearl to follow Ancre and discover what she could about his movements and intentions. Then she herself accompanied Matthew and Peter to Beaumont's room to discuss what they'd overheard. When Beaumont returned an hour or so later they told him of the conversation.

The commodore noted the news of General Ancre's presence on the island without surprise, adding merely, 'Yes, I must say he's a cool customer, conducting his business on a British possession. The man has great style, I'll say that for him.'

'But why would he run the risk of arranging a meeting on Jamaica, sir?' queried Peter. 'It seems foolhardy.'

Beaumont shook his head, smiling. 'This world is changing rapidly. If General Ancre didn't want to be seen by anyone on his own side, surely this would be the ideal place for a secret liaison.'

'But, why would he be watched by his own side? Didn't

you say he's the head of their Naval Secret Service?' asked Peter.

Beaumont nodded. 'All the more reason his rivals in France would have him spied upon. I'd bet five gold guineas to a tin penny that if he'd held such a meeting on a French island, reports of it would be on the boat to France this afternoon.'

'What do you think he's buying from the Americans?' asked Nancy.

Beaumont shrugged. 'Heaven knows. He may well be doing something for Napoleon. Who can tell?'

Nancy shook her head. 'And they say women are the tricky ones.'

Just then the servant girl Pearl returned. 'Where did Ancre go to?' asked Nancy.

'To the British admiral's house,' Pearl replied. 'Didn't Mr Beaumont tell you? I saw him and the admiral shaking hands on the steps with the man, General Ancre.'

Nancy, Matthew and Peter all shot confused glances at the commodore.

He laughed and threw up his hands. 'You might as well be among the first to know. The preliminaries of a peace treaty between France and Britain have been proposed. It will be signed in October and ratified next year. As well as conducting his own business with the two Americans, General Ancre was paying his respects to the admiral because we will soon no longer be enemies.'

'So, that'll be it, sir?' said Peter. 'All friends again?'

'Hardly, old chap. There's still a hostile fleet out there, call them pirates, corsairs, privateers, what you will, but they're about the toughest sailors the French have. It was fortunate to meet General Ancre. This will fit in with our plans very well.'

'*Our* plans, sir?' said Peter, unable to disguise the hint of sarcasm in his voice.

'Yes, *our* plans, Mr Raven. I may think them up, but you will be assisting me in their execution, never fear.'

'Aye, aye, sir,' said Peter, this time more respectfully.

'Why was your meeting Ancre a good thing?' asked Nancy, confused.

'Because we still have no idea where Vallon's headquarters are,' Beaumont replied. 'And we won't find out by aimlessly sailing about the Caribbean. I've got a strong suspicion General Ancre knows where to find him. If he accepts our offer to take him to Santo Domingo, by the time we get there – in these new days of peace – I shall have become his good friend and may pry something out of him.'

'But surely he will already have arranged his own passage, sir?'

Beaumont shook his head ruefully. 'Yes, he has. He told me so this morning. But sadly, the ship that was to take him has caught fire. A tragic accident. Luckily, no lives have been lost, but he will have to accept my kind offer.'

'When did his ship catch fire?' asked Nancy.

Beaumont looked at his pocket-watch. 'Let me see,' he said, 'he's lunching with the admiral, and they should just be starting their soup. I should say the ship will be burned out by pudding time.' He looked up and said, 'Do you know, there's something I'm not going to be able to enjoy for a long time to come.'

'What would that be, sir?' asked Nancy.

'A dish of tea.'

'I'll have Pearl make you some,' said Nancy.

Beaumont rubbed his hands together enthusiastically. 'As soon as we've drunk our tea, we shall be off to the naval yards. I've had the crew of the *Wasp* rounded up so I can address them.'

'The *Wasp*?' asked Peter, unfamiliar with the ship.

Beaumont nodded. 'The French don't control all the privateers on the high seas, Mr Raven. The *Wasp* is British. She came limping into Port Royal a month ago with the captain and the first and second officers dying of yellow fever. They'd captured a Portuguese merchantman and she was loaded to the gunnels with coffee from South America. The merchantman was unarmed, but its escort vessel put up a harder fight than expected. She nearly finished the *Wasp* off before they managed to sink her. The *Wasp's* crew got her in here for repairs, but since then they've lost their captain and officers. But I arranged to have Petty Officer Connors infiltrated into the crew some time ago.'

'What are we going to do with her?' asked Peter.

Beaumont continued. 'The men of the *Wasp* want their prize money for the merchantman so they can get back out to sea and pick off some more ships.'

'But won't they have to stop their plundering if there's peace with France?' asked Nancy.

'Quite so,' replied Beaumont. 'So I've decided to offer them a prize they can't refuse.'

'And what would that be, sir?' asked Matthew.

'The offer of treasure beyond their wildest imagination, Mr Book. I've never known a privateer yet who could resist the chance of stealing a chest full of gold.'

Chapter Thirty-five

THE MEN OF THE *WASP*

Peter, Beaumont and Matthew stood beside the dry dock where the *Wasp*, once a captured French brigantine, was having her copper bottom repaired.

Before them stood her silent crew, a truly villainous looking collection of human beings. Even the officers looked like the worst kind of desperadoes. Their newly elected captain, a young man called Brough, with long black hair worn in braids, had obviously once been handsome. However, a slash from a blade had left him with a livid white scar that ran from forehead to chin. The wound had taken out his left eye, which was now covered with a patch.

The first lieutenant was a squat powerful man with his right forearm missing. The ivory replacement was fitted with a short spike rather than a hook. His flaming red hair grew from his head and chin in a shock of ragged stubble.

There were one hundred and twenty-four of them. They were colourfully dressed in silks and velvet, and all burned nut-brown, liberally scarred, tattooed, and heavily armed. On British warships, guns, pistols and swords were kept under lock and key until they were required. These men looked as if they were permanently prepared for a boarding party.

Their weapons were the finest they could steal. They each carried at least a brace of the best quality pistols carelessly tucked into their sash or belt, and beautifully crafted swords and knives with horn, gold or ivory handles. Some had cavalry sabres, and one man had a curved Persian dagger with a jewel-encrusted sheath stuck in the silk sash about his waist. Peter noticed the dagger first, but when he looked into the man's face he recognized Petty Officer Connors, who gave him a sly nod.

The men watched Beaumont with mild interest as they lounged about the dry dock where the *Wasp* was being repaired. There was no hint of deference in their manner, as there would have been if they were seamen from a British man-o'-war. All they'd been told was that an influential man wanted to address them, so they were prepared to listen, but Peter had the impression that if they didn't like what they heard, Beaumont would be pitched into the sea, or worse, impaled upon the numerous sharp weapons that were so evidently at hand.

There was no threat of the lash or of being clapped in chains to control these men, and Beaumont's service rank

meant nothing to them. To gain their respect he would have
to win them over with the power of his personality, and a
sizeable bribe.

But he got their attention as soon as he began.

'Gentlemen of the *Wasp*. Allow me to introduce myself.
I am Commodore Paul Beaumont of His Majesty's Royal
Navy. As I am an officer in the King's service and you are
pirates, it could be said I am your sworn enemy.'

A buzz of amused comment passed through the *Wasp's*
crew at his bluntness. But Beaumont held up a hand and
they fell silent.

'However, this is a changing world, and wise men will
profit from the changes. I have not come here to talk to you
of patriotism, or to urge you to face the perils of the sea in
the name of King and country. I have come to explain your
new situation and to offer you a business proposition that
entails work far better paid than you have ever known.'

Now he really had their attention.

'You may not know it yet, but France and England will
soon sign a peace treaty.'

This caused further exchanges of comment among the
sailors.

'Please, hear me out,' said Beaumont. 'Now that peace
is about to be restored, the British Government no longer
needs you as privateers. Your letter of marque is to be
revoked, which means you will no longer be licensed to
seize the vessels of other nations. And they are not going to
let you keep the last prize you took. I regret to have to tell

you that the merchantman you seized after such a desperate fight has been impounded.'

A growl of anger came from the crew, and weapons were drawn.

'Gentlemen,' Beaumont called out. 'The ship you took was Portuguese, and Portugal is now potentially an ally of England. Such an act of piracy may well have been over-looked in the past, when your services were valued. But peace will change everything. You may not even be allowed to keep the *Wasp*.'

The crew was now shuffling forward in a thoroughly ugly mood, and Peter hoped that Beaumont wasn't going to drive them to immediate insurrection before he'd persuaded them to do his bidding.

Once again the commodore held up his hand for silence. 'Hear me! I have a new friend who is a representa-tive of Napoleon, First Consul of the French Republic. If you sail to France with me in the *Wasp*, you will be permit-ted to take the Portuguese merchantman with you. Coffee has been in short supply in Europe because of the British blockade. Sold on the open market the cargo will be of inestimable value.'

'What's in this venture for you?' called out Captain Brough. To Peter's surprise he spoke like an English gentleman.

'On behalf of His Majesty's Government, I want half the profits,' said Commodore Beaumont. '*And* to direct the future operations of the *Wasp*.'

'He's asked for too much,' Peter muttered to Matthew.

'No,' replied Matthew softly. 'They wouldn't have believed him had he asked for less.'

'So, what happens after we deliver the coffee?' asked another member of the crew.

Beaumont had them. 'Those who wish to take their profits may do so, and there will be letters of pardon for the crimes the French claim you've committed against them.' He paused just long enough for that to sink in: like all good orators, Beaumont understood the art of timing. 'But for those who wish to stay in my service aboard the *Wasp*, there will be more gold to be had than you could imagine in your wildest dreams.'

'Gold?' 'What gold?' 'From where?' clamoured several voices.

'I know where Count Vallon keeps his treasure trove,' said Beaumont, speaking so softly the crew of the *Wasp* leant towards him, hanging on to every word.

'We all know where he keeps it,' called a scornful voice. 'Roc d'Or. But the island is said to be impregnable, even if you knew where it was. We once toasted a Frog privateer's feet for a week and still he was too terrified to say where it is.'

'Nonetheless, I know how we can steal Vallon's gold.' Beaumont smiled at the men.

Peter saw he had their complete attention. Just as there is always someone who will buy a dubious treasure map, so all privateers were willing to follow anyone who promised them a chance to steal a fabulous treasure.

The crew of the *Wasp* took a vote there and then, with no prior discussion, and immediately declared themselves loyal to Beaumont. The commodore thanked them heartily, and said he would be in touch within forty-eight hours to make final arrangements for the voyage.

Peter was deeply impressed. As they walked out of the privateers' earshot, he said, 'So, you arranged all that this morning in just one hour, sir?'

'Certainly not, Mr Raven,' Beaumont replied blithely. 'I wasn't quite sure what I was going to do this morning. Now, I've got to tell the admiral I'm taking possession of a prize ship of enormous value and returning a gang of villainous cut-throats to the high seas. And what's more, I must also persuade General Ancre to sail with us to France.'

'How will you do that, sir?' asked Matthew. 'He looks a pretty tough old bird.'

'There may be one way,' replied Beaumont. 'He thinks I am a mere commodore in the Royal Navy. When I tell him I'm a British spy he may find my company somewhat more desirable.'

Chapter Thirty-six

THE BEST LAID PLANS

The Culpepper brothers had departed in the afternoon, so Nancy put a *No Vacancies* sign on the front
door of the boarding house and set about organizing a special farewell dinner for Beaumont, Peter and Matthew and
two other guests. While the meal was cooking, Nancy
entertained them in her parlour, which was as splendidly appointed as any drawing-room Peter had ever
been in. Oriental rugs and silk-covered furniture graced
the room. On the walls a gold ormolu mirror hung on
each side of a large painting of shepherdesses, and there
were also several portraits of grim-faced, bewigged aristocratic gentlemen.

When Peter and Matthew complimented Nancy on the
décor she replied, 'I bought it all from a Dutch privateer
who stole the cargo from a French ship eight years ago. He
said it had all been on its way to some fancy estate on

Martinique.'

She was about to pour another rum for Matthew and a glass of wine for Beaumont when there was a thunderous pounding on the front door. When she answered it, they heard shouts of friendly greeting and she returned with Lieutenant Harington.

'Ah! Just as I imagined it, Beaumont,' he smiled, tugging one side of his excessive moustache. 'A feast – I swear I could smell the roasting geese from the harbour.'

'How did the boat-burning go?' asked Beaumont as Harington accepted a glass of wine.

'We fired an old wreck and whisked the boat General Ancre had hired away to a cove along the coast. He wouldn't know the difference when he saw the charred timbers bobbing about.' After swigging down his wine, Harington held out the glass to be refilled, saying, 'So, what's the plan, Commodore?'

Beaumont stretched out his legs and raised his eyes to the ceiling. 'The same as ever. To find out what Napoleon's plotting with Count Vallon and spike it.'

'Even though we're almost at peace?'

Beaumont shook his head. 'We'll never be at peace with France, not until Napoleon's toppled, Richard. I've made a study of him. I've read his dispatches and captured letters to his friends. I know what's in his heart. He hates Britain, or at least he hates our rulers. He wants to depose the King and rule over us with his own men in power.'

'Well, he won't have much difficulty finding them. There's plenty in Britain who are sympathetic to him,' said Harington.

Peter knew the lieutenant was right. He'd even heard conversations in his own home in which neighbours had spoken in favour of the ideals of the French Revolution. To some in Britain, Napoleon was a great man.

'That's not our concern,' said Beaumont. 'We all swore an oath to the King. That's enough for me.'

'I drink to your sentiments,' said Harington, draining his glass. 'Now, is it true you're off to France? I thought you intended to hunt down Count Vallon?'

Beaumont sighed. 'We've had no success in locating Roc d'Or. And God knows we've tried hard enough. Besides, I've received new orders.' He unfolded a piece of paper taken from his pocket. 'I picked this up today.'

Peter could see that the message was in code, but Beaumont read it out effortlessly, as though it were written in plain English.

'Information has come to His Majesty's Government that by secret treaty, the Spanish have returned Louisiana to the French.

'This being so, the United States of America are anxious to negotiate with the French Government to purchase the port of New Orleans and to secure the right to use the Mississippi River, thus allowing the passage of goods produced by their western territories. They intend to dispatch the lawyer Robert R. Livingston as their Minister for France and special envoy to Paris to negotiate the purchase.

'Our late agents in Paris reported that Foreign Minister Talleyrand claims the French intend to build a new empire on the
North American continent once the territories known as Louisiana
are returned to them. They also plan to possess Florida, and thus
own sea ports dominating the Gulf of Mexico.

'If these territories are returned to France it would become
master of the Caribbean and ultimately control the gold and silver
mines of South America. In this eventuality, the United States
would become dominated by the French, Great Britain would be
squeezed out of Canada, and France would gain ascendancy over
the entire Western Hemisphere.

'It is the opinion of His Majesty's Government that His Britannic Majesty's best interests would be served by preventing the French
from carrying out their plans and encouraging the Americans to
expand to the west.

'We also have unconfirmed reports that Napoleon intends to
send an army to the island of Santo Domingo. It is very important
that we know Napoleon's intentions in the West Indies in order to
maximise disruption of his plans.

'With these objectives in mind, you are hereby ordered to proceed to Paris, so that we may receive the latest information you are
able to gain there.'

Beaumont nodded. 'It's a sound move for me to return
to Paris. What happens out here is first decided there. It is
vital now that we obtain our information directly from the
horse's mouth.'

Lieutenant Harington then asked him, 'What did it
mean by "our *late* agents in Paris"?'

Beaumont looked up. 'Our three best men in Paris were found floating in the river Seine a month ago. It was reported in the French papers. They were all Swiss – or at least that was their cover.'

In the silence that followed, there was another loud knock on the door. 'That should be our last dinner guest,' said Beaumont.

'Who else are we expecting?' asked Harington.

'I thought we'd entertain General Ancre. After all, we shall be shipmates tomorrow, I hope.'

The others looked at each other, astonished by Beaumont's latest tease. But the new arrival was a messenger from Professor Manichi in Port-au-Prince.

Beaumont scanned the letter quickly but before he could tell the others its contents there was another knock. This time it was General Ancre. He wore a plain buff-coloured coat but still looked very much a soldier.

Ancre was delighted that everyone spoke French. 'My English is very poor, almost non-existent, I fear,' he said haltingly before changing to his own language. He seemed particularly taken with Nancy. After kissing her hand he gestured about the room. 'Mademoiselle, permit me to compliment you on the fine taste you display in the furnishing of your private rooms.'

He examined the portraits on the walls before adding, 'I take it these people are relations?'

Nancy nodded with a smile.

'Extraordinary!' said Ancre, smiling in a satisfied way.

'My dear young lady, do you realize that they bear an extra-ordinary likeness to the relatives of the Marquis Guvion on the island of Martinique? I know this because I was born there, and was well acquainted with the look of the family.'

Nancy didn't flinch. 'It must be a coincidence, sir. My family name is O'Reilly.'

'Quite so,' said General Ancre. 'I'm sure it is impossible that you could be related to the Guvions. They are all com-pletely without charm, and certainly lack your grace and manners.'

It was some measure of General Ancre's aplomb that he could approach dinner with a lodging-house keeper, an unlikely Spanish schooner captain, an English naval officer, a midshipman and a petty officer with such ease. When he took his place at the table in Nancy's private dining-room, it was as if he were joining a collection of old acquaintances.

The meal was delicious and General Ancre congratulat-ed Nancy on keeping such an accomplished chef. Then he laid down his napkin and spoke to Beaumont: 'I suddenly find I am free to take up your offer of a passage to Santo Domingo, Commodore. As you may have heard, my boat rather surprisingly caught fire. Although on examining the fragments of burnt wreckage I was a trifle surprised to see that the colour of the paintwork had mysteriously changed from turquoise to light blue.'

Beaumont shot a glance of reprimand to Harington who rolled his eyes to the ceiling in embarrassment.

'Let us lay our cards on the table, General Ancre,' Beaumont began. 'I am a member of the Royal Navy Intelligence Service. And you are head of the French Secret Service in the West Indies.'

Ancre smiled. 'And I take it Mr Raven is your bodyguard. I saw him practising with his pistol in Port-au-Prince.'

'I didn't see you, sir,' said Peter.

Ancre now addressed Beaumont. 'You've done a very good job, Commodore. I have admired your efforts for some time and made a great effort to bring them to an end.'

'And I yours,' replied Beaumont, smiling pleasantly. 'But perhaps we can now be of assistance to one another, General.'

'What do you have in mind?' asked Ancre.

'I think, in your heart, you want the destruction of Count Vallon as much as we do.'

'Ah, Count Vallon,' said Ancre, accepting a cigar and a lighted taper from the servant. He blew smoke towards the ceiling before continuing. 'And why should you imagine I wish him any harm?'

Beaumont leant forward clasping his hands together. 'You are a man who loves his native island, General. Now that we shall be handing Martinique back in the peace treaty, you will be able to return home.

'We know you have some business venture in mind. If you are to conduct it in these waters, Count Vallon could be as great a menace to you as to Britain. Besides, we all know he is insane. There is no place for the likes of him in a war between civilized nations.'

General Ancre smiled wearily. 'Something of a contradiction, don't you think? A war between civilized nations.'

Beaumont shrugged. 'Surely, if we must have wars, isn't it better to conduct them within the boundaries of honourable rules?'

'Yes,' replied Ancre. 'But it is an old-fashioned concept, Commodore. I fear we are all servants of our masters. Napoleon wishes to make a friend of Vallon, so who am I to . . .?' He ended the sentence with an expressive shrug.

'But in your heart I know you would like to see us destroy him,' said Beaumont with unexpected passion.

Ancre remained impassive, and Peter was put in mind of an old leopard sitting on a sunny rock.

'It is my duty to serve Napoleon Bonaparte, the First Consul of France,' he replied carefully. 'I am expected to meet with Count Vallon and return with him to France. That is why I accept your offer to take me to Santo Domingo, where he awaits me.'

Beaumont shook his head. 'Not according to the information I received just before your arrival, sir.' He pulled the letter from his pocket. 'This tells me that Count Vallon, accompanied by a large retinue of trained men, has already sailed without you. He is aboard the *Columbine*.'

General Ancre hardly paused before replying. 'In that case, my dear Beaumont, I shall be delighted to sail with you all the way to France.'

Chapter Thirty-seven

PASSAGE TO FRANCE

Although the crew of the *Wasp* looked like desperate ruffians, they proved to be first-class seamen. However, Beaumont had decided it would be unwise for Peter to carry out his midshipman's duties as if he were aboard a Royal Navy vessel.

'These men will not respond well to the orders of a youth, Mr Raven,' Beaumont had explained as they sat in the captain's cabin on the morning they were due to leave Jamaica. 'Captains of Royal Navy ships can expect their crews to obey the orders of boys, but privateers are different. Their world is rather more democratic. They even elect their own officers. It would be a needless provocation to expect them to take orders from you.'

'Aye, aye, sir,' replied Peter, reluctantly admitting the sense in the commodore's words.

'Besides,' continued Beaumont, 'I have other tasks for

you. I have given orders that you are to question the men to establish how many of them can speak French.'

Peter nodded. He'd already noted that several men spoke the language. Four black seamen he guessed were escaped slaves. Five of the crew had spent time in the French-speaking region around the lower reaches of the Mississippi. And he expected to find others, as it was common for ships that had spent a long time in Caribbean waters to have hands that spoke other languages.

'How well do you require them to speak French, sir?' he asked.

'I'm not looking for men with the skill of a diplomat,' replied Beaumont. 'A rough and ready grasp of it will do.'

'Aye, aye, sir.'

'Oh, and another thing,' Beaumont remembered. 'I've asked Petty Officer Connors to teach you some special fighting skills.'

'Fighting skills?' said Peter, puzzled. 'Is Connors a pugilist, sir?'

Beaumont gave a short barking laugh. 'I doubt if any pugilist would last very long against Petty Officer Connors, Mr Raven.'

'But he's not very big, sir.'

'Precisely. And neither are you. So you can find out how a smallish fellow like Connors has managed to stay alive so long. Carry on.'

'Aye, aye, sir,' replied Peter, and rose to leave. As he reached the cabin door there was a single rap, and General

Ancre came in. He was expected for breakfast. Crouching slightly to avoid hitting his head on the overhead beams, he greeted Beaumont and took the seat he offered. Sighing, he looked about him and said, 'You sailors are amazing. The more ships I sail in the more I'm reminded of coffins.'

Beaumont smiled. 'In the Royal Navy, we officers actually sleep in our coffins. They bury us in the bunks we use.'

Matthew entered and swiftly spread a tablecloth and cutlery. Although he'd been promoted to petty officer he was acting, on his own suggestion, as Beaumont's steward and cook for the journey to France.

'This crew wouldn't be quick to trust a new petty officer, sir,' he'd explained. 'And besides, I can't see a man among them who could cook worth a damn. As I'll be eating the same food, I thought it better you leave the matter to me.'

General Ancre accepted with pleasure the offer of eggs and bacon. 'A splendid dish,' said the old soldier when it was served. 'It is a fine thing to face the day with a hearty meal inside you rather than a mere piece of bread.' He did, however, decline tea in favour of coffee.

This was Beaumont's first real opportunity to speak at leisure with the general. For the past three days he had been studying the crew as they prepared the ship for sailing. All had impressed him. The men were exceptional and he was well pleased with the officers. It transpired that the scar-faced Captain Brough had served as a lieutenant in the Royal Navy and earned his distinguishing wound at the

Battle of the Nile. Van Alders, the red-bearded lieutenant, was a Dutchman and had been a second mate on trading ships before becoming a privateer.

'How long do you think our passage will take?' asked Ancre, accepting another cup of coffee.

Beaumont shrugged. 'Who can tell? We could be in France twenty-five days from now, or two months.'

'Of course,' accepted Ancre. 'It was a silly question. I know ships are the servants of the weather. That was something it was difficult to make Napoleon understand.' Ancre raised his shoulders in a shrug. 'As you know, I am not a sailor, but I have no problem grasping that.'

'How did you get into the spying game, General?' asked Beaumont. 'You have the reputation of being a formidable soldier. It seems perverse to take a successful fighting general and make him the head of naval intelligence.'

General Ancre smiled. 'I think since we are to share such confined quarters it would be acceptable for you to call me Ancre.'

The commodore inclined his head in a slight bow, saying, 'Beaumont,' and the two shook hands.

'Beaumont,' said the general thoughtfully. 'Such a French name.' Then he continued. 'To answer your question: as you know, our Navy has been in some disarray in the years since the Revolution began.

'Bonaparte doesn't trust the senior naval officers at all, so he appointed me to be head of the West Indies Station — because I was born in this part of the world, I suppose.

Most of my fellow soldiers wouldn't know the geography of the Caribbean from the coast of Brittany!'

Beaumont nodded. 'May I make something clear, Ancre? I am not an enemy of France – just of Napoleon.'

Ancre smiled again. 'My dear fellow, the First Consul would say the two are one and the same.'

Chapter Thirty-eight

CONNORS' WAY

The following afternoon some of the *Wasp's* off-duty crew watched Peter's first fighting lesson with Petty Officer Connors. It was a fine day and the ship dipped in and out of the water like a dolphin, cutting through the sapphire blue waves towards the windward passage between Cuba and Santo Domingo.

The men were in a good mood and shouted encouragement to Peter, who was armed with a crude wooden cutlass. As instructed, he was attempting to stab or slash the evading Connors. The petty officer was armed with Peter's midshipman's dirk, but the point of the dagger had been sheathed in a protective cover of burnt cork.

A few of the men were smoking pipes, which surprised Peter. On Royal Navy ships smoking was strictly forbidden, except in specially restricted areas lined with brick, because fire was such a hazard on a vessel made of wood, tar, hemp and paint. The danger of fire was even greater in the tropics, where long periods of intense sunshine so completely dried out the fabric of ships. Smoking was yet another example of how privateers were expected to discipline themselves, and Peter saw that the men were careful with their pipes.

'Always use the roll of the ship,' Connors told Peter. 'Whenever your opponent has to shift his balance to stay on his feet you'll have an advantage over him.'

As the ship rolled again Peter lunged with his wooden cutlass. Connors nimbly stepped aside and lightly stabbed at Peter's stomach, leaving yet another charcoal smudge on his shirt, which had been clean on that morning.

'That's enough with weapons for today,' said Connors. 'Now we'll try some hand-to-hand work.'

Peter felt more confident about that. Isaac had given him lessons in fisticuffs from the time he was able to walk. He squared up to Connors, fists held up in the prescribed manner of a pugilist, and the wiry little man smiled and casually kicked him under the kneecap with the edge of his bare foot.

Peter collapsed on to the deck, clutching at the searing pain in his leg. Connors leant over him and said, 'Good job I wasn't wearing shoes and kicking hard, eh, Mr Raven?'

'That wasn't fair fighting, Mr Connors,' replied Peter through gritted teeth.

Connors pulled him to his feet. 'Never again confuse

sport with fighting, Mr Raven. Boxing is for those who find fun in men battering the brains out of each other. What I'm teaching you is a matter of life and death.'

Peter leant against the gunnels holding a ratline while Connors continued. 'When you've only got your bare hands and feet against an opponent armed with a weapon, he might assume he has the advantage and relax just enough for you to surprise him. If you learn what I tell you, the bigger your opponent is, the better.'

'How so?' asked Peter, intrigued despite his aching leg.

'A big bullying sort of man always thinks we little fellows will be easy to beat,' said Connors.

'So you are, runty,' taunted a tall, powerful man named Wyman whom Peter had already noticed swaggering about the ship. Unlike the good-natured derisive banter from the other men, his words were a challenge.

Connors winked at Peter before he turned around, saying, 'If you'd like to take Mr Raven's place, Wyman, I'll be glad to demonstrate how runts like us deal with blowhards.'

Wyman needed no further urging. He charged at Connors, leaning forward in a wrestler's crouch and reaching out to seize his arms. Connors sidestepped him easily, and knocked the legs from under him with a sweep of his leg.

'Do you see, Mr Raven?' Connors called out cheerfully. 'I used his own momentum and weight to bring him down.'

But Wyman was already up again and had changed tactics. He rushed at Connors punching with his ham-like fists.

It was clear that if one of his blows struck home, Connors' jaw would be cracked like a walnut shell.

Connors moved with the grace of a dancer, avoiding the flailing fists that never once found their target. Wyman, breathing hard from his exertion, stopped to take stock. Connors casually beckoned to him. Wyman roared in rage, and lunged forward.

Connors stood his ground and half raised his own left hand, which wasn't bunched into a fist. Instead, the fingers were extended and stiffly grouped together. He ducked under Wyman's grasping hands and jabbed forward as if to deliver a straight left to his jaw, but his actual target was the hollow in Wyman's throat beneath his Adam's apple.

Connors' blow connected and the big seaman fell to the deck as if pole-axed, grasping at his throat and making a dreadful gurgling sound. Two men hurried to his aid and Connors said to them, 'Don't worry, he'll be all right soon. But his throat will be sore for a few days. Give him a stiff tot of rum.'

Then he turned back to Peter. 'You see, Mr Raven? And that's only one way of bringing down a big one. Of course, in a real fight I would have finished him off. Tomorrow, I'll show you a few ways to do that. Now, think of the places where I stabbed you. Those are the spots on the body where you'll do the most damage with a sharp weapon.

'In a fight, it's much harder to kill someone with a knife than folks think, if they aren't trained to the job. The body of a pig has a lot in common with a man's. Later on, I'll show you the most vulnerable places on the live pig we have on board.'

'If you insist, Mr Connors,' replied Peter with an obvious lack of enthusiasm.

The next day, still limping slightly from the kick he'd received from Connors, Peter reported to Beaumont on the French speakers on board. 'Nineteen in all, sir,' he began. 'Eight of them are fluent, the rest rough and ready.' He passed the commodore a sheet of paper with the names written on it.

'Excellent, Mr Raven,' answered Beaumont. 'I shall interview them all personally. The most I shall require is ten.'

The commodore's examination produced a few welcome discoveries. Of the Englishmen who spoke French, one called Forbes had been a valet before the Revolution, working for a gentleman of leisure in Paris. Another, named Rawlings, had been tutor to the children of a French aristocrat. The third, Benson, had also worked in France as a senior clerk in an import and export house specializing in spices.

'We'll make good use of these chaps,' said Beaumont happily.

Fine weather continued to ensure that the voyage of the *Wasp* passed pleasantly enough. Beaumont and General Ancre played a good deal of chess: both the actual game, with equal skill and passion, and also a metaphorical version in which they probed for each other's hidden thoughts and intentions by setting conversational traps for one another.

By the time the *Wasp* reached Le Havre the two men had formed a genuine attachment, each seeing in the other a reflection of themselves that bound them in a deep friendship that overrode any difference in nationality. So it was with real regret that the commodore bade his new friend farewell on his departure for Paris.

By good fortune, Benson quickly located an old contact from the spice trade, and with a judicious bribe he set in motion the purchase of the merchantman vessel together with its fabulous cargo of coffee. The sum they were finally offered was even higher than Beaumont had anticipated: enough to buy a man a country estate in England and provide a lifetime's comfortable income.

Beaumont, having distributed lavish amounts of cash for ready spending to each of the *Wasp's* crew, made further arrangements with a merchant bank to deposit funds in their London branch in the names of all the men. They were all delighted with the arrangement and pledged their everlasting loyalty to the commodore.

Meanwhile, Beaumont asked the ten selected French speakers on the *Wasp* if they would like to accompany him, Peter, Matthew and Connors to Paris. They were to pose as servants, but in reality they would be bodyguards and must expect danger.

The men accepted readily.

'It's a strange thing,' mused Peter to Matthew later. 'Had the commodore just offered the men jobs as servants, I'm sure they would have refused to do it. But knowing they'll be engaged in subterfuge and risking their lives makes them all the more willing to do it.'

'That's privateers for you,' answered Matthew, who was cooking a joint of beef in the *Wasp's* galley. 'They would set fire to their own shirt tails rather than be bored. They're the kind of men who live for excitement, Mr Raven. It's not so much the treasure they want but the dangers they'll encounter to acquire it.'

'Quite so, Mr Book,' said Beaumont. 'That's why I must keep the rest of the crew busy while we are about our business in Paris.'

When they'd eaten, Beaumont remembered a task he'd been meaning to put in hand for some time. He cleared the table in the little cabin, and produced two very large sheets of good quality paper, a fine-nibbed pen and a bottle of ink. Then he set Matthew to make maps of the Roc d'Or fortress and the domain beyond, urging him to include as much detail as he could remember.

'It's years since I was there last but I recall everything, sir,' Matthew said confidently, and he proved his claim to be correct. The first map, showing the surrounding country-side, was excellent.

'And do you think you've drawn it to scale, Mr Book?' asked the commodore, looking pleased.

'Yes, sir,' Matthew assured him. 'I've made charts

before, when I was aboard a Dutch merchant ship.'

'Count Vallon could have changed things over the years,' ventured Peter.

Matthew shook his head. 'It's not in his nature to change things, Mr Raven. Count Vallon is a completely obsessed man. Once he has made a decision, nothing will ever change his mind. He designed every inch of the domain. I'll bet my life it's still just as it was when I was a boy.'

Beaumont accepted Matthew's word, and was even more impressed by his map of the fortress defences and the harbour. It even included the approximate depth of the water at high and low tides. Beaumont studied the sketch for a while, then asked, 'These guns mounted on the parapets to defend the entrance to the harbour – can they be reversed to fire inside the harbour itself?'

'Yes, and they're not at too high an elevation. Only fifty or so metres above the water line at high tide. You can easily see the gunners from the dockside inside the harbour.'

Beaumont nodded and continued to study the maps for a while. Then he placed them in a tubular leather case in the chart locker.

Matthew guessed what was in Beaumont's mind. 'You couldn't get even one ship into Roc d'Or, sir,' he said. 'Let alone the fleet you'd need to destroy Vallon's ships that shelter in its harbour. Even if the guns on the ramparts don't manage to blow you out of the water as you approach the harbour entrance, you'd never be able to get past the boom. Only a fish could get under that.'

Beaumont thought for a while, then stood up with a smile and called for Captain Brough.

Almost three weeks had passed since General Ancre had left the ship to make his way to Paris. During the time the *Wasp* had been docked at Le Havre, Peter and Matthew had gone about the town quite a bit, enjoying the sensation of treading on soil that had so recently been forbidden territory.

They had missed whatever instructions Beaumont had given to Captain Brough. But the commodore had then spent the best part of a day writing letters to England, and the following morning he informed Peter, Matthew and Connors that they would be taking rooms in a nearby tavern. No sooner had they gone ashore with their gear than the *Wasp* slipped away on one of Beaumont's mysterious missions.

Finally, Beaumont was ready to start the journey to Paris with his own party. He'd sent Forbes and Rawlings ahead to find them a suitable residence and had received a letter by post rider from Rawlings that very morning, telling him that he and Forbes had found a furnished house in the best part of Paris.

The other French speakers who were to accompany him, Peter, Matthew and Connors had purchased new clothes and had all visited the barber. Two had even been fitted with false teeth, having lost their own through violence rather than old age. The privateers looked almost respectable, although they all still wore their swords, and their jackets had been cut generously enough by the tailor to conceal their pistols and knives.

None of the men could ride with any skill, but four of them were able to manage teams of horses well enough, so Beaumont had purchased two carriages for the journey to the capital. As they bowled along the well-paved road lined both sides with newly planted saplings, Peter looked out of the window, fascinated by the French countryside. This was the land of the enemy he had heard of since he'd been an infant. It looked remarkably peaceful and pleasant – not unlike England, he thought, slightly puzzled.

Chapter Thirty-nine

A SUMMONS FROM
GENERAL ANCRE

Lucy Cosgrove had spent a long and enjoyable summer in Paris, but the autumn was even more intoxicating. Determined to consign the bloody horrors of the Revolution to the past, Napoleon had declared that he wished to heal the wounds inflicted by the fanatical Jacobins and make France one happy family again.

In that cause a decree had been issued, informing all those who had fled abroad that they were welcome to return home, providing they were loyal to Napoleon's government. A surprising number of aristocrats who had been in exile took the opportunity and flocked back to Paris, which became, as the First Consul had intended, a city of dazzling light.

It was a time of fashionable gatherings, at which grand hostesses competed to entertain the most interesting and exceptional members of society in their salons. Artists, writers, philosophers, poets, scientists, even those who had little to offer but their amusing conversation or their wealth, mingled in an atmosphere that Mrs Hargreave sometimes found hard to breathe. But Lucy adored every minute of it.

Since she'd won Napoleon's approval with her skills as a markswoman, Lucy had been invited to every splendid occasion. Every evening there was a ball or a glittering dinner party, a new theatrical production or another opera to attend. And as the nation lived to the rhythm of the ten-day week introduced after the Revolution, weekends were so far apart that Mrs Hargreave frequently yearned for an old-fashioned quiet Sunday.

There were other Americans in town, and Robert R. Livingston was soon to arrive with his wife and two daughters and their husbands. It was already common knowledge that Livingston was coming to Paris to negotiate the purchase of New Orleans and that he could expect a difficult time from Talleyrand, who as Foreign Minister was being tantalizingly vague about whether or not the French were interested in selling the vital sea port.

Lucy and Mrs Hargreave had attended lunches, dinner parties and various social occasions organized by fellow American visitors, but Lucy usually found them dull by comparison to the gaiety of their Parisian counterparts.

One glorious autumn afternoon, Lucy was strolling with

Joséphine in the garden of Malmaison, the Bonapartes' private retreat. Jack Cobden was amusing the children of Joséphine's first marriage by pretending to be a grizzly bear. They shouted with enjoyment and clambered over his broad back when he pretended to lie down asleep.

'So, you already know this Monsieur Livingston who is coming soon to Paris. Is he not supposed to be something of a bore?' asked Joséphine.

'He loves France, Madame, but he has never acquired the Parisian habit of laughing at life's adversities,' said Lucy, who found the French habit of speaking frivolously about important matters quite captivating and practised it herself whenever possible.

'But he is a great man, is he not?' asked Joséphine. 'We are told he administered the oath to George Washington.'

'Oh, Mr Livingston is a dear,' said Lucy. 'But I really had no idea how provincial my country is, compared to Europe. Last night, I spoke to a man who claimed there is no God and that the ancient Greeks were better off with their pagan worship. If he'd even suggested such a thing in the Hudson Valley he'd have been ridden out of town covered in tar and chicken feathers.'

'Do not be deceived, child,' said Joséphine, gently. 'Not so long ago, my first husband was guillotined for saying the wrong thing.'

'I'm so sorry for your loss, Madame, but hasn't all that changed now?' said Lucy. 'I didn't know anywhere could be as wonderful as Paris. And it was all brought about by the

First Consul. You must be immensely proud, Madame.'

'I am,' smiled Joséphine. 'But let me tell you a little secret. Life is splendid with my husband, but sometimes I too crave a little extra diversion. So, I have persuaded him to accept the invitation of an extraordinary man who has just arrived in Paris.'

'Who is he?' asked Lucy, intrigued to hear there was someone who actually impressed Joséphine.

'Heir to one of the most ancient families in France,' answered Joséphine. 'And he is reputed to be fabulously wealthy. He is holding a ball tonight. Would you care to accompany me?'

'I should be most honoured, ma'am,' replied Lucy respectfully, never forgetting the importance of Napoleon Bonaparte's wife.

Just then Jack Cobden stood up, as if he had scented danger. He looked hard until he saw Lucy strolling safely beside their hostess.

The house they had rented on the Rue Tivoli was as splendid as Beaumont had stipulated to Forbes and Rawlings, but for the moment it was in chaos, which did nothing to improve the commodore's temper. Unusually for him, he'd dozed only fitfully, often fidgeting and groaning as they'd travelled through the night. However, Peter, Matthew, Connors, and the three other men who'd shared his carriage had all apparently slept like babes.

The arrival of the group was proving to be a noisy affair.

Seamen on ships tended to work quietly, but today they were clattering about the house carrying sea-chests and shouting to each other as they got themselves organized. The commodore eventually shut himself in the library on the first floor, where he dozed in a large and comfortable chair until Peter interrupted his rest by bringing him a note.

Beaumont read the message and was instantly awake. 'It's from General Ancre,' he said softly. 'He wants to meet you and me in Notre Dame at twelve o'clock.'

'Me, sir?' said Peter, surprised to be included.

'That's what the note says. Go and tell Forbes to have one of those infernal carriages ready in half an hour. We might as well arrive in style.'

Peter was nervous as he passed through the mighty decorated doors of the cathedral. For a moment he wondered if, just by entering these awesome precincts, he might be committing some sin in the eyes of his own religion.

All his senses were struck by the gloomy grandeur of the vast enclosed space, the pervading scent of incense, the beauty of the choir's singing, and the magnificence of the gigantic stained-glass windows which filled him with wonder as he gazed up at their glowing colours.

'Keep up, Mr Raven,' said Beaumont softly. 'You look as if you've seen a ghost.'

'Do you think we should be in here, sir?' whispered Peter, worried.

'What do you mean?' asked Beaumont, pausing to glance about them.

'As Protestants, sir. Should we even *be* in a Roman Catholic cathedral?' asked Peter, disturbed by his misgivings.

Although his parents prided themselves on being enlightened, they had always been rigorous in observing their faith within the Church of England, considering it part of their duty to the King, as well as the cornerstone of their beliefs. Peter had never even met a Roman Catholic until he'd visited the West Indies.

'Have you been in a cathedral before, Mr Raven?' asked Beaumont lightly.

'Yes, sir. Canterbury, with my parents,' answered Peter in a hushed voice.

'Well, just remember that it used to be a Catholic cathedral before Henry the Eighth appropriated it from Rome. Just do as I do,' he added. 'I'm sure it's all the same to God.'

Beaumont dipped his hand in the Holy Water provided, and crossed himself as he genuflected. Peter did the same. Then Beaumont tugged Peter's sleeve and they walked down the great aisle to take a pew behind a man whose head was bowed in prayer. Feeling very small in the interior vastness, Peter realized it was General Ancre who half-turned and smiled at him.

'Good morning, gentlemen. I'm glad to see you in church.' He sighed and gazed up at the intricate tracery way above them. 'Beautiful, isn't it?' he continued. 'Religion was abolished as being unpatriotic at the height of the Revolution, but a lot of peasants like me find it hard to put aside all the old ways. And now Napoleon has ended discrimination against the church. Who knows, one day, we might even find him in here himself.'

'Why did you call us here?' asked Beaumont, concerned. 'Is there any danger?'

'On the contrary,' said Ancre. 'Napoleon is anxious to meet you both.'

'Napoleon?' said Beaumont, unusually taken aback. 'Napoleon wants to see *me*?'

'Actually, he's more interested in meeting Mr Raven,' added Ancre with a chuckle.

Peter gasped. 'Why would he want to meet me, sir? I'm just a midshipman.'

'Ah,' said Ancre. 'This is typical of the First Consul. He has the most amazing interest in all manner of subjects. Who makes the best bridges? Or buttons? Should soldiers wear boots rather than shoes? Is wheat better than corn for bread?

'He is still puzzled that the British make more successful sailors than the French. When I spoke with him this morning, he again raised the subject. I told him you were both in Paris, so he wants to question you, to see for himself the kind of stuff you're made of. He is attending a reception at the house of the Duc d'Allorais this evening. So shall you, if you agree.'

'Has the Duc himself invited us?' asked Beaumont.

'Napoleon has, and that is sufficient to ensure you will be welcome.'

'Do I have to go, sir?' asked Peter. It sounded far more formidable than leading a boarding party against an enemy ship.

'We can't miss this opportunity, Mr Raven,' said Beaumont. 'It may interest you to know that Count Vallon's family name is d'Allorais.'

Suddenly transfixed, Peter could feel his heart pounding and the familiar hatred welling up inside him. He made no further objection.

But Beaumont was puzzled. 'If there's no danger, why did you arrange this clandestine meeting, Ancre?' he asked.

The general smiled. 'Gentlemen, I simply thought a visit to Notre Dame would be good for your souls,' he replied with a chuckle.

Chapter Forty

BEAUMONT BEWITCHED

Beaumont had his dress uniform packed in his sea-chest, but Peter's was lost along with the *Torren*. So before they returned to the house, they stopped at a military tailor recommended by Ancre and presented one of the general's signed cards. It was enough to ensure the tailor's promise to make a fair representation of a British midshipman's dress uniform and have it delivered by early evening.

'That's fast going,' said Peter, impressed.

'We keep uniforms already partly made up. The only difficulty will be the buttons, sir,' explained the tailor's bemused assistant, who had measured Peter.

'Just use the buttons of a French naval uniform, my dear fellow,' said Beaumont.

'It will be a unique creation,' said the man, raising an eyebrow.

In the carriage as they drove back to the house, Beaumont chuckled. 'Think of it, Mr Raven, you'll be the only midshipman in the Royal Navy to have his uniform made by the tailor who sews for the marshals of France.'

But Peter wasn't listening. Ever since Beaumont had mentioned Count Vallon his mind had been racing with the memory of the man who had given the order for his ship-mates to be killed, and their dying screams.

As arranged, General Ancre was waiting for them outside Count Vallon's house. He was enjoying a cigar in the balmy evening air. Because Napoleon was attending the occasion, there were sentries of the elite guard posted outside. They presented arms to Ancre, Beaumont and Peter as they mounted the steps together.

'One day when you're an admiral, Mr Raven, you'll remember that salute,' said Beaumont as they stepped into a massive marble hallway where footmen took their cloaks. After mounting the stairs, they were ushered into an already crowded ballroom, brightly lit by several huge crystal chandeliers. The walls were lavishly adorned with large and extraordinary paintings.

Peter found the perfumed atmosphere almost overwhelming. An orchestra played, and light glittered on women's jewellery and on the decorations of the many uniformed soldiers among the guests.

'Rather impressive for a bunch of revolutionaries, eh, Mr Raven?' Beaumont whispered.

'It certainly is, sir,' Peter replied, but he was more interested in the paintings, which he recognized as scenes from Greek and Roman mythology. He'd never seen works of art on such a grand scale and executed with such breathtaking skill. Peter reminded himself that all this glorious extravagance had been brought together by the monstrous creature he had vowed to destroy.

However, the crowd had eyes only for one another. The most important leaders of Parisian society had flocked here in the hope of meeting the man whose presence had set Paris chattering.

His mind sharpened by his hatred and his need to control it, Peter noticed that despite the powdered wigs and white gloves worn by the footmen serving champagne, they were all hard-looking men. Beaumont and General Ancre talked to one another but were also listening to the crowd gossiping, mostly about the Duc d'Allorais.

Whispered stories passed from group to group. Someone claimed their host had been forced into exile by the threat of the guillotine, another that colossal debts had driven him from his homeland, and that he never used his family title, preferring to be known as Count Vallon.

A dandified figure dressed in extravagantly fussy clothes, his hair glistening with pomade, confidently informed a group of women that the duc had killed three men in a sword fight over the reputation of an heiress, and since that day had been hunted by avenging assassins.

'My dear General Ancre!' A pleasant female voice rose

above the general babble.

Ancre, Beaumont and Peter all turned to see Joséphine Bonaparte smiling at them. She was accompanied by two beautiful young women and a handsome, fair-haired man in the gold-encrusted uniform of a general. Peter, suddenly shy, noted the delicacy of the evening dresses worn by the three women. Arms and shoulders bare, they wore gowns made of the lightest silk, gathered in beneath their breasts so that it drifted gently about them as it fell in flowing lines to their bejewelled sandals. All three women wore their hair drawn up high on their heads, with curling ringlets plucked from it to fall artfully about their faces.

General Ancre presented Beaumont and Peter, first to Joséphine Bonaparte, then to Napoleon's dark-eyed sister Pauline and her husband General Victoire-Emmanuel Leclerc, and finally to Lucy Cosgrove.

Peter thought Lucy outshone all the other women in the room, including the classical beauties in the paintings. He blushed as he took her hand, and to his astonishment she grinned and winked at him. Only then did he realize she was not much older than his sisters, and he managed to grin back.

But Peter's favourable impression of Lucy was as nothing compared to the startling effect she had on Beaumont. The commodore had been under fire many times in his naval career, but never from a weapon of such devastating power as Lucy Cosgrove's smile. Peter was surprised by the sudden change in the commodore's usual easy confidence;

Beaumont seemed unable to shift his gaze from Lucy's eyes.

As Beaumont's lips brushed Lucy's proffered hand, he felt strangely weak, as if he'd just run an exhausting distance. But before he'd gathered his senses enough to form a polite greeting, the unmistakable figure of the First Consul joined them, and he was glowering at the ladies.

'You must be cold, my dear,' he said to Joséphine, eyeing her bare shoulders. Then to his sister Pauline he declared, 'I do wish the women of my family would set a better example. Those who choose to parade half-naked are never shown proper respect.' But for Lucy he had a softer smile. 'Ah, Miss Cosgrove, your presence continues to enhance our fair city.'

Having chastised his wife and sister, Napoleon's mood improved and he warmly greeted General Ancre, who in turn presented Beaumont and Peter to him.

As Beaumont exchanged formal greetings with the First Consul, Peter studied the man who had always been described to him as a monster. He wanted to know how Napoleon would compare to Count Vallon, who was yet to appear.

Bonaparte wore a dark green uniform coat with red cuffs, and doeskin breeches with tasselled boots. He was not grotesquely ugly as English caricaturists invariably depicted him. Nor was he exceptionally small, or humpbacked. Even with the heady mix of perfumes in the air Peter was aware that Napoleon smelt of eau de Cologne. His long fine hair framed a smooth pale complexion, but his eyes were dark and piercing.

Napoleon gave Beaumont his full attention during their conversation, then turned to Peter. 'So, Mr Midshipman Raven,' he said. 'Do you approve, now that you've studied me so intently?'

Peter replied with as much confidence as he could muster. 'Please forgive me, sir. I did not intend any rudeness by my gaze.'

Napoleon laid a hand on his shoulder. 'Do not apologize, young man, I also stare at what interests me. We who stare see more than those who merely look.' He smiled, touching one of Peter's uniform buttons. 'French, eh? Did you know that in my youth I wanted to join the *British* Navy?'

Before Peter could reply to this unexpected information, an aide in military uniform leant close and spoke quietly to the First Consul. 'Forgive me, sir, but your host, the Duc d'Allorais, requests a private audience with you.'

Peter flinched as he caught the count's name.

'Does he?' replied Napoleon, raising his eyebrows at General Ancre. 'I expected him to be here to greet me. Where is he now?'

'There is a private chamber two floors up.'

Napoleon sighed. 'These houses are too big,' he complained. 'I marched shorter distances campaigning in Italy. Have him informed I shall be along quite soon,' he then instructed the aide.

Before making a move, Napoleon asked General Ancre,

'How long has Count Vallon been in Paris?'

'A few days, sir. He first visited his family estates.'

'Is there much left to see?'

Ancre shook his head. 'Not any more. The chateau was burnt to the ground in the Revolution.'

Napoleon sighed. 'What a waste. Tell me, Ancre, why does a mob always assume the intelligence of its most stupid member?'

The aide had sent a footman ahead with Napoleon's message and was now waiting to escort the First Consul. Keeping his hand on Peter's shoulder, Napoleon said, 'You may come with me, Mr Raven. We shall continue our conversation while I make this tiresome trek.'

Napoleon walked slowly from the vast room, all the while shooting questions at Peter, who walked beside him doing his best to describe the training given to, and the duties expected from, a midshipman aboard a British ship.

The First Consul seemed to be giving all his attention to Peter's answers, and prompted him to elaborate on certain subjects. Peter was interested to realize that he, in turn, felt deeply flattered and wanted somehow to please and to gain the approval of this extraordinary man.

'And what is your favourite subject?' asked Napoleon as they stood before two great doors, two floors above the ballroom. The First Consul nodded for the aide to thrust them open.

'Gunnery, sir,' Peter replied without hesitation as they both strode into the darkly-panelled room. 'But I like the calculations as much as the bangs.'

Napoleon laughed delightedly, totally ignoring Count Vallon who stood glowering before him dressed in black silk. 'And it is also mine,' Bonaparte said. 'I was trained as an artillery officer, did you know that?'

'No, sir,' answered Peter, fighting to contain himself. He feared his heart might burst from the rage now coursing through his body at the proximity of his sworn enemy. But his mind was never so alert. The room surprised Peter. He realized it must once have been a private chapel; there was even a confession box against one wall.

'The big guns,' Napoleon continued, still ignoring Count Vallon. 'They always control the battle. Infantry and cavalry have their part to play, but cannon, they are the real deciders in war,' he enthused. 'But we must part now, Mr Raven. Let us hope that you and I may never have to turn our guns upon each other.'

Peter could see that Napoleon had deliberately taken him into the room and continued their conversation in front of Count Vallon. It was clearly meant as an insult to the count for not greeting him on his arrival. But had fate presented Peter with this opportunity? He gripped his dress dirk and wondered if he could kill Vallon now, before Napoleon's escort mistook his action as a threat to the life of the First Consul.

Realizing such an attack might fail, Peter came to attention and gave a smart salute. Napoleon returned it, and Peter marched from the room. Slightly dazed by his encounter with Vallon, Peter began to walk along the empty corridor to return to the ballroom, but he noticed the next door along was slightly ajar.

Glancing into the room, Peter saw it was a picture gallery with even more paintings than in the ballroom below. After a quick look up and down the corridor he slipped inside.

Chapter Forty-one

CUPID'S SECOND ARROW

Pauline Bonaparte was accustomed to receiving a great deal of flattering attention, so it irked her that the handsome British commodore had eyes for no one but Joséphine's American protégée, Lucy Cosgrove.

Joséphine had already been drawn into an animated conversation with another group nearby, so when the orchestra began to play Pauline tapped General Leclerc on the epaulet with her fan and indicated with a sweep of her dark eyes that she wanted to dance. Obediently, Leclerc led his wife towards the dance floor, leaving Beaumont alone with Miss Cosgrove.

'Are you enjoying your stay in Paris, Miss Cosgrove?' Beaumont ventured, desperately wishing he could think of something witty and memorable to say.

'Thank you, yes.' Lucy's reply was polite but cool, because Beaumont was a British officer, and her family had fought a bloody war to gain freedom from the Crown of England. Even so, she had to admit this young man with a sunburnt face and broken nose was, in an odd sort of way, quite attractive.

'Would you care to dance, Miss Cosgrove?' Beaumont asked hopefully.

Lucy considered the request. She did love dancing, and at least this man was young and presentable.

'If you wish,' she replied, and Beaumont led her to the floor. He was so nervous in her presence he could barely breathe, and as much as he racked his brains he could think of absolutely nothing worthwhile to say. Then fate dealt him a kind card.

'Jack Cobden!' Lucy suddenly exclaimed. 'How did that sly fox get in here?'

Beaumont followed her gaze to see a tall man with alert eyes watching them intently. He was a good head taller than everyone else around him. Beaumont laughed, and in that instant his overwhelming awe of Lucy, which had inhibited his natural ease since they'd met, evaporated.

'Are you laughing at me, sir?' Lucy demanded.

'Only with the deepest admiration, Miss Cosgrove,' Beaumont said, easily now. 'I'm simply delighted we share such an expressive language.'

'That is *all* we share, sir,' Lucy replied sharply. 'I was raised to believe you English are a cruel and vicious race, who delighted in burning the homes of the American people during our War of Independence.'

'I was a very young boy in Ireland during the American rebellion, Miss Cosgrove,' Beaumont answered lightly. 'I am of course loyal to King George, but as for being English, my name is French and my mother is Irish. Whereas Cosgrove is a fine old English name.'

Lucy tried her best to keep a straight face, but the crooked nose and the smile of the young commodore melted her resolve, and she chuckled.

'Now you are laughing at *me*, Miss Cosgrove,' said Beaumont.

'Only because I've just thought of the dreadful oaths my grandfather would utter at the thought of me dancing with an Englishman – even one with a French name.'

Lucy's laughter proved even more devastating to Beaumont than her coolness. He danced on, happier than he could ever remember, and totally distracted from his real mission.

Peter paid no attention to the paintings in the gallery, but made directly for an ornate closet standing against the wall at the far end of the room, his footsteps silenced by a long carpet that covered most of the floor.

Like the entire mansion, the empty gallery was well lit – a mute boast of Count Vallon's fabulous wealth, as good-quality candles were expensive. Peter quietly opened the door of the large wooden closet and stepped into its confined space. A single seat stood beneath a small grill between the gallery and the room next door. Peter was in the other side of the confession box he'd seen in the room where Napoleon was meeting Count Vallon. The door of the confessional on the other side of the wall was half open and he could see into part of the chapel.

'So, my dear sir,' Napoleon was saying. His voice, coming quite clearly through the grill, sounded conciliatory now. 'You have decided to accept my offer.'

'Why else would I be here, First Consul?' replied Count Vallon.

Napoleon ignored the veiled insolence and continued. 'I hardly think you would bother to come all the way to France to *reject* the offer of a throne.'

'You are correct, First Consul,' replied Vallon, almost dreamily. 'King of Louisiana is a title with the proper resonance, don't you think? The throne of England was tempting, but I have no desire to live there. I would rather put all my golden eggs together in one basket and accept your American offer.'

'So, you will be content with Louisiana?'

Vallon laughed. 'With one slight addition. As well as King of Louisiana, I also wish to be the Duke of New Orleans. I intend to have a son, and that would be a fitting title for him.'

There was a slight pause before Napoleon said, 'I was not told you were married?'

'I am not, nor yet even betrothed,' replied Count Vallon. 'But I have decided to give the matter of wedlock my urgent attention.'

'I am delighted you are so decisive, sir,' said Napoleon. 'It is never too early to think of one's successors. Now, when can you hand over my money?'

'As soon as I receive the legal charter for Louisiana bearing your signature, I shall send for the first payment,' Vallon answered. 'If the winds are in your favour, gold to the value of one million pounds sterling will arrive within two months; possibly sooner.'

'How will you safeguard the passage of such a prodigious sum from the West Indies?' asked Napoleon.

'I now command the *Torren*, a first-rate British man-o'-war. I shall use her to transport the gold. And, what is more, now you are about to sign a peace treaty with the British, they will be unable to attack her as she will be considered one of the legitimate spoils of war. Rather amusing, don't you think?'

'A splendid irony,' Napoleon replied. 'As for the subsequent instalments, I shall require you to pay them directly to General Leclerc, who will shortly be embarking with a French army for Santo Domingo. I look forward to you keeping your part of the bargain, Your Majesty.'

'The feeling is mutual, First Consul,' answered Vallon. 'Now, if you will excuse me, my other guests await me. I have been neglecting my duties as host.'

Peter could hear Vallon's footsteps departing and the opening of the doors. There was a short silence before Napoleon spoke again. 'What do you think?' he asked his aide.

'He is a dangerous madman, First Consul,' replied the aide bluntly.

'He is,' answered Napoleon. 'But his treasure is the golden key with which I shall unlock the door to America.'

'You'll need to be careful, sir,' warned the aide. 'Count Vallon could slam the door in your face. I cannot see him accepting the throne of Louisiana, then bending a knee to France.'

Napoleon sighed. 'Yes, I suppose he will inevitably become yet another little king I shall have to pull down, like all the others.'

Peter could barely wait to report what he'd overheard to Beaumont, but he forced himself to stay in the confessional box until the aide had closed the chapel doors behind Napoleon. When he was sure the corridors were clear, Peter hurried down to the ballroom, only to find Beaumont dancing with the American girl, Lucy Cosgrove. Count Vallon, accompanied by the French Foreign Minister, was graciously making his way through the crowds skirting the dance floor. Talleyrand, who seemed to have assumed the role of his personal ambassador, was introducing the clusters of people wanting to meet their host.

Waves of loathing were still flooding through Peter, but he knew he had to control his almost overwhelming desire to attack Vallon. Holding in his rage he made his way towards the count, never once taking his eyes off the man's face. Eventually, he was just a few feet from Count Vallon and Talleyrand.

Peter saw Vallon glance at Lucy and Beaumont as they danced by. For a moment the count seemed oblivious to all else. It was the second time that evening that Peter had observed a man become suddenly enthralled by Lucy Cosgrove.

'Foreign Minister,' said Vallon, reaching out to touch Talleyrand's arm without taking his eyes from the dance floor. 'Who is that dancing with the British naval officer?'

Surprised, Talleyrand followed his gaze and answered, 'Miss Lucy Cosgrove, a young American visitor. Joséphine Bonaparte has taken her up as her protégée.'

'American!' Count Vallon exclaimed. Instantly, his customarily languid manner became one of undisguised excitement. 'It is fate that *she* should be an American. I have been sent a goddess for a consort.'

'Fate, Count?' queried Talleyrand. 'Forgive my slow wits, but I'm afraid I don't understand what you mean.'

With his eyes following Lucy as she danced, Count Vallon said, 'She looks as if she were created to be Queen of America.'

'A Queen of America,' echoed Talleyrand. 'What an amusing concept.'

'We are in a new century, Foreign Minister,' said Vallon, still staring at Lucy, who had now become aware of his unsettling gaze. 'Extraordinary things shall come to pass. Please present me to Miss Cosgrove. That English sailor must not be allowed to monopolize her.'

When the music ended, Talleyrand limped across to

Lucy, and with a slight nod to Beaumont he introduced Count Vallon. He immediately requested the next dance, and she accepted. As Beaumont reluctantly left the floor, those who remained began lining up for a quadroon, which was one of Lucy's favourite dances.

Lucy had attended many balls in Paris and had grown used to the flattering attentions of a legion of young men. Most were drawn to her beauty, but many also found the large fortune she was expected to inherit equally attractive. Her attitude to all these suitors varied enormously, depending on their ability to amuse her. The most tiresome were the youths who sought to impress with their looks, their poetic souls, or their superior intellects. Lucy much preferred those who simply strove to make her laugh.

Many of the young men had declared their undying love for Lucy, but she knew she could never feel more than a friendly interest in them, and indeed felt more affection for her favourite deerhound at home.

Now, dancing with Count Vallon, she was becoming unsettled. In the space of an hour she'd found herself attracted to two different men. While giving every impression of remaining poised and unruffled, she had no idea how to make sense of the inner turmoil she'd begun to feel.

After her initial hostility, her encounter with Beaumont had been a happy one. She'd loved dancing with him, laughing at his teasing remarks and responding to them in equal measure. Count Vallon was different. He was older than the commodore, and Lucy found the attentions of this elegant, charming aristocrat enormously flattering.

Until now, most of Lucy's romantic convictions had been formed during girlhood conversations with her friend Mary Van Duren. She'd always firmly stated that when she fell in love it would be all-consuming, and the man who captured her heart would do so to the exclusion of all others.

Although she'd recently become a confidante of Joséphine Bonaparte and her sophisticated circle of female acquaintances, Lucy had not yet grown accustomed to their shocking gossip. They frequently talked of casual affairs of the heart, and Lucy secretly thought less of them for the apparent shallowness of their affections. Now here *she* was, utterly bewildered to find herself indulging in romantic fantasies about two very different suitors. And there was no doubt in her mind that both men were genuinely ardent in their admiration of her.

As she danced with Count Vallon, Lucy said how much she enjoyed the music.

'Had I known to expect someone of your beauty, Miss Cosgrove,' he replied with a charming smile, 'I would have had a symphony composed for you.'

'I am amazed and pleased, Count, that you could find an American girl equal to the beauties of Paris,' she answered, blushing.

'There is no comparison, Miss Cosgrove,' Vallon continued to flatter her. 'The upstarts you see about you this evening are scarcely fit to be in your company.'

'Surely they are not all upstarts, sir,' Lucy teased. 'Was not Madame Bonaparte a great lady before the Revolution?'

Vallon laughed, and Lucy was astonished to find herself flirting with the man who Joséphine Bonaparte had proclaimed was the catch of the season.

Standing agitatedly in a less crowded part of the ballroom, Peter watched Count Vallon with Lucy Cosgrove. He wanted to shout out and warn her that she was dancing with a madman capable of the most unspeakable depravities.

Beaumont was in deep conversation with General Leclerc, but Peter could see that his eyes kept watching Lucy Cosgrove. Frustratingly, Peter had found no opportunity to report the conversation he'd overheard between Vallon and Napoleon.

When General Leclerc was once more summoned to dance with his wife, Peter hurried over to the commodore. 'I've discovered something important about Count Vallon, sir,' Peter whispered urgently.

'Not here, Mr Raven,' replied Beaumont, smiling at General Ancre who was talking with some of the other guests nearby. But Beaumont's eyes quickly returned to watching Lucy Cosgrove dancing with Vallon.

Peter followed his gaze. 'I wish we could kill him now, sir,' he said bleakly.

'Enough of that, Midshipman, keep a hold on yourself,' warned Beaumont. 'We have a greater duty to perform before that can happen.'

As General Ancre rejoined them, Peter noticed Count Vallon shoot an equally hostile look in Beaumont's direction.

As she danced alternately with each of her two admirers, Lucy could not help but make more comparisons. Beaumont was deliciously funny. Mischievous as his smile was, she also noticed that she felt oddly safe whenever he took her hand, and she felt his palm was rougher than might be expected for a gentleman.

Vallon was quite different. He had an attractively mocking smile, and his strange long features caused other women in the ballroom to stare at him. But there was something unknowable in the count's hooded eyes; he seemed burdened by some untold secret. The mystery of it intrigued her.

Although her two suitors were quite opposite in style and character, both were powerful men, and Lucy felt charmed by them in a way she'd never before experienced. Beaumont was somehow warm, welcoming and protective. But there was a sense of danger about Vallon that induced a nervous excitement in Lucy. Both Commodore Beaumont and Count Vallon were infatuated with her, but she was simply revelling in the first stirrings of her romantic feelings.

Despite the warning glares she received from Jack Cobden, Lucy continued to dance with the two men. At each change of partners they icily ignored one another, and their rivalry quickly became the subject of excited gossip throughout the ballroom.

Eventually, an equerry informed Lucy that Napoleon and Joséphine were preparing to depart. As one of their party, she was expected to leave with them. But both Vallon and Beaumont had already extracted her permission to call upon her great-aunt the following day.

After the First Consul and his party had finally left, Peter and Beaumont also took their leave. At last Peter could get enough of Beaumont's attention to begin to tell him of the conversation he'd overheard.

Beaumont had taken the sensible precaution of ordering an escort from among the *Wasp's* men. Two of them were stationed outside Vallon's mansion, waiting for Peter and Beaumont's departure. They drew their swords for the walk through the dark, rubbish-strewn side-streets back to their rented house.

Within a couple of hundred paces, they were indeed set upon by four assassins, whose flurry of pistol shots went awry in the darkness. Having no stomach for a fight with other armed men, the attackers ran off after two of them had received sword thrusts.

'Damnation!' Beaumont cursed as he examined one of his shoulders by the light from the window of a house.

'Are you hit, sir?' asked Peter, sheathing his dirk.

'A bullet nearly took off one of my best epaulets,' Beaumont replied ruefully. 'Never mind, Connors is good with a needle and thread.'

'Do you think they were Vallon's men?' asked Peter.

'Maybe,' answered Beaumont. 'I hope they were, if that was a demonstration of their fighting abilities.'

As they resumed the walk home, Peter told Beaumont everything he'd overheard of Napoleon's conversation with Vallon.

'What an extraordinarily fortunate day,' said Beaumont thoughtfully as he avoided stepping in the sewage channel down the centre of the roadway. 'This makes the relationship quite clear,' he continued, striking a fist into the palm of his other hand. 'Napoleon must desperately need Vallon's money to finance a new colony in the Americas. That's his Achilles heel, Mr Raven. If we can cut off Napoleon's supply of gold, we may yet rend his plan asunder.'

'Why don't we just kill Vallon now, and put an end to it, sir?' urged Peter again.

'Don't be so bloodthirsty, Mr Raven,' said Beaumont, shaking his head. 'Our time will come, but not just yet.'

'But *why* not yet, sir?' asked Peter.

'Because if we kill Vallon now, someone else will be appointed in his place. We must see that the entire enterprise fails before we put an end to him. Have a little patience, Mr Raven, I beg you.'

'Are you going to warn Miss Cosgrove about Count Vallon's true nature, sir?' asked Peter.

Beaumont thought for a while, then shook his head. 'I can't give her any details about Vallon, and if my warning were simply that he was a detestable character, she would think I only spoke out of jealousy. Besides, she might even discuss it with Joséphine Bonaparte and that would be like telling Napoleon himself. Fortunately, Miss Cosgrove has a sly fox to protect her when I'm not there.'

They walked on in silence, Peter vowing to try harder to control the seething hatred he felt.

Chapter Forty-two

THE COURTSHIPS OF
LUCY COSGROVE

In the weeks following the ball, the public attention paid to Lucy Cosgrove by Commodore Beaumont and Count Vallon was the talk of Parisian society. While Lucy didn't mind being the centre of such talk, Mrs Hargreave was horrified by the very idea of it. By her standards all gossip was to be abhorred, and the idea that the name of her great-niece was being bandied about the drawing-rooms of Paris was hateful to her. Finally, she resorted to something she'd always considered an impossibility. She consulted Jack Cobden.

'Even the Livingston family are talking about Lucy and her two suitors. What do you think I should do, Mr Cobden? I'm at my wits' end,' she complained. Cobden had joined Mrs Hargreave in the conservatory for morning coffee. Lucy was still asleep, having been up late at yet another ball, chaperoned by Joséphine Bonaparte.

'Lucy behaves with every propriety,' Cobden reassured her. Mrs Hargreave was again reminded that this savage man, who went nowhere without a great hunting knife tucked under his jacket, was actually a properly educated gentleman.

'How do we know?' she wailed. 'These days, I'm not always about to keep my eye on her. She could be up to anything.'

'But I'm *always* there,' replied Cobden, sipping his coffee appreciatively.

'Always?' asked Mrs Hargreave.

Cobden nodded. 'Lucy is smarter than you think. She may take a stroll in a garden with Beaumont or Vallon, but I go too. And even if neither of them sees me, Lucy always does.'

'She sees you?'

'I taught her to keep her eyes open.'

Mrs Hargreave sighed deeply. 'It's still not good enough. I'm considering taking her home, away from all this. What do you think?'

Cobden put down his cup and looked into her eyes. 'Mrs Hargreave,' he began. 'What exactly was your purpose in bringing Lucy to Paris?'

Mrs Hargreave straightened her shoulders defensively. 'I wished her to know something of the wider world before she settled down to marry an American boy of her own social standing.'

'After all this head-turning frivolity in Paris, do you

really think Lucy will meekly return to the Hudson Valley and settle down with a rich lad who has never been further than the boundaries of his father's estate?' Cobden shook his head. 'You set this hare running, Mrs Hargreave. Now you must watch it finish its course.'

'What do you mean with all this backwoods talk?' she said stiffly. 'I'm sure I don't understand a word you say.'

'My meaning is plain. Which one will she settle for? Commodore Beaumont or Count Vallon?'

'Oh, no!' Mrs Hargreave moaned. 'Beaumont is *British!* That's unthinkable. And despite all his grand titles, the other one has all the appearance of an adventurer. Besides, he's far too old for Lucy.' She sat up, sudden resolve written on her features. 'I shall prepare for us to return to America immediately.'

'I think that would be extremely unwise,' warned Cobden.

'Pray, tell me why?'

Cobden poured himself more coffee from a delicate silver pot before he answered. 'If you try to harness Lucy, she will just kick out. It's in her nature to do so. Since she's had no mother to guide her, she's always followed her own instincts. Tell her she's barred from doing something and the outcome is guaranteed: she'll go ahead and defy you.'

Mrs Hargreave knew it was true. 'So, all I can do is wait?' she said numbly. 'And I can't even decide myself which of the two men is the most unsuitable.'

'That's easy,' said Cobden with a wintry smile. 'Beaumont is by far the better man. Count Vallon is a creature whom I might yet have to kill. The trouble is, Beaumont is British. Try breaking that news to her grandfather. He'd rather she wed Lucifer himself.'

'Why do you call Count Vallon a *creature?*' asked Mrs Hargreave, suddenly interested by Cobden's choice of words.

'Beyond the Allegheny Mountains there's a tribe of Indians called the Crow. I lived with them for a time and they taught me that all men and women are in their nature some kind of animal or bird.'

'So, what kind of creature is Count Vallon?'

'He's a wolverine.'

'A *wolverine?* What is that?'

'Wolverines kill for pleasure, ma'am. They rip their victims to pieces. They also have an interesting habit of utterly destroying any human habitation they come upon. Some Indians call them the devil wolves.'

Mrs Hargreave pondered on this, then could not resist asking, 'And what kind of an animal am I, Mr Cobden?'

'Why, you're not an animal at all, Mrs Hargreave. You're a swan,' he answered without a smile.

In another part of Paris, Commodore Beaumont stifled a yawn. He was seated next to Peter Raven on a comfortable sofa in the recess of a large bay window in a great house overlooking the river Seine. The coffee they were drinking was so good the commodore wondered if it had come from the shipment he'd sold in Le Havre.

'I've brought Midshipman Raven with me as part of his education, my lord,' Beaumont explained to their rather fat host. 'And, I must say, he is coming on apace. It was he who eavesdropped on Napoleon.'

Lord Denton raised a quizzical eyebrow and said, 'Capital work, Midshipman. I say, it's a jolly good wheeze to use him, Beaumont. I salute you, sir.'

Peter had to grin at his lordship's enthusiasm.

'Now, my dear fellow,' said Lord Denton, whose comical demeanour and air of being perpetually surprised was enhanced by the extravagance of his clothes. 'Tell me everything you've learnt. The fellows at home are keen as mustard to know all, so leave out no detail.'

Despite talking like an over-inflated schoolboy, Denton was one of the sharpest men employed by His Britannic Majesty's Secret Service.

Beaumont yawned again and apologized. 'Forgive me, my lord, I was dancing until the early hours.'

Denton waved his excuse away. 'Yes, yes, but what about Napoleon's immediate plans?'

'All is as we assumed. But the key for us is his lack of money. As you suspected, he intends to crush the black insurgents on Santo Domingo and push on into Louisiana, but he desperately needs cash to do it. That's where Vallon comes in. To create his vast French colony on the American continent, Napoleon Bonaparte needs Count Vallon's gold.'

Lord Denton nodded. 'You have to admit Napoleon

thinks on a grand scale, even when France is as broke as a gambler on Derby Night. No handful of little islands for him, by George. He wants the whole bag of marbles to himself. They're all the same, bully boys. Play the game my way, or I'll give you a good thrashing. But one thing still puzzles me.'

'What's that?'

'Why is Vallon going to hand over the cash? What's in it for him?'

'Napoleon has promised him some fancy titles in return. He's to be King of Louisiana and Duke of New Orleans. We are sure of this because Mr Raven overheard Vallon and Napoleon make the agreement. The money is definitely coming from Count Vallon.'

'All of it?' said Lord Denton, surprised. 'Vallon's going to steal all of it? It needs a dashed lot of cash to pay for armies, don't you know? That's why we're signing the peace treaty. Britain is beginning to feel the pinch, too, as well as being tired of this damnable war.'

'Vallon has been plundering the Caribbean with his fleet of privateers for years. He already has a fabulous treasure locked up, and his fleet will be adding to it even as we speak.'

'Remind me, Beaumont, why don't we just send a squadron of warships and destroy him and his base once and for all?'

Beaumont shrugged. 'I'm reliably informed that his fortress is impregnable. Send a fleet and it will be sunk by the batteries of cannon defending the harbour walls.'

'So, you know all about its defences?'

Beaumont smiled ruefully. 'I have detailed maps. The trouble is, I don't yet know its actual location.'

Denton ran a finger under the high, starched neckcloth at his throat. 'Hmmm,' he ruminated. 'That is a trifle difficult. So, what are your plans? We can't have Napoleon building a vast new French colony in America. It wouldn't do at all. Much better for us if the Americans push further to the west. They wouldn't ever want to go to war with us over Canada if they've got all that land about the Mississippi to plough, plant and graze.'

'I must remind you there are no armies in that part of the world, my lord,' said Beaumont. 'We British have but a handful of soldiers in the West Indies and they're constantly depleted by yellow fever. The Americans have no army at all to speak of. A single regiment of French soldiers could make Louisiana safe for France.'

'Napoleon is a sharp fellow,' said Lord Denton. 'He'll keep holding out the possibility of selling New Orleans to the Americans, and their man Livingston will move heaven and earth to get him to make the sale.'

'As long as Vallon is going to deliver the cash for his army, Napoleon will never sell New Orleans,' replied Beaumont.

'So, what's the answer?' asked Lord Denton, throwing up his hands.

Beaumont put down his coffee cup. 'I intend to provoke

Vallon into returning to the Caribbean. I will confront him there and somehow destroy his headquarters and prevent his wealth from ever reaching the French.'

'And I am going to kill him, my lord,' added Peter, who hadn't spoken until this moment.

'You, sir?' said Lord Denton, half amused. 'You're going to kill the King of Louisiana? And how shall you do that?'

'A petty officer called Connors showed me a way.'

Chapter Forty-three

THE PROPOSAL

It was a November evening in the Tuileries Gardens, and the sky above was lit with the glittering explosions of thousands of fireworks. All Paris was celebrating the preliminary peace treaty signed by England and France. It was also the night Miss Lucy Cosgrove received her first proposal of marriage.

Commodore Beaumont had managed to whisk her away from the attentions of Count Vallon by dancing her straight out of the ballroom. It was harder than he'd expected to find a remote part of the great gardens where they could be alone; they were thronging with people who'd come to see the fireworks of Napoleon's Festival of Peace.

But in the midst of these historic events, Commodore Beaumont had more personal and romantic matters on his mind. For some weeks he had, with the help of his friend

General Ancre, arranged to be at virtually all of the social events to which Lucy Cosgrove had been invited. They had also ridden together in the park, attended dinners at the finest restaurants, soirées at the grandest salons, and on several occasions they had shared a box at the opera, reluctantly chaperoned by Mrs Hargreave.

But Count Vallon had been equally attentive, and Lucy along with her disapproving great-aunt had been in his company just as frequently. Since the first night they had all met, Lucy had scrupulously avoided flirting with either Commodore Beaumont or Count Vallon. But it was clear to the rest of Parisian society that both men were completely smitten by the young American.

Indeed, the astonishing success of Lucy's restrained attitude towards her two suitors had so impressed the other ladies of fashion that they had begun imitating her warm and friendly yet always ladylike manner, hoping it would prove equally attractive to their own suitors.

'Miss Cosgrove,' Beaumont began nervously, well aware that Jack Cobden had followed them into the gardens, although he was still out of earshot. 'I am sure it must be clear to you what I feel in my heart.' Beaumont paused to judge her reaction to his words, and to glance about for Cobden. Mercifully, he was keeping his distance, and was about to be joined by a woman. Beaumont continued haltingly with the speech he had rehearsed earlier.

'Our nationalities may seem to be a barrier to our true happiness, but I can only pray it will not be an insuperable

one, and in time we will be able to breach it. I am a plain
sailor by profession, so I will state my hopes and desires
without further elaboration. Will you marry me, Miss Cosgrove, and make me the happiest man alive?'

The last sentence was delivered in a rush, as Beaumont
could see Cobden striding towards them, accompanied by a
young woman he didn't recognize.

Lucy was looking up at the commodore, smiling sweet-
ly. 'Commodore Beaumont, I am deeply flattered by your
proposal but it is all so sudden. I cannot, for the life of me,
give you an immediate answer.'

'But you do not say *no*?' asked the commodore hopefully.

'I do not say *no*,' she answered. 'Nor yet, *yes*. I must
give your offer proper consideration.'

Beaumont bowed. 'The reason I press my suit this
evening is because I must leave Paris on urgent business. I
could be gone for some weeks. May I hope to receive your
answer on my return?'

'I have no wish to dally with your affections, sir, but I
cannot guarantee my answer in that time. However, I shall
do my best.'

Just then a voice called out, 'Lucy! Lucy Cosgrove, it's
me!'

Lucy leapt to her feet in astonishment and embraced the
young woman who had arrived with Cobden. 'Mary Van
Duren,' she cried. 'I can't believe it's you! Even though I
had heard you were coming to Paris.'

'Well, I heard you were the toast of the city, so I've

come to set up as your rival,' said Mary, laughing. Then she shook her head. 'No, I've even better news. I am soon to be Mrs Thomas Lansdowne. We are to be married when my fiancé arrives in France.'

Beaumont stood awkwardly as the two friends chatted excitedly. 'How long have you been engaged?' Lucy wanted to know.

'Since the summer,' replied Mary. 'He came to New York from Washington to work in my father's law firm. Now he's coming over to be part of Robert Livingston's staff at the embassy. I came ahead with my father, who is to be a legal adviser there. I thought you and I could share at least a few weeks together before I become a married woman.'

'Oh, Mary, there's so much to show you,' said Lucy, suddenly seeming younger than Beaumont had ever seen her before. Then she recalled his presence. 'Oh, Commodore Beaumont,' she gasped. 'Please excuse my appalling manners, but Mary is my oldest friend and we haven't seen each other in such a while.'

'I understand, Miss Cosgrove,' said Beaumont. 'I must go now, but I shall live in hope until we meet again.'

With a sweeping bow that clearly impressed Mary, he walked away, but gestured for Jack Cobden to follow. When they were out of earshot Beaumont became serious. 'Keep Miss Cosgrove safe while I am away, Mr Cobden. I think you may share my concern about Count Vallon's true nature?'

'I do,' replied Cobden tersely.

Beaumont looked up as more fireworks exploded in the sky.

'I want you to know, Mr Cobden, that Miss Cosgrove has my heart in her possession, and it is as dear to me as she is herself.'

Chapter Forty-four

MORE LESSONS FOR MIDSHIPMAN RAVEN

Peter was pleased when Commodore Beaumont informed him they were departing for England the following morning.

'Will we take bodyguards, sir?' Peter asked.

Beaumont shook his head. 'No, we shall be safe enough in England.'

'So, are we going on leave, sir?' he asked hopefully.

Beaumont thought for a moment or two, then nodded. 'Yes, Mr Raven, you may have a few days to yourself. I am going to the north country for a few weeks, and there will be no need for you to accompany me. But I've thought of a way for you to pass the time. You might as well enjoy yourself in London.'

'But *not* by going home, sir?' ventured Peter.

Beaumont shook his head regretfully. 'I'm sorry, Mr

Raven. I'm afraid that is quite out of the question.'

'Aye, aye, sir.' Peter had answered matter-of-factly, but he suddenly felt a need to be on his own. Beaumont's quarters took up the whole of the first floor, and the rest of the men shared a large room close to the kitchen, or galley as they insisted on calling it.

Seamen were gregarious by nature, but Peter occasionally felt a need to be alone. At sea the answer was to climb a mast. In this house he had found a way through the attics to the flat roof, the only place where he could be guaranteed solitude. He stood there looking over the darkened city, thinking of home. It was his father's habit to read aloud on winter evenings, and Peter remembered sitting before the log fire in the living-room, his mother and sisters sewing as they all listened. He could not recollect the last time he had felt quite so melancholy.

Then, from below, came the sound of the men singing *Admiral Benbow*, a song popular with British sailors. Peter listened and smiled grimly, his sentimental mood quite dispelled by the grisly words.

Brave Benbow lost his legs
By chain shot, by chain shot,
Brave Benbow lost his legs by chain shot.
Brave Benbow lost his legs,
And all on his stumps he begs,
Fight on my English lads,
'Tis our lot, 'tis our lot.

Peter knew there was no going back to the warm, safe

world of his childhood. He had seen men die or lose their limbs in battle, and he told himself he still had a score to settle.

'*Fight on my English lads,*
'*Tis our lot, 'tis our lot.*'

He echoed the words as he went below to join in the singing.

Two days later, Peter was back in England, and feeling slightly strange. His surroundings were familiar enough, and the constant sound of his own language was pleasantly reassuring, but he felt he had changed beyond recognition.

They took a fast coach from Dover to London. The recent cold weather had made the roads hard enough to ensure a swift journey. Beaumont arranged rooms at a modest hotel in Bond Street, and Peter turned in soon after supper. Service aboard a man-o'-war had quickly endowed him with the sailor's habit of snatching any opportunity to get a good night's sleep. He no longer considered an early bedtime as something only children had to endure. But Beaumont stayed up in the public room, writing a letter to Lucy, Peter guessed.

Late the following afternoon, dressed in civilian clothes, Beaumont and Peter called at the town residence of Lord Denton in Park Lane, where Beaumont was to make his report. Peter was not required to be with them, so he took a seat in a vast leather chair in the library. Warming himself before a blazing coal fire, he read a copy of the *London*

Gazette while Lord Denton spoke with Beaumont in the adjoining office.

Eventually, the connecting door opened and Peter heard Lord Denton say, 'And what will you do with Mr Raven while you're out of town?'

'He's going back to school, sir,' answered Beaumont intriguingly.

When at last they were seated in a cab, Peter asked Beaumont, 'What school am I to attend, sir?' He sounded slightly disappointed, as the commodore had promised something amusing to occupy his time.

As usual, Beaumont was keeping the secret to himself for as long as he could. His face expressionless, he replied, 'You'll see in a few minutes, Midshipman.'

From the window of the cab, Peter saw they'd stopped in the Haymarket. Beaumont paid off the driver, and they crossed the bustling pavement to hurry down a wide alley-way thronging with a riff-raff of fruit-sellers, chestnut vendors and some villainous looking loafers. Peter was intrigued as he followed Beaumont through the stage door of a theatre. He made his way backstage with as much ease as if he were aboard a frigate.

Eventually, Beaumont rapped on a dressing-room door, and was answered by an imperious, 'Come.' They entered a small cluttered room, where Peter found himself staring at the reflections of a man and a woman, who were looking at them equally enquiringly from the long mirror they were facing.

The man had big features, dominated by a straight nose

that he was emphasizing with broad strokes of dark make-up. The woman was young and exquisitely pretty with hazel eyes and tumbling ringlets of blond hair framing an oval face. Her make-up was paper-white and her mouth and cheeks scarlet with rouge.

'My God!' said the actor, obviously surprised to see Beaumont. 'The black sheep of the family.'

'My darling Paul,' chimed in the young woman, who also smiled at Peter. 'It's been so long since we last saw you, we thought you must be dead and buried by now.'

'I'm very much alive, as you see, Harriet,' replied Beaumont cheerily. 'And I need a favour.'

'I can't lend you any money,' said the actor, applying more make-up so that the broad lines on his face softened and he appeared much younger.

Beaumont reached into his pocket and took out a fat leather bag which he slapped down on the table top beside the man. 'One hundred and fifty guineas, plus some extra for being a decent sort of fellow,' he said. Then he remembered something and pulled out another bag. 'I'm sorry, Mr Raven, I quite forgot,' he apologized. 'Here is your share of prize money. Lord Denton gave it to me this afternoon.'

Peter took the bag in astonishment and was delighted to feel its weight.

'And who is your rich young companion?' asked Harriet as she expertly painted a beauty patch on her left cheek.

'Midshipman Peter Raven,' answered Beaumont, slumping down on a well-worn sofa and indicating Peter should take a vacant wooden chair. 'Mr Raven, this is my brother, Mr Anthony Beaumont and my sister-in-law, Harriet Walters. Mrs Beaumont still uses her maiden name in the theatre.'

'I'm delighted to meet you,' said Peter gravely, rising from his chair to give a half bow. 'I've heard of you both. You're very famous, even in Richmond. I had no idea the commodore was your relative.'

'Polite young beggar, ain't he?' said the actor to his wife. Then he looked at Peter. 'And what exactly are you doing in the company of my elusive young brother, Midshipman?'

Peter glanced at the commodore, unsure what he should reply.

'He works for me, Anthony,' said Beaumont quickly. 'And I want you to do me a favour.'

'Fire away, old thing,' said Anthony Beaumont, rattling the bag of guineas before returning to his make-up. 'Your credit is good once again.'

'I've got to go away for a bit,' explained Beaumont. 'I want the two of you to take Mr Raven under your wing. Put him up and teach him a few tricks of your trade, as you did the others I sent you.'

Peter had no idea what Beaumont was talking about, or who the 'others' were, but Anthony Beaumont and his wife seemed unfazed by the sudden imposition of a total stranger upon their household.

'Very well, old dear,' replied Anthony easily. 'I only

hope you'll approve of your new lodgings, young fellow.'

'I'm sure I shall be happy anywhere the commodore recommends, sir,' replied Peter.

'When are you off, Paul?' asked Harriet.

'Tomorrow morning – early,' he answered.

'Then you can both watch the performance tonight and buy us supper afterwards,' insisted his brother.

Chapter Forty-five

A MAN IN HIS TIME

After lodging with the Beaumonts for a week, Peter appreciated that although the couple's daily routine would be considered unconventional by his parents' standards, it was as rigidly observed as life aboard a Royal Navy ship. Everyone in the household slept late and breakfasted at noon, on a substantial meal of eggs, bacon, kidneys, sausages, tomatoes and soda bread. It was prepared by Mrs Burke, the formidable Irish housekeeper who had been nursemaid to Commodore Beaumont and his brother when they were children.

The living conditions of Anthony Beaumont and his wife were quite unlike anything Peter had ever experienced. They lived in a row of ramshackle, oddly leaning terraced houses off the Strand, near the new Somerset House.

Although the house was comfortably furnished, four rooms on the third floor had been abandoned as they were filled by massive wooden buttresses propping up the walls. Anthony Beaumont explained that this was to prevent the house from caving in under the pressures of the buildings on either side. None of the doors shut in their crooked frames, and networks of cracks ran across the plaster ceilings, which occasionally shed largish lumps when people trod too heavily on the floors above.

'But it's cheap, old fellow,' Anthony explained. 'Even though it's a bit like living with the aftermath of a volcano.'

After breakfast, regardless of the weather, the Beaumonts took a vigorous walk for more than an hour in Hyde Park.

'Acting is a strenuous profession, both mentally and physically, dear boy,' Anthony told Peter, who accompanied them on the first day of his stay. 'Many a good actor has finished off his career by being unfit to tread the boards in the more physically demanding roles.'

When they returned from their walk, both took hot baths and napped for an hour. After that, Anthony said they would normally read quietly until the evening's performance. But during Peter's stay, this period was to be taken up by his lessons.

Peter often accompanied them to the theatre, as the company frequently changed the production and he'd seldom had the opportunity to watch professional actors at work. Afterwards, he would join Anthony, Harriet and others in the company for long and noisy suppers.

The passing days had stretched into a month by the time

a letter finally arrived from the commodore explaining that he had been delayed, but would return to London quite soon. By now, Peter had learnt his lessons well and was accomplished in the various arts of disguise and deception.

Anthony Beaumont taught him that the key to assuming another identity was to think of oneself as that sort of person. 'But you must always remember the voice comes first,' said Harriet. 'There's no point in looking like a chimney sweep's apprentice if you sound like the squire's son.' For half an hour each day, they had Peter repeat the same passage of the Bible, each time in a different accent.

Soon, Peter was able to alter his stance to give the impression of being shorter or taller. He could also deceive others as to his real intelligence by the control of his facial muscles.

'The slacker they are, the more stupid you will appear,' explained Anthony. 'If you want to be taken for a total idiot, leave your mouth open and your eyes unfocused. Stupid people never notice anything.'

Harriet taught him how to apply make-up. Padding his cheeks made him look fatter, and the slightest amount of greasepaint could give him the appearance of being either ill or in robust health, or even to look rich or poor, which Harriet explained was generally evident in one's complexion.

'I'm sure you appreciate by now, dear boy, that changing yourself convincingly is not just strutting about wearing wigs and painting your face,' Anthony explained.

'Remember, you won't be on the stage, where over-acting is necessary,' added Harriet. 'Acting in real life must always be far more subtle.'

'Now,' said Anthony one afternoon, 'I want you to act out being a messenger boy delivering a bouquet of flowers to a lady from a gentleman admirer. Start with a knock on the door.'

Peter gave several sharp raps then swaggered towards Harriet and spoke in a convincing London accent.

'Present for you, missus,' he said, tugging a lock of hair and holding out an imaginary bunch of flowers. 'A gent at the stage door says, are you free for supper?'

'Good!' exclaimed Anthony. 'The accent is excellent and the walk just right. Messenger boys are always confident and cheerful, it helps no end in getting a tip. I liked the forelock tugging as well. Just the right amount of insincerity. And the innuendo implied in the supper invitation was masterful. Your own mother wouldn't have known you, Mr Raven.'

Peter smiled at the compliment, and an idea sprang into his mind.

Beaumont finally returned to London on Christmas Eve. Having collected his mail from the Admiralty, he called at Lord Denton's Park Lane residence briefly before going on to his brother's house. Harriet and Anthony were about to depart for their evening performance.

'Paul!' Anthony exclaimed as they met on the doorstep.

'A surprise, as usual. Are you spending Christmas with us? Mrs Burke is to roast two capons as usual. It's the only day we actors get off, you know.'

'Actually, I was looking for Midshipman Raven,' Beaumont replied. 'How has he been getting on?'

'He's done splendidly; a real talent,' replied Harriet. 'But Peter isn't with us at the moment. He's gone off by himself to spend a few days in the country.'

'I must say, he's an independent lad for one so young,' added Anthony.

'He's seen and done things that made him grow up faster than most boys,' said Beaumont thoughtfully. Then he remembered his brother's offer. 'Thank you, Anthony, but no. I don't think I shall be able to stay. Is Thompson's livery stable still where it always was?'

'Yes, but it may be closed on Christmas Eve.'

'I'll knock him up if it is,' said Beaumont, and headed off for Long Acre Mews. Then he called back, 'Merry Christmas to you both.'

'And a merry Christmas to you,' replied Anthony. 'No doubt we'll see you again in a few more years.'

It was pitch dark on the road west, but Beaumont calculated he must be close to Richmond, even though he was unsure of the final part of his route. Eventually, drawn by the lights, he stopped at a public house on the Lower Richmond Road and offered five shillings to any man who knew the locality well enough to carry a lantern and lead his horse to his destination.

'Here we are, sir,' announced his guide after they'd plodded on for nearly an hour. 'Saint Mary's Church.'

Beaumont dismounted and tied his horse to a yew tree next to the gate. Then he stood for a moment in the churchyard, observing the light glowing through the stained-glass windows and casting patches of colour on to the lichen-covered gravestones.

Inside, the congregation was singing *The Holly and the Ivy*, which had always been one of Beaumont's favourite carols. As it came to an end, he slipped into the church and stood near the door with a cluster of other latecomers, for whom there were insufficient pews.

He looked along the crowded rows of worshippers a number of times before finally recognizing Peter Raven, who was seated in one of the back pews. The collar of his civilian greatcoat was turned up and he had a long scarf wound about his lower face.

As the Reverend Raven finished the service and blessed his parishioners, Peter got up and quickly eased his way through the crowd making for the door. Beaumont caught his eye and indicated with a movement of his head that Peter was to meet him outside. As the congregation filed out Peter found Beaumont in the shadows.

'They had no idea I was here, sir,' said Peter softly.

'I know, Midshipman,' replied Beaumont.

'Your brother showed me how to make myself look anonymous,' continued Peter. 'I passed right by my sisters and they didn't even notice me.'

'What about your mother?'

'That was a bit odd,' admitted Peter. 'I know she didn't see me, but several times during the service she glanced around as if she were looking for someone. I've never seen her do that before.'

Beaumont smiled. 'Mothers often surprise us, Midshipman. My brother tells me you've done very well in your lessons. Now I've got a reward for you.'

'Sir?' said Peter, puzzled.

'You're no longer the *late* Midshipman Raven.'

In the dim light, Peter could see him smiling. 'I don't understand,' he said.

'We have received word from our agents in America. The privateers who now control the *Torren* had a particularly bad passage from the West Indies. She could make no headway for weeks, and then encountered such violent storms she was almost lost. The privateers had to put into Charleston in Carolina for extensive repairs. Naturally, the word got out. Now the world knows that the *Torren* wasn't sunk. Embarrassing for the Government, but it means you may now return from the dead.'

'Sir, does this mean—?'

Beaumont interrupted him before he could finish. 'Yes, Mr Raven. You may spend Christmas with your family.'

Peter's expression of pure joy made Beaumont almost laugh aloud with pleasure.

'Will you join us, sir?' asked Peter without hesitation. 'I

know my parents would be honoured by your presence.'

Beaumont hadn't been looking forward to the cold return journey to London and the terrible prospect of Mrs Burke's overcooked capons on Christmas Day.

'I too shall be honoured, Mr Raven,' he replied.

Chapter Forty-six

TRUE LOVE'S PATH

Some things had changed in Paris when Peter returned from his leave towards the end of January. He dumped his gear and made his way to the galley, where Petty Officer Connors brought him up-to-date with the gossip. Like all sailors, Connors dearly loved to pass on rumours and speculation along with the facts.

'The men have all been behaving themselves. Except for Forbes. He got drunk three times last week and had a fight with two French Grenadiers in a tavern. Everyone else has been as good as gold. A bit of a miracle, really, for privateers.'

'Anything else happened?' asked Peter.

'Napoleon's brother-in-law, General Leclerc, has left with an army for Santo Domingo,' he said, as they sat watching Matthew prepare a massive casserole for the men's dinner.

'Tell him about Pauline Bonaparte,' said Matthew.

'Oh, yes,' continued Connors. 'Madame Leclerc, you mean. It seems she didn't want to go to Santo Domingo with her husband, but preferred to stay and have a good time in Paris. So Napoleon had her carried on to the boat kicking and screaming.'

'Anything else?' asked Peter, chewing on a peeled carrot he'd taken from Matthew's pile of prepared vegetables. 'Any news of when the *Torren* arrives with Vallon's gold on board?'

'Nothing yet,' said Connors. 'But the Americans are here in strength. Robert R. Livingston and his family are the top social catch. But Talleyrand's been leading him a merry dance on the question of New Orleans.'

'What about Vallon?' asked Peter, unable to keep the loathing from his voice. Matthew and Connors exchanged glances before Connors answered.

'He's still here, chasing after the American girl. As is our Commodore Beaumont. They've both proposed, by all accounts, but Miss Cosgrove is keeping the pair of them dangling.'

'Odd rivals,' said Peter grimly.

Matthew spoke while expertly slicing a piece of pork. 'Well, she'll soon enough be a widow if she chooses to marry Count Vallon. I've never known a man so many others wanted dead.'

'Where's the commodore now?' asked Peter.

'Picking up another dress uniform. He needs three to

keep up appearances these days,' said Connors. 'He has a social engagement every night.'

'Where's he going this evening?' Peter wanted to know.

'The Americans are giving a ball,' Connors told him.

Although she was glad to be among old friends at the Livingstons' ball at the American Embassy, Mrs Hargreave was not happy. She watched with her customary disapproval as Beaumont and Vallon reserved dances with her great-niece.

Lucy remained in a torment of indecision. Although Beaumont had returned from London some weeks before Peter, she had still not given him an answer to his proposal. Nor had she answered Count Vallon, who had also asked for her hand.

Mary Van Duren's presence in Paris had not helped Lucy resolve her dilemma. Although Mary's fiancé had arrived and taken up his work with the American Embassy, Mary was, if anything, dizzier than she'd been in her school days. Enjoying the romantic drama, she constantly urged Lucy to put off any choice between the suitors, praising each in turn, then pointing out their flaws. Much as Lucy cared for Mary, she'd begun to have grave doubts about the wisdom of her advice. Her misgivings about her own behaviour had increased to the point where she had begun to feel quite heartless.

'It's all so deliciously exciting,' said Mary as they stood watching Beaumont and Vallon glowering at each other from opposite sides of the ballroom. 'Do you think they'll come to fighting a duel over you?'

'I sincerely hope not!' replied Lucy, appalled and slightly frightened by such a thought. This simply cannot go on, she told herself.

'But it would be so romantic,' sighed Mary. 'Like knights jousting. You would be the envy of every woman in Paris.'

This comment finally decided Lucy. Mary's girlish images of jousting knights and duelling rivals made her realize how foolish, and unforgivably coy and insulting, her indecisive behaviour had been towards both men. The thought of them exchanging pistol shots, and the sudden and dreadful vision of Beaumont lying on the cold ground like a finished animal, was quite unbearable. And, she realized, it was the death of Beaumont she had most dreaded.

Having finally made up her mind, she offered her excuses to Mary and walked determinedly towards her great-aunt. She was at last resolved to tell her she loved Commodore Beaumont and had decided to accept his proposal of marriage.

Before Lucy had reached Mrs Hargreave where she sat with the female members of the Livingston family, a man arrived with a note for Beaumont. He read the message immediately, then hurried away without even a glance in Lucy's direction.

Beaumont did not go to his own house after leaving the Livingstons' ball. In response to the note he'd received, he hurried to General Ancre's apartment. Beaumont had been surprised earlier that the general had not been at the evening's event.

He was shown into the study, where General Ancre sat in his waistcoat slumped before a low fire. He had been drinking, and Beaumont could see it was dark rum from the almost empty bottle on the table beside him. As Ancre looked up, Beaumont saw that his eyes were filled with sorrow.

'Join me in a memorial toast, my friend,' said Ancre quietly as he filled a glass with the fierce liquid.

Beaumont waited for him to continue.

'Let us drink to Anne-Marie Ducourt,' Ancre said, looking towards the last flickering flames in the grate. Then he glanced up at Beaumont. 'You didn't know Anne-Marie, of course. She was one of my agents, who worked as a maid in Vallon's household here in Paris.'

The general took a long swallow of his drink before he continued.

'Two days ago, she told me that a room had been prepared with great iron bars at the door on the third floor of Vallon's mansion. It contained only a huge iron box intended to hold a fortune in gold coin. Napoleon's first payment arrived on the *Torren* off the coast of Le Havre at the beginning of the week. It was transferred to a smaller boat and secretly transported to Paris. It arrived under heavy guard in the small hours, this morning.

'So, the money to buy Vallon's American kingdom is finally here,' said Beaumont.

'You know all about that?' asked Ancre.

'Yes,' Beaumont replied. 'But my information is less up-to-date than yours. I received reports that the *Torren* was due any day. I was going to leave for Le Havre tonight to work out a way of stealing the bullion.' Then he asked, 'Ancre, why did you say we are drinking to the memory of this Anne-Marie?'

The general stood up slowly and stirred the embers in the fireplace with a long poker. 'Early this morning, Anne-Marie was found in the doorway of this house. She was not dead, but every bone in her body had been broken. The work had been done so expertly she was still just alive, although suffering unbelievable agony. Each breath she took tore at practically every nerve in her body.'

'Vallon's work?'

'Who else? He'd had it done as a warning to me not to interfere. He sent the tortured body of a poor young girl to make his point.'

'I'm deeply sorry, General,' said Beaumont, knowing how inadequate his words were.

Ancre shook his head. 'I'm growing old,' he replied. 'I have seen too much pain and bloodshed. We must do what we can to bring it to an end. Vallon has to be stopped, or his wealth will fund a perpetual war. Napoleon offers glory, but he will cause the blood of France to flow like a river until the nation is utterly destroyed.'

General Ancre reached out to the table and took up a notebook, which he handed to Beaumont. 'Do what you can with this.'

*   *   *

The sound of the front door crashing open brought Beaumont's men rushing into the hall, their weapons drawn. But it was the commodore himself who strode grim-faced into their midst. Shouting for all the men to assemble in the living-room, he threw off his cloak and stood before the great fireplace, his back to the flames.

'Gentlemen,' Beaumont began in deliberately conspiratorial tones to make the men edge closer. 'The great fortune we have been waiting for has arrived at Count Vallon's house. It has been secured in what Vallon thinks is a thief-proof safety box.' He paused dramatically before adding, 'We are going to steal it!'

A roar of cheers filled the room in anticipation of some action. 'Will there be fighting, sir?' Rawlings asked keenly.

'I'm sure it will come to that, Mr Rawlings,' Beaumont replied. 'But the fighting will be the easy part. The prize is gold coin. The concealment and transport of it afterwards will be the risky part of this robbery. Bring me paper and a pen and I will show you my plan for taking the treasure.'

Peter could not remember a more eager group than the seamen who gathered about the table while Forbes hurried to fetch the writing materials. With the exception of Matthew, who rarely betrayed much emotion, the rest of the men looked like excited children on Christmas Eve.

'Will we have to use those blasted carriages to escape, sir?' asked Connors, before the commodore had even begun to outline his intentions. 'I was rattled like dice in a cup the last time.' Being more used to the motion of ships at sea, none of the men had enjoyed being buffeted about in the dusty carriage interiors.

'No,' answered Beaumont, then added enigmatically, 'I think we may well use a far slower means of escape.'

Chapter Forty-seven

THE SKILL OF SAILORS

Despite staying up well into the small hours going over the commodore's plan, everyone in Beaumont's household was up and about their appointed tasks well before dawn the following morning.

By the time the first grey light began to show in the east, two sturdy carts pulled by teams of work horses had been acquired and a variety of other equipment hired from a building contractor, a type of business that also started work early. Beaumont had already gone off on his own to make other arrangements.

Under Connors' direction, Matthew, Peter and two of the other men spent most of the morning spying on Vallon's mansion. They confirmed what Beaumont had already learnt from General Ancre: the ground floor of the great house was heavily guarded and had steel bars at all the windows.

The road was a wide, well-paved, tree-lined avenue of identical massive houses. Each had a short flight of steps leading up from the pavement to a pillared portico. A short gap of about three metres separated each building from its neighbour. At the rear, the houses had high walls topped with spikes enclosing cobbled yards.

At midday, Beaumont examined the quick sketches Peter had made and nodded. 'It makes sense for him to have a house with only a smallish garden, Mr Raven,' said the commodore. 'That allows him to turn the ground floor into a fortress with no large perimeter to guard. Because he thinks no one can penetrate the ground floor, he feels safe. Now, General Ancre has informed me there's an empty house in the same street?'

'Five along from Vallon's,' answered Matthew. 'The property is all shut up, as the owners are away.'

'And is it identical to Vallon's house?'

'Precisely the same, sir,' replied Matthew. 'I talked with a neighbour's gardener. He worked for the builder when the houses were going up. The foreman used exactly the same plan for each property.'

'I want a team of men on the roof of the empty house this afternoon, obviously cleaning the chimneys. You can be a sweep's boy, Mr Raven. Make me an accurate map of the roof and give me your best estimate of how much load it will take.'

'Aye, aye, sir,' replied Peter.

* * *

By nightfall, Beaumont's instructions had been carried out and his men were ready for action. 'Speed is of the essence, gentlemen,' said Beaumont when he briefed them for the first stage of the operation. 'Fifteen of Vallon's men are guarding the ground floor. We must account for every one of them. What about our party going on the roof?'

'We're ready, sir,' said Peter, after a nod from Connors.

'Then good luck to you,' said Beaumont. 'And good hunting.'

The operation began at two a.m., long after Vallon had been observed returning home and the house locked up for the night. The neighbours to the right were also asleep, unaware of the vital role their house would play in the operation about to be executed.

At Beaumont's signal, Peter Raven and four of the men silently swarmed up the outside of the neighbouring house with long lengths of twine tied to their belts. They easily found footholds in the ledges, decoration, guttering and stone copings of the building. In little more than a minute, they were over the low parapet and on the gabled roof.

The twine was in turn tied to ropes attached to builder's equipment below, which they now hauled up. A landsman seeing them work would have been amazed at their silent dexterity, but to seamen accustomed to manning the topsails of a ship riding out a storm their task was simple enough.

They quickly brought up some long building spars, and quietly transferred this equipment to the roof of Vallon's house across a temporary bridge spanning the gap between the two houses. In minutes, by rigging a triangle of crossed spars lashed down with cables, they had fashioned a crude but robust crane. It jutted out over the edge of Vallon's roof, and was fitted with a well-oiled block and tackle.

Peter attached himself to the line, and they lowered him down to dangle outside the room in which General Ancre had told Beaumont they would find the great iron box full of gold. Peering through a gap in the curtains, Peter was able to see into the unfurnished room. The doors leading to the rest of the house were fitted on the inside with great iron bars, but only a single guard armed with a brace of pistols was on duty inside.

The guard, with a blanket draped over his shoulders, sat on a hard wooden chair next to the box, a candle flickering beside him. To his great relief, Peter noted there was no fire in the grate, and that the man was asleep.

He signalled to be pulled back up to the roof, where he and Connors held a whispered conversation.

'Are you sure you can do it, Mr Raven?' asked the petty officer anxiously.

'Quite sure,' replied Peter. 'It's the only way. If we try breaking in through the window, the guard will have time to discharge his pistols and warn the entire household.'

'And you're sure you know which chimney to go down?' asked Connors.

'Yes, certain. I had a good look at the layout on the other house,' said Peter, stripping off his jacket and checking his own pistols. 'I'll give a whistle to let you know I've succeeded.'

Another line was attached to Peter, and this time he was lowered into one of the massive chimneys. 'Two men stand to the pulley,' ordered Connors in a whisper. 'You others prepare to descend when I give the order.'

Inside the chimney, just above the fireplace in Vallon's strongroom, Peter paused in his descent and held his breath to listen intently, until he heard a rasping snore come from the guard. Now blackened from head to foot and moving as quietly as he could, Peter emerged from the huge fireplace.

He'd only taken two steps towards the guard when soot, loosened by his passage, fell into the grate. The man awoke instantly, but was so startled by the candlelit apparition standing before him that he didn't even manage to cock his pistols before Peter had clubbed him unconscious.

On hearing Peter's whistle, Connors and two of his men slithered down the outside of Vallon's house, while the other two remained to man the block and tackle. Peter opened the barred window and hauled in the cable they had lowered. He attached it with a bowline to the ring set in the lid of the mighty iron box.

Connors had given a long piercing whistle before he and his men had swarmed down ropes from the roof. At the sound of the whistle the rest of the privateers, led by Beaumont, galloped the two carts to the front of the mansion.

Alerted by the sudden clatter of hooves, the guards on duty inside threw open the shutters on the ground floor to see what was causing the commotion. A fusillade of shots greeted them from the carts, causing them to duck their heads below the windowsills. Although surprised by the sudden ferocity of the attack, the men manning the ground floor quickly began to return the fire. As the battle raged, hefty wooden beams were being lifted from the carts and lashed across the portico, preventing those inside from coming out to engage with the men in the carts.

Beaumont's plan had worked. Vallon had assumed that any attempt to steal his gold would come from ground level and that the guards inside the house would provide enough of a force to fight off any intruders. He had not anticipated being imprisoned inside his own headquarters as the treasure was lowered down the outside of the building.

Still working with impressive speed, and ignoring the shots coming from inside the house, Beaumont's men seized the other end of the cable which ran through the crane's block and tackle, then down into the room where Peter had attached it to the great iron box. On Connors' command they hauled on the cable, and with a crash of broken glass they swung the box through the half-open window with Peter sitting astride it like a blackened imp.

A top-floor window was flung open and Vallon, his face contorted with rage, leant out to discharge two pistols at Peter. The bullets struck the iron chest on either side of his legs, missing him by only a hair's breadth. The count's fury had hardly spoilt his marksmanship.

The bullion was swiftly lowered into the leading cart,

and the horses lashed into a wild gallop down the cobbled street. Piling into the second cart, the rest of Beaumont's assault team made their escape.

With the horses galloping at full stretch, the carts careered wildly through the darkened streets of Paris. Finally, they clattered alongside the river Seine until Beaumont ordered them to stop. Used to working in pitch darkness, the men swiftly hauled the treasure aboard a waiting barge. Once unloaded, the carts continued to gallop towards the north gate of the city.

Chapter Forty-eight

TAKING LEAVE OF THE FIRST CONSUL

The empty carts headed for Calais, driven as decoys by men whom Beaumont had hired from the owner of the barge he'd rented. Beaumont's men, with Vallon's captured treasure concealed beneath a cargo of iron pots and pans, coasted gently down the river Seine towards Le Havre.

By choosing this method of absconding with the gold, Beaumont calculated that Vallon's own manic nature would put him off the scent. Gambling that it would never occur to him that anyone might make their escape by such a slow method of transport, Beaumont had taken an enormous risk, but it had paid off.

Humiliated by the raid, Vallon had reluctantly informed the Prefecture of Police, but they held out no hope of recovery when they heard that the stolen fortune was in gold coin.

'It could be in a thousand different hands by now,' the policeman explained with infuriating deliberation. 'And who is able to identify a gold coin as their own, Monsieur?'

Count Vallon, in an explosive rage, expected nothing from the officials. He had no choice but to remain in Paris till he received information about the stolen bullion from the riders he himself had dispatched on all the major roads out of the capital.

The waiting made him a dangerous man to be near. He'd already attacked a manservant who, terrified by his master's restless twitching, had begged him to remain still while he was being shaved. Enraged by such insolence, Vallon had snatched the razor from his hand and slashed the man several times.

The only person who could speak to him without incurring a violent rage was Captain McGregor, who was now in Paris after sailing the *Torren* from Roc d'Or. 'For the Devil's sake, man, what is your plan of action?' McGregor asked on the third day of Vallon's frustrating wait.

The blunt words had a sudden and curiously calming effect on the count, and for a few moments he was quiet. 'I intend to make a certain lady my bride,' he replied, sounding quite balanced now. 'Then we shall return to Roc d'Or where I shall obtain more gold and make the delivery directly to General Leclerc on Santo Domingo, as the First Consul requested.'

'Have you seen Napoleon since the English took his money?' asked McGregor.

'I have not,' replied Vallon shortly.

'Will he be angry that you haven't delivered as promised?'

Now that his rage had subsided, Vallon could think with greater clarity. He shook his head. 'No, he will not. I think he will welcome the fact that I've been humiliated. Napoleon will be scornful, but secretly he will be pleased at my discomfort. However, he knows there's plenty more gold to come; he's lost nothing.'

'You seem to understand the man very well,' said McGregor, impressed. 'To be able to look into his heart like that.'

Vallon even managed a smile. 'I can certainly do that – just as he can look into mine.'

'And who are you going to marry?' McGregor asked.

'A young American. And it's time I got on with that business.'

When Count Vallon appeared at Mrs Hargreave's house to demand an answer from Lucy to his proposal, he was a long time knocking before a maidservant finally opened the door. She informed Count Vallon that Mrs Hargreave, Miss Cosgrove and Mr Cobden had left for America that morning. They were accompanied by Miss Mary Van Duren, who was so distressed about Miss Cosgrove leaving France and missing her wedding, that she was keeping Miss Cosgrove company as far as Le Havre, her port of departure.

The maid also offered the information that going home was quite against Miss Cosgrove's wishes and that Mr Cobden too had seemed uneasy. But Mrs Hargreave was determined that they should depart immediately, and had accepted an offer of passage to America from Le Havre in General Ancre's new ship, the *Maid of Martinique*.

Vallon knew what he must do. Within a short time he had presented himself at the Tuileries and was demanding to see the First Consul. After an exasperatingly long wait, Count Vallon was granted an interview. He was shown into Napoleon's study, where the First Consul had been dictating a variety of letters to an array of secretaries. To Vallon's pique, Napoleon had not deemed it necessary to see him alone, and was making him conduct his business in the presence of eavesdropping minions.

'I understand you have been careless with the money you owe me, Count,' said Napoleon coldly as soon as Vallon entered the warm room. 'I was relying on the sight of all that glittering gold to stiffen the resolve of the laggards in my government.'

'My apologies, First Consul,' Vallon answered through gritted teeth. 'I thought at least the streets of Paris would be safe from British pirates.'

'Are you sure they were British pirates, Count? I find that hard to believe,' Napoleon replied. 'The British are now our friends. Maybe you have other enemies. Men who are cruel to women are seldom popular with Frenchmen.'

Vallon ignored this veiled reference to Anne-Marie Ducourt's murder. 'I come to tell you, First Consul, that I am setting out for the West Indies immediately. My intention is to make the second payment of our bargain to your brother-in-law General Leclerc on Santo Domingo as soon as possible.'

'Then you have my permission to leave, Count Vallon,' replied Napoleon coldly, and returned to his dictation.

Chapter Forty-nine

THE FATE OF THE
MAID OF MARTINIQUE

When the treasure barge was just a few miles from the docks at Le Havre, the crew were surprised to be hailed by a horseman calling Beaumont's name from the embankment. Steering closer to the grassy edge, Peter and the commodore recognized General Ancre. He was accompanied by a mounted groom, and they each led a second saddled horse. As Beaumont's men tied up the barge, he and Peter stepped ashore.

'Nicely timed, General,' complimented the commodore, who had previously informed him how he intended to escape with the gold.

'I have news for you,' said the general. 'Since you left Paris, Mrs Hargreave has insisted that Miss Cosgrove return home with her to America.'

Shock and disappointment flashed across Beaumont's

face. 'Have they already sailed?' he asked.

Ancre shook his head. 'No. In fact, I have offered to take them. It will be the maiden voyage of my ship, the *Maid of Martinique*.'

'Are they on board yet?' asked Beaumont desperately. 'Will I be able to see her?'

'We are making the final preparations on the ship, something about trimming her, I believe.'

'Yes,' said Beaumont. 'It's a question of adjusting the ballast to make her balance better in the water.'

The general nodded. 'While the work is being done, Mrs Hargreave and her party are staying at a hotel on the outskirts of Le Havre. We planned to embark this evening.'

'Where is the hotel?' asked Beaumont. 'Do I have time to get there?'

'Certainly – that is why I brought you the horses.'

'Do you ride, Mr Raven?' asked Beaumont.

'After a fashion, sir,' replied Peter, taking the reins from the groom and mounting the smaller bay mare.

Shouting instructions to Connors to continue to Le Havre and dock the barge as close to the *Wasp's* anchorage as possible, Beaumont hauled himself up into the saddle of the black stallion led by Ancre. The general set off at a good pace, and Peter had his work cut out to stay in his saddle as they crossed the countryside at a canter.

As they galloped up the drive towards the forecourt of a country house hotel, Peter could see that all was not well.

A carriage and horses stood unattended on the gravel, and bodies were sprawled awkwardly on the ground.

Shouting Lucy's name, Beaumont leapt off his horse and ran in through the hotel's open door. Peter and General Ancre remained outside, staring at the scene of carnage.

Face down, some distance from the carriage, lay Jack Cobden, the back of his head and the side of his face clotted with dark blood. Two discharged pistols lay discarded by his side. Still clutched in his hands were his great hunting knife and a tomahawk; both blades were covered in blood. Six men lay dead on the ground around him.

'Cobden put up a great fight,' said Ancre, impressed. 'The dead men were armed with pistols and swords, and still he managed to kill six of them.'

'He's still alive, sir!' said Peter, leaping down from his horse.

'My God,' exclaimed Ancre. 'What a formidable warrior.'

A trembling manservant appeared at the hotel doorway, and stood gaping at the dead men on the forecourt. 'Fetch water and bandages,' ordered the general. But the man was too stunned to move. He just stood there, motionless, his mouth open in shock. Ancre strode over to him and delivered a sharp slap, which seemed to rouse him from his torpor.

'Find the kitchen, Mr Raven. Get water, while I question this dolt.'

When Peter returned with a basin and towels, Beaumont and Ancre were crouching over Jack Cobden. Cradling his head they washed the blood from his face, and his eyes flickered open. The man's usual mahogany complexion was tinged with a grey-green pallor.

'You're a lucky man, Mr Cobden,' said Beaumont. 'A bullet has made a nice dent in your skull and you've got a few sword thrusts through you, but you're going to live.'

'Lucy and Mary! Where are they?' he asked urgently, his voice barely above a whisper.

'Not here, my friend,' replied Ancre.

'Mrs Hargreave?'

'Inside, unharmed but in a state of shock. I've seen to it that she gets a large dose of brandy,' said Beaumont.

'It was Vallon,' whispered Cobden weakly. 'He rode up in a carriage with outriders, bold as a brass cannon, announcing Lucy was to go with him as they were to be wed.' He waved at the bodies about him. 'These are the wolves he brought to back him up.'

'I see you disagreed with him,' said Beaumont grimly.

'I could hear them talking when they thought I was dead,' murmured Cobden. 'They're taking the two girls aboard the *Torren*.'

Beaumont nodded. He was calm now. 'We'll get a surgeon to tend your wounds and prepare ourselves to sail in the *Wasp* tomorrow.'

'Take me with you!' said Cobden, gripping his sleeve. 'I won't be left behind.'

'Rest easy, sir,' replied Beaumont. 'You'll sail with us on

the morning tide.'

'Tomorrow?' queried General Ancre. 'Why not today?'

'Explain the relative strengths of our ships, Mr Raven,' said Beaumont, 'while I get Mr Cobden into the carriage.'

'There's no point in us hurrying after the *Torren*, sir,' Peter told the general. 'She's got more than a hundred heavy guns. But the *Wasp* is faster than she is. We'll shadow her and await our opportunity. If we just came up to her she'd blow us out of the water as easily as swatting a fly.'

Beaumont lifted Cobden's blood-soaked body as though the big man were as light as a child. While he was arranging him as comfortably as he could inside the carriage, Ancre questioned Peter further.

'So, what will you do?' he asked.

'The commodore will outwit Vallon, sir,' Peter replied confidently.

'Your loyalty is touching, young man, but how can you be sure?'

'He was a captain at the Battle of Cape St Vincent. He destroyed two enemy warships, both bigger than his own frigate. He'll find a way of overcoming Vallon, you'll see.' As he spoke, Peter looked in the direction of the port. A tall column of smoke rose into the air.

'Looks like there's a ship on fire. Poor devils,' said Beaumont, rejoining them.

With a groom driving Mrs Hargreave's carriage, they rode into Le Havre. General Ancre became agitated as they approached the burning ship in the dockyard. Finally, his worst fears were confirmed: the *Maid of Martinique* was ablaze from stem to stern.

As the port authority's boats fought to control the fire, Ancre, Beaumont and Peter stood watching the beautiful vessel burn to ashes.

'What a destructive monster the man is,' said General Ancre with a sigh. They were in no doubt that it was Vallon's work. 'He could gain nothing by doing this, save to wound me.'

'Ships can always be built anew, General,' said Beaumont with brisk but genuine sympathy.

General Ancre shrugged. 'That vessel represented my life's savings. I am as poor again as I was when I first signed on as a trooper in the King's army.'

'What did you want her for?' asked Beaumont, his curiosity momentarily overcoming his concern for Lucy and Mary.

General Ancre raised his arms to shrug in a gesture of regret. 'I was going to start a brand new enterprise – in this new century – and in a new world. A business like no other, Commodore.'

'What business was that, sir?' asked Peter, as curious as Beaumont.

'The ice trade,' said Ancre, smiling sadly.

'The ice trade?' echoed Peter and Beaumont, puzzled.

The general nodded. 'Experiments have proved that if large blocks of ice are packed in straw to insulate them, they can be transported to the tropics and beyond without melting. Once there, they would be stored in ice houses underground. People in the West Indies yearn for ice to cool their drinks, but more importantly to protect their perishable foods. They could even make ice-cream. Think of it, a supply of pure ice available all year round, and customers who would always want to replenish their supplies.'

'Where would it come from?' asked Peter, intrigued by the idea.

'My partners, the Culpepper brothers, would have it cut in vast quantities from the frozen winter lakes of the North American states. I don't know what the Culpepper brothers will do now. I fear I have let them down badly.'

Beaumont slapped Ancre on the back. 'Don't worry, General. You shall have *two* new ships to conduct your business. You forget, we are in possession of a considerable fortune and you have earned a fair share. I will not see your help to us go unrewarded.'

'Napoleon will see it differently,' Ancre said with a wintry smile.

'Perhaps it is time you decided whether to continue serving that tyrant or to be your own man,' said Beaumont briskly.

'I have already made that decision, Commodore,' replied Ancre resolutely. 'When we have seen this venture concluded I intend to become an American citizen.'

General Ancre's spirits were somewhat lifted by Beaumont's comforting offer, but now it was the commodore who seemed agitated. Excusing himself, he strode off along the dock. Beaumont's anxiety abated only after he'd located the *Wasp* at anchor and had been assured by Captain Brough that his mission to England had been successful.

Chapter Fifty

A RELUCTANT BRIDE

The weather in the mighty reaches of the Atlantic Ocean proved kinder than it had on the *Torren's* last crossing. But even though the great ship made good progress as she headed south, it did nothing to alter Count Vallon's vicious mood.

During the months he'd lingered among Parisian society, Vallon had controlled his temper so successfully in public that the majority of people he'd encountered had found him quite delightful. His vast wealth also helped to disguise his true nature, as those in possession of fabulous fortunes were expected to act with unthinking disregard towards their inferiors.

Throughout his life, Vallon had allowed his moods to dictate his behaviour. Even after the atrocity he'd committed as a youth had caused his banishment from France, he'd always blamed his father for any injustice, rather than admit his own actions were responsible for his punishment. Vallon could also display remarkable charm and cunning, which allowed him to convince others that he took their feelings and wishes into account, but it was all mere play-acting.

To Count Vallon, the kidnapping of Lucy Cosgrove was entirely justified. When he'd decided they should wed he could not imagine that she might object, and simply took her refusal to accept immediately as a female ruse. So, once he had Lucy aboard the *Torren,* he was quite unable to accept her repeated refusal to reciprocate his romantic feelings.

His confusion lay in his madness. To understand her rebuff, he would have to admit that he'd committed an outrage, and that was impossible for him. The contradiction drove him even deeper into his insanity. Finally, after weeks of rejection, he resolved the conflict raging inside his mind by simply telling himself that Lucy's rejection was due to an illness. From then on he became more cheerful, and beseeched Mary Van Duren to nurse her friend until she recovered from the 'fever' that had 'unbalanced' her mind. Mary, who was in a constant state of terror, was sensible enough to go along with the charade.

For her own part, Lucy continued to treat Vallon as she would a wild animal. She'd seen Jack Cobden fight the men who had come to kidnap her, and had seen him fall. Nonetheless, she was sure he could not be dead. She could feel only hatred and an ice-cold contempt for the man who could do such vile deeds.

Convinced now that Lucy would turn to him when her 'illness' had run its course, Vallon looked elsewhere for entertainment during the long and tedious sea voyage. There were prisoners aboard the ship, a few men Vallon had taken from the *Maid of Martinique* when he set fire to her.

One night, when Lucy and Mary had retired to the cabin they shared, they heard strange grunting noises coming from the poop deck, accompanied by savage laughter and wild shouts of encouragement. Then came a series of horrifying howls more terrible than anything the two young women had ever heard. Lucy had once heard the death screams of a deer caught and killed by a grizzly bear, but they were nothing like as frightening as the sounds they were now hearing on the *Torren*. She finally appreciated the depth of Vallon's insanity, and to keep herself and Mary alive she decided it would be wise to appear cooperative.

Vallon was delighted by her new attitude and announced that Lucy was well on the way to 'recovery'. He continued to observe the social proprieties and left Lucy in the company of her companion. Mary, however, was less able to control her fear of Vallon and visibly shrank away whenever he came near her.

But a new problem began to plague the count. Ever since they'd murdered the crew of the *Maid of Martinique*, the rumour of a ghost had circulated about the ship. Men reported seeing the white shape of a seaman flitting about the decks during the night watches. Vallon tried to quell the rumours, but they persisted despite the sailors' fear of Vallon's cruelty.

Each evening, weather permitting, Lucy and Mary dined in Vallon's quarters, striving hard to disguise their repugnance for the man. For his part, Vallon now spent most days playing the clavichord in his state room, and the plangent sound was driving the two women to distraction.

They had been at sea for little more than a month when Vallon casually announced after dinner one evening that they were close to the end of their journey.

'And what shall we see to tell us our voyage is at an end, sir?' asked Lucy with more warmth than usual.

Vallon, pleased by her manner, described Roc d'Or with a passionate intensity that he imagined had finally won her over. 'So, prepare yourself, my dear Lucy,' he concluded with a smile. 'For the week after we land we shall be wed.'

'What is to become of me?' asked Mary, her voice fluttering nervously.

'My sister likes to keep pets,' said Vallon. 'I shall give you to her.'

That night, when the two young women were in their cabin, Lucy whispered to Mary, 'I stole this knife.'

She showed Mary the delicate piece of silver cutlery she'd taken from Vallon's dinner table.

'Oh, Lucy,' said Mary hopelessly. 'Surely we'll never be able to protect ourselves with that.'

'It may keep us alive,' said Lucy. 'But you must do exactly as I say.'

'Do you think there's any hope for us?' asked Mary forlornly.

'While we live there's always hope, but we must be ready to give ourselves a chance,' said Lucy firmly. 'Jack Cobden taught me that.'

'What shall we do?'

'Mary, can you swim?' asked Lucy.

'Yes,' she replied. 'I'm a good swimmer. I learnt one summer in the pond at my uncle's house in Virginia.'

'Good,' said Lucy, relieved. 'When the ship is close enough to the shore we must leap into the sea and swim for it.'

'They'll come after us.'

'It will take them time to lower boats. And once we're ashore, I can keep us alive in the jungle.' As Lucy talked, she was scavenging around the cabin. Any objects she thought might be useful to help them survive she placed into a bag with a long loop attached.

Mary sat on her bunk, still making objections. 'I'll not be able to swim far in wet clothes,' she said.

Lucy handed Mary the silver knife. 'Start preparing yourself,' she ordered. 'Cut through most of the stitching in your clothes so you can tear them off when we leap into the water.'

'Tear them off!' said Mary, appalled. 'Those dreadful men will see me unclothed.'

Despite their predicament, Lucy couldn't help laughing. 'Oh, Mary, thank goodness you're here to cheer me up,' she managed to whisper.

Mary took the knife and, with the sharp point, furiously began to attack the stitching on the seams of her outer garments.

Jack Cobden's wounds had healed by the time the *Wasp* reached the Caribbean. The journey had taken longer than they'd hoped, as they'd encountered storms in the middle passage which had blown the ship far off course. But in the seventh week of their voyage, Beaumont stood on the quarterdeck taking the night air with Peter, General Ancre, Matthew, Jack Cobden and Captain Brough. The sky was clear and a full moon laid a shimmering silver streak across the dark blue ocean.

'We'll put into Santo Domingo tomorrow,' said Beaumont easily. 'But I'm afraid there can be no shore leave for the men.'

'They'll take that hard,' observed Captain Brough. 'It's been a long run from Le Havre.'

'It can't be helped, I'm afraid,' replied Beaumont. 'You'll just have to keep their spirits up with promises of the booty to come.'

'They won't need the hope of booty to follow you, Commodore,' Captain Brough said matter-of-factly. 'You've obviously won their hearts.'

Beaumont smiled. He already knew he could trust the

crew of the *Wasp*, but it was good to have it confirmed. The commodore had been keeping an iron grip on his emotions throughout the voyage. He'd had to, otherwise he would have driven himself mad with anxiety about Lucy.

'How long will we be in port, sir?' asked Brough.

'Just a few hours. Enough time for General Ancre and myself to obtain reports from our respective agents. It is imperative that we press on for Roc d'Or. I need hardly remind you what is at stake.'

'How will we find the way, sir?' asked Peter, astonished. 'Did you work it out, Matthew?'

'Not me, Mr Raven. I escaped from Roc d'Or overland. I couldn't find the way by sea.'

'We owe that information to General Ancre,' answered Beaumont. 'He very wisely made secret navigational notes when he first travelled there to meet Vallon.'

'And you've kept that news until now?' said Peter, grinning. 'No wonder they call it the Secret Service, sir.'

Peter was on watch the following evening when the *Wasp* put into Port-au-Prince. The crew had accepted the order to remain on board. The harbour front blazed with lights, and the water was filled with small boats plying between the merchantmen and eight French warships riding at anchor. Peter could see fires in the mountains beyond the port.

Beaumont and General Ancre returned from their separate missions ashore within half an hour of each other, and both had a similar story to tell.

'The island is in chaos,' Ancre began. 'General Leclerc's forces are fighting a savage war against the black army led by Toussaint L'Ouverture. Leclerc seems to be winning the battles but Toussaint's men are fighting with incredible ferocity, even though some of his generals have gone over to Leclerc.'

'I heard the same,' said Beaumont. 'But Leclerc is losing even more men to yellow fever than to the opposing forces. The French troops are dropping like flies. Santo Domingo has become a hell hole.'

'I have news about Vallon,' said Ancre. 'General Leclerc has no money at all. He is desperately short of cash. He's even tried borrowing from the Americans, but so far he's had no luck. Apparently, he's already sent an emissary to Vallon to hasten the first payment.'

'I thought it was impossible to contact Vallon, sir,' said Peter.

'Count Vallon gave me the name of one of his agents here when we were still on speaking terms. I passed that name on to Leclerc,' Ancre explained. 'The *Torren* made a far quicker journey than we did,' he added. 'Vallon was lucky and just missed the storms that delayed us. They docked here in Santo Domingo weeks ago. Count Vallon dropped off Captain McGregor. He stayed in Port-au-Prince for a while before travelling on to Roc d'Or.'

'Did your agent know which ship Vallon is going to use to transport the gold to Leclerc?' asked Beaumont.

'The *Columbine*,' answered General Ancre.

'You're sure?' said Beaumont. 'It would be much safer on the *Torren*.'

'Some news has filtered out from Roc d'Or. One of Vallon's captains finally had the courage to desert. He was in Havana, but my man got the information from him and brought it here to Santo Domingo. It seems the captain also brought a lot of men off with him. Even Vallon can't get sailors to serve aboard the *Torren* since her voyage from France.'

'Why not, sir?' Peter asked.

'They're all convinced it's haunted.'

'It is,' replied Peter grimly. 'By *me*.'

'Did the deserting captain have any other information?' asked Matthew.

'If he did, he won't be telling it now,' said Ancre. 'Vallon's reach is still long. The man was found with his throat cut.'

'One thing is certain,' said Beaumont. 'We must capture the *Columbine* – or send her to the bottom before she delivers that gold shipment to General Leclerc.'

'How can we intercept her if we don't know what route she will take?' asked Cobden.

'It should be easy enough,' answered Ancre. 'Two French warships, the *Eloise* and the *Arian*, are to rendezvous with her. They are preparing to sail as we speak. Vallon would not, of course, give the French the exact location of Roc d'Or, so the meeting has to take place at sea, close to an uninhabited island. I have a note of the position.'

'Well done, General. I congratulate you on your choice of agents,' said Beaumont. Taking the slip of paper he laid a chart out on the table and rapidly made the necessary calculations.

'About one hundred miles south-west of Jamaica,' he announced. 'We must get under way immediately. If we sail before the French warships, we should just have enough time to finish her off.'

'Or take her as a prize,' Captain Brough suggested.

Chapter Fifty-one

ENCOUNTER WITH THE
COLUMBINE

The weather was perfect. A westerly wind blew the *Wasp* all the way under full sail, and within four days they were at the position Ancre's agent had given him. On Beaumont's orders, they heaved to in anticipation of intercepting the *Columbine*. It was an anxious time, with double the usual lookouts posted. They prayed Vallon's ship would reach them before the French frigates.

The first sighting came from the crow's-nest on the mainmast. 'Sail on the port bow,' called out the sailor.

To their relief it was the *Columbine*. She made a pretty sight in the sunny weather, tacking towards Jamaica as though she were on a yachting cruise.

'Action stations,' commanded Beaumont.

The crew ran out the guns, in case of resistance from the schooner. But Peter felt more like a hunter closing in on his prey, rather than experiencing the nervous excitement he'd feel facing a more powerful enemy. If it came to a fight, the *Columbine* would be no match for the *Wasp*.

'Stay with me, Mr Raven,' Beaumont ordered. 'I may need you to take messages about the ship if they're foolish enough to put up a fight.'

'Aye, aye, sir,' replied Peter, busy with his pistols. Connors had found him a matched pair that were smaller and lighter than the usual service issue.

'Looks to me as if they were made for a lady, Mr Raven,' the petty officer told him. 'But they're just as deadly for all that, and even more accurate because they're rifled. You'll be able to pick off sharpshooters in the enemy's maintops with those, I shouldn't wonder.'

'They're heaving to,' came a shout, and it was clear to all that the *Columbine* was uncertain of the *Wasp's* intentions.

'Run up French colours,' ordered Beaumont. 'With any luck they may take us for their escort.'

The ruse seemed to work, and by the time they bore down on the *Columbine* she stood no chance of running before the wind. The mere sight of the *Wasp's* open gun ports was enough to convince the *Columbine's* captain that her opponent's superior fire-power merited surrender, and he gave the order to heave to.

'I shall lead a boarding party,' Beaumont announced.

'May I join you, Commodore?' requested General Ancre.

'As you wish, General,' replied Beaumont.

With Peter at his side, Beaumont and a party of twenty men swung aboard the *Columbine*, and met no resistance. Captain McGregor, on the quarterdeck of the *Columbine*, was philosophical about the turn of events when he was ordered aboard the *Wasp*. 'The greatest treasure you'll ever take, man,' he said. 'And not a shot fired.'

'Fortunes of war, Captain,' said Beaumont.

'What are you going to do with us?' asked McGregor frostily. He showed no sign of fear, obviously suspecting Beaumont was too much of a gentleman to put him and his crew to death.

'You may take the small boats from *Columbine*, with sufficient food and water to get you to Jamaica. But only if you tell me what has become of Miss Lucy Cosgrove, whom Vallon was holding prisoner aboard the *Torren*.'

'Which one was she? The fair-haired wench?'

'No,' replied Beaumont. 'That was Mary Van Duren. Miss Cosgrove has black hair.'

'Ah, that one,' said McGregor triumphantly, as if he had just solved a great mystery. 'I never saw what happened to *her*, man. They told me she vanished.'

'But you were on board *Torren* – you brought her over from France,' protested Beaumont.

'I only went as far as Santo Domingo. I stayed there for a few days, then made my way to Roc d'Or.'

'How do you mean, the girl "vanished"?' queried General Ancre.

'I only know what I was told,' said McGregor, glancing

contemptuously at Ancre. 'Vallon heaved to off Roc d'Or to exchange signals, as is the custom when ships are coming in. It seems something peculiar then happened aboard *Torren*.'

'In what way *peculiar*?' demanded Beaumont, having difficulty containing his temper.

McGregor continued, unperturbed. 'It was a clear day apparently, but the ship was suddenly engulfed in dense fog. When it cleared, the black-haired girl had vanished. The other one just stood there like a ninny, struck dumb with terror. There was no sign of the missing one in the water, and they couldn't find her anywhere on the ship. Vallon was still out of his mind with rage when I last saw him. I've never seen him worse. His sister had to dose him with a potion to calm him.'

'What happened to Mary Van Duren?' asked Jack Cobden.

McGregor shrugged. 'It seems Vallon's sister took a liking to her fair hair. She's made her one of her pets.'

'She has human pets?' asked Ancre, horrified.

'For as long as they live,' replied McGregor, glaring at General Ancre. 'Now, sir, if you will be kind enough to provision our boats. I have no wish to dally in the presence of traitors to France.'

All the time they and been speaking, Peter had been studying the rigging of the *Columbine* with an uneasy feeling. Now he saw two men half-concealed in the furled mainsail. Their muskets were aimed at Beaumont.

'Ambush!' he yelled, drawing his pistols and firing at the marksmen. The first of his shots went wide, but the second hit one of the sharpshooters. His musket fell from his hands and clattered on to the deck. The second marksman's shot ploughed a deep furrow in the planks between Beaumont's legs.

McGregor stood with his claymore at his side, not yet having offered the two-edged broadsword in surrender. Now, with a sudden twisting motion and screaming an old battle cry, he drew the great gleaming blade.

Beaumont had half turned to fire his own pistol at the remaining marksman in the rigging and was unprepared for the attack, but General Ancre reacted immediately. He had not once taken his eyes from McGregor, and throughout the conversation he'd kept a hand in the pocket of his jacket.

As McGregor raised the sword above his head to strike Beaumont down with all his strength, Ancre swiftly drew a small, multi-barrelled pistol from his pocket and let go with all charges. Seven bullets slammed into McGregor's chest, throwing him backwards on to the deck before he could deliver his blow.

It was clear from the reaction of the rest of the *Columbine's* crew that they were not going to offer any further resistance.

'Mr Raven, General Ancre, thank you. I owe you both my life,' said Beaumont, ruefully looking down at McGregor who was still clutching the claymore in his death grasp. 'That will teach me to disarm captives, even when I'm foolish enough to imagine them to be gentlemen.'

'My dear Beaumont, you are most welcome,' answered Ancre. 'I never did trust the gleam in that man's eye.'

The crew of the *Columbine* quickly clambered aboard the small boats, lest they too should share McGregor's fate. 'It's a risk, giving them their freedom,' Cobden commented as they watched the crew of the *Columbine* pull away.

'I know, but I have no stomach for murdering them in cold blood,' said Beaumont, anxious to be under way before the French frigates turned up. 'If there'd been a battle, that would be different.'

'You're too charitable,' said Cobden.

Beaumont smiled, well aware he was lucky to be alive after McGregor's attack. 'Most sailors are quick to put themselves in the other man's shoes,' he answered.

Beaumont quickly selected a crew to man the *Columbine*, and instructed them to make her ready to follow the *Wasp*. Beaumont calculated their position in relation to New Orleans, then matched it with the set of navigational notes and timings written in the notebook Ancre had given him in Paris after Anne-Marie Ducourt's murder.

Three days later, just after first light, the officer of the watch called Beaumont to report that the *Wasp* had made landfall. In sight was a mountainous coastline thick with jungle growth and soaring trees, just as General Ancre and Matthew Book had described.

Realizing they could be within cannon range of Count

Vallon's concealed fortress, Beaumont put about and lay well off, fearing they may be spotted by his lookouts. 'According to my calculations this is the approximate position of Roc d'Or,' he explained to Ancre, pointing to the chart spread out on the table. 'Will you be able to recognize any of the coastline from the shape of the mountains?'

'Yes,' said Ancre immediately. 'I do believe I will. From a side angle, the three mountains to the south of Roc d'Or look like the profile of a man with hardly any forehead, a blunt nose with a large wart on the tip and a very weak chin. Look, I will draw it for you.'

He made a rapid sketch.

'We'd better proceed to the next stage,' said Beaumont, and he asked Peter to summon Matthew, Jack Cobden, Captain Brough and Connors. When they were all assembled in the captain's small cabin, Beaumont summarized his intentions. 'Our objectives are to rescue Lucy Cosgrove and Mary Van Duren, destroy Vallon's capacity to wage war, and do our best to take his remaining treasure,' he began. 'Before we make a detailed plan of action, I will be grateful for any comments.'

'I'd like to go in first and attempt a rescue of the girls,' said Jack Cobden.

'I understand your anxiety, and believe me I share it completely, Mr Cobden,' Beaumont replied sympathetically. 'But we have no idea where they are. And remember, McGregor told us that Lucy and Mary have been separated.'

'I know where Lucy is,' said Cobden without hesitation.

'How can you possibly, sir?' said Ancre doubtfully. 'Vallon's domain is huge.'

'I trained that girl from the time she was a child,' Cobden told them. 'McGregor said she *vanished*. Well, if she isn't dead, she'll be in hiding, and once she's hiding they'll never find her. But I can.'

'In that case, Mr Cobden, where will she be?' asked Beaumont, hope sounding in his voice as he spoke.

'Lucy won't be hidden on the ship. She doesn't know anything about boats. She'll make for the woods, where she'll be at home, or in this case the jungle. I always drilled one thing into Lucy. If ever we were separated in a fight, she was to make for the highest ground and I'd find her. No matter how long it took.' Cobden reached over and tapped the warty-nosed mountain Ancre had drawn. 'That's where she'll be, on top of that big hill.'

Beaumont looked at Matthew. 'Can you lead Mr Cobden to that spot, Mr Book?'

'I think so,' replied Matthew, nodding at the sketch.

'No offence intended, Mr Book,' said Cobden firmly. 'But I don't want to go crashing about in a jungle as if we were taking our seats in a Paris concert hall. I move kind of quiet when I need to.'

Matthew smiled. 'I think you'll find me equally soft-footed, Mr Cobden, and I know that terrain.'

'Just as long as you understand that I'll leave you behind if I have to.'

'What will you do if you locate Lucy?' asked Beaumont.

'Go on and rescue Mary Van Duren,' answered Cobden.

'Just the two of you?' asked Captain Brough.

'The *three* of us,' said Cobden. 'Lucy is better than most men I know.'

'Make sure you proceed with the utmost caution,' warned Ancre. 'Vallon's domain is well guarded.'

'Stealth will be our watchword,' said Matthew. 'And I know how we can enter the domain from the jungle and avoid the militia guards Vallon keeps posted at the villa. I also know the easiest ways in. They keep the windows open to cool the building.'

'I wasn't aware of any militia post nearby,' said Ancre.

'You can't see the barracks from the house, or the stables; they're obscured by trees,' said Matthew. 'The landscape was altered to conceal them in a vast depression so Vallon and his sister would enjoy an uninterrupted view of the mountains. Were we to attack the villa with a large party, the guards might well beat us off. But I know how to steal in there.'

'What about Miss Van Duren?' Peter asked.

'I'm pretty sure they'll have imprisoned her in a cage in the cellar,' continued Matthew. 'We will find her, I promise.'

'You sound like the man for me, Mr Book,' said Cobden approvingly.

'The greatest problem will be Vallon,' added Matthew. 'Wherever he is, he always has the best of his guard about him, and he thinks fast. He will make the job tough at the villa.'

'We shall create a diversion in the port,' said Beaumont. 'It will be an explosion of sufficient magnitude to bring Vallon and his guard to the dockside.'

'How will you do that?' asked Ancre.

'Lay a vast explosive charge against the harbour boom. Then we will go on to destroy the fortress.'

'That can only be done from inside the harbour. How will you get in?' asked Ancre. 'You can see it's impenetrable. Vallon's gunners will blow you out of the water before you can get close enough to the boom to lay a charge. Courage alone will not do the job, Commodore.'

'Believe me, Ancre, I have a way of doing it,' answered Beaumont.

Chapter Fifty-two

FULTON'S ANSWER

'What about me and the crew of the *Wasp*, sir?' asked Captain Brough as they were eating a breakfast of cold chicken and hard biscuits served on the quarterdeck. 'What shall we be doing?'

'Rest easy, Captain Brough, there'll be plenty of work for all of us,' Beaumont reassured him as the *Wasp* crept up the coastline. Ancre stood at the rail scanning the terrain for the shape of the mountains he would recognize.

'Do you know if there are any good quality muskets on board, Commodore?' asked Cobden, joining them.

'I think we can do better than that,' said Beaumont. 'Captain Brough, have someone break open the crate of Baker rifles we bought in England.'

'Baker rifles?' queried Cobden, unfamiliar with the maker's name.

'Fine pieces of work, Mr Cobden, made by Mr Ezekiel

Baker of Whitechapel Road, London. See what you think.'

A few minutes later, Cobden was examining a rifle that was still coated in its protective grease. He set to work cleaning the weapon with a cloth and, when he was satisfied, balanced the rifle in his hands.

'They're shorter than the long rifle you're used to,' said Beaumont, 'but they're remarkably accurate. Shall we test-fire it?'

Jack Cobden shot first and, even at a long range, easily hit the bobbing bottle that had been cast overboard. Matthew also proved to be a fine marksman. Cobden expressed admiration for the rifle, but had one reservation. He didn't like the length of time it took to tap the ball down the grooved barrel. Turning to Captain Brough he asked if there was any equipment aboard for casting smaller bullets.

Brough assured him it would be an easy matter. Cobden and Matthew experimented for more than an hour until finally Cobden was satisfied.

'Well, I don't know if Mr Ezekiel Baker would approve,' he told Beaumont, who'd found him on the quarterdeck laying out the equipment he and Matthew would take ashore. 'But if we use the smaller ammunition we've cast, we're able to load and fire five shots a minute. That's a pretty fair rate of fire.'

'Did your shots remain accurate?' Beaumont asked.

'You should see, sir,' said Peter, who had been tossing various targets into the sea for Matthew and Cobden. 'They can hit anything.'

'What's this?' asked Beaumont, picking up a buckskin shirt and breeches rolled around a pair of long moccasins that Cobden had taken from his luggage. The bundle smelled faintly of wood smoke.

'Lucy's clothes,' replied Cobden. 'I had a feeling she might need them again, so I brought them along.'

Beaumont held the bundle for a moment, then put it down again with the rest of the kit, laid out on a hatch cover.

Cobden looked over the pile, saying, 'I think we have all we require, Mr Book. Shall we check?'

Matthew called out, 'Miss Cosgrove's buckskins. Three knapsacks, two coils of rope, three Baker rifles, extra powder horns and ammunition pouches. Three hunting knives, three tomahawks. One compass. One steel signal mirror. A tinderbox, two days' rations of salt pork and ship's biscuits, three water canteens, and three leather bottles of rum.'

'So much rum?' asked Beaumont.

Matthew grinned. 'We're going to put it on our arms and faces, sir. The jungle mosquitoes don't care for it.'

Beaumont nodded, looking down at Lucy's buckskins. 'What do you think she'll be wearing now?' he asked.

'She'll be coated in dust and chewing leaves to keep her mouth moist until we get there, I'd guess,' said Cobden.

'There are springs high on that mountain,' said Matthew.

'Good,' said Cobden. 'Then she won't be chewing

leaves, and she'll be smeared with mud.' He straightened up and added, 'We're ready to go, Mr Beaumont. When we hear your explosion we'll hurry like hell to get to the port, so look out for us.'

'We shall, Mr Cobden. Expect to be picked up by a ship. I intend to sail out of Roc d'Or or die in the attempt.'

'How shall we know which ship?'

'She'll be flying the Union Jack.'

At dawn the following morning, the *Wasp's* cutter dropped Cobden and Matthew ashore and the two men vanished into the dense jungle. Aboard the *Wasp*, Beaumont began his own preparations for the assault on Roc d'Or. Under his instructions, Captain Brough and the crew rigged blocks and tackle, and with help from men on the capstan, they began to slowly winch out a huge boxwood packing case that had been concealed deep in the rear hold of the *Wasp*. It was gigantic – at least twenty paces long, and as wide and deep as Peter was tall.

'Another of the commodore's little mysteries, I suppose, sir,' said Peter to General Ancre, who'd asked him if he knew what it contained. They both looked on, intrigued, as the packing case was broken open and a protective layer of straw and sacking removed to reveal a cylindrical metal contraption, shaped something like a ship, but without mast or rigging. At the rear it had a propeller above a rudder, and towards the prow there was a bulbous turret with a viewing window. There were small paddle wheels on either side.

'What kind of vessel is that?' asked Peter, intrigued by the extraordinary craft.

'I do believe it is a submersible, Mr Raven,' replied Ancre.

'Quite right, General,' said Beaumont. 'You are looking on the future of naval warfare, Mr Raven. As the general correctly guessed, this is a submersible. It was built in the Lake District of England.'

'So that's what you were doing when you were away in the north for so long, sir?' asked Peter, slightly irritated that Beaumont hadn't told him of the craft earlier.

'Don't sulk, Mr Raven,' answered Beaumont lightly. 'Suppose you'd been captured and tortured by Vallon. Secrecy is always necessary in our work. It may save lives – even yours.'

'Sorry, sir,' replied Peter, regaining his good humour. 'You say *we* built this one?'

'Yes, I stole the plans of Robert Fulton's invention from the French. Remember when you rescued me from the Seine estuary?'

'Of course,' replied Peter and an image of Otto Guttman momentarily flashed through his mind.

'As I said,' Beaumont continued, 'she was built near Windermere in the Lake District, well away from prying eyes. While you stayed with my brother in London, I went there to acquaint myself with some additional changes our engineers suggested. Captain Brough took delivery of her for me when we were in Paris. He tells me it was a devil of a job getting her to the coast.'

'It certainly was, sir,' said Brough, grinning.

'So, this is how you're entering the harbour,' said Ancre. 'But how will you get close enough? Surely Vallon's lookouts will see you leave the *Wasp* from the battlements of Roc d'Or?'

'She lays very low in the water, and there is a small triangular sail attached to a collapsible mast so the wind will take us close inshore. If a lookout sees us, he'll never guess what she is. We shall submerge then, and power her by cranking her paddles ourselves,' said Beaumont. 'She'll be armed with two very powerful bombs to create the maximum amount of mischief.'

'One for the boom?' guessed Ancre.

'And the other for the fortress,' added Beaumont.

'Then what?' asked General Ancre.

Beaumont slapped the side of the submersible, which produced a deep hollow-sounding note like a great gong being struck. 'Having destroyed the boom, once we're inside the harbour, we will employ her special devices and set her running automatically to ram the fortress wall of Roc d'Or, thus exploding the second charge with which she's fitted.'

'And what will you do then?'

'After abandoning the submersible, we will board the *Torren*,' Beaumont explained.

'But you don't know where the *Torren* will be moored.

And what about the men already aboard her?' asked Ancre, his concern clear to all.

Beaumont picked up Matthew's map of the harbour and jabbed his finger at the jetty opposite the fortress. 'She will be tied up here, General, exactly where you saw her last. It is by far the best position in the harbour for a ship of her size. As for guards, I very much doubt if anyone is on board the *Torren*, considering her reputation for being haunted.'

Despite his reservations, Ancre was deeply impressed. 'And what of the *Wasp*?'

'Following the destruction of the boom, Captain Brough will sail the *Wasp* into the harbour, where the crew will set fire to her and put her on a course to ram the privateers.'

'And the crew of the *Wasp*?'

'When Mr Brough is satisfied the burning *Wasp* is properly on course, he and his men will abandon ship and join us aboard the *Torren*. We shall wait until Mr Cobden's party arrives, then, if necessary, fight our way out of the harbour.'

'What about the treasure Vallon has stored at Roc d'Or?'

Beaumont gave a grim smile. 'I think the key to this plan must be flexibility, Ancre. But if the opportunity arises, we shall do our best to seize Vallon's gold as well.'

'You place too much of your fate in the hands of the gods, Beaumont. In this respect you remind me of Napoleon,' said Ancre, exasperated. 'How will you command the winds to allow you to sail, at will, in and out of Roc d'Or?'

Peter smiled; he could answer that question. 'We'll rely

on common weather conditions in the tropics, sir. We've checked with Mr Book that they apply to Roc d'Or, and he assures us that they do. During the heat of the day, a wind blows from the sea to the land. At night the reverse happens. That's why the operation is timed to take place before and after sunset, when the breeze reverses its direction.'

General Ancre looked at the resolute faces before him and said, 'Gentlemen, I salute your courage. But I must say, I believe it is a desperate venture.' He slowly shook his head. 'I would not give much for your chances of survival, even if you are successful in destroying the fortress.'

Captain Brough spoke for them all by saying with a grin, 'We wouldn't have joined the commodore, sir, if we couldn't take a laugh.'

The general raised his arms from his sides and let them fall again, making the gesture his final comment.

Most of the day the men laboured to prepare the submersible for action, pausing only when Beaumont insisted Peter give her a name. Holding a bottle of rum in his hand, he said, 'I name you His Majesty's ship *Revenge*. May God bless you and all who sail in you.' The men cheered when he smashed the bottle on her side.

Next, Beaumont carefully supervised the loading of the two massive explosive charges, which were sealed in watertight containers. Then he filled the boilers of the steam engine with water and their fireboxes with highly flammable spirit.

Earlier, he'd announced that the crew of the submersible would consist of himself, Connors, Peter and
Wyman, the strongest of the *Wasp's* crew, who had become
a firm friend of Connors since their fight.

When she was lowered over the side, the commodore
demonstrated to them how the submersible was to be
operated. 'It is quite simple, gentlemen. We enter through
the airtight hatch which we seal behind us,' he explained.
'We'll pump sea water into the ballast tanks to take the
craft below the surface. We can vary our depth by pumping
water either in or out of the tanks. She's driven by means of
crank handles which we use to turn the propeller. When we
reach the boom at the harbour entrance we stop and attach
the first charge, which is secured to the upper hull.'

'How do we attach the bomb, sir, if we're underwater?'
Wyman asked.

'You will notice the charge I've attached to the outer
hull had a series of upward-pointing spikes,' Beaumont
replied. 'When we are under the boom, we pump water
out of the ballast tank so that we rise up enough to make
contact with its underside. The spikes will drive up into the
wooden boom and secure the bomb, which we shall detach
from inside the submersible. One of the spikes is
retractable and that will trigger a mechanism to fire the
explosive charge after a short delay.'

'How long a delay, sir?' asked Wyman.

'Fifteen minutes. That is enough time for us to pump
more water into the ballast tank and distance ourselves

sufficiently to survive the explosion.'

'How far will that be, sir?' asked Peter.

'We'll shelter behind the *Torren*. Her bulk should protect the submersible from the worst effects of the shock waves.'

'What about the second charge, sir?' asked Peter.

'That will be a little more tricky, Mr Raven,' said Beaumont. 'You will notice that the nose of the submersible also has a spike.'

'Yes, sir.'

'When that is primed, it becomes an instantaneous detonator.'

'An *instantaneous* detonator, sir?' queried Wyman. 'How do you mean?'

'Upon impact it retracts to strike a percussion cap filled with an entirely new sort of explosive that has just been developed. That in turn will explode the much greater conventional explosives with which the whole prow of the submersible is filled.'

'Begging your pardon, sir,' said Wyman. 'But where will we be when this last charge goes off?'

'Having directed the submersible at its target by fixing the tiller connected to the rudder, we shall abandon ship and swim away to board *Torren*.'

'But what will power the submersible if we're no longer turning the paddle crank?' asked Peter.

'There's the genius of it,' said Beaumont with a grin. 'The little steam engines it has on board. They work off burning spirits. The engineers have calculated that there will be enough air inside the hull to allow the engines to continue to burn until they thrust the submersible on to her target. The whole contraption will explode with enormous force. It will be made even more powerful by having taken place underwater, where the shock waves will greatly increase the magnitude of the explosives. At least that's the theory.'

'Do the engineers have some doubts about it working, then, sir?' asked Wyman.

'Well, they tested all the components separately and they were a great success,' replied Beaumont, choosing his words carefully. 'But I must confess they didn't actually try to blow anything up with it, as this is their only prototype.'

Wyman seemed to accept the answer philosophically, and set to with the others to make himself familiar with the workings of the extraordinary vessel.

Chapter Fifty-three

LUCY'S COMPANION

Jack Cobden was relieved to find that Matthew Book was indeed able to move through the jungle undergrowth as silently as himself. For the first three hours they climbed steadily. The heat in the overpowering gloom was stifling, but at least the rum they'd applied so liberally kept the mosquitoes at bay. Even so, the lush undergrowth snarled their passage, and they were relieved when their surroundings eventually gave way to different species of trees that had covered the ground with a soft carpet of leaf mulch. It grew cooler as they continued to clamber steadily upwards through the forest.

The trek took them more than half the day, with only a brief pause to eat their rations. As they approached the summit in the middle of the afternoon, Cobden held up a warning hand, gesturing for Matthew to stand closer. 'Someone ahead,' he whispered.

'Miss Cosgrove?' asked Matthew softly.

Cobden shook his head. 'A man. He's been at sea for a long time, and he hasn't washed very often. He smells of fear too.'

'What about Miss Cosgrove?'

Cobden shook his head again. 'I haven't caught her scent yet.'

Following Cobden's nose, they soon found a trembling man with ash-blond hair and an unhealthily pale complexion. He was wide-eyed with fear, crouching at the foot of one of the great trees close to the summit of the mountain. He whimpered in alarm when they seemed to materialize out of the gloom before him.

'Batty!' Matthew exclaimed in astonishment.

'You know him?' asked Cobden, who had seized hold of the trembling man to prevent him from running away.

'He must have been hidden on board the *Torren* ever since Vallon took her,' said Matthew. 'Lucy must have found him.'

'On the contrary, he found me,' said a voice nearby.

Still holding the wretched Batty by the tatters of his grubby shirt, Cobden said in a low voice, 'You can come out now, Lucy.'

Matthew stepped back in surprise as the carpet of leaves by his feet erupted and a young woman emerged. Just as Cobden had predicted, her body and undergarments were smeared with dried mud.

'Don't be afraid, Batty,' said Matthew, turning back to

Cobden's captive. 'This is Jack Cobden. He means you no harm.'

To confirm Matthew's reassurance, Cobden released Batty and patted him gently on the shoulder.

'Mr Batt rescued me,' said Lucy, as she quickly wriggled into the buckskins thrown to her by Cobden.

'What about Mary Van Duren?' asked Cobden.

Lucy shook her head. 'She was terrified, and ran into the fog Mr Batt had made. I couldn't find her afterwards.'

'So, how did you get away?' asked Matthew.

'Mary and I were going to jump into the sea when the ship was close enough to the shore, and swim for it. I thought I'd persuaded Mary to trust me.'

'So?' asked Cobden.

'Vallon had brought us up on to the deck. He seemed proud of his castle, like a child showing off his toy fort and tin soldiers. Well, there we were on the deck, and I was all set to dive overboard with Mary, when this strange fog suddenly enveloped everything. Next thing, I felt a hand take mine. I tried to drag Mary with me, but she couldn't move. Then she pulled her hand free and ran away.'

'Did you go over the side?' asked Matthew.

'No,' Lucy replied. 'That was where Mr Batt was even more clever. We went below instead. He hid me on the ship. You should have seen him; he was like a rabbit down a warren, and he dragged me after him. He'd made rat-runs all over the ship's hold, cut passages through bulkheads, made tunnels under piles of rope and crates of supplies.

They searched and searched, but couldn't find us. Finally, when the *Torren* was berthed for a few days, I persuaded him to come with me. One night we escaped and made our way here to the high ground, as you would have expected, Jack.' Then she said to Cobden, 'I knew they couldn't have killed you.'

'They came pretty close,' he admitted.

'How did you make the fog, Batty?' asked Matthew.

'I used wet oakum to make the smoke and rum to make it burn,' he said proudly. 'I'd strung buckets over the side all around the poop deck. The oakum was floating in rum. After a time, the twine tying the buckets burnt through and they fell into the sea. By then the smoke was so thick they couldn't see them floating away.'

'How did you light them?'

'I used a fuse from the powder store. It was easy, but the men on board the *Torren* thought it was ghostly magic.'

'Thank you again, Mr Batt,' said Lucy. 'It certainly saved me.'

'Why did you do it, Batty?' asked Matthew.

'The man, Vallon,' said Batty. 'I saw him do terrible things to the men he captured. I couldn't let him harm Miss Lucy.'

'You're a true gentleman, Mr Batt,' said Cobden. 'For what you've done I shall forever be your friend.'

'And now we must find Miss Van Duren,' said Matthew.

'We'll signal the *Wasp* first, then get going,' said Cobden. 'How long will it take to get to the villa from here?'

'It's all downhill,' replied Matthew. 'A two-hour descent, then an hour to reach the villa if we move fast. Say, three hours in all.'

'I'll signal three and a half,' said Cobden. 'That'll give us a little margin as we've got Mr Batt with us.'

'How can you signal from here so they'll be able to see it?' asked Matthew, puzzled.

Cobden grinned. 'I'm good at climbing trees,' he answered.

Three hours had passed since a joyful Beaumont had read the message flashed with mirror from the mountain top and learnt that Lucy was safe. The final arrangements had already been made aboard the *Wasp*. The treasure they'd stolen from Vallon in Paris, and all else of value, had been transferred aboard the *Columbine*, along with General Ancre. The submersible was now moored to the side of the *Wasp* and riding on the calm sea.

Beaumont was the last to board the *Revenge*, and before they cast off he gave one last order. 'When you hear the sound of the boom blowing up, sail the *Wasp* into the harbour as fast as you can, Captain Brough.'

'Aye, aye, sir. Good luck,' he replied.

Wyman winched up the short mast that supported a rigid sail, and they steered for the harbour. When they judged they were close enough to be seen, they lowered the sail and sealed the hatch from inside.

Sitting inside with their backs to either side of the hull,

they all began to crank the propeller to drive the craft towards the boom. It was hot work in the cramped interior. The observation window stayed just above the surface of the water until they closed on the harbour mouth, then they pumped in extra ballast to take her down lower.

Inside the metal cylinder, they had only a small candle to provide light for them to read their chart and Beaumont's calculations. The first leg of the operation went without a hitch. They successfully attached the mine by driving the spikes deep up into the underside of the wooden boom. When they detached from the mine they pumped the submersible even lower, then cranked with all their might to propel themselves across the enclosed harbour until Beaumont judged it was time to stop.

As they pumped out more ballast to raise the observation window above the water line, there was a tense moment until they were satisfied they'd completed the journey without the lookouts on the fortress walls raising the alarm. Beaumont's calculations had brought them within easy reach of the *Torren's* mooring. In the still waters of the harbour they tied the three-quarters submerged vessel to the warship's side. Peter slipped out of the hatch and climbed a heavy chain dangling from a mooring ring so as to look over the town square.

All was quiet in the marketplace. The late afternoon sun beat down on the empty stalls and the square was deserted. The only sign of life was a scavenging dog exploring a heap of rubbish.

'Still siesta time,' he called down quietly to Beaumont. Then he shinned up a rope dangling from *Torren's* side. The commodore's assumption proved correct: there was no one on guard. Vallon's superstitious sailors had obviously been too frightened by the 'ghost' to remain on board. The crew of the submersible began to set the equipment to drive her, unmanned, towards the fortress.

Beaumont, thinking a youth would create less curiosity than an unknown man, sent Peter to scout around the harbour. He strolled lazily along the jetty to stand opposite three privateer ships at anchor in the middle channel. They appeared to be unmanned, but Peter guessed there would be a watchkeeper on each vessel. Pausing to kick a pebble into the still water he continued to glance about idly.

The taverns lining the waterfront were not observing the siesta, each one spilling out its share of music and raucous laughter. On the battlements of the fortress across the harbour, bored sentries paced slowly past the embrasures that housed the heavy cannons. All seemed very peaceful.

Peter returned to clamber quickly back on to the deck of the *Torren*. In the water below, Beaumont, Connors and Wyman were working fast, lighting the submersible's steam engines, readying her to steer a course towards the walls of the fortress.

The mountain Cobden and Matthew had climbed was not conical but wedge-shaped. Its highest point formed part of a long blunt ridge stretching far back into the valley. They hurried along this undulating route until, looking down through the fringe of trees on the summit, they could see Villa Royale in the middle of the plateau on the valley floor.

Using the ropes, Cobden, Matthew, Batty and Lucy began scrambling down the almost sheer mountainside. Their descent was faster than Matthew had estimated: the lower slopes had been burned clear of foliage many years before and the bare rock was less sheer and easier to get down, but Batty was a problem and occasionally had to be reassured and encouraged as if he were a nervous child.

Eventually, they stood on flat ground, and bending double to pass through a wide strip of tall scrubby grass at the foot of the mountain they reached a tall palisade of mahogany logs topped with spikes. They used the ropes to scale the wall and abseil down the other side, avoiding the tripwires which Matthew showed them had been strung there to warn Vallon's men of intruders.

They'd just crossed the gravel road at the base of the high wooden wall when Matthew suddenly gestured for them to take cover in a ditch. They lay silent in its long grass as two mounted militia men passed by, their horses moving at a slow walking pace. One of the men was smoking a cigar, and its scent lingered long after they had gone.

Pressing on with Matthew in the lead, they were soon crossing wide, cultivated fields. Avoiding the occasional farm buildings, they kept to the narrow paths between the plantations of poppies. Soon, they could see the walls of Villa Royale glowing like gold on the plateau ahead.

'How many guards can we expect?' asked Cobden.

Matthew shrugged. 'There used to be more than a hundred of them. And the same number off duty in the barracks behind the villa. The guards always had strict orders to keep as quiet as possible. Any man making excessive noise was severely punished.'

They climbed over the villa's surrounding wall and moved stealthily through the gardens towards the main building. An orchestra was playing a Handel symphony, which reached them clearly in the warm evening air. It was suddenly interrupted by the sound of an agonized scream.

Watched warily from a respectful distance by his steward, Le Croix, Count Vallon stood in the late afternoon sun on the battlements of Roc d'Or harbour, blithely unaware that the defences in which he took such pride had been penetrated.

He was drinking wine from a large silver cup and reading a book which he held in his other hand. He looked up, and glancing through the camouflage of vines to the shimmering sea, he sighed deeply. Since Lucy's mysterious disappearance from the deck of the *Torren*, the count's behaviour had become even more wildly unpredictable. His mood swung from bouts of maniacal high spirits, when he would be filled with feverish energy and reckless generosity, then into sudden deep, self-pitying gloom.

The gloom was so all-consuming he would be unable to eat, converse or move from his couch, where he would simply drink bottle after bottle of claret. But unknown to Vallon his sister, filled with concern for him, had begun to dose him with larger and larger amounts of laudanum to dull his despair. Either she or Le Croix would add it to his wine. The drug controlled the excessive mood swings, but made him lethargic and often mawkishly sentimental.

Vallon beckoned Le Croix, who approached his master as warily as a dog accustomed to receiving blows. But Vallon simply held up his empty cup for Le Croix to refill from the large silver decanter he carried.

'Will I ever find my Lucy again, faithful old friend?' asked Vallon.

'I'm sure you will, sir,' Le Croix soothed. 'Would you not care to return to the Villa Royale?' he urged. 'Your sister intends to burn one of her pets on the terrace this evening.'

Vallon shook his head. 'I prefer to be here,' he replied almost in a whisper. 'Perhaps the ocean will be kind and return my love to me.'

He was still gazing over the sea when the colonel in command of Roc d'Or's artillery strode towards him. 'Forgive this intrusion, sir,' said the colonel. 'But a sentry says he thought he noticed a light flashing on the mountain. And the lookout reports a ship passing almost within cannon range.'

Vallon lowered the silver cup from his lips and looked towards the *Wasp*, which was running a course parallel to the fortress. 'Ships often pass close to Roc d'Or, Colonel,' he replied, unconcerned, his mind still dulled with the effects of the wine and laudanum. 'You know we are quite invisible from the sea. There's absolutely nothing to be concerned about.'

Just as he finished his sentence, a mind-numbing explosion shook the battlements. The shock wave smashed painfully against their eardrums, and for a moment the sky flashed even brighter. Seconds later, a series of booming echoes returned from the mountains enclosing the valley.

Moments later, a debris of splintered wood and chunks of iron showered down on the battlements where Vallon, Le Croix and the colonel stood. So jarring were the shock waves from the explosion, all three men were temporarily dazed. Vallon was the first to realize the boom blocking the harbour mouth had been destroyed.

'Man the guns!' he ordered the colonel, then added with a drug-induced calm, 'That damned ship is intending to enter my harbour.'

'We'll all be killed!' Le Croix squealed in terror.

'Get out of the way,' ordered Vallon, snatching the wine decanter from his steward's hand. Le Croix scuttled off towards the stairs leading down into the interior of the fortress, feeling safer with each step that carried him below.

Artillerymen ran to man the great cannons concealed within the walls. Vallon watched the preparations unconcerned, as the fog of wine and laudanum lifted from his mind. The great boom was utterly destroyed. Not even a stump remained, but Vallon could clearly see there was only one ship approaching Roc d'Or. She was taking advantage of the last of the sea breeze to make the difficult manoeuvre into the narrows at the harbour mouth. Even as he watched his harbour invaded, Vallon admired Brough's seamanship.

'Send runners to the taverns to order all crews to get to their vessels,' he instructed the colonel of artillery. 'If this ship gets past the fortifications, they'll have to finish her off. Also, have half the guns on the battlements turned to fire on her in the harbour.'

'They won't pass our defences, sir,' assured the colonel.

'I think she might make a fair job of the attempt, Colonel. Best you follow my instructions or I shall roast you on a spit like a pig.'

Vallon watched the frightened colonel hurry off to carry out his orders.

Chapter Fifty-four

NEMESIS

Beaumont, Connors and Wyman were making the final adjustments to the submersible as the first of the guns on the fortifications opened fire on the *Wasp*. She was already turning into her approach upon the harbour entrance.

'Steady as she goes, my brave lads,' muttered Beaumont, glancing up as the first salvo ripped into the *Wasp's* billowing sails.

'All ready, sir,' said Connors, emerging from the submersible's hatch, which was the only part now visible above the water line. 'The steam engines are running and her rudder is set.'

'Let her go!' said Beaumont.

Connors slammed the hatch, screwed her tight, and pulled hard on an outside lever to engage the paddle wheels with the steam engines. The submersible, just visible below the surface, thrust across the harbour, accelerating with deadly accuracy as the *Revenge* ran true towards the wall of the fortress. Beaumont, Connors and Wyman clambered aboard the *Torren* and waited in eager anticipation for the second explosion.

But nothing happened.

'Dear God, a dud,' muttered Beaumont in horror.

As the fortress guns lashed the *Wasp*, her crew used flaming torches to ignite the barrels of tar positioned about her decks. 'She's alight, men. Everyone over the side!' shouted Brough as the first flickering flames showed on her superstructure.

From the *Torren*, Peter could see Brough lashing the *Wasp's* wheel into position, setting her final course towards the privateers' ships anchored further along the harbour. He then ran to the side and dived overboard to strike out with the rest of his crew towards the *Torren*.

The moment they'd heard the howling scream, Cobden had abandoned his original intention of scouting around the Villa Royale.

'It came from the rear terrace,' called Matthew urgently.

'Here, Mr Batt, into these bushes,' cried Lucy.

Matthew had to push the petrified Batty into the hiding place. Then Cobden, Lucy and Matthew ran forward, skirting the mansion through the ornamental gardens.

Emerging at the foot of the marble steps, they found an execution cage had been erected with bundles of firewood piled at its base. On the terrace, Lady Anne looked down and saw the intruders. Her long face contorted into a grotesquely savage mask and she screamed again. Three long scratches on her left cheek were bleeding. Lady Anne turned impatiently as two uniformed guards struggled to force a desperately fighting Mary Van Duren to her knees. Lady Anne, clutching a razor-sharp knife, hovered over the girl, ready to slash her face at the first opportunity.

Lucy didn't hesitate. The Baker rifle came to her shoulder in one fluid movement and her shot sent the threatening knife spinning from Lady Anne's hand.

Stunned, the guards stood open-mouthed for a moment, then tried to snatch up their muskets. But Cobden moved faster, killing them both with his hunting knife.

Lady Anne was too insanely angry to be frightened by the appearance of strangers. 'How dare you enter without permission?' she demanded, stamping her foot in rage. Bizarrely, Vallon's orchestra continued to play inside the villa. Lucy, having reloaded her rifle, was now supporting the suddenly faint Mary.

A look of crazed puzzlement replaced Lady Anne's expression of anger. 'This girl must be punished! She scratched my cheek!' she screamed, touching the wounds on her face. Staring down at the bodies of the guards she added, 'My brother will have you all burnt alive for this.'

She moved to retrieve her knife, but Cobden seized her hair and held her at arm's length as he would a poisonous snake.

Mary now said in a faint voice, 'Oh, Lucy, I'm so glad to see you. But why are you wearing those awful clothes again?'

Lady Anne began to whine like a spoiled child denied a treat. 'I want to burn her,' she hissed petulantly. 'She scratched me, and she needs to be punished. I *demand* you let me burn her.'

Cobden dragged the mad woman to the open cage, and kicking aside the bundles of firewood as he lifted her bodily, he thrust her inside it and clicked on the lock. He then looked anxiously towards the screen of trees concealing the barracks.

The orchestra had finally stopped playing and the musicians were now peering out on to the balcony, too timid to leave the villa. 'Where are the guards?' Cobden asked a trumpeter who, braver than the rest, was first to venture on to the terrace.

'Most of them are gone,' the man answered.

'Gone?' repeated Matthew, puzzled. 'Gone where?'

'Some weeks ago Count Vallon became convinced there were traitors among them,' said the trumpeter. 'He began to torture the guards he suspected, and they blamed others to try and save themselves from his wrath.'

'His madness was worse than I have ever seen it,' said the cellist who had joined them. 'But he finally realized that he'd gone too far and they were all terrified for their lives—'

The trumpeter interrupted. 'Then he seemed to think

he could buy back their loyalty. So he gave the remaining guards money and leave to visit Havana. He even provided a ship to take them. The only guards left are the few that patrol the fences.'

'What about the horses?' asked Lucy.

'They're in the stables,' said the trumpeter. 'The slaves exercise them in the mornings now.'

'Why haven't the slaves run away?' asked Matthew.

The trumpeter shrugged. 'Where would we all run to? Besides, it may all be one of Count Vallon's tricks.'

'It's no trick, man,' said Cobden.

More of the orchestra crowded out on to the balcony, where they saw Lady Anne trapped in the cage. 'Are you leaving her here?' asked a cellist.

'We don't want her,' answered Cobden.

Gaining confidence, three of the musicians approached the cage to peer at Lady Anne as if she were a savage beast.

'Keep away!' she screamed, sensing they wished to harm her.

Slowly, one of the musicians raised his flute and played a hideously discordant note. Lady Anne shuddered as if he had plunged a knife into her. Matthew Book covered his ears. Seeing Lady Anne's discomfort, more of the musicians took up the torture and the dreadful cacophony caused her to convulse in agony.

'I must get away from this noise,' gasped Matthew desperately.

Suddenly, the thunderous explosion of the boom being

destroyed blasted across the countryside.

'The stables,' said Cobden. 'We must head for the port as fast as we can.'

In the harbour of Roc d'Or, a furious artillery barrage had begun. Vallon had turned his guns on the blazing *Wasp* as it bore down on the privateer ships riding at anchor. The *Wasp's* crew clambered aboard the *Torren* and frantically ran out her starboard guns. Within minutes they were returning fire, and although heavily outgunned they made a valiant effort to knock out the fortress batteries.

Peter yelled a warning to Beaumont. More than three hundred privateers had been routed out of the taverns by Vallon's guards and the sound of the artillery. Seeing the burning *Wasp* was about to ram and set fire to their own vessels, the captains formed their crews into a single, heavily armed force. Drunk with rum to the point of fighting madness, they ran towards the *Torren*, roaring their defiance.

'Captain Brough!' Beaumont shouted. 'Man six of the portside cannons and load them with grapeshot.'

But before the gun crews were in place, help came from an unexpected quarter. From all the buildings lining the waterfront came men, women and children. Armed with kitchen knives, axes and machetes, and with their bare hands, the slave population of Roc d'Or fell upon the privateers. Many of them were killed or wounded at the first fusillade, but then the slaves were fighting hand-to-hand with the privateers before they had time to reload.

Vallon gave the order for his men to ignore the *Wasp* and directed all his artillery at the *Torren,* which he saw posed the greater danger. Helped by the last of the sea breeze, the *Wasp* ploughed into the privateers' unmanned ships. Flames leapt to their decks, and within minutes they too were burning fiercely. But the fortress guns had found their range and the *Torren* was taking a greater number of hits.

Suddenly, there was a lull in the weather. The air became momentarily still, then the land breeze began to blow from the valley. The crew of the *Torren* were anxious to take advantage of the expected wind, but Beaumont shouted that they must wait for Cobden's party to arrive before they made their escape.

As is the way in the tropics, darkness fell abruptly, but the harbour remained dramatically lit by the blazing ships ignited by the burning *Wasp.* On the poop deck of the *Torren*, Peter swept the opposing fortress with a telescope. Together with Beaumont they were shouting directions to individual gun crews, alerting the captains to targets where they were to make hits.

Peter saw something gleaming at the base of the fortress. It was caught in the light cast by the burning vessels, which were now drifting out of control in the harbour like gigantic floating funeral pyres.

Directing his telescope, Peter saw that the receding tide had revealed half of the *Revenge*. It was lying at the base of the fortress wall, jammed among the heaps of massive rocks piled there. The vessel had wedged itself between two of the larger rocks, the detonating spike not quite touching the wall. Unable to make the necessary impact, the charge had not exploded. Peter considered directing guns to try and explode it, but rejected the idea. No cannon on board the *Torren* could be that accurate, and they needed all their firepower to distract the gunners on the fortress batteries.

Hurrying below, Peter raced down the familiar companionways towards the magazine deep in the bowels of the ship. In the powder store the sweating crew were passing the cartridges of powder with desperate speed. Peter searched among the barrels and found what he was looking for, a good length of fuse. Back on top, he raced through the withering gunfire that was sweeping the deck from the fortress. Near the galley, he located a closet where he knew foul-weather tarpaulins were stored.

With feverish haste, he took his knife and hacked off a square to protect the fuse, found a tub of lard in the galley and smeared it thickly on the outside of the tarpaulin before thrusting the gooey mess under his shirt. Then, running to the side, Peter dived overboard.

It was a long swim to the fortress, and the harbour's waters were made dreadfully perilous by the drifting hulks of burning ships. But Peter battled on, thunderous cannon-fire rending the air above him. Finally, he reached the rocks at the foot of the fortress, which were slimy with lichen and encrusted with sharp barnacles exposed by the outgoing tide. Making a supreme effort he hauled himself out of the water.

Cobden, Lucy, Mary, Batt and Matthew galloped on to the cobbled square and into the midst of the devastation. Cannon-fire from the fortress directed at the *Torren* had smashed into the buildings, reducing some of them to rubble and making a fine wreckage of the market stalls.

Hundreds lay dead among the debris, but the force of privateers had been utterly destroyed by the rebelling slaves, who had killed more than half and taken the rest prisoner. They'd now withdrawn from the line of fire, to await the outcome of the artillery battle.

'Cobden's party, Commodore!' shouted Captain Brough. 'Do I have your permission to get under way, sir?'

'Prepare the ship for sailing, Captain,' answered Beaumont. 'But keep the guns firing. We must keep their heads down.'

Looking about him, Beaumont shouted, 'Where is Mr Raven?'

Dismounting from their horses, Cobden, Matthew, Mary, Lucy and Batt all raced aboard the *Torren*. Batt and Mary hurried below while the other three directed their rifles at Vallon's gun crews.

'Mr Raven!' Beaumont continued to shout, his voice roaring out between rounds of gunfire.

'I can see him, sir,' yelled Matthew, pointing across the

harbour. 'He's at the foot of the fortress.'

Beaumont found Peter's discarded telescope, and by the light from the burning ships, trained it to where Matthew had indicated. Peter was aboard the *Revenge*.

'My God, he's entering the hatch of the submersible,' Beaumont called out. Then he saw sharpshooters on the battlements firing down on Peter. But Cobden, Lucy and Matthew had also spotted them, and the moment they showed themselves again after reloading they were instantly picked off.

The *Revenge* was stuck at the point where the fortress bulged away from the long arm of the rocky promontory, thrusting out into the waters of the harbour like a vast squat barrel. As the shots from the *Torren* smashed into the fortress, chunks of masonry showered down, threatening to bury the *Revenge* and crush Peter. Beaumont ordered the *Torren's* gunners to fire on another part of the fortress while they watched anxiously, trying to work out what Peter was attempting to do. Then he emerged from the submersible's hatch.

'By the Lord Harry,' said Beaumont excitedly. 'The boy's run a fuse to the explosives. Well done, Mr Raven,' he shouted, though there was no chance of his praise reaching Peter.

'He'll kill himself with the explosion if he ignites the mine from there,' shouted Cobden.

'No,' answered Beaumont, half to himself. 'Not if he works his way around the belly of the fort. If he tucks himself in there, where that flight of steps is, he may well avoid the blast.'

The pistol Peter drew from his belt was wet, but still provided a shower of sparks when flint struck metal. He cocked and fired the mechanism repeatedly until the gun-powder-impregnated fuse caught fire.

Throwing the pistol aside, Peter dived back into the water and swam desperately around the mighty swell of the fort to where the wall joined the bare face of the rocky promontory. Scrambling ashore once more, he huddled into the recess, under a flight of stone steps that led up to the battlements.

The explosives packed in the nose of the submersible detonated with an earth-shaking explosion even greater than the one that had destroyed the boom.

Those on board the *Torren* watched in awe as the outer face of the fortress, which until a few moments before had seemed so impregnable, now dissolved as if blown inwards by the breath of a colossus. A great billowing column of dust rose up, illuminated by the burning ships. Once more, booming echoes returned from the mountains.

'The explosion must have set off the fortress's powder store,' shouted Beaumont, peering anxiously towards the obscured fortress. 'Look out for Midshipman Raven.'

To Peter, crouched with his hands pressed over his ears, the shock came like a massive hammer blow striking his entire body, even though he was not directly in the line of the explosion.

The detonation had punched away virtually all of the fortress. As the dust cleared, the onlookers could see that more of the weakened battlements that had held the guns were slowly falling away to crash down on to the rocks below.

The entire edifice had been destroyed except for a narrow remaining strip of battlements built on the rock promontory itself, and the connecting portion of the structure to which the steps that had sheltered Peter were attached. A few surviving members of the gun crews lay on the narrow irregular strip, still stunned by the explosion.

'Dear Lord!' said Cobden in amazement as the dust slowly settled.

'Will you credit that, now?' exclaimed Connors as a new and extraordinary phenomenon presented itself to the onlookers.

The interior of the great cavern excavated by the explosion was glowing with a light of pure gold lit by the flames from the still-burning ships.

'What the devil is that?' asked Captain Brough, as puzzled as the rest of the *Wasp's* crew.

'The bullion!' exclaimed Beaumont. 'Vallon must have stored his gold in there as well as his powder magazine. The explosion has plastered it all over the rock face the fortress is built against.'

Now that the opposing guns had been silenced, the crew of the *Wasp* began a ragged cheer.

'Mr Raven is alive,' said Beaumont steadily, as he looked through the telescope. They all watched as Peter began to climb the steps towards the shattered remains of the battlements. When he reached the top step, one of the defenders rose up like a spectre from the only remaining sector.

'My God,' uttered Lucy, who now held the telescope. 'It's Vallon! He's survived the explosion.'

'I can't get a clear shot,' said Cobden, lowering his rifle. 'The boy is standing right in front of him.'

Blocking Vallon's way, Peter stood on the narrow remains of the crumbling battlements leading to the path along the promontory. He did not look at all formidable. Torn by the sharply encrusted rocks, his clothes hung in tattered rags, and exhaustion made him sway unsteadily. Rents in his shirt revealed that the barnacles had raked Peter's body with a hundred cuts, so that blood glistened through his coating of dust.

Vallon's own clothes and face were also thick with dust, and there were stinging cuts on his hands and face. He was in no mood to be defied. But he drew his sword carelessly, as if about to slash at an offending bramble.

'Who are you, boy?' he asked, his voice barely above a menacing whisper. 'What are you doing here?'

'I am Midshipman Peter Raven of HMS *Torren*,' croaked Peter, drawing his dirk and speaking with some effort. 'And I have come to hold you to account for murder, Count Vallon.'

Vallon now looked with more caution at the grimy

bloodstained boy confronting him in the light from the burning ships. It was not a respectful glance, more the sort given to a wild animal crazed with pain. Vallon realized it was just possible this reckless creature might do him some actual harm, like a bite from a mad dog.

Raising his sword, Vallon lunged forward, intending to put a swift end to this upstart. But Peter managed to stumble back on to a wider section of the battlements.

From the deck of the *Torren*, Cobden, Lucy and Matthew all trained their rifles on the ruined battlements, but the light from the burning wrecks flickered, and the two figures moved deceptively in and out of deep shadows, making a clear shot impossible.

Vallon advanced on Peter with no thought in mind other than to finish him off with a killing thrust and make his way to the promontory's pathway. But as Vallon pursued the insolent creature, the clumsy stumbling youth kept managing to just avoid the probing point of his sword.

'He's getting weaker,' Brough called out anxiously. Everyone aboard the *Torren* held their breath when Peter tripped again, and fighting weakly for his balance he fell forward on to his knees.

Vallon made a sweeping cut with his sword.

Peter held up his dirk to parry the blow, only to have it go spinning from his hand into the void.

The watchers on the *Torren* gave a collective groan of helplessness. As Vallon drew back his sword, he once more presented a half possible target in the flickering light.

Cobden shouted, 'My shot!' But before he could squeeze the trigger, Peter once more swayed to his feet, blocking Cobden's view of Vallon. This time he seemed to be about to fall forward and Vallon unhurriedly drew back his sword ready to thrust it casually through his helpless opponent.

As Vallon's sword arm drew back to its full extent, Peter swiftly straightened up, and with surprising agility stepped closer to Vallon. Using his hand like a short jabbing sword, Peter's stiffened fingers caught the unprepared Vallon full in the hollow beneath his Adam's apple.

His eyes wide with sudden fear, Vallon dropped his sword and clutched at his searing throat. His body jerked upright as he fought to regain his choking breath. Peter stepped forward, and using the whole weight of his body he struck Vallon with his shoulder.

Completely unbalanced, Vallon was thrown backwards. His feet scrambled frantically to keep him upright, then he tumbled from the edge of the parapet. As he fell, three rifle bullets from the *Torren* struck his body before he smashed on to the rocks at the water's edge and rolled into the sea. His corpse finally came to rest floating face down on the outgoing tide.

A cutter was sent to bring Peter back across the wreckage-strewn harbour, and he eventually joined his companions on the quarterdeck of the battered but victorious *Torren*, where the wounded were already being attended to.

'I thought you were a goner, Mr Raven,' said Beaumont

after the clamour of Peter's welcome abated. 'You gave us a few bad moments.'

'I had more strength left than it may have appeared, sir,' answered Peter modestly. 'Your brother's acting lessons certainly came in handy. Vallon thought I was done for too, so he underestimated me, just as Petty Officer Connors would have predicted.'

'We did a good job of work here,' said Cobden, looking across the harbour at the ruined fortress and the smouldering wrecks of the privateers.

'And paid the price,' said Captain Brough, glancing down at the row of the *Wasp's* dead, already covered with tarpaulins.

'What about the slaves, sir?' asked Matthew, gesturing at the mass of people in the market square, where they had fought the privateers with their bare hands.

'I see no slaves, Mr Book,' replied Beaumont evenly. 'I see only free men and women who fought to call this place their homeland.'

Chapter Fifty-five

LOOK HOMEWARD

S ome weeks had passed at Roc d'Or while the *Torren* was being repaired in the shipyard. She was back at her mooring next to the *Columbine*. The wrecked buildings round the market square were also gradually being restored, and in the process Batt had finally found a new home. It transpired that he had been a plasterer before he'd been press-ganged into the Navy, and his old skills were welcomed by the townsfolk.

Commodore Beaumont had supervised the reposition-ing of a battery of cannon salvaged from the destroyed fortress. They were manned to guard the harbour from those of Vallon's privateers still at sea who might return and attempt to re-establish their dominance. Roc d'Or was no longer impregnable, but even without the boom in place it would still be a foolhardy task to try and force an entry.

Beaumont had also supervised the recovery of a great

deal of the gold embedded in the rock face. Great chests of it were now under guard in the hold of the *Torren*, ready to be handed over to the British authorities in Jamaica. But still gleaming in the nooks and crannies there was a fair amount that he had instructed should be left to pay for rebuilding the town.

The crew of the *Wasp* were satisfied with the arrangement, as they still had on board the *Columbine* their share of the bullion taken in Paris. But Beaumont, Connors, Batt, Matthew and Peter, as the only members of the Royal Navy to have retaken the *Torren*, would share the prize money for it, as well as receiving part of the value of the gold salvaged from Roc d'Or.

The *Columbine* had made a run to Santo Domingo, taking Lady Anne to the insane asylum in Port-au-Prince, and returned with Doctor Antrobus, who told them of the appalling conditions he'd left behind on the island. The savage war continued there, but the French were suffering greater losses from the ravages of yellow fever than from the battles. It was well known that General Leclerc was desperate for money to support his troops.

'Well, he won't be getting any cash from here,' said Beaumont to Lucy as they strolled along the waterfront at Roc d'Or with Peter and Matthew.

Lucy had long since put away her buckskins and she, Mary Van Duren and Jack Cobden were soon to return to America in the *Columbine*. General Ancre was to accompany them, and with the aid of Lucy's grandfather he intended to apply for American citizenship.

Beaumont had appointed Matthew Book to be his agent in Roc d'Or after Matthew had confided in Peter that he intended to marry Nancy O'Reilly and settle down in his place of birth. 'I had no idea you and Nancy had such feelings for each other, Mr Book,' he said. 'That was a lightning courtship.'

'Like you and Miss Cosgrove, I suppose, sir,' said Peter.

'But Miss Cosgrove has yet to agree to marry me, Mr Raven,' Beaumont replied gravely.

Lucy smiled. 'My answer shall be *yes*, Commodore, if you will but seal your intentions with one more act of outstanding courage.'

'You have but to name it,' answered Beaumont ardently.

'You must sail up the Hudson River and ask my grandfather for my hand.'

'That day will come, Miss Cosgrove,' said Beaumont with quiet conviction.

Approaching them, Petty Officer Connors held something aloft. It was a sword.

'They found this in the wreckage of the fortress, sir,' said Connors. 'It belonged to Count Vallon.'

Beaumont took the blade and made a swift slashing motion. 'A beautiful weapon,' he said.

'A pity it was used for such evil,' said Lucy with a slight shudder.

'A short duelling sword, sir,' said Connors. 'The finest I've ever seen.'

'I think you have earned this, Mr Raven,' said Beaumont, presenting him with the weapon. Peter took the sword and felt the craftsman's balance in the forged triangular blade.

'I think it will find better service in the future,' said Matthew Book prophetically.

POSTSCRIPT

General Leclerc's army bled to death on Santo Domingo. Napoleon had promised his brother-in-law ample funds to fight the war, but no money ever came. Leclerc's men suffered appalling casualties, both from battle and from yellow fever. On November 2, 1802, General Leclerc himself died from the disease.

For a few months, Napoleon planned to send yet another army to Santo Domingo under the command of General Victor. But he and his troops were trapped by winter ice in Holland, and gradually he seemed to lose interest in his plans for an empire in America. In April 1803, to the astonishment of the world and the outrage of many leading citizens of France, Napoleon Bonaparte sold virtually the entire mid-west of America to the United States for the knock-down price of $15,000,000, which worked out at about four cents an acre. Known as the Louisiana Purchase, it was the greatest bargain in the history of the world.

With the agreement of the British Government, the English bank Baring Brothers actually loaned America all of the money for the Louisiana Purchase, and Napoleon used every penny of it to prepare for another war against his most hated foe, Britain.

PARTS UNKNOWN
INDIAN NATIONS
Hudson Bay
LABRADOR or NEW BRITAIN
CANADA
St Lawrence
UNITED STATES
Boston
New York
LOUISIANA
Bermuda
MEXICO
Gulf of Mexico
Cuba
WEST INDIES
Jamaica
Santo Domingo
Caribbean Sea
PACIFIC OCEAN
Galapagos Isles
R. Amazon